PRAISE FOR

NEW YORK TIMES BESTSELLING AUTHOR

KAREN WHITE

"One of the best new writers on the scene today."
—The Huffington Post

"Truly gifted."
—*Las Vegas Review-Journal*

"[Karen White] gives you everything you could want."
—*New York Times* Bestselling Author Kerrelyn Sparks

"A master storyteller."
—Fresh Fiction

"*The Time Between* is a lyrically written, beautiful novel about atonement, love, and letting go. Engrossing and unforgettable."
—*New York Times* Bestselling Author Eloisa James

Praise for
The Time Between

"From its mesmerizing first scene, *The Time Between* propels you into the sunbaked world of the South Carolina Lowcountry and a childhood tragedy that haunts the lives of two unforgettable sisters in love with the same man. In clear and gorgeous prose, White spins a luminous tale of love and loss, of betrayal and redemption, and of a harrowing family secret buried in the upheaval of the Second World War. This is storytelling of the highest order: the kind of book that leaves you both deeply satisfied and aching for more. No one weaves together the present and the past with greater magic than Karen White."

—Beatriz Williams, *New York Times* bestselling author of *A Hundred Summers*

"*The Time Between* is a lyrically written, beautiful novel about atonement, love, and letting go. Engrossing and unforgettable."

—*New York Times* bestselling author Eloisa James

"White . . . once again crafts characters who transcend their romantic roles through their frailties and weaknesses." —*Kirkus Reviews*

"White moves smoothly between narrators as well as different time periods, crafting an intriguing and romantic family drama." —*Booklist*

"White writes complex, heartbreaking novels with just enough pathos and plenty of redemption." —*RT Book Reviews* (top pick)

"Set in South Carolina's idyllic Lowcountry against the bittersweet notes of a piano in mourning and a prophecy spoken in Gullah, *The Time Between* weaves a story as intricate and sturdy as a sweetgrass basket, with the fresh, magnetic voices of its headstrong characters." —ArtsATL

More Praise for the Novels
of Karen White

"[White] describes the land and location of the story in marvelous detail. . . . [This is what] makes White one of the best new writers on the scene today."

—The Huffington Post

"Tightly plotted . . . a tangled history as steamy and full of mysteries as the Big Easy itself." —*The Atlanta Journal-Constitution*

continued . . .

"Readers will find White's prose an uplifting experience as she is a truly gifted storyteller." —*Las Vegas Review-Journal*

"White entwines historical fact and research seamlessly through the lives of these strong and intriguing women." —*Library Journal*

"White's ability to write a book that keeps you hankering for more is her strong suit." —*South Charlotte Weekly*

"White . . . weaves together themes of Southern culture, the powerful bond of family, and the courage to rebuild in the face of destruction to create an incredibly moving story her dedicated fans are sure to embrace."
—*Moultrie News* (SC)

"White's ability to showcase her characters' flaws and strengths is one of the best in the genre." —*RT Book Reviews*

"Expertly written, White's emotionally tender story of intrigue, love, and modern-day natural disasters sets her apart as the ultimate voice of women's fiction." —Fresh Fiction

"Karen White delivers the thrills of perilous romance and the chills of ghostly suspense, all presented with Southern wit and charm."
—*New York Times* bestselling author Kerrelyn Sparks

"Brilliant and engrossing . . . a rare gem . . . exquisitely told."
—The Book Connection

"White creates a heartfelt story full of vibrant characters and emotion that leaves the reader satisfied yet hungry for more from this talented author."
—*Booklist*

"You savor every single word . . . a perfect 10."
—Romance Reviews Today

"A terrific, insightful character study." —*Midwest Book Review*

"A story as rich as a coastal summer . . . a great love story."
—*New York Times* bestselling author Deborah Smith

"As lush as the Lowcountry . . . unexpected and magical."
—*New York Times* bestselling author Patti Callahan Henry

New American Library Titles
by Karen White

The Color of Light

Learning to Breathe

Pieces of the Heart

The Memory of Water

The Lost Hours

On Folly Beach

Falling Home

The Beach Trees

Sea Change

After the Rain

The Tradd Street Series

The House on Tradd Street

The Girl on Legare Street

The Strangers on Montagu Street

Return to Tradd Street

the time between

KAREN WHITE

New American Library
Published by the Penguin Group
Penguin Group (USA) LLC, 375 Hudson Street,
New York, New York 10014, USA

USA | Canada | UK | Ireland | Australia | New Zealand | India | South Africa | China
penguin.com
A Penguin Random House Company

Published by New American Library, a division of Penguin Group (USA) LLC. Previously published in a New American Library hardcover edition.

First Trade Paperback Printing, May 2014

NAL Trade Paperback ISBN: 978-0-451-46811-6

The Library of Congress has cataloged the hardcover edition of this title as follows:

White, Karen.
The time between/Karen White.
p. cm
ISBN 978-0-451-23986-0
1. Self-realization in women—Fiction. 2. Family secrets—Fiction. 3. Sisters—Fiction. 4. Edisto Island (S.C.)—Fiction. I. Title.
PS3623.H5776T56 2013
813'.6—dc23 2012050076

Printed in the United States of America
10 9 8 7 6 5 4 3 2 1

Set in Bembo Book MT
Designed by Alissa Theodor

PUBLISHER'S NOTE

This is a work of fiction. Names, characters, places, and incidents either are the product of the author's imagination or are used fictitiously, and any resemblance to actual persons, living or dead, business establishments, events, or locales is entirely coincidental.

To my husband, Tim.
Thank you for your love and patience for the last twenty-five years.

ACKNOWLEDGMENTS

First and foremost, I thank my readers for your enthusiasm and kind words, and for allowing me into your lives. I couldn't do what I do without you!

Thanks also to my terrific team at New American Library—sales, marketing, and publicity—who do such a wonderful job of getting my books out there. And to the awesome art department for the remarkable cover on this and all of my books. You always manage to pinpoint the true spirit of a book and create something special every time. And a huge thank-you to my editorial team—Cindy Hwang, Claire Zion, Kara Welsh, and Leslie Gelbman—for your words of encouragement and support. As you know, authors are incredibly thin-skinned, yet you always manage to make me believe that I actually know what I'm doing. Thanks also to my agent, Karen Solem, who has been with me since the beginning.

To Agnes Joo, Gabi Stevens, Edith Stefel, and Walt Mussell for your generosity of time and your patience with my questions regarding Hungarian phrases and terms. Just please don't ask me to try to pronounce any of them!

Thank you to the lovely people of Edisto Island, especially those at the Edisto Bookstore, for all the terrific research materials, and to our excellent tour guide Dottie from Tours of Edisto. You made the island and all its rich history come to life.

Again, thank you, Diane Wise, RN, MSN, CNM, for your professional insights on pregnancy and childbirth. You've helped me with so many books and yet you still cheerfully answer all my questions with patience.

Thank you to my BFFs and critique partners, Wendy Wax and Susan Crandall. I can't believe you're still taking my calls after surviving yet another deadline with me. Thank you for all your hard work on my behalf—and my editor thanks you, too!

Last, but certainly not least, thank you to my long-suffering family—Tim, Meghan, and Connor. I might not cook for you, but that doesn't mean I love you any less.

For time is the longest distance between two places.

—Tennessee Williams

CHAPTER 1

Eleanor

The first time I died was the summer I turned seventeen. I remember the air being so hot you could smell the pluff mud baking in the sun, the scent sulfur-sweet and strong enough to curl your toes, the tall stems of sweetgrass listless, their tips bowed in submission. Blood sat like melted copper in my open mouth as I rose above my broken body, splayed like a rag doll beside the dirt road. *Let me go,* I thought as I hovered, weightless. But I felt the pull of a gossamer thread of conscience and retribution that tethered me to this earth. Before I heard the screams of the sirens and my mother's wailing, I knew I wouldn't stay dead for long.

I watched, suspended between this world and the next, as my mother bent over Eve's body, my sister's legs bent in ways they shouldn't have been. Two paramedics worked on her, trying to push my mother away, while another noticed me, my body nearly hidden in the thick underbrush by the side of the road. He squatted next to me, his fingers reaching for the pulse in my neck. I felt none of this. I watched passively, as if I were a spectator in a movie theater.

I noticed that the paramedic was young, with thick blond hair on his head and muscled forearms that reflected the sunlight and reminded me of the sweetgrass. I was studying him so intently that I didn't realize that he'd begun to perform CPR. Still I felt nothing. I was more focused on my sister and on my mother, who hadn't looked in my direction yet. I hadn't really expected her to.

And there was Glen, tall and slender and strong, moving between Eve and me, helpless to do anything, his frantic pacing only stirring up dust.

I heard my name called and thought for a moment it might be my father come to take me away—away from the two broken girls and screaming mother and the air that moved in hot, thick waves. Flies buzzed and dipped over the thin trail of blood from my open mouth, but I couldn't hear them or feel them. I was thinking somebody needed to swat them away when I noticed for the first time the wooden church set back behind the trees. When Eve and I had walked our bikes down the dirt road just a short time before, giggling like the little girls we had once been, I hadn't seen it. It seemed impossible that I couldn't have.

The bright, whitewashed walls and tall steeple shone like a benediction in the relentless sunlight. The words PRAISE HOUSE were hand painted over the top of the arched red door, and a fence with a rusty gate swung as if spirits were passing through. It made no sense for the church to be where it was, nestled between the giant oaks and bright green undergrowth. But the white paint glowed in the sun as if brand-new, the wood steps leading up to the front door smooth and worn from the tread of hundreds of feet. Seated on the bottom step was a large woman with skin the color of burnt charcoal, her fingers working her sewing bone through the strands of a sweetgrass basket. She wasn't looking at me, but I was sure it was she who'd called my name.

"Who are you?" I wanted to ask, but all I could do was watch her and her fingers and the grass as it was woven into the pattern of the basket.

Grasping the basket in one hand, she stood and began walking toward where I lay. She stopped for a moment, looking down on me, her shadow blocking the sun from my baking body like the angel of mercy. Slowly she knelt by the paramedic and leaned toward me. He didn't seem to notice the woman as she bent close to my ear. Her words were clear, and I thought I could feel a cool breeze on my cheek from her breath as she spoke. "All shut-eye ain't sleep; all good-bye ain't gone."

The pain struck me like a fist as I was pulled back toward earth, down into the body I'd inhabited for seventeen years, and gasped with one long, icy breath. I opened my eyes, meeting the blue eyes of the startled paramedic. I turned my head, searching for the woman, but she and the church were gone. Only the sound of a rusty gate and the lingering scent of the heat-scorched sweetgrass told me that she'd been there at all.

I heard my mother crying out my sister's name over and over as I stared up at the clear blue sky, where a white egret circled slowly overhead. *All shut-eye ain't sleep; all good-bye ain't gone.* I didn't know what she meant, but I reasoned I'd been given another lifetime to figure it out.

Almost fourteen years later, I was still trying.

CHAPTER 2

Glen was waiting for me as I struggled up the peeling porch of our North Charleston house with the grocery bags, the change from my bus fare still clutched in my hand.

"You're late," he said softly as he walked toward me, his long legs and movements as graceful as a dancer's.

It was those long legs that had saved Eve's life—and probably my own—on that hot summer day all those years ago. He'd run for help on those legs, which had made him a track star in high school and the first two years of college. He'd never been mine, even back then. From the first moment Eve saw him at Carolina's sipping a Coke with fellow Citadel cadets, he'd been hers.

I smiled at him in the failing light. "Mr. Beaufain needed me to finish a project for him before I left."

Glen took one of the bags from me, his fingers lingering on my hand. He was close enough that I could smell his scent and see the damp tendrils of his dark hair that touched the collar of his shirt. He still wore his tie and I wondered if he'd even gone inside yet or had sat here waiting for me.

"How are you, Eleanor? How are you really? It seems I barely see you anymore."

I glanced nervously at the windows. "Don't," I said, the word as familiar and sharp as a razor's blade.

His voice was quiet so as not to be overheard. "I'm not doing anything to be ashamed of, Eleanor. I would never dishonor you that way."

"Don't," I said again, turning from him and feeling the stain of his touch and the slow burn of his gaze on my back.

My mother jerked open the door. "We've been worried sick. Where have you been? Your sister is just about starving to death, and I can't take my medication on an empty stomach." She took the last bag from my hand as I stole a glance at Glen, who gave me a sympathetic shrug.

Eve sat in her wheelchair in front of the bay window, where the grand piano had sat for a short time. When we'd lived on Edisto Island, my favorite place had been sitting on the piano bench next to my father, who smelled like the ocean and whose hands were coarse and roughened by shrimp nets and ropes. But his fingers had an elegance to them, holding within them the magic to translate the music from mere piano notes to flesh and blood, a living thing. Without any formal training himself, he taught me how to see the music in my head, to create food for the soul from black marks on a page. He bought books so I could learn how to read music, but his lessons taught me so much more. While my mother traveled with Eve to pageant after pageant, our father made plans for me to attend the Juilliard School in New York.

Eve glanced up at me. "Hello, Eleanor. We were beginning to wonder if you were going to come home at all."

I slid off my jacket and hung it on the back of a chair. I didn't answer her, afraid to let them know that I had thought of little else as I rode from downtown Charleston with my old friend and coworker Lucy Coakley in her ancient Buick Regal and then in the swaying, lurching bus for the second leg. "I'm sorry. I got held up at work." Lucy would refuse, but I'd insist on paying her for waiting two hours. I wouldn't tell them that, either.

A delicate furrow formed between Eve's brows. "You should tell Mr. Beaufain that you expect to be paid overtime if he wants you to work past five o'clock."

I thought of my boss, not much older than myself, with serious, slate gray eyes and a quiet manner; he sometimes brought me lunch and accepted my early departures and late arrivals without question. He knew I took my sister to her doctor's appointments, and although I knew nothing of his personal life except that he was divorced and had a young daughter, he seemed to understand everything my absences implied.

"I'll try and remember to tell him," I said, my eyes avoiding hers as my gaze strayed to the bay window behind her. It faced the rear garden once cultivated by my mother, until her arthritis had become too bad. It had gone mostly wild, and I found I liked it that way—liked the way the untamed vines crept around the bowed and chipped lattices like a child clinging to its adoptive mother. It was a symphony of unexpected colors, the bastardized floral arrangements of the uncultivated garden creating new chords that had never been heard before. When I stood in their unplanned perfection, I almost imagined I could hear their music.

My gaze returned to my sister's pale, perfect face as she lifted her mouth for Glen's kiss, her tiny hand with its gold band on the third finger gripping his arm. She was a china doll, with porcelain skin and violet eyes, hair as black as our mother's had once been, her limbs long and elegant. She wore a lavender silk housedress—made over by Eve from one of her pageant dresses—which set off her eyes and creamy skin. Most people saw only the beauty and the wheelchair and the delicate ankles and useless feet. It made them overlook the steely determination in her eyes and her unforgiving nature. But perhaps I saw them because I was the only one allowed to.

My mother disappeared into the kitchen, her voice trailing behind her. "Eve will need her bath tonight. She's had a headache for most of the day, and I know she'll enjoy one of your good head massages, too."

I followed her into the kitchen, already rolling up my sleeves. I wouldn't have time to change and hoped the smell of frying chicken wouldn't cling to my work clothes. I had two good skirts that I rotated with five blouses, and I couldn't imagine the smell of fry grease would be familiar or welcome at the investment firm of Beaufain & Associates.

I began to mix the flour, salt, and egg for my batter as Mama washed the chicken in the chipped porcelain sink. I was humming quietly to myself, keeping rhythm with the symphony that always seemed to be playing in the back of my head, when my mother shut off the faucet. She dabbed the chicken dry with a paper towel, her eyes focused on her task. "Are you playing at Pete's tonight?"

Dip, flip, roll. I concentrated on covering the chicken with the batter, hoping to hide the slight shake of my hands. "Pete hasn't called me. I guess they've found another piano player who could come more regularly. Besides, Eve needs her bath."

The grease popped in the fryer as she blew away a frizzy clump of graying hair from her face. It was only the end of May, but the heat of a Charleston summer had already begun to lay its stifling hand on the city.

"Eleanor, since when do you wait for him to call you? Just show up and play for a couple of hours. He pays good money. And you can help Eve with her bath in the morning before you leave for work."

I wiped my forearm across my forehead, feeling the beads of sweat. "I'm real tired today, Mama. I don't know."

Her silence shouted all the words that hung between us, everything about a hot summer day fourteen years ago and how I'd killed Mama's dreams.

"You can take the car," she said, as if I'd already argued and lost. Which, in a way, I had.

Dip, flip, roll. "Yes, Mama," I said, placing the first chicken leg into the fryer and watching its skin bubble in the heat.

After a nearly silent dinner, I cleared the dishes, then retired to my room to change. I slid on the red satin sheath dress that hugged my body and nestled too low between my breasts. My mother had it made from another one of Eve's old pageant dresses when she'd discovered that Pete's Bar, in a nearby North Charleston neighborhood, was looking for a piano player on weekday evenings, somebody who might encourage the down-at-luck crowd to buy one more drink.

My mother was washing dishes in the kitchen as I came down the stairs, Glen and Eve sitting next to each other on the couch watching television. Eve had her hand on Glen's arm, and they both looked up at me as I walked to the front door.

Glen jumped up. "I left my jacket and wallet in the front seat. Let me get those before you leave." He stood and took the car keys from the hall table.

Eve's eyes glittered as she watched Glen escort me out the front door. He followed me down the front steps to the curb, where he'd parked the car, being very careful not to touch me. He handed me the keys.

"You don't have to go, Eleanor."

Does he know? I stared up into his earnest eyes. "It's only for a few hours." My gaze skittered down to my hands, to the closely cropped nails I still kept short even after all these years.

"You don't have to go," he repeated, his words almost too soft to hear, and I felt certain that he did know—knew that when the music died from the piano I would look for somebody to give me what he could not. I hated myself for my weakness, for my inability to take my just punishment and live the life I'd been given. But I'd never forgotten the music my father had given me or the dreams that refused to die. I had once been like Icarus, flying too close to the sun, and in those nights in the smoky bar with the piano and the men with their sad, admiring glances, I could allow myself to believe—if just for a short while—that I was still flying.

The scent of Confederate jasmine flitted stealthily in the night air, sending a wave of fragrance before snatching it away like a serpent's tongue. I put my hand on the door handle of the car as Glen took a step closer. I held my breath at his rapid movement, his arm rising before he brought his hand down in a stinging slap on my forearm.

We both looked down in surprise as he lifted his palm to reveal a mosquito, dead and bleeding my blood against pale skin. Glen took a handkerchief from his pocket and held my arm carefully as he wiped away the mess, his gentle touch as startling as the sting from his slap.

I reached inside the car and brought out his jacket, the front pocket heavy from the weight of his wallet, and handed it to him. Our eyes met, and I wondered if mine looked as resigned as his did.

"It won't always be this way," he said softly. "I'll have my degree soon and I'll get my promotion so I can start making real money. Things will change."

"Will they?" I asked before slipping into the driver's seat. Staring through the windshield, I could still see Eve's wheelchair and my mother's sad eyes. There were some things in this life that could never change.

"Don't wait up," I said as I closed the door, knowing that he would lie awake in his bed next to Eve, listening for my footfall on the front porch, imagining he could smell another man's scent clinging to my skin.

I pulled away from the curb without looking behind me. I listened to the thrum of the tires against the pavement, hearing again the words of the Gullah woman. *All shut-eye ain't sleep; all good-bye ain't gone.* With a crushing sense of defeat and frustration, I realized that I was no closer to understanding what she'd meant than I'd been the day I'd touched the sun and been sent crashing down to earth.

CHAPTER 3

In the back corner of Pete's Bar, I sat on the piano bench, sipping my third scotch and soda, and felt the edges of my life begin to blur. I never got so drunk that I couldn't play, just drunk enough. The bar had begun to empty, leaving behind the stale air of loneliness and a haze of cigarette smoke that swirled under the ceiling fans like confused ghosts looking for the way out.

Draining my glass, I placed it on the piano before spreading my fingertips over the white keys. My fingers were long, like my father's, and I'd been able to reach an octave since I was seven years old. Unlike the rest of me, my hands hadn't changed much in the years since, except for the small scar near the top of my right index finger, as if I needed another reminder of what I'd done to Eve.

A middle-aged man with sad, red-rimmed eyes sat at a nearby table, his gaze never wavering from me. His collar was dirty, his tie stained, but as I began to play, the music transformed us into the people we had once dreamed of becoming.

I played "Summertime," a Gershwin standard that didn't require too much of me or my audience. Sometimes when I played it, I'd have a drunk make his way to my side to sing half-remembered lyrics. But I was left alone this time, just me and the music and the man with the sad eyes who'd shredded the label of his beer bottle and was now rolling up the little pieces of paper. He was building up his courage to approach me, I knew; I'd seen it enough times to recognize the signs.

I returned my focus to the music, in my head hearing my father's rich baritone as he sang to a younger version of my mother, a mother who'd not yet lost her beauty or dreams and still remembered how to smile. I felt my own smile curve my lips as I played the last chord as a slow arpeggio, each key separate and singing until the final note. I held it down with the pedal, allowing the sound to fade like the smoke from a blown-out birthday candle.

As soon as I lifted my fingers from the keys, I felt his presence beside me, smelled his breath full of beer and cigarettes and a hastily chewed mint. I turned to meet his eyes, noticing that he had probably once been a nice-looking man. But life and all its burdens were clearly marked in the deep ridges and lines of his face, like text on a written page in which each word had been carved with force.

The second thing I noticed was that Pete's wasn't as empty as I'd thought. Another man sat on a stool at the bar, the glare from the piano light hiding his face in shadow. But there was something familiar about him, in the shape of his head and broad shoulders. I blinked hard, annoyed that I couldn't see. He wasn't a regular; I knew that much. His back wasn't hunched with defeat, and his pants were pressed with a neat crease down the middle, his shoes burnished to a dull shine.

A throat cleared beside me. "Excuse me."

I looked up and smiled, remembering the distant feeling of skin against skin. "Yes?"

He cleared his throat again, his own smile shaky. "You've been playing for a while and I was wondering if you might be hungry. If you, that is, if you are, if you'd like to go with me. To get some food."

Tilting my wrist to read my watch, I saw that it was nearly midnight. Underneath the scotch and soda my stomach was empty. "I'm done here, and yes, I'd like that." I picked up my purse from beneath the bench and stood. I had to grab hold of the piano to steady myself, then picked up the tip jar and carefully upended the contents into my purse. Keeping my smile intact, I said, "I just need to go powder my nose, if you'll excuse me for a moment." I touched his arm, and his eyes met mine in understanding.

Concentrating on putting one foot in front of the other in my high heels, I began to make my way to the ladies' room. I had just passed the bar when I felt a firm hand on my arm.

"Eleanor?" Although it was spoken as a question, there was no doubt in the man's voice, a voice I recognized.

I twirled around too suddenly. My head spun and I had to strike out my hand to steady myself. I found myself gripping the sleeve of a fine gabardine jacket and looking into the dark gray eyes of my employer, Mr. Beaufain.

I blinked twice, as if I could somehow make him be somebody else. I realized I was still gripping his jacket sleeve and quickly let go. "Mr. Beaufain," I stuttered, my tongue feeling thick. "I didn't think you lived around here."

His eyes were hard, but I saw the edge of his lips soften slightly in the start of a reluctant smile. "I don't. I had a business meeting, and I needed a drink."

I lifted my eyebrows. Even in my not-quite-sober state I couldn't imagine anyone in *this* neighborhood having any kind of business that would interest Mr. Beaufain.

He looked behind me toward the piano, where the stranger was anxiously shifting from one foot to the other. Speaking loudly, he called out, "I'm taking the lady home."

"You have no right—"

He cut me off. "You're drunk, Eleanor. And I don't think you should leave this bar with a stranger."

Anger flickered to life beneath the haze of the alcohol. "How do you know he's a stranger?"

He didn't answer as we both listened to the front door slamming and I realized I hadn't even asked the man for his name.

Softly, Mr. Beaufain said, "I'll drive you home now."

"I have my own car," I insisted, still too embarrassed to meet his eyes.

"You're in no condition to drive. I'd rather make sure you get home safely than lie awake all night and wonder."

I felt my cheeks flame as I thought of him lying awake and thinking about *me*.

"But my brother-in-law will need the car in the morning," I continued, desperate to leave this scene behind.

"What time does he leave?"

"Nine o'clock," I replied, sure this would be the end of it as I gave him my address. My North Charleston neighborhood wasn't a convenient commute from his south-of-Broad home. I knew for sure where he lived only because Lucy had once driven me by his house on Gibbes Street. It was old and grand and so far out of my world that it might as well have been on another planet.

He lifted his BlackBerry and pushed a number, then spoke quietly into the phone. After a moment, he lowered it and regarded me with a grim smile. "Done." He held his hand up and I dropped my keys in his palm without hesitation. He was my boss, after all, and I was used to following his orders.

I hadn't heard his conversation because my head and stomach had begun to churn in opposing directions. "Excuse me," I said. I quickly walked past him and went to the restroom, where I promptly emptied the three drinks of scotch into the toilet. After rinsing my mouth and splashing cold water onto my face, I felt marginally better. I stared at the woman in the dirty mirror, at the spots where the silvering had begun to flake off, creating holes in her face. But it seemed like it was my true reflection, the only honest assessment of what I looked like from the inside.

Mr. Beaufain's black Mercedes was parked at the curb, and the thick scent of leather wafted out as he opened the door to let me into the passenger side. I put on my seat belt, then sat with all of my limbs locked and my hands clutching my purse on my lap. I felt like one of the old women on my bus who feared a mugging from every stranger.

"Here," he said, shrugging out of his jacket and reaching to place it over my shoulders. The car's air-conditioning cut through the humidity like a cold knife, giving me goose bumps, but I felt sure that his jacket wasn't to keep me warm.

I clasped the lapels together, grateful but still acutely embarrassed. "Thank you," I said as he started the car and pulled out into the deserted road. I stole glances at him in the passing flicker of streetlights and noticed a tightness in his jaw that wasn't normally there, and I remembered what he'd said about having business in the area and how he'd needed a drink. Feeling a need to fill the silence, I said, "I've never seen you at Pete's before."

He didn't answer right away. "I've never been. I was doing a favor for a family member—and I was supposed to meet somebody at the bar." I felt his gaze on me. "How odd that I'd find you there."

"I go there sometimes to play. Pete gives me fifty dollars an hour under the table plus tips." I wanted to slap my hand over my mouth. I didn't want to remind him of the humiliating scene he'd witnessed.

Mr. Beaufain was silent for a long moment. "I didn't know you played the piano, Eleanor. You're very good."

I stared at him, his strong profile outlined against the side window. Although I'd worked at his firm for more than two years and he signed my paychecks, I hadn't expected him to know more than my name and that I was always available for overtime. Or that I had a sick sister and had to sometimes come in late or leave early but I always made up the time. It surprised me that he'd expected to perhaps know more.

I looked back at my fingers, which were still clutching my purse. "My father taught me when I was little. He wanted me to go to Juilliard." I wasn't sure why I'd told him this, as if the darkness had somehow transformed the inside of the car into a confessional.

He didn't say anything. I wondered if it was because he knew what childhood dreams were, knew how easily they disappeared as the realities of getting older crept up like a tidal surge, stealing everything in its retreat back to the sea.

"It's never too late, you know. To become what you want to be. My daughter tells me that all the time." His cheek creased slightly, as if he were trying to remember how to smile. I'd never met his daughter, or even seen her, but Lucy had told me that she'd been very sick a few years ago and lived with Mr. Beaufain and not her mother. I'd never thought to wonder why.

"What does your father say now?" he asked.

His question caught me by surprise. "He drowned. When I was fourteen." I turned away from him, feeling the sting in my eyes and the spray of salt water as I remembered sitting on the pier and waiting and waiting, even after the storm became so bad that the police chief had to carry me to his car. "I stopped playing after that. And then Mama sold the piano . . . later."

I didn't continue, the memory too painful even in the plush confines and dark anonymity of a confessional.

"I'm sorry," he said, pulling up to a red light with his left blinker flashing. His voice seemed deeper in those two words, as if he understood the weight of grief, the years like strands of yarn that wound around themselves tighter and tighter until it was impossible to find where they'd begun.

"It was a long time ago," I said quietly. I smelled his jacket and the clinging scent of his cologne and felt oddly comforted by it. A plaid hair ribbon lay in the console between us, reminding me of what he'd said about his daughter.

"What's your daughter's name?"

His face softened in the dim light, making him appear younger than he was, and I realized that seeing him now, like this, away from the office, made me notice how handsome he was, how his eyes betrayed his emotions if one looked close enough.

He gave me a half smile that I was beginning to recognize. "Her mother named her Genevieve, but I usually call her Peanut."

A chuckle erupted from the back of my throat before I could call it back. There was something sweet about this serious man in the black suit calling his daughter Peanut.

"What's so funny?" He didn't sound offended.

He slid the car up to the curb in front of my house, and I wondered at the stab of disappointment in the pit of my stomach. I stared down at my hands, embarrassed again. "My father called me Ellie. He was the only one. Everybody else calls me Eleanor."

"Ah," he said, and I knew he understood.

He made a move to open his car door, but I stopped him.

"That's not necessary. I'm fine from here."

It looked like he might argue, so I quickly opened my door and stepped out into the muggy night air, my head surprisingly clear. I leaned down into the car. "Thank you, Mr. Beaufain. I really do appreciate the ride, although it wasn't necessary. You've got a long drive back to Charleston."

"I'm glad I was there." He smiled softly. "My name is Finn, by the way." His face was serious suddenly. "I was wondering . . ." He stopped as if measuring his words, then said, "Do I pay you enough?"

It took me a moment for his question to register. "Yes. Of course," I stammered.

He shook his head slightly. "I'm sorry. That didn't come out the way I intended. I suppose I wanted to ask you if you'd be interested in some extra work. Different from what you're doing now, and just a few hours a day. But I'd pay you well."

The thought of never having to go back to Pete's Bar brought back my light-headedness. "What kind of work?"

His gray eyes were contemplative under the domed light. "I don't really have a job description yet, but it would be as sort of a companion to an elderly lady—my great-aunt. She's in the hospital now but will be coming home in the next week." He spoke a little faster, as if he needed to work harder to sell me on the idea. "She has a large house on Edisto Island that she won't leave, and I don't like her being there by herself all day long."

Something warm and soft like hope fluttered in my chest, then just as quickly died. "I would have no way to get there and back."

"I can provide transportation." He said it suddenly, as if he'd just made up his mind.

I stepped back from the car, imagining I could smell the wet scent of the ocean. "I grew up on Edisto. I might know your great-aunt."

Something flickered in his eyes. "It's late. You should go inside. We can talk about this tomorrow."

I felt unsettled under his gaze. "Yes," I said. "I'd like that. Good night, Mr. Beau . . ." My voice trailed away. I felt odd calling him by his first name, but it seemed just as strange calling him by his formal name now, too. So instead I let the silence fall between us.

"Good night, Eleanor. I'll see you in the morning. And don't worry about your car—it'll be here."

"Thanks again," I said, then turned and hurried up the peeling porch steps, suddenly aware of how shabby our house must appear to him and grateful once again for the darkness that hid from sight all the things best kept hidden.

I felt him watching me as I turned the key in the lock and let myself in, not looking back as I closed the door. I listened as the soft hum of the engine disappeared down the street, hearing, too, the sound of quiet footsteps above me and then the creak of bedsprings.

I inhaled deeply, smelling the stale scent of fried chicken and the faint, expensive cologne that clung to the jacket I'd forgotten to give back. I pulled it closer around my neck as I switched off the hall lamp and made my way up the stairs.

Far away the sound of distant thunder rumbled in the sky, and I stared out the darkened window of my bedroom, feeling the storm brewing. For the first time in a long while, I thought of my childhood home and the sound of the wind blowing from the ocean to tease the house's eaves and make them sing the mermaids' songs. My father had taught me that so I'd never be afraid of storms. And until the day he'd died, I'd believed him.

Knowing I wouldn't sleep, I sat down on the bed, keeping the jacket on my shoulders, and allowed myself to think of possibilities while I waited for the rain to come.

CHAPTER 4

The Piggly Wiggly bag crinkled at my feet as Lucy braked sharply in the early-morning Charleston traffic, and the loose front bumper—held in place by twine and a prayer—clattered against the front end of the car. The air conditioner, having breathed its last sometime the previous summer, gasped out only warm air. A sheen of perspiration coated Lucy's dark brown skin even though it was barely eight thirty in the morning. I didn't bother looking into the mirror on the visor, knowing I looked similarly disheveled despite the extra time I'd spent dressing.

It was my fault we were late. I'd missed my bus because I'd realized too late that I couldn't walk into Beaufain & Associates with Mr. Beaufain's jacket draped over my arm and that I needed something to put it in. I'd run back inside the house to grab a grocery bag and had been waylaid by my mother wanting to know where the car was. Not having the time to get into an explanation or argument, I'd told her not to worry and then slammed out of the house again, for the first time in my life happy I didn't own a cell phone.

"You're not going to tell me what's in the bag?" Lucy asked for the second time. We'd known each other since we were in diapers growing up on Edisto and had never not shared a secret. Until now.

"It's just something I borrowed and need to give back," I mumbled, thinking of how I'd finally fallen asleep just as dawn cracked open the sky, Mr. Beaufain's jacket tucked firmly around my shoulders.

"Um-hmm," she said, her chin jutting out to show me that she meant exactly the opposite.

She turned sharply into the lot behind the office building on Broad Street and parked, first lowering all four windows. The car had a better chance of melting from the inside than being stolen.

I slid my ID into the slot in the back door and let us in, the sound of a distant telephone ringing muted by the soft carpet. We stood for a moment allowing the air-conditioning to brush over us before silently going our separate ways—Lucy to the accounting department and me to client services.

I had just made it to my desk and was trying to figure out the best place to put the bag where it wouldn't be noticed—having already decided to sneak into Mr. Beaufain's office when he left for lunch to place it on his chair—when I heard my name spoken. It reminded me too much of the night before, when he'd called my name as I walked toward the ladies' room at Pete's. I pretended to fumble with the bag under my desk until I composed myself.

"Eleanor," Mr. Beaufain said again. Even though he'd told me his first name, I couldn't see him as anything but Mr. Beaufain of the dark suits and murmured conversations with important clients.

I stood suddenly, clipping my head on the edge of my desk. I briefly saw stars but was too mortified to cry out in pain or rub the spot, where I was sure I'd have a bruise. I forced myself to meet his eyes as if I hadn't been in his car the night before telling him about my father or Edisto, as if I hadn't slept with his coat around my shoulders. "Yes?"

His gray eyes were dark and shuttered, making it easier for me to pretend that this man and the one from the previous night were separate. "After you get settled, can you come to my office, please?"

I nodded, my head hurting from the bump. "Yes. Just give me a few minutes, if that's all right."

His gaze flickered over my face with a look of concern before he curtly nodded and retreated to his large office, which faced Broad Street. I felt the interested gaze of his personal secretary, Kay Tetley, as she sat perched at her big mahogany desk pretending to open mail.

I turned on my computer and made a show of storing my purse in a drawer and stacking my to-do pile in the middle of my desk next to my Geechee Girl mug—a gift from Lucy—before retrieving the Piggly Wiggly bag and heading to Mr. Beaufain's office. I'd resisted the urge to freshen my lipstick, even though my lips felt dry and cracked, not wanting Kay's interest to be piqued any further. The crinkling grocery bag was enough.

He stood facing his window near the bank of computers that were never shut down, a cup of coffee steaming in his hand. He wore a black suit, even in this heat, but the cuffs of his shirt were starched bright white, a gold cuff link reflecting the light. The office itself retained the charm of the old building, which had once been a grand house and had then been converted to offices for Beaufain & Associates by his great-grandfather.

Prior to this visit, I'd been in his office only briefly to deliver documents. The tall ceilings were edged in egg-and-dart molding, and an antique chandelier surrounded by an elaborate plaster medallion dangled above the center of the room. Elegant paintings decorated the walls, including a watercolor by local artist Mary Whyte. I recognized it from an exhibition I'd seen at the Gibbes Museum, remembering the way I'd wondered how it would feel to be able to own such an object of beauty, to stare at it anytime you wanted.

The floors in here were the original heart pine, with a large Persian rug done in deep hues of burgundy and navy covering the center of the room. Only one framed photograph sat on his desk. Its back was to me, but I knew it held the picture of a brightly smiling young girl. My lips twitched as I remembered the nickname her father called her. *Peanut*.

The room smelled of books and furniture polish and the faint scent that I recognized from his jacket. I found myself blushing at the thought and was glad he couldn't see me.

"Beethoven's *Pathétique*. That's what you were playing last night when you thought nobody was there." He turned to face me. "Am I right?"

Too surprised to be embarrassed, I nodded. "I'm surprised you recognized it. I'm a little rusty on my classical repertoire."

He took a sip from his mug as his eyes assessed me. "Would you like some coffee?" He indicated a silver coffee service on a tray on an antique sideboard on the far wall.

I desperately needed the caffeine but was too nervous to be able to pour and drink without spilling something. "No, but thank you."

He watched me for a moment before pointing to the leather armchair on the other side of his desk. "Please, sit down." He waited for me to sit, then said, "I'm hoping your brother-in-law made it to work on time?"

It took a moment for me to figure out what he was referring to, and then I remembered the car I'd driven to Pete's and how Mr. Beaufain said he'd make sure it was brought back in time for Glen to get to work. There'd been no calls to the office from home, so I assumed everything had worked out. "Yes. Thank you. For everything," I added hastily.

As if he were as eager to move from the subject as I was, he cleared his throat. "I mentioned to you last night the possibility of extra work."

Slowly I said, "I'd like to hear more, but I'm afraid my . . . obligations at home might make adding hours to my work schedule not possible."

"Caring for your sister, you mean?"

I nodded. "My brother-in-law works long hours and my mother has really bad arthritis so that it's difficult to do things for Eve. I appreciate the flexibility that you've given me here." I felt a moment of panic as I thought that the reason why he was offering me another job was because of this very thing, that he wanted someone more reliable in my current job, someone who could work longer hours when necessary and who didn't need to leave sometimes in the middle of the day.

He interrupted my thoughts. "I don't want to add to your burden. I simply thought perhaps that an arrangement could be mutually beneficial. I wouldn't have to worry about my great-aunt being all alone all the time, and you'd have an extra source of income."

My gaze dropped to my hands. My voice was barely above a whisper, but I needed to say it. "Would you have thought of me for this position if you hadn't seen me at the bar last night?"

Gently, he said, "Let's call it serendipity. I became aware last night that my aunt wished to return to her home right before I ran into you. And then I heard you play."

I looked up. His face was serious, his eyes measuring.

"My great-aunts—my grandmother's sisters—were great musicians." He paused. "My aunt Helena is grieving right now. Her lifelong companion, her sister, has died, and she'll be returning to the house they shared alone. I'll be there as much as I can, and I'll have twenty-four-hour nursing care for her, but I was hoping for something . . . more."

"But why me?"

He didn't hesitate. "Because I see how you care for your sister, how responsible you are not just for her well-being but also for the work you do here. And when I saw you last night . . ." He stopped and moved to the sideboard to pour himself another cup of coffee. He moved with a taut grace, and I noticed how tall he was and how measured his movements, as if he was wound tightly and ready to spring. He focused on stirring his cup. "I'd pay you double the hourly rate of what I pay you here, and I'd start with five hours a week—hours of your choosing—plus I'd pay for the time it takes to get there and back. And you'd have a car for your exclusive use to drive to Edisto—or anywhere else."

He faced me and I saw a flicker in his eyes, making me think that there was something he was holding back.

"What's your aunt's last name? I might recognize it."

"Szarka. It's Hungarian. They moved here from Hungary." His steady gaze held mine, almost like a dare.

I knew the name, of course. It was the last name of the two old ladies who lived in the big white house on the wide Steamboat Creek—although they would have only been in their sixties and seventies when I lived on Edisto. They'd seemed old to us children, with their graying hair contained in tight buns and their unfashionable long skirts and thick accents. They were everywhere, it seemed, volunteering at shrimp festivals and house tours, organizing coat collections in the winter and school supply donations in the fall. And they'd always had the best candy at Halloween. I was ashamed to admit that we children had mimicked their accents and strange, foreign ways, but Eve and I were always the first in line at their door on Halloween.

"Yes. I remember them. And there was a boy. . . ." I stopped, my eyes widening in recognition. I remembered the boy I'd seen only from afar, sailing his paper airplanes down into the creek from the Steamboat Landing dock. I'd found one on the bank of the creek once. I was amazed at the myriad folds and tucks in the single piece of paper. It must have taken hours to make, and I remembered thinking how each fold contained an unanswered prayer or an unspoken dream, all of which had been too heavy to keep it aloft.

He moved to stand in front of me, leaning against his desk, his arms folded. "My mother died when I was nine, and my father sent me to Edisto during the summers to get me out of his hair, I suspect."

"I think I saw you a few times," I said carefully. But I didn't tell him how Eve would notice him around town or at church with his aunts and would dismiss him because he was a town boy from off island who didn't know how to set a crab trap. At least in the beginning, before Eve noticed boys and the boys started noticing her. I'd ignored him, too, but I'd never forgotten that paper airplane or its precise, delicate folds, which a boy had turned into wings. "You never came out to play."

"As an only child, I was what you would call overprotected. I wasn't allowed to go down to the beach or hang around with the island children. But my aunts were good to me, and I loved the island."

"Szarka," I said out loud for the first time, the hard consonants odd against my tongue. I knew that was their name, of course, although Eve and our friends had always simply referred to them as the "old ladies in the big house." But the name sounded familiar for another reason, too, as if I'd heard the name recently but couldn't remember where. "I'm curious, though. How did they end up on Edisto?"

He took a sip of coffee. "The house had belonged to my father's family, but my grandfather gave it to my aunts to live in when they came here from Hungary during the war. They wanted to be near family—but not too near—and Edisto seemed to be a good spot."

"I remember your aunts," I said. "They were always kind to us children, although I can't say we returned the favor."

He nodded, his eyes expectant, but I wasn't sure what he wanted me to say. I cleared my throat. "Your aunt Helena is the surviving aunt. What was her sister's name?"

"Bernadett."

I felt somehow ashamed, as if I should have known their first names—should have known them as individuals with names and distinct personalities, who had been doting aunts to a lonely little boy. I frowned, thinking. "You said that Helena was in the hospital following Bernadett's death. Were they both ill?"

Mr. Beaufain pushed away from his desk and returned to the window, studying the traffic on Broad Street. "Bernadett died in her sleep. And Aunt Helena . . ." He shrugged. "I don't think she wanted to live without her sister. She didn't eat or drink anything, and waited to die. I was lucky that I discovered them when I did."

I wanted him to face me again so I could look into his eyes. Maybe then I could see what it was he wasn't telling me. I fidgeted, the bag with the jacket crinkling at my feet, where I'd placed it on the floor beside my chair. "I need to speak with my mother and my sister, to see if this might work. . . ." My voice drifted away; I was unsure what else I should say.

Without turning around he said, "They have a grand piano, a 1926 Mason and Hamlin. You could play it as often as you'd like. Aunt Helena would like that. And I know she would enjoy your company."

I felt a small stirring in my chest again, a hard, dead thing startled into taking a breath. I waited a moment before I answered. "Can I let you know tomorrow? I really do need to discuss it with my mother and sister."

"Of course. And if you need to reduce the hours or make them more, that's fine. This sort of thing has to be a flexible arrangement. For all of us."

I thought again of the piano, a Mason & Hamlin, like the one my mother had sold, and I couldn't help but wonder why he thought he needed to bribe me with it.

"We'll talk tomorrow, then."

I stood suddenly, realizing that I was being dismissed. "Yes. And thank you." I felt awkward, not sure if I was thanking him for the opportunity or for driving me home. I didn't want to elaborate.

I headed out of his office, sensing his gray eyes following me until I'd closed the door, belatedly realizing that I'd left his jacket in a heap inside a Piggly Wiggly bag on the floor. I stared at the closed door to his office for a moment, telling myself I would tell him no regardless of what my mother and Eve said.

But I was unable to erase from my mind the image of a young boy on the dock sailing paper airplanes up into the air, weaving an invisible ribbon in the wide sky, then watching them crash into the water.

CHAPTER 5

Eve

I knew Eleanor was home even before I heard her key turn the latch. Ever since I can remember, my sister has been an extension of me, a disembodied limb that I have no control over. But she belongs to me, just the same. When she was born, Daddy put that tiny baby in my arms and said she was mine. Mine to love and take care of. I don't think he ever imagined things turning out the way they did.

"Mama?" Eleanor stood inside the door, bringing with her the scent of rain.

I looked up from the dining table, where I'd been sewing row upon row of endless sequins on a majorette costume for a sixteen-year-old. Mama's arthritis had gotten too bad to do the fine work, but I'd surprised us both by taking over with stitches as straight and precise as hers had once been.

"She's resting," I said, watching Eleanor slide out of her wet shoes, the blue pumps that had been polished so many times that they rubbed the inside of her ankles blue. "And Glen's working late again."

I watched her closely. I could read her face as if it were my own, but there was something in her expression now that I didn't recognize, something that reminded me of a long-ago birthday when she'd handed me a present and told me what was inside because she couldn't stand waiting any longer for me to open it.

She walked over to the table and turned on the overhead light. I hadn't noticed how dark it had grown outside or how I'd been straining my eyes. I blinked in the glare. "Thanks. Mama said to go ahead and start supper when you got home. She'll need to take her medicine when she gets up."

Eleanor nodded without seeming to really hear me, a nearly imperceptible humming zinging off her skin and scalding me like a spray of boiling water. As an afterthought, she turned to me. "I forgot to go to the store on the way home. I guess we'll do leftovers."

Her gaze strayed down to the majorette costume, to the tiny silver stars stitched within the sea of sequins. "You're as good as Mama." Her short, clipped nail touched one of the stars, making it move and shimmer in the overhead light.

"I'm trying," I said. I didn't want praise from her, from the baby who'd been given to me to protect but who'd forgotten our decreed roles along the way.

She nodded as she turned away to disappear into the kitchen, and I soon heard the refrigerator door being opened and closed, followed by the banging of pans.

After dinner, as the three of us sat swallowing the last of the reheated macaroni casserole and the salted tomatoes Mrs. Crandall had brought from next door, Eleanor put down her fork and straightened the napkin by the side of her plate.

"Mr. Beaufain has offered me another job. Not to take the place of the one I have, but something extra. Just five or so hours a week to start, and then we can adjust if I need to." She paused, as if trying to gauge our reactions. "He said he'd pay me twice what he pays me now."

Mama was frowning, but I could tell that the mention of the money had piqued her interest. "Doing what?" she asked, and I felt embarrassed for a moment for Eleanor, thinking of that dirty bar where she played the piano. I had never pretended not to know why she would come home late, and I knew this was why she avoided my eyes now.

"Acting as a sort of companion to his great-aunt. She's been in the hospital and she's coming home, but Mr. Beaufain doesn't want her to be alone with just her nurse. She lives on Edisto."

She had our mother's full attention now. "I don't remember any Beaufains on the island."

Eleanor shook her head. "She's his grandmother's sister. Szarka is the last name."

I saw recognition in my mother's eyes. "Helena and Bernadett?"

"Yes. They lived in the big white house on Steamboat Creek. They always had the best Halloween decorations and candy."

I sat back, remembering the two old ladies with their dated clothes, and the reek of mothballs that clung to them in the same way I imagined the memories of their homeland did. My mother was shaking her head as she stood and pulled a newspaper from the stack on the step stool. She flipped through a few pages before pulling out a middle section and placing it on the table in front of Eleanor. Pointing at an article, she said, "This Helena and Bernadett Szarka?"

Eleanor leaned over to read, the thrumming energy that had been pulsing through her since she returned home diminishing like a dying firefly. "It says only that Bernadett died of natural causes."

"And that it's under investigation," my mother pointed out.

"But that's usual when a person dies in the home, isn't it?"

"That might be, but they don't explain why Helena was almost dead when they found her. That doesn't sound right."

Eleanor was shaking her head, the movement almost frantic. "Mr. Beaufain explained that after Bernadett died, Helena stopped eating, not able to imagine life without her sister. But she's better now. She's coming home to Edisto to get better."

I heard the desperation in her voice, like the sound of a small animal caught in a trap. *Welcome to my world,* I thought. The thrumming had returned, making me wonder what it was about this job offer that was causing this reaction.

Mama continued. "Last weekend I ran into our old neighbor from Edisto, Mrs. Reed. I hadn't seen her in years, and there we both were at that huge discount fabric store on Sam Rittenberg Boulevard. She told me about poor Miss Bernadett and how people were talking about how strange it was that there was no funeral announcement. There was more gossip, but I don't see the need to repeat it." She shook her head. "The fact is, things aren't all right in that family, and I don't like the idea of you being all alone in that big house with an old woman. Besides, we need you here. Eve needs you. Especially now."

Mama shot a glance at me, and I knew what she was about to say. It had been my secret until that morning, when Mama had caught me throwing up in the garbage can after breakfast, and I wasn't sure I was ready to tell my sister. Eleanor looked at me, too, with no sign of understanding.

Turning back to Mama, she said. "My hours would be completely dictated by me, and he'd give me the use of a car so I could get there and back quickly. And they have a grand piano. I would be allowed to play it. . . ." She stopped suddenly, as if just now hearing our mother's words. "What do you mean, 'especially now'?"

Mama's smile was triumphant. "Eve's pregnant. She and Glen are going to have a baby."

The blood rushed from her face so suddenly that I thought she would pass out. I turned away, unable to look at her pain. Despite our past, which lay like an unweeded garden between us, she was still my sister.

She managed a smile, the corners of her lips not quite making it. "Congratulations," she said, leaning over and surprising us both with a kiss on my cheek. But her lips were cool and I thought I felt a tremor go through her before she pulled away.

Mama spoke again. "She'll have a lot of doctor's appointments. With Glen's long hours, and my arthritis making it difficult for me to drive, you'll be the one who'll have to take her to most of them."

Eleanor stood and began to gather the dinner plates, including the empty one she'd put on the table for Glen just in case. I knew she'd make him a plate of food and leave it warming in the oven. When we were younger, I'd wished to be just like her: strong and confident. So brave. But that was the old Ellie, the one I'd sent away the day I'd fallen from a tree and awakened to a broken body and an anger directed at the one person I could blame who wouldn't fight back. I made her understand that she had to work for my forgiveness.

But forgiveness is an elusive thing, like trying to hold a song in your hand. It was because of this that I didn't correct my mother by telling her that Glen and I could manage, that we didn't need Eleanor. Because I held the songbird tightly in my fist and I no longer knew how to let it go.

Eleanor surprised us by coming out of the kitchen immediately instead of doing the dishes. She stood with her hands gripping the top of Glen's empty chair. "They have a Mason and Hamlin grand," she said again, and in those words I heard her defiance overruling my mother's objections, saw the reckless, wild girl I'd once admired, and averted my eyes.

Yes, I thought, unable to say the word out loud. Just as I'd always been unable to tell her that I'd seen the Gullah woman that day, too, had heard what she'd whispered into Eleanor's ear. Nor could I tell her what the words had meant. She'd have to figure that out on her own.

Without returning to the kitchen, my sister headed outside into the rain, barefoot and without an umbrella, while Mama and I watched her go.

Eleanor

I dreamed of the old Gullah woman again that night for the first time in a long while. I'd walked in the rain for more than an hour, unaware of how wet I was, or how rough the pavement beneath my bare feet. I could feel only the startled panic I'd felt at learning of Eve's pregnancy and recall the flicker in Mr. Beaufain's eyes when he'd told me how his aunt had died. Maybe my mother was right to be concerned. But at that moment all I could think about was getting away from Eve and Glen and my mother, of having something in my life that had nothing to do with them. Whatever secrets Mr. Beaufain and his aunt kept, they couldn't touch me; I was already too numb.

When I lay down to sleep, the rain from my hair seeping into my pillow, I dreamed of Edisto, of the sunset over Russell Creek and the feel of pluff mud beneath my toes. I sat on a pier, the same pier where I'd waited for my father, and I knew I was waiting still; I just wasn't sure for what. And then she was there again, sitting on the pier next to me with her sweetgrass as she wove each strand in and out, her fingers like words as they told a story of the basket she was making.

Her dark skin gleamed with sweat, although I didn't feel hot at all but could feel the cool breeze of the ocean as it kissed my skin, bringing with it the tang of salt and my own sweat. These were the smells of my childhood, the background scent of the music I had created there with my father. A cold dryness swept through me, a desolate wind of grief that wound itself into a ball in my throat, choking me.

I wanted to cry, but I felt the hard, dark stare of the woman beside me and I reluctantly turned to meet her gaze, afraid I'd miss whatever I'd been searching for on the horizon.

Must take care of de root for to heal de tree.

I wasn't sure if she'd spoken aloud or if I'd just heard the words in my head. But I knew I wasn't alone in fighting my demons, and the tight ball in my throat suddenly unfurled, like a thread pulled on a hem until all the stitches were gone.

I leaned toward her to ask her what she meant, but I was back in my bed again, the pillow still damp from my rain-drenched hair. I sat up, wondering what had awakened me. I blinked in the predawn light, noticing that my door was open.

"Eleanor?"

I swung my legs to the floor, feeling dizzy as I sat up. "Glen? What are you doing in here?"

He closed the door softly behind him but stayed where he was. "I wanted to talk to you—alone. To see . . ." His voice drifted off, but I knew what he'd been going to say. He'd always been very easy to read.

"Congratulations," I said, my voice at odds with the word. "You and Eve must be very excited." We stared at each other through the dimness, the hazy light of early morning like smoke on a battlefield.

"Eve wants children. . . ." Again he seemed unable to finish his sentence.

"I know," I said, wanting to scream at him or cry but remaining silent instead. My heart ached as I watched him, longing to smooth his hair, still damp from his shower—wanted him to want me enough to take a step forward. But he stayed where he was and I nearly sagged with relief.

He opened his mouth to say something else, but I held up my hand, unable to bear it. "She's your wife, Glen. You don't need to justify anything to me."

His jaw clenched and he stood ramrod straight, just like the soldier he had once wanted to be. "I hope you can be happy for us."

"Of course," I lied. "I'm going to be an aunt."

He winced. "I didn't mean for this to happen. Not the baby part," he explained quickly, "but you and I."

I remembered his hurried words before I'd headed out to Pete's Bar and his promise that things would be different. He just hadn't told me how much. I couldn't help but laugh, the sound like the dry wind over the desert. "There's never been a you and I. Besides, I don't think the universe cares too much about what we want."

A slice of sun pierced the crack between my curtains, illuminating his face in time for me to see him flinch. The sound of an alarm from down the hall startled us both.

"I just wanted to make sure you were okay," he said, pausing for a moment before opening the door and sliding from my room as stealthily as he'd entered it.

I listened as the house awoke, listened to the gurgling sound of water running and my mother's careful steps on the old wooden floorboards, as if nothing had changed. I rose from the bed and headed for the shower, listening to the soft murmur from my mother's room as she said her morning prayers.

The cold spray of the water felt good on my warm skin, reminding me of my dream of sitting on the pier and staring at the horizon as I waited for something I could not name, and I wondered how it was possible to mourn what I had never even had.

CHAPTER 6

Being born and raised on Edisto meant that I had never wished or hoped to live anywhere else. The island rests along the South Carolina coast halfway between Bluffton and Charleston, guarding St. Helena Sound like an osprey guards her nest. Like most islands in the Lowcountry, it's been inhabited and fought over for thousands of years, but it always seemed to me that the beauty of my Edisto was in the colors of the sky and the grass and the creeks that changed with the seasons and that made visitors want to stay. And pulled at the hearts of those who had been forced to leave her.

I smelled the pluff mud as we crossed over the Dawho River Bridge on our way to Edisto, imagining I could hear the teeming insects that lived in the tall marsh grasses of the tidal creeks and estuaries that sprawled like arthritic fingers around us. I focused on the distant horizon, the line where ocean met land, as if expecting to see my father's shrimp boat. But his boat was long gone, as were all the other shrimpers who had once called Edisto home. It had been a dying industry even when my father plied these waters, and like him, all that was left of the industry were memories and faded photographs and the stories of the old folks who still remembered the glory days before gated communities and golf courses had crept into the Lowcountry like untamed kudzu.

"How does it drive?" Mr. Beaufain—Finn—asked. I found it easier to call him by his first name when we were away from the office. He was referring to the white Volvo SUV he'd given me to drive. It was normally used by Genevieve's nanny, who was currently at home in Belgium with her family until the beginning of the school year in the fall.

"Great," I said. "Drives like a car instead of a truck. Just don't make me parallel park it." I'd never had the regular use of a car, so it felt odd to be sitting behind the wheel of any vehicle, especially one that still smelled like new leather.

He smiled and I barely recognized him. Gone were the black suit, French cuffs, and tie, replaced with a collared knit golf shirt and khakis. His businesslike demeanor seemed to have been shed with the suit, leaving behind a man who looked a lot more relaxed and knew how to smile but still carried shadows behind his eyes.

"Don't think there will be much call for that. There's plenty of room for parking at Aunt Helena's house. And I have a carriage house behind the house on Gibbes Street. Just in case you need to stop by to pick up some of my daughter's things," he added hastily, realizing at the same time I had that he was assuming I'd come to his house. He continued. "When Aunt Helena is feeling better, I'd like the two of them to spend some time together."

I nodded, flicking on my blinker as he indicated a turn onto Steamboat Landing Road. I had rarely driven on Edisto. I knew every road, every beach access point, but mostly from the seat of a bike or johnboat. I had left the island after I'd been issued a driver's license, but I'd still preferred to get around by boat or bicycle.

We turned again, down the narrow dirt road that led to the large white house overlooking Steamboat Creek, near the dock where I'd once seen Finn tossing his paper airplanes into the wind. I'd been in the johnboat with Lucy, eagerly paddling in the opposite direction so he wouldn't see us, afraid the off-island boy would want to come with us. I hadn't told Finn, unsure if he'd welcome the knowledge that I'd witnessed that, had seen his aloneness as a child.

The tires crunched over the unpaved drive, past the wax myrtles and a stand of pecan trees, until I reached the white house with the red roof. It had stood near the bend of the creek where it met the North Edisto River for nearly two hundred years, and it was clear from its defiant posture that it was planning on remaining there for at least as many more. A carved wooden sign that seemed to be almost as old as the house had been stuck into the earth right past the pecan orchard, announcing the house's name: LUNA POINT.

I pulled up behind a large white Cadillac, a relic of the eighties. Finn caught my gaze and gave a wry grin. "I need to get rid of that, but I don't want Aunt Helena to feel like I've taken away all of her independence, even if she knows she'll never drive it again."

I nodded in agreement. If it weren't for Lucy and her Buick, I would have felt like a mouse in a maze with no exit. I turned off the ignition and we sat for a moment in silence. His long fingers drummed on his thighs and I realized with some surprise that he was nervous.

Feeling a tinge of alarm, I asked, "She knows I'm coming, right?"

He didn't respond right away, which answered my question. I focused on not sagging against the headrest. "So what happens if she doesn't want me to stay?"

He turned cool gray eyes on me. "She's unable to determine what is in her best interests right now. As her guardian and only surviving adult relation, I have to decide what she needs. And what I need. I can't be with her all the time, but I know she wants to stay in her house. This is the only way I can make that work for both of us."

"All right," I said, smoothing down my skirt and opening the car door. I glanced across the seat at him. "I just wish you'd explained that to me before . . ." I'd almost added *before I set all of my hopes on this.*

He looked at me with understanding, and I wondered how I hadn't noticed this about him before, hadn't realized that his gray gaze missed nothing yet at the same time created a barrier to seeing what lay behind them.

"It'll work out, Eleanor. It will."

I was tempted to believe him if only because he said so.

The house was much as I remembered it, a raised cottage with a tabby foundation and front and back porches as wide as the house, each with a vista of creek or river. I was surprised to see that it was in good repair, having pictured it as being old and sick like the owner, then remembered that Finn was in charge of its upkeep.

The white clapboard siding gleamed in the buttery morning sun, the smells and sounds of the island pulling me back for a moment as I remembered my happy childhood spent barefoot on the beach, digging for clams with Lucy and Eve and the summer children. Something like pain pressed at my heart, reminding me of why I never looked back at those days. Remembering made everything so much harder, like the flash of a camera that blinded you and sent you stumbling.

Empty flowerpots sat on the steps leading up to the porch and on either side of the front door, the soil inside dry and brittle. Six white wicker rocking chairs faced sightlessly out toward the river, swaying like ghosts. Finn didn't knock on the thick wooden door or press the doorbell before opening the door and motioning for me to enter.

I found myself blinking in the sudden dimness. Although windows covered most of the house's façade, it was startlingly dark inside. I stood in a high-ceilinged foyer where a stairway with heavy wood balustrades led the way to the second story.

Wainscoting encircled the walls in the hallway and alongside the staircase, the steps carpeted with a navy blue oriental runner. All the wood was painted white, saving the interior from being overwhelmingly dismal. As my eyes grew accustomed to the darkness, I saw that the draperies were drawn over the windows. And as I allowed my gaze to scan the walls over the wainscoting, I began to understand why.

A collection of oil paintings of various sizes hung on the walls in the foyer, their colors protected from the sun and muted by shadows. These weren't the typical paintings one found in a house, much less an island house. Knowing virtually nothing about art, I could still tell that these were very old. Stepping closer to what appeared to be a naked Greek god holding a trident and lounging on a cloud surrounded by cherubs, I could see small cracks in the paint. I could also tell that the paintings hadn't been professionally stretched and framed. The canvases hung loosely in the frames, faint undulations still visible, as if the paintings had been kept rolled up for an extended period of time.

As if anticipating my question, Finn said, "The aunts brought them from their home in Hungary. I've stopped begging them to allow me to get them restored and properly framed. Or even appraised. Aunt Helena didn't want me to touch them."

I looked across the foyer to what appeared to be the dining room, where a large still life of a fruit bowl was centered by faded rectangular patches where other paintings had apparently hung.

"She moves the paintings from time to time, taking some down and hanging new ones or not replacing them at all. I've spent virtually every summer of my childhood here and watched her move the paintings, but never once have I been able to encourage her to talk to me about them. I just gave up, figuring it was one of her eccentricities."

I raised my eyebrows. This was the first I'd heard about any "eccentricities."

"They're all adorable, I assure you," he said, a faint smile teasing his lips.

I almost laughed, wondering if that was the first time he'd ever spoken the word "adorable" out loud. "What about Bernadett?" I asked. "Did she have any say about the paintings?"

He shook his head. "Helena was the oldest and Bernadett deferred to her. I suppose if one had to die before the other, it happened the way it should have. As much as Helena would prefer not to live without her sister, Bernadett couldn't have." Something shifted behind his eyes. "I loved them both, but Bernadett just seemed . . . broken."

He stopped as if suddenly realizing he'd spoken aloud and regretted it.

The sound of footsteps from the back of the house made us both turn. A mature redhead wearing a bright floral dress and sensible shoes came and stood at the bottom of the stairs. She was short and stout, and she had to look up as she approached. Her face brightened when she recognized Finn.

"I thought I heard voices. Mr. Beaufain—it's so good to see you." She frowned, a deep V forming between her brows. "I'm afraid Miss Helena isn't having a good day." Her gaze slid to me in reproach. "I don't think she's up for visitors."

"Aunt Helena hasn't had a good day in a while. I think it's time we changed that, don't you?" He indicated for me to step forward. "Nurse Kester, this is Eleanor Murray. She'll be spending time with Miss Helena while she recuperates to give you and Nurse Weber a break and to assist in my aunt's convalescence in any way that she can." He smiled, but it wasn't necessarily a pleasant one. It was more like the smile of a person used to getting his way. Or that of a talk-show host who already knew what was behind the curtain. This was the man I recognized.

He continued. "Unless she's having a medical emergency that I wasn't informed of?"

Nurse Kester flushed. "No, sir. She's just being uncommunicative and wouldn't eat. She's finally sleeping."

Finn nodded. "We'll let her rest for a bit, then, while I show Eleanor around. Please let me know when she wakes up."

The nurse left and I began wishing that I could open the drapes. I craved light. I had ever since I was a child. Maybe it was because I'd grown up beside the great Atlantic, where the sun touched us first every morning, the reflected light illuminating our world as if the dark had never been.

"I've hired two full-time nurses for the time being, and they work out their schedule so that there's always one of them here. There's an old maid's room off the kitchen that we've made into a little bedroom where they can sleep near Helena. I'm afraid she doesn't allow them too much rest." He stepped back. "Let me show you around."

Opposite the front door was the short hallway where Nurse Kester had come from, which appeared to lead into a kitchen and the back of the house. Across the hall from the dining room was another room, with a matching fluted arch painted a bright white that separated it from the foyer. From where I stood, I could see the back legs of what looked like a wooden bench with a padded seat. A small tingle began at the base of my spine.

Finn's cell phone rang and he excused himself for a moment to answer, leaving me to move forward on my own. I stopped in the room's threshold, my fingers itching to throw open the drapes to allow in the light. The walls were papered in a bloodred floral pattern, making the room seem even darker. A large crystal chandelier dangled from the high ceiling. I searched the wall inside the doorway for a light switch and turned it on. The bulbs shone weakly through the crystal drops of the light fixture, their glow barely parting the dimness to illuminate several badly framed paintings. I didn't look too closely at the art, as my attention was distracted by the large black piano that dominated the room.

The tingle that had begun at the base of my spine edged out with little fingers, like a river slowly flooding its banks. The piano was ebony satin, like ours had been, and was a little over six feet long. Its elegant legs tapered at the bottom into brass casters. It sat on an oriental rug, undoubtedly to protect the wood floors from the weight of the instrument, but the rest of the floors were left bare. I could only imagine the sound it would create in this room of high ceilings and virtually no other furniture besides two small chairs and a love seat.

But the top of the piano was closed, as was the fall board, and although it showed no sign of dust, it seemed to have been abandoned, its music silenced as if in mourning. I thought of the old women who'd lived here and of Bernadett's death and Helena's near death, and it occurred to me that the whole house was mourning along with the piano. I'd closed up my own piano after my father's death, as if it contained all my good-byes. It had remained that way through our move to the North Charleston house and then until the new owners had come in a large truck to take it away.

"When Helena's better, I know she'll welcome the sound of music in here again."

I turned, startled to hear Finn's voice behind me. I nodded, my throat crowded with memories that blocked my voice. I stayed where I was, unwilling to move forward, as if by doing so I would somehow make the piano disappear. I seemed to do that with all the things I'd ever loved.

Swallowing, I said, "Does Helena play?"

His gray eyes seemed to be assessing me, and I found I couldn't meet his gaze. It was as if he knew something I didn't and was wondering if he should tell me or let me figure it out for myself.

"She did," he said. "She and Bernadett were wonderful musicians. They both sang and played piano. But Helena was the better pianist, although it's hard to describe how." He paused for a moment, thinking. "Bernadett was technically brilliant, but Helena became the music she played."

I looked away from him, ashamed to find my eyes stinging. I remembered my father saying the same thing about me, how it was possible to learn all the technical attributes of the music, but the way I felt when I played was something that couldn't be taught.

"Maybe she'd like to play for me," I managed to say.

He shook his head. "Her arthritis is too bad now. She hasn't played for years. I've come to think of this as Bernadett's piano, since she's the only one who's played it for as long as I can remember. She might not have been as gifted as Helena, but she loved to play."

I glanced back at the silent, closed piano, wondering whether this one held as many good-byes as mine had.

"Come on," he said, gently touching my elbow. "Let me show you the rest of the house."

I followed, eager to leave the room and all its possibilities behind me.

The house was large, with four bedrooms, a dining room, a music room, and a nice-sized recently updated kitchen. A sunroom had been created along the northwest corner of the house to encompass the creek and river views and was accessed through the kitchen. As a child, I'd wondered about this room as I regarded it from the vantage point of my johnboat, what it must be like to be inside a place with glass walls.

Two well-worn armchairs sat facing the river, the table between them littered with books; more books—including one that was opened and face-down—were piled on ottomans with worn fabric that matched the armchairs. The room had an air of abandonment, but it seemed as if the occupants had just put down a book and left, expecting to return soon. A small carriage clock ticked on a low shelf, keeping time for no one. On the wall with the door, the only wall not made of windows, were tall bookshelves overflowing with books and knickknacks and a large collection of sweetgrass baskets. Of all the rooms I had seen so far, this was my favorite.

A shallow oval sweetgrass basket sat on top of one of the shelves, and as I looked around I saw that not only the shelves but most surfaces were full of the baskets, all in assorted shapes and sizes. I'd seen a few larger baskets in the rest of the house, but the sheer number of them in this one small room was almost overwhelming.

"Aunt Bernadett collected them," Finn explained. "She couldn't drive down Highway Seventeen without stopping at a basket stand or visit the Charleston Market without buying one. She loved the stories that were woven into each basket." He picked up a small round basket with a lid and examined it for a moment. "They're probably worth a small fortune now, but I doubt Aunt Helena will ever get rid of them."

I touched a deep, round centerpiece basket on the floor filled with old catalogs. "My friend Lucy's mother and grandmother had a stand on Highway Seventeen. I used to watch them create their baskets, and Lucy and I would try to memorize the patterns and guess which one they were making. And then I moved. . . ." My voice drifted away and I looked up to find him watching me intently. I walked past him, out of the room, eager to continue the tour.

All of the bedrooms were upstairs, but the downstairs parlor, with access from the dining room and the kitchen, had been converted into a room for Helena. We walked quietly past the closed door as Finn led me toward the stairs and the upper level.

"You probably won't have much need to be up here, unless you decide to spend the night on occasion. I have a housekeeper, Mrs. Adler, who comes three times a week and cooks and cleans and stocks the refrigerator, so there are always fresh sheets on the beds. My daughter has a room since she comes here occasionally, too, although not lately." I caught his frown as he turned back down the hall toward the staircase, past four doors, three of which were closed.

"The guest bedroom is at the end of the hall—it was Helena's room until about five years ago, when the arthritis in her knee got too bad and we had to move her downstairs. And Gigi's room is next to that." He paused in front of the remaining closed door. "This was Bernadett's. Helena doesn't want anybody in there."

I nodded, remembering how I'd wanted to keep the back hall with my father's jackets and boots left alone like a shrine. But it had been the first area cleaned out when Mama had decided we needed to move.

I moved to stand before the one door that stood ajar. "What's in here?"

Finn stopped directly behind me, his warm breath brushing the back of my hair. "A relic."

I pushed the door open wider and stood where I was, taking it all in. The twin-sized trundle bed was covered in a navy blue quilt with various astronomical bodies stitched precisely in brightly colored thread. Star charts and framed photographs of spaceships covered the walls, while what seemed like hundreds of tiny hooks dotted the ceiling, each holding a small fishing line attached to a flying object: model rockets, war planes and passenger jets, planets from the solar system, and elaborately folded paper airplanes.

I turned to him, unable to hold back my grin. "This was your room."

His face remained unreadable. "Yes. Every summer from the time I was about nine until I went to college. The aunts never saw a reason to change it. To them I stayed that small boy."

I tried to reconcile the man I knew now with the boy who'd lived in this room, had made the airplane models and rockets, had folded each fold in each paper plane, but I couldn't. That boy was long gone, and I couldn't help but wonder if he saw holes, too, when he looked at his reflection in a mirror.

"I wanted to be an astronaut," he added quietly, his expression showing that he was as surprised as I was with his admission.

I looked closely at him. "I saw you once. When you were about twelve, I think. I might have seen you before, but that was the first time I realized you were the nephew who stayed with the two old ladies in the house in the summer but wasn't allowed to play with us." I blushed, realizing what I'd just said. I kept speaking to hide my embarrassment. "You were playing with a paper airplane and you tossed it over the creek, but it turned and got stuck on the bank. I went looking for it the next day and found it."

"I know," he said softly. "I saw you. From our dock. That's as close as I was allowed to get."

It was my turn to frown. "Did you know who I was, then? When you hired me?"

He shook his head. "Not until I saw you that night at that awful bar and you told me you'd grown up in Edisto. That's when I realized I knew who you were. I remembered seeing you with your mother and sister in church."

You remember Eve, I wanted to say. I'd wear the same skirt and blouse every Sunday—the only dressy clothes I'd owned—but my mother would dress Eve up like she was competing in a pageant. Nobody noticed me at all.

"What a small world," I said, stepping back into the hallway, away from the ghost of the little boy who still lived in the room.

His answer was the sound of the door snapping shut behind us. Nurse Kester appeared at the top of the stairs at the end of the hallway. "Miss Helena is awake, Mr. Beaufain. I told her you were here with Miss Murray, so she's pretending to still be asleep."

Finn's cool eyes met mine. "Are you ready for this?"

I wasn't sure if I was or not, but I seemed to have run out of options. "Yes. I'm ready."

I followed him and Nurse Kester down the stairs and toward the back of the house, sensing the waiting presence of the ghost boy who'd once wanted to be an astronaut and that of the silent piano waiting patiently for the music to start again.

CHAPTER 7

Helena

I heard the girl's voice from far away, probably because it sounded like my Bernadett's—soft like the way a hurricane starts with the gentlest breeze. I turned my head, half-prepared to rise and greet her before I remembered. My sister was gone, vanished like morning frost that fades as you watch. I closed my eyes and turned my head toward the wall, wanting to imagine, just for a few more moments, that I was still in my bedroom in our little house on Uri Utca in the Buda hills, which overlooked the Danube, my beautiful Bernadett in the twin bed beside mine.

"I can come back another time," the girl said. But I heard Finn's footsteps approaching, just as firm and purposeful as they had been since he was a five-year-old boy, and I knew he was not going to leave until he had done what he had come here to do.

I felt them in the doorway, watching me, and I practiced slow, even breaths while remembering the grocer across the street—remembering him, not his name—shouting out in my native tongue to the Laszlo boys, who made it a game to steal Linzer cookies from the bin at the front of his store on their way home from school. I could almost smell the sweet honey scent of *anyukám*'s baking *mézeskalács* in the bakery on the first floor of our house, making me crave food for the first time in a very long while. I felt that if I kept my eyes closed a little longer, I would see Bernadett rise from her bed to begin her morning prayers. I was desperate to speak to her; did she not know that? *Please hurry and wake up, Bernadett. Please.*

"Aunt Helena?"

Finn's voice rushed at me, erasing my old bedroom as quickly as a crashing wave takes over a sand castle. Slowly, I turned my head and looked up into my great-nephew's face, the face with Bernadett's eyes, framed by the same wide brow. I wondered sometimes if this was why I had always loved him so, if I somehow saw him as a second chance.

"Aunt Helena?" he said again, taking my hand. I had not realized how cold I was until I felt the warmth of his skin against mine.

"I am not dead, if that is what you are wondering." My "g" still came out like a "k," something I had not been able to stop even after all these years.

His eyes smiled but without the rest of his face, something my sister had perfected, too. It was disconcerting at first, never knowing what they were really thinking.

"I've brought Eleanor to meet you. I told you about her, remember?"

I squinted as the slight figure beside him moved forward, and I felt Nurse Kester place my glasses on my face before tucking another pillow beneath my head so I could partially sit up.

I frowned at the skinny girl with the light brown hair and wide blue eyes, wondering what Finn had been thinking to bring her here. I imagined she seemed timid to others, her shoulders curved forward as if bracing for a blow. But she moved forward and did not hover behind Finn, and her eyes met mine instead of staring at a place behind my head. She reminded me of the Russian stacking dolls my mother had given me for Christmas one year, a smaller doll nested inside each one, hidden from sight until you opened the larger one.

I frowned. "Yes, you did. And I told you not to bother. I do not need anybody else in this house making noise. I have Mrs. Adler and my nurses, and the way they poke and prod at me with all of those needles, I am surprised I do not look like Swiss cheese. If I have any more 'help' like that, I will be dead in a month."

Finn winced almost imperceptibly, and I knew we were both remembering that day when he had found me on the floor by Bernadett's bed, courting death like an old lover. "I am fine," I added more gently.

"But I'm not," he said. "I can't be with you all the time, and I think you might get lonely here by yourself with just nursing care. Eleanor can read to you, or talk, or discuss books or movies. And when you're feeling up to it, she can take you to church or out to see friends."

I stilled, wondering how he could think that I could return to my old life, as if all that had happened had been a made-up story like the old movies Bernadett and I would sometimes watch. And then I remembered. *He doesn't know.* My secret was mine alone now, like a piece of ripe fruit perfect on the outside, its rotten core visible only after one had bitten into it.

I turned my face away, afraid that he could read my thoughts.

"She plays the piano, Aunt Helena. As well as Aunt Bernadett, I think. When you're feeling better, you can ask her to play for you."

The girl tensed, and I turned to study her again, her coltish body seeming to cleave to the shadows. She had one of those delicate, lovely faces that one sometimes overlooked in the presence of blatant beauty, a tulip in a garden of red roses. And it was almost painfully clear that she had no idea of her own beauty.

"She does not look like a musician," I said, watching the girl closely.

Her chin rose slowly, her fine eyes taking their measure of me. "Neither do you."

Finn looked at her in surprise, while I forced my mouth to remain in a frown. "Who is your favorite composer?"

Keeping her eyes on mine, she said, "We can talk about that once you've eaten something. I believe Nurse Kester said she'd left your lunch in the fridge. Would you like me to get it?"

I shook my head. "No, let Finn do it. You may stay."

Finn glanced at the girl and she nodded. "I'll be right back," he said.

We watched him leave, and then I closed my eyes. "I do not want you here. It would be better if you told Finn that you do not want this job anymore. Tell him I am too much trouble, too feisty for you. That I am not worth your time."

She was so quiet, I wondered if she had left. But then she spoke. "I can't do that. I'm sorry."

I do not know what made me angrier—her refusal or her apology. How could she be sorry? I was the one who was sorry—sorry that I had not been allowed to die with Bernadett and silence the sorrowful songs that haunted me still. My voice trembled. "Have you ever known grieving that ends only when your own heart stops beating?"

I wanted to look away, my own pain mirrored in her darkening eyes.

"Yes," she said, so quietly that I did not hear her. But I felt the word as if I had been struck, the waves of pain slow and undulating. *Ah.* I closed my eyes in understanding, knowing now why Finn had brought her. I just had no idea how to tell him that he was wrong, that a broken heart stayed broken even in the company of another.

"I'll be back on Saturday," she said, her chin lifting slightly before she turned and headed toward the door. She paused on the threshold, then spoke without turning around. "My favorite composer was Chopin, but his music reminds me too much of my father." She stepped aside to allow Finn and Nurse Kester to enter with a food tray. Facing Finn, she said, "I'll meet you in the foyer when you're ready to leave."

We watched her go, listening to her unhurried tread on the wood floors of the hallway, and I imagined Bernadett's ghost nearby, applauding.

Eleanor

As a child growing up on Edisto, I spent as much time with Lucy's family as with my own, loving how they kept a spot open for me at their Sunday supper table, and grasped my hands during the blessing as if my pale skin wasn't any different from their own.

It was to their house I'd run after my father's boat was found, where I'd gone to be gathered tightly into the large bosom of Dah Georgie, Lucy's grandmother. I had stayed with them until my mother came to get me, saying she needed help planning the funeral. I had never gone back to their small house near Store Creek, wanting my memories of it to fade so it wouldn't hurt so much.

But I could still hear their voices. The Gullah language, a mixture of West African dialects and English, had always seemed like music, a symphony of words, the lilting cadences and rounded vowels the notes. Sometimes if I pressed her really hard, Lucy would speak in Gullah, but only if we were alone where nobody else could hear. I once asked her why she was so reluctant, and she told me it was because Gullah is the language you cry in.

I remembered that as Finn and I drove away from Luna Point, with its dark rooms and the lonely old woman. Her accent wasn't as strong as it had once been, as if the ocean's waves had weathered the harsh consonants like a battered shore. But I wondered if she thought in Hungarian, and if it was the language she still cried in.

"So, what do you think?" Finn asked, his eyes nearly translucent in the glare from the sun.

"Shouldn't I be asking you that?" I kept my eyes focused on the road ahead, feeling his steady gray gaze on me.

"I still want to hire you, if that's what you're asking. I just want to make sure you're still interested. I know Aunt Helena didn't make the best first impression."

I nodded, making the turn onto Highway 174, passing the landmarks of my childhood, prominent on the landscape like bookmarks in my memory. "I have a sister, too. And I understand her pain." I paused, remembering something Helena had said. "But I think there's something more than grieving for her sister. Like she doesn't want to be here anymore. Do you know what I mean?"

Without looking at me, he said, "Yes."

I waited for him to say more, but we rode in silence, the air heavy with the scent of salt water and marsh. "Show me your house," he said suddenly. "Where you used to live as a girl."

I braked in surprise, throwing us both forward. Pressing my foot on the accelerator again, I asked, "Why?"

He shook his head. "I'm sorry. Never mind." He rubbed his hand over his jaw, as if suddenly uncertain, and I was once again struck by how different he was here than at the office. There, dressed in dark suits and a serious demeanor, he was confident and unapproachable. Except now I'd seen his eyes when he spoke of his daughter and had seen his boyhood room with the model rockets and paper airplanes. I was beginning to learn that there was much more to Finn Beaufain than the person he usually allowed most people to see.

"I'll show you. It's not there anymore—it got hit by lightning in the late nineties and burned to the ground. It was on Russell Creek, near the Brick House ruins. We rented the house from the family that still owns the ruins. I used to think it was the most wonderful place in the world and I'd never see anything more beautiful." I was silent for a moment, thinking about the years following my father's death, and of the house in North Charleston that was filled with silent accusations and stale penance and where music never played. "I still do," I added, surprised I'd spoken aloud.

We drove in silence down Highway 174 to Brick House Road. Just before the gates with the NO TRESPASSING sign, I turned left on a dirt road. We traveled a short distance until I saw Russell Creek and stopped the car, letting the engine idle. "Have you ever been here before?" I asked, nodding toward the distant skeleton of the old mansion, its missing roof and windows like the mouths of baby birds in a nest waiting to be fed.

"A few times," he said, and then was silent for a while, so I thought he was done speaking on the subject. He unbuckled his seat belt, and then, staring straight ahead, he said, "I brought my ex-wife to Edisto right after we were engaged, to meet my aunts. I hadn't been back since I'd finished high school, and I'd never been allowed to explore the island, so I thought it would be fun to discover it with Harper. It's funny, really; I'd only ever known such a small corner of Edisto, but I'd loved it. It's what I always thought of as home when I was away at school." He paused and looked at me. "I wanted her to love it, too."

"And did she?"

His mouth twisted. "No." He shrugged. "She's from Boston, so I probably shouldn't have brought her in the summer. She couldn't stand the heat or the bugs or the smell of the marsh. Or how casual and shabby everything is allowed to get here. We were supposed to stay a week and we ended up leaving after two nights."

I felt personally affronted at her dismissal of my beloved island, knowing where the flaw lay. A distant memory of my father and me brushed through me, and I turned to Finn. "Did you take her to see the sunset? When my father was home and the weather fine, we would watch it together. I don't think there's anything else on earth more beautiful than an Edisto sunset."

"I did. Aunt Bernadett gave us one of her sweetgrass baskets with a bottle of wine and two glasses and sent us out to go watch. But the mosquitoes wouldn't leave Harper alone and we were back inside before the sun had even begun its descent."

The image of his ex-wife being bullied by mosquitoes made me want to laugh, and I had to bite my lip and look away.

"Are you laughing?"

I shook my head, although by now I couldn't hold it in, and an unladylike snort came out of my mouth. I looked up at him, mortified. But he was smiling and I felt myself relaxing again.

"It was a good bottle of wine, even though I ended up drinking it by myself."

"I'm sorry," I said.

"Me, too." He opened his car door and stood while I turned off the ignition.

The sun was directly overhead, the heat pricking my skin. But a breeze stirred the tall grasses like the breath from a ghost, and I felt light-headed for a moment, remembering my father in this place. With the house gone, it was almost as if he'd never existed at all.

We walked toward the creek, the ruins of the old house behind us. The chorus of insects rose and whirred, the staccato sound of the cicadas keeping tempo for the rest of the band. For a long time after moving from the island, I'd had a hard time going to sleep with the silence, missing the night music of the marsh.

"It's beautiful here," he said, turning his face into the breeze. "I wonder sometimes how different things would be now if I'd grown up here instead of in Charleston." His hair at his temples and at the back of his neck had darkened with sweat, and again I had to work hard to reconcile this man with the cool and crisp Mr. Beaufain. It was as if two souls lived within his skin, separate but not. But maybe everybody was like that, all of us living the lives we had to while dreaming of the lives we wanted.

"What a great spot for watching the stars at night."

I cupped my hand over my forehead to shade my eyes as I looked up at him. "And at your aunt's house, too, I would guess."

He nodded. "I used to have a telescope in my bedroom at their house, but I brought it with me to college. Then things got in the way and I didn't have time anymore to study the sky. I don't really remember what happened to it."

I wanted to be an astronaut.

His words came back to me and I found I couldn't look at him, afraid that I might see the disappointment in his face, afraid I'd see my own reflection.

A blue heron flew overhead, its wings seeming to mock us humans, with our clumsy feet, who had to rely on planes to make us airborne. I wondered if watching the shorebirds was what had once made a little boy stare up at the sky and dream of reaching the moon.

"Why did you want to come here?" I asked.

His eyes were sharp and clear as he assessed me, and I had the feeling that he'd been waiting for my question. "Aunt Bernadett once brought me here—we snuck out while Aunt Helena was at one of her meetings for the historical preservation society. She brought me here because she wanted me to see the ruins. And because the last time she'd been there, she'd heard something that she'd wanted to share with me."

He paused. "We were standing right about here when I heard piano music coming from the house that used to stand there." He indicated the empty space where my family home had been. "It was a cool evening and the windows were open. We stayed here for about an hour, listening to the music and staring up at the sky as the stars appeared one by one. It's one of the only childhood memories I have where I remember being completely happy."

My throat felt tight, like I'd swallowed a ball of cotton. "And you wanted to know if it could have been me playing that night."

His BlackBerry buzzed and he pulled it from his pocket to answer and have a brief conversation before ending the call. Without looking at me, he said, "We've got to go. I have an issue at work that can't wait until Monday."

He began walking toward the car, his long strides making it hard for me to catch up. "Did you ever come back? Before that time with Harper."

"A couple of times. It was hard to get away without Aunt Helena noticing. But I never heard the piano again."

I felt the odd compulsion to apologize to him for not being there to play when he needed to hear me. Instead I reached into my purse and pulled out the car keys. "Would you like to drive?"

He looked almost relieved, and I recalled how his hands had clutched at the armrest on the way over. He took the keys and smiled gratefully. "Thank you."

He held the passenger door open for me and I slid in. We rode in silence for most of the way home as I tried to remember a night when I'd felt the presence of somebody outside my window, and thought of a little boy staring up at the night sky and dreaming of one day touching the stars.

CHAPTER 8

Lucy slid her Buick into a spot at the curb on Gibbes Street in front of Finn's house, then looked at me with raised eyebrows. "You sure you don't want me to come in with you?"

I rolled my eyes. "Come on, Lucy. Everything about this new position is completely legit—I've even met the elderly great-aunt. There's nothing to worry about."

She stuck out her chin. "Um-hmm. Well, when he starts asking you to call him by his first name, you just let me know. 'Cause that's when you *really* need to start worrying."

I concentrated on gathering my purse from the floor so she couldn't see my face. "Give me a call if you want me to drive you to work for a change. I'll have the Volvo for at least the rest of summer—until the nanny gets back."

Lucy looked with disdain at the white Volvo SUV with the Ashley Hall sticker on the window. She snorted. "I wouldn't be caught dead in that car. I prefer a vehicle with a lot more personality."

I leaned into the open door. "It's got air-conditioning."

She looked at me without blinking. "I'll let you know."

I shut the door and waved as she pulled away. "See you at work tomorrow. If not, you can call the police."

She was still shaking her head as she drove out of sight, the sound from the broken muffler unfamiliar in this neighborhood.

I stood outside the black painted wrought-iron gate, the scent of something sweet and green heavy in the air. As with most all Charleston homes south of Broad Street, the front and side gardens were filled with flowers, a busy array of colors and scents that always found ways to surprise the senses. They made no sound, yet I'd always thought that if I hadn't been a musician, I would have been a gardener. But I'd had no desire to be either for a very long time.

I pushed open the gate and stood on the brick-paved walk that led up to the raised house, a split staircase rising to the main entrance on the first floor. I had never been interested in studying or knowing much about architecture, but from staring up at the house from the walk, I could tell it was very big and very old. It faced the street, and although it didn't have a piazza, there was a small half-circle porch at the front door held up by two columns. The door was painted black, with a leaded glass transom over it, and a brass carriage light hung by a chain from the ceiling.

The house was painted yellow, the inside ceiling of the porch painted haint blue, just like Dah Georgie's house. But that's where the resemblance ended. This house was pristine, perfect from the fresh paint to the orderly flowers lined up in the garden like marching soldiers in their bright finery. It was a beautiful house, but it didn't feel like a home. I couldn't imagine large numbers of family members gathered for Sunday dinners any more than I could see Finn sitting with his daughter on the empty joggling board set up in the side garden.

Before I could talk myself out of it, I reached up and pushed the doorbell, then waited. And waited. I looked at my watch, making sure I had the right time. Finn had asked me to meet him at his house at five thirty. He would have driven me himself, but he'd been called away from the office. I'd been glad to meet him here, not wanting to have to explain to my coworkers why I was driving home with Mr. Beaufain.

There were no warning footsteps, just the sound of the latch being sprung from the other side of the door, followed by it opening slowly. I looked down and saw a young girl, older than in the photo on Finn's desk, with white-blond hair cut in a short pixie style and held back with a pale pink fabric headband. Her eyes were large and round and much too big for the tiny face that peered up at me. They were dark gray, like her father's, and had the same steady intensity as his. But seeing those eyes in a young face was unexpected, like finding a pearl inside an oyster's shell.

Despite her appearance, I knew Finn's daughter was about ten, although she could have easily passed for a six-year-old. The skin on her face was so pale it appeared translucent, and her stature small enough that I could probably span her waist with both of my hands. But her smile was broad and welcoming, and the hand she put into mine, though tiny, was warm.

"Eleanor Murray?"

"Yes," I replied, startled at her firm grasp. She shook my hand, then let it go before pulling the door open farther to allow me inside.

"And you must be Genevieve." I smiled down at her.

A round-faced woman with bright red hair and freckles came hurrying into the marble-floored foyer, wiping her hands on an apron. "Miss Murray?"

I nodded. "Yes. Mr. Beaufain is expecting me."

"It's so good to meet you. I'm Mrs. McKenna, the housekeeper. Mr. Beaufain called to say he's running a bit late. He said he'd let you go ahead and take the car, but he has the keys in his briefcase. He wanted to know if you could wait."

I glanced at my watch, realizing I didn't really have an alternative unless I wanted to call Lucy and make her come back and get me. "Sure, that's fine. Is there someplace I can wait?"

Before the housekeeper could say anything, Genevieve spoke up. "I can show you my room if you'd like."

Mrs. McKenna beamed. "That's an excellent idea. If you don't mind, Miss Murray?"

Not really knowing what I should say, I shook my head. "Of course not. I'd love to see it."

Genevieve slid her hand into mine again and tugged me toward the graceful staircase that rose in a spiral to three levels from the foyer. Passing by a large floral centerpiece holding court on a round table in the middle of the marble foyer, I noted the antique furniture and custom draperies as we ascended the stairs, marveling at how perfectly beautiful it all was, how it looked like somebody had re-created it from a painting that showed the way an elegant home should be. But I found myself wanting to push aside the draperies to allow the light to shine into all the corners, to see the father with his collar unbuttoned or the mother reading a magazine in bed. But I neither saw nor felt either one.

When we reached the first-floor landing, Genevieve led me down a long hallway covered with plush carpet toward an open bedroom door, keeping up a constant chatter. "You don't have to call me Genevieve," she said solemnly as she faced me on the threshold. "Madame LaFleur—my ballet teacher—calls me Genevieve, but everybody else calls me Gigi. Well, except for Mommy and Daddy."

"And he calls you Peanut," I said, smiling at the memory of our conversation in the dark car.

She looked surprised. "He told you? Mommy won't call me anything but Genevieve because she says nicknames stick to people their whole lives until everybody forgets your real name. I like Gigi better, so it doesn't matter. But when Mommy's here, you need to call me Genevieve."

I nodded. "Of course. And you can call me Eleanor."

She frowned, her eyes serious. "You don't look like an Eleanor."

"And what should an Eleanor look like?"

She shrugged her small shoulders. "I don't know. Somebody bigger, I think? Maybe with curly hair who knows how to play tennis really well." She frowned again, thinking. "Somebody who doesn't dream when they sleep at night."

Gigi dropped my hand and slid into the room. I wanted to ask her what she'd meant, but I stopped inside the room, my words temporarily deserting me. A large white four-poster canopied bed dominated one corner of the large room. It and the windows and the stuffed armchairs gathered in another cozy reading corner were covered in a whimsical pink lace fabric, yards and yards of it draped over the four posts and over the drapery finials, which were in the shape of ballet slippers. A ceramic chandelier, a replica of a fairy-tale castle, hung suspended by a rope of the same material in the center of the room. A mural covered the wall opposite the bed, what looked like a scene from *The Nutcracker.* On closer inspection, I realized that the little girl at the center of the stage was Gigi.

"I like pink a lot," she said, not apologetic at all.

I realized that the walls had been painted a soft hue of her favorite color, and even the rug was the palest pink. I turned my back on the little girl, overwhelmed with . . . what? Anger? Jealousy? I couldn't explain it, other than to admit to myself that this was the room I'd always wanted, the kind of room my own father had promised me I'd one day have once he'd saved enough money to send me to school and had a little extra left over. This was the kind of room a devoted parent created for a beloved daughter. A room that could have been mine if things had been different.

I pretended to stare at the mural, keeping my back to Gigi while I tried to check my emotions, tried not to miss my father so much that being in this room felt like a blade sliding across my skin.

"Do you like it?"

I managed to nod. "Yes. I like pink, too," I stammered. My gaze drifted to a bulletin board hanging on the wall adjacent to the mural. There were several photos of a tutu-wearing Gigi with her father and a single picture of her with a beautiful slender woman with dark hair who I assumed was her mother. I realized then that this was the first time I'd seen anything personal in the house. From what I could tell from my brief glance from the foyer, the downstairs was immaculate: no discarded shoes or backpacks or books splayed open as if the reader had just left. It was as if the heart of the house had been confined to this one room.

Tacked along the edges of the bulletin board were neatly folded paisley scarves in every color—although there were several in varying shades of pink.

"That's my collection," she said at my elbow, startling me. I hadn't heard her approach. "I don't wear them anymore, but they're pretty so I keep them."

I looked down at her, feeling I was missing something. "They are very pretty. Which is your favorite?"

A small finger with chipped pale pink polish pointed at a fuchsia scarf. "That one," she said matter-of-factly as she unpinned it from the board and then handed it to me to examine more closely. "Mommy said I should venture out into different colors, but I keep coming back to pink. I do try, though. Last week I wore green tights with a pink leotard. Mommy said that didn't count because the tights had pink polka dots on them. I think that the way we dress is as much a part of expressing ourselves as when we dance."

I found myself smiling down at her. There was something eminently likable about her. Although she was a child, she had a depth to her, a gravity to her movements and expressions that made me think she could have been years older.

Facing her, I said, "And did you figure that out all by yourself?"

An impish grin lit her face. "No. Madame LaFleur said it first. But I'm pretty sure I thought it even before she said it out loud."

Despite myself, I laughed. "I somehow don't doubt it, Gigi."

"It's time for your vitamins, Gigi. Mrs. McKenna's waiting for you in the kitchen."

Finn looked like a shadow in his dark suit as he stood still against the doorframe, and I had no idea how long he'd been there.

"Daddy!" Gigi ran to her father with outstretched arms, and he scooped her up. After kissing her on the forehead, he set her down.

"I'm glad to see you two have met. Now, say good-bye to Eleanor and run on downstairs. You'll see her again on Saturday when we go to Edisto."

Almost sedately, she walked back toward me and extended her hand. "It was a pleasure meeting you, Miss Eleanor, and I look forward to seeing you on Saturday."

Her eyes sparkled, belying her formality, as if to tell me she was performing for her father.

I took her proffered hand and smiled back. "It was a pleasure meeting you, too, Genevieve, and I look forward to spending more time with you this weekend."

She grinned up at me, but instead of turning back to her father, she paused, a questioning look on her face. "Can I call you Ellie? You look much more like an Ellie than an Eleanor, don't you think, Daddy?"

I wondered if he could hear my quick intake of breath.

"I think you may be right, Peanut." His eyes, a calm and cool dark gray, stared back at me over his daughter's head. "But it's up to Eleanor to decide what she wants you to call her."

Ellie. Nobody had called me that since my father had said good-bye to me the morning he disappeared into the sea. And until this moment, I hadn't realized how much I'd missed it.

I smiled. "I like Ellie. If you'd like to call me that, it's okay with me."

Her own grin widened. "Great! See you Saturday!" She skipped out of the room and, with a final wave, disappeared down the hallway.

I found myself looking awkwardly down at the fuchsia scarf in my hand, the skin at the base of my skull beginning to prickle. "Why does Gigi have so many scarves?"

"She was diagnosed with leukemia when she was five years old. She's in remission now—almost four years. We've got another year to go before we'll start breathing again."

"I'm sorry," I said. "I didn't know. . . ." I remembered how I'd felt when I first saw her bedroom, my misplaced anger at a little girl. *She had leukemia.*

I turned abruptly back toward the bulletin board, blindly looking for the thumbtack that had held the scarf in place, afraid that if he saw my eyes he would know.

"It's not something I like to talk about. I was gone from work a lot when she was first diagnosed, but that was before you came to work there, so you wouldn't have known." He stopped. "Those were very dark days."

I found the tack and replaced the scarf before facing him again. "I understand. It's just . . . I'm glad I know now. She's a great kid."

He smiled his warm smile, the rare smile that made the sides of his eyes crinkle. "I think so, too." He tilted his head toward the hallway. "Let's go downstairs. All this pink makes me a little dizzy."

I nodded, relieved to leave the little girl's bedroom behind me. I waited in the foyer while he collected his briefcase and set it on top of the hall table. After pulling out the Volvo's keys, he handed them to me.

"I had the people at Volvo give it a little tune-up and make sure everything was in working order, so it's good to go. I'm sorry things took a little longer than I'd anticipated."

I clutched the keys in my hand. "It's not a problem. I really appreciate the use of the car." I smiled, feeling awkward again. "I guess I'd better go. Before the traffic . . ." My voice trailed away as I fumbled for the door latch.

"Would you like to stay for dinner? Mrs. McKenna always makes plenty in case I have a client over. To make up for you missing your own dinner at home."

My hand paused on the doorknob as I looked back at Finn. "Thank you, but I need to get back. They'll be waiting for me to make dinner."

His face remained impassively polite. "Well, then, you'll need to get home. Sorry to have kept you."

I pulled open the door and stepped out onto the portico, then faced him again. "I'm curious. Did Gigi design her own room?"

"No, actually. I did—with the help of a decorator friend. But I knew exactly what she'd want."

I nodded, trying not to smile at the image of Finn Beaufain sorting through rolls of pink tulle and lace.

"Why?" he asked.

I wasn't really sure of the answer, only that the almost-forgotten edge of pushing my boundaries had suddenly poked its way up through the clouds of self-doubt and penitence. "Just wondering. It's the kind of room every girl dreams of. And I thought maybe her mother had done it as a sort of homage to her own girlhood dreams."

His eyes darkened. "Harper wouldn't have known even where to begin."

I felt chagrined, as if I'd been Bluebeard's wife caught peeking into the locked room. I took a step backward. "About Saturday—I'm going to shoot for eleven o'clock. Traffic in the summer can be unpredictable."

"That's fine. Peanut and I are going to be there Friday night, so no rush. We'll see you when you get there."

"Well, good-bye, then," I said.

He nodded in response and then watched me walk through the gate to the parked car. I didn't look back, not wanting to ruin the mental image of Finn Beaufain standing in a puddle of pink tulle as he created the dream bedroom for his little girl. I unlocked the door and paused for a moment, remembering how Gigi had called me Ellie, and wondering what she'd meant when she'd said that people named Eleanor didn't dream when they slept at night.

CHAPTER 9

When I arrived home, Glen and Eve were sitting outside on the front porch swing. A pizza box sat on the table in front of them, and I felt a stab of guilt.

"We were hungry," Eve said, her eyes on me. "There's another whole pizza in the fridge if you haven't eaten."

Glen wiped his hands on a napkin and stood, making sure that the swing didn't rock too much and disturb Eve. "Nice car, Eleanor. Where'd it come from?"

I wondered if the hint of accusation I heard in his voice was real or imagined.

He came down the steps toward the car, and I saw the way the sun hit his dark hair, turning the edges of it copper. It reminded me of the first time I'd ever seen him, wearing his Citadel cadet uniform and sitting with fellow cadets in the adjacent booth at Carolina's restaurant in Charleston. His back was to me, and the sun through the window had lit his hair on fire just like a beacon. And then I'd turned to Eve and dared her to go say hello.

But I didn't fall in love with him until his first date with Eve. He'd come to pick her up in a friend's borrowed Honda, and I'd been instructed to offer him something to drink on the front porch and keep him entertained while Mama helped Eve get dressed. The first thing he did when I answered the door was take off his hat, something no member of the opposite sex had ever done in my presence before. He'd been a first-year student at the Citadel—a knob—and his hair had been shorn so close that you could see his scalp. But his eyebrows were dark, with coppery edges, and nicely shaped, and his eyes were so brown they'd seemed almost black.

He was probably the most handsome boy I'd ever seen—not that I'd seen many—which made me so nervous that when I returned to the porch with a Tupperware pitcher of lemonade and two plastic tumblers, I'd tripped, sending the tray and its contents down the steps.

He hadn't laughed, and his first concern was for me, to make sure I hadn't been hurt. I might have fallen in love when he'd wiped the drip of lemonade off my nose and gave me a silly grin, or perhaps it was when he'd been the one to suggest making another pitcher while he cleaned up the mess so that I'd have nothing to explain to Eve and Mama. Or maybe it was when he'd escorted Eve down the porch to his car, her delicate hand tucked inside the elbow of his arm, and he'd turned around to wink at me.

He was still the tall, lanky, and broad-shouldered young man he'd once been, but his eyes weren't as bright, and his step was now heavier, as if the burden of years rested heavily on him like a yoke tethering him to the life he'd made for himself.

"It's for my new part-time job. I'll be taking care of an elderly woman living on Edisto a couple of days a week. She's Mr. Beaufain's great-aunt, so he's made a few allowances for my work schedule at his office downtown, and I have the use of the nanny's car for now."

Glen leaned down to peer into the driver's side window. "Looks like it's brand-new."

I shrugged. "Could be—it smells new."

I climbed up the stairs and took the seat next to Eve, and she leaned back, almost imperceptibly. When we were children we'd sometimes shared a bed when I'd been afraid of the dark or a storm and needed the comfort of a familiar touch. It had been at Eve's request, telling our father it was part of her job as oldest sister to protect me.

Clearing my throat, I said, "The days that I'm in Edisto, I'll be staying there for dinner. I'll try to make sure you have leftovers to reheat, or you can order pizza. The extra money I'll be bringing in will make going to a restaurant once in a while a little more affordable."

I'd been staring at my hands, then slowly raised my gaze to meet Eve's violet eyes. They'd been compared to Elizabeth Taylor's, yet Eve's were opaque, not allowing any light to shine through them. They hadn't always been that way but had changed as she'd grown older, as if she'd chosen that to happen in the same manner she'd chosen to start wearing shorter dresses or to cut her hair.

"How nice for you," she said. "I'm sure we'll be fine surviving on pizza and fast food."

"Eve." Glen's voice held a note of warning, but my sister and I both knew that whatever it was between us was impenetrable, a thick, dark place where we wallowed yet allowed no one else entry.

I stood and walked toward the edge of the porch and looked out at the dried grass and dead flowers I'd planted earlier in the spring and then forgotten. Nobody had bothered to water them. "To start, I'll be going to Edisto every Wednesday and Saturday, although we might add a day or two, depending on how it goes. If you need help getting to your doctor's appointments, please schedule them on the days I'm here. Or maybe schedule them during Glen's lunch hour so he can take you."

I didn't turn around, afraid they'd both see my uncertainty, my unease with this person speaking and using my mouth. But all I had to do was focus on Eve's pregnancy, and it all became so much easier.

I heard Glen climbing the porch steps and then the sound of the porch swing straining from the ropes that held it to the ceiling. "That won't be a problem," he said, and I pictured him placing a restraining hand on top of Eve's, and the thought made me want to cry.

A heavy thrumming bass from a radio blared as an old white pickup truck with giant tires slowly passed in front of the house. It slowed to a stop and the driver leaned out, his cigarette hanging from his fingers, which drummed against the door to the beat of the music.

The volume lowered as the driver leaned out of the car and shouted my name. "Eleanor!"

I stayed on the porch, recognizing Rocky Cooper, a boy I'd gone to high school with. A boy who'd once appointed himself my partner in crime. I lifted my hand in greeting, wanting him to move on. I peered past him toward the passenger seat to a man I didn't recognize who was raising a bottle to his lips.

"Hey, Rocky."

"Haven't seen you in a long time," he said, his once boyish face now darkened to leather by the South Carolina sun. I'd heard he worked in construction now, flitting in and out of jobs depending on his sobriety. "Thought you'd moved away. Then again, I don't get back to Edisto too often." He smirked. "Somebody's always complainin' about somethin'."

I nodded, as if I agreed. "Been working. Keeping busy." I stayed where I was, hoping he'd get the hint.

He jerked his head toward his companion. "Me and Jimmy was planning on going out for some fun tonight. Why don't you hop on in and join us?"

I tried to make my smile genuine. "I'd like to, but I've got a lot of work to do."

He looked behind me to where Eve and Glen still sat, then returned his gaze to me. "Looks like a real party." He took a drag on his cigarette. "If you change your mind, you know where to find me."

Jimmy lifted his bottle in a salute as Rocky gunned the engine, the music returning to its previous volume, the throbbing tempo lingering long after I could no longer see the truck.

"Sure miss having him around," Eve said primly.

"Me, too," I replied without any hint of sarcasm as I headed toward the door. "I'm going to reheat a slice of pizza."

Her voice called me back. "You haven't asked me when the baby's due."

I felt like someone had poured a large bucket of iced water down my back. I faced her, surprised to see the uncertainty there. "I thought you had to see the doctor first to confirm a due date."

"We will. But my guess would be January." Her look was almost hopeful. "You'll be an aunt in January."

I was suspicious of this olive branch, wondering if it would snap back and slap me. "A winter baby, then. That'll be nice for you, not having to go through the last months of pregnancy in the heat of summer."

"And I can wear some of Glen's sweaters in the cold weather to save money on maternity clothes." She leaned her head on Glen's shoulder as her hands rested on her flat belly.

"Great," I said. "I'm going to go eat my dinner now."

I quickly opened the door, letting it slam behind me as if I could shut out the memory of when I'd died and come back to life, and how I still couldn't figure out why.

Eve

I sat in my wheelchair, facing the dining room sideboard, which hadn't been used for food in years. It was an antique, from our mother's family, and had probably once been worth something. But years of neglect and a broken hinge on the front successfully hid any potential.

Mama had been using it for storage space for her costume making, a necessity since the arthritis in her knees made climbing up and down the stairs to the bins that lined the walls in her bedroom impossible. And now that I'd pretty much taken over her business, I realized that I'd have to do the same thing. Either that or wait until Eleanor or Glen came home to fetch things for me.

I stared in dismay at the crammed interior of the sideboard, with scraps of fabrics, bead boxes, several pairs of scissors, and glue bottles—a few which appeared either empty or so old that their contents would be useless—and even magazine clippings. Mama had once subscribed to *Vogue* when we could afford it. I knew her mother had had a subscription while Mama was growing up in Charleston, before she met Daddy, and that Grandmother—whom I'd never met even though she'd died less than a year before—had used the magazine to plan her wardrobe. Mama had just used it to get ideas for costumes. I knew these clippings had been pulled from the magazines in doctors' offices when nobody had been looking. Eleanor and I had simply looked away, accustomed for too long to Mama's idiosyncrasies.

The slamming of a drawer and then the sound of hard footfalls came from upstairs. I hadn't meant to make Eleanor angry. Or maybe I had. It was almost a relief to see the old spark in her. It was her fault, really. I wanted my sister back. The girl she'd been before Daddy died; the girl with the easy laugh and the brave heart. Even the wild girl she'd become afterward would have been preferable to the ghost she was now. Maybe that's what she was. She had died that day, after all. Maybe she just hadn't realized yet that she wasn't still dead.

Her bedroom door opened and I listened as she stomped across the hall to the bathroom, and then the door slammed shut. I sighed, then leaned forward into the cabinet, the sound of the television annoying me more than usual. Mama did little else these days, and it took all I had not to yell at her and tell her that the less she moved, the less she'd be *able* to move. I did my physical therapy every day for that reason. I might be confined to my wheelchair, but I refused to be a prisoner in my own life. Sometimes I felt as if I were living in a haunted house, cohabiting with the spirits of the walking dead.

I peered into the back of the cabinet. A rectangular package—what looked to be a dress pattern—had slid behind one of the drawers and was trapped between the drawer and the back of the sideboard. Pressing the side of my face against the front, I leaned forward with my outstretched hand and, grasping the corner, tugged until it came loose. Sitting back in my chair, I looked down to see what I'd rediscovered and felt a smile curl my lips.

"Eleanor!" I shouted, then waited until the bathroom door opened, her footsteps hurried as she ran down the stairs.

"Is everything okay?" she asked, her face flushed from the cold water she'd been splashing on her face, which still couldn't hide her red-rimmed and swollen eyes.

"Look what I found." I handed over the dress pattern.

I could tell by the way her face softened that she recognized it, too. "My suit," she said softly.

It was a *Vogue* pattern that she and I had picked out at the fabric store on her fourteenth birthday, a classic women's suit with a Chanel silhouette of pencil skirt and bracelet-length sleeves. It was the suit she would have worn for her interview at Juilliard, and I was going to make it for her when she was old enough to wear it and I was old enough to operate my mother's sewing machine. We had purchased it about a month before our father died, a month before Eleanor had closed up the piano and stopped dreaming.

"I can't believe we still have this," she said, her fingers gripping it tightly. She looked over at me with uncertain eyes, as if she wasn't sure if we were sharing a memory or if I was tossing her dreams up in the air to see them scatter like confetti.

"It's still a beautiful pattern," I said. "With a more updated fabric, of course. No one wears those colors in plaid anymore."

We looked at each other, our smiles fading, as if realizing simultaneously that we didn't do that anymore, that the last thing we'd been in agreement on was a trip to see who could climb the highest in an oak tree.

"No, probably not," she said. "If you're going through stuff to give away, I guess you can toss this in the pile."

Don't, I wanted to yell at her. *Don't, don't, don't.* She had made her own purgatory, with me her fellow prisoner. Except she seemed to think that I had the key to our cell. Maybe I did, but I didn't spend my time dwelling on it. It wasn't my nature. Eleanor needed to find her own escape, make her own key. Because I was growing weary of watching her fling herself against her life like a moth to a light.

"Sure," I said, wanting my words to sting, if only to see if I could resurrect that spark again. "I'll just give it away, since I don't see anybody in this house needing it."

"Are we expecting visitors?" Mama called from the family room.

Eleanor placed the pattern on top of the sideboard as we both turned toward the front window. A black Mercedes sedan had just parked in front of the house, and an impossibly pink little girl was climbing from the backseat, something clutched in her hands. We watched as the driver exited the car and took the girl's hand before they both climbed the steps to the front door.

"Oh," Eleanor said, nervously glancing at the stairs as if looking for an escape. Then she bolted for the front door and threw it open before the visitors could press the doorbell and discover it was broken.

She smiled the smile I hadn't seen in a long time as she spoke to the little girl first. "Hello, Gigi. I didn't expect to see you so soon."

"You forgot your purse. You left it in my room."

I recognized the old brown leather satchel that Eleanor had been using as a purse.

The man placed his hand on top of the girl's head, and the gesture made me stare a little harder, move a little closer. It had been an unconscious movement, but it said so much about this man and how he felt about the world.

I could see that Eleanor was trying to move them all back onto the porch, so I wheeled my chair closer so they could see me from the doorway.

"Aren't you going to introduce us, Eleanor?"

She stood so still that for a moment I thought she would refuse. But then she took a step back, opening the door wider. "This is Finn Beaufain and his daughter, Genevieve. It seems I left my purse at their house this afternoon when I went to pick up the car."

I nodded hello, studying the man. I stared at him a little longer than necessary, wondering why he seemed so familiar. He was tall and lanky, like Glen, and I assumed he probably played tennis or ran or both. But his eyes were an unusual shade of gray, the kind of eyes that seemed friendly and easily readable until you got to know the man. Shadows clung to him in the way they clung to Eleanor, and I wondered if they'd recognized this in each other.

"This is my sister, Eve Hamilton," Eleanor continued, and Finn took my hand in a firm clasp and shook it.

"It's a pleasure meeting you," he said. His voice was deep and accented with old Charleston, sounding very much like our mother's. She'd used it to her advantage to gain customers for her costume designing, making them feel that class and prestige could be stitched into each seam. But Finn Beaufain had no need for his accent to impress others. His bearing and those eyes commanded all the attention and deference he needed.

Genevieve took my hand, too, and shook it. I found I couldn't take my eyes off her. She reminded me of an angel in one of Raphael's paintings, with perfect pink and white skin and wide gray eyes like her father's that seemed to miss nothing. But it was her smile that was truly captivating, a smile that suggested things might not be all right in her world but she'd chosen to smile anyway.

"It's nice to meet you," she said. She leaned forward, as if to study me more closely. "You look like an Eve," she said, tilting her head. "Eleanor said that I could call her Ellie because she definitely looks more like an Ellie."

My gaze shot to Eleanor. Ellie had become the name I'd associated with my lost sister, the sister with the infectious laugh and mischievous bent who could play the piano as if the music tethered her to heaven. I studied her face, wondering if hearing the name had conjured Ellie's spirit, but I saw only Eleanor.

Our mother approached the door, smoothing down her hair, which hadn't seen a comb all day, and running her fingers down her housecoat as if to make sure everything had been buttoned properly. Her slippers slapped across the wood floor, but all of us had been raised too well to allow our expressions to register anything besides a polite regard.

"I'm Dianne Murray, Eleanor and Eve's mother. It's so good to finally meet you." She made the statement sound more like an accusation, as if Mr. Beaufain should have issued an invitation long before now to meet her. "I used to be an Alston. I believe my father, James Ravenel Alston, and your grandfather were classmates at Porter-Gaud."

Finn's face betrayed no emotion at the blatant name-dropping as he grasped my mother's offered fingertips as if she stood in the foyer of a grand mansion and wore a ball gown. Judging from Finn's expression, one could believe he saw her that way, too.

"I see where your daughters received their good looks, Mrs. Murray," he said, his Southern drawl a little more pronounced as he spoke to her, as if he were an actor in a play. Which, I supposed, we all were.

Mama actually blushed, as did Eleanor, and just as I thought the moment couldn't get any worse for my sister, Glen returned from his run, tanned and muscular and drenched in sweat. He must have noticed the Mercedes at the curb, because he opened the door with caution, peering inside like a child watching the lid of a jack-in-the-box.

Flushing scarlet, Eleanor made the introductions again, and I watched as Glen took his measure of Finn Beaufain. "It's a pleasure to finally meet you. We've been curious about the man who demands such long hours from his employees."

Nobody said anything for an extremely long moment as we all tried to decide where to look.

Finn's eyebrows rose. "Eleanor is an extremely conscientious employee who makes sure the work gets done regardless of how long it takes. Which is one of the reasons why I thought of her for assisting with my great-aunt's care." He smiled at Eleanor, whose color was now a faded shade of rose.

Glen moved to stand closer to Eleanor, and I wondered if anybody else could see the way she leaned toward him, like a magnet searching for true north. Glen, still breathing heavily from his run, was working his jaw, tasting his words first. Before he could say anything else, I rolled my wheelchair closer. "We all appreciate the opportunity that you've given Eleanor."

"Especially now that Eve is expecting," Mama said, unwilling to be left out of the conversation.

Finn shot a glance at my sister, something like realization crossing his face. "Congratulations, to both of you," he said to Glen and me.

My sister wore her Eleanor smile, the bland smile she put on to face the world in the same way a widow would wear black. *Go,* I wanted to shout at her. *Run.* Whatever she thought she felt for Glen was part of a life that no longer existed, or maybe never had. And I had given her the perfect escape with my pregnancy. But just because we were sisters didn't make me a fair jailer. I sat back quietly and just watched.

"I wasn't aware you didn't have a cell phone, Eleanor," Finn continued. "I would like to be able to reach you when you're with Aunt Helena, so I'm going to go ahead and get you one—at my expense, since I'm requesting it."

He wasn't asking, like he was accustomed to giving orders and people following without question. Eleanor bristled but didn't argue, and I could see it pained her. It reminded me of the times as a child when our father would remind her to practice the piano. She practiced all the time, but on her own schedule, and only balked when *told* to do it. I had secretly admired this about her, wishing that my mother's requests wouldn't send such fissures of alarm through me. It was as if I'd known, even then, that what Eleanor had was real and solid. And that what I had, the looks and the pretty costumes, was like powdered sand in a windstorm.

It was probably why, when Eleanor wanted to play chicken with cars or hitchhike to Myrtle Beach, I was her willing accomplice. I needed to believe that I had a little bit of Eleanor in me.

Genevieve tugged on her father's hand. "It's getting dark and we haven't stopped for ice cream yet."

Finn smiled down at his daughter, and it was in that unguarded moment that I knew why he seemed so familiar to me. He was that boy on Edisto who never joined our group, who sat in church and stared at Eleanor instead of me. I remembered still how much that had bothered me, and how I'd worn more and more outrageous outfits to church so he'd notice me.

"It's a pleasure meeting you all," he said politely as he led his daughter to the door.

I watched him carefully as they walked out onto the porch before giving a final wave as they tucked themselves into the black car. But Eleanor was looking at Glen, and then he was touching the small of her back as he followed her inside.

Go! I shouted to no one at all. *Run!*

But nobody did. Instead they both joined my mother on the couch in front of the television set. Slowly, I wheeled myself to the sofa and waited for Glen to lift me and place me next to him, my hand holding his tightly as I thought again of the unused suit pattern and how nothing had turned out the way it was supposed to.

CHAPTER 10

Eleanor

As a child, I spent long hours with Lucy watching Dah Georgie make her sweetgrass baskets. She'd give us a nickel for each bundle of grass, palmetto leaves, and pine needles we would collect for her, and then we'd sit at her feet watching her build her baskets. There was a rhythm to it that sank into my skin as she fed layer into layer, adding rushel for color, using pine needles and palmetto strips to start. It was like watching a symphony being written, or a painting being painted, as each layer revealed more and more of the artist. Dah Georgie called the basket patterns names like Dreams of Rivers and Path of Tears, but all the baskets with lids she'd call secret keepers.

She taught us that building baskets was like building a life, finding materials from different places—bits and pieces with their own purpose—and creating a vessel that could pour out or keep in. I thought about this now, driving to Edisto, wondering what sort of basket my life would be and what it would be named.

I pulled down the Volvo's visor to block the morning sun, then flicked on the GPS. I knew how to get to Edisto, the roads and bridges across the marshes and creeks as much a part of me as the blue veins that ran under my skin. But I wanted to see them in color on the GPS screen, as if I needed to make sure that all of this was real and not some crazy and dangerous adventure I'd imagined to create a bump in the flat road of my life. I was supposed to have outgrown that need years ago.

Despite the heat, I rolled down the windows to catch the scent of my island before I even reached her. I left the radio off, not wanting to be distracted. No matter how mundane, I couldn't have music playing without focusing my attention on it and relegating everything else to the background, and I had no intention of damaging the Volvo with distracted driving. Still, I found myself humming to the beat of the tires on the pavement, my fingers playing an imaginary melody on the steering wheel.

Helena's white Cadillac stood in the driveway next to a blue Toyota, presumably belonging to the nurse on duty. Finn had called me earlier to say that he was taking Gigi to the beach and would be back sometime in the late afternoon, so I hadn't expected to see them when I arrived.

Although Finn had told me to walk right in, it felt odd, so I rapped on the front door a couple of times and waited, unwilling to use the doorbell in case Helena was asleep. Eventually the door was opened by a frazzled and tall blond woman who started speaking before she'd even opened the door.

"I'm so sorry to keep you waiting!" she said in a thick Southern accent. "I was in the kitchen up to my elbows in wood stain trying to fix those kitchen chairs. They've been bothering me since I first started working here. I'm thinking I need to make cushions and curtains, too, when I'm done, but I suppose I need to ask Mr. Beaufain first. Not that I'd want him to pay me; I just enjoy that sort of thing." She paused long enough to catch her breath and stick out her hand. "I'm Teri Weber, by the way. You can call me Teri, but Mr. Beaufain and Miss Szarka like to call me Nurse Weber."

I shook her hand and introduced myself, asking her to call me Eleanor, and smelled the distinctive scent of wood stain wafting from the back of the house. Her fingers felt a little sticky to the touch. "I'm sorry to bother you. I didn't feel right just walking in."

"Don't worry about it—I told Mr. Beaufain that I'd be listening for you just in case, and see, I was right! He said you'd be here to keep Miss Helena company, but she's sleeping now, so I guess you can do whatever you like. I have the TV on in the kitchen watching my shows, but you're more than welcome to watch something else. I'd be happy for the company."

"Thanks," I said, "but I think I'll explore the house a little more, become familiar with it while I wait for her to wake up. Will you give me a shout when she does?"

"Absolutely. I put a baby monitor in her room so I'll know the second she opens her eyes." She beamed at me, then excused herself to return to the chairs and the wood stain.

I stood in the entranceway, wondering what I should do after I was done exploring if Helena still wasn't awake. Maybe I could make lunch or mop a floor, but I'd already learned that the housekeeper and nurses took care of all that. My gaze strayed to the room with the piano; then just as quickly I glanced away, focusing instead on the paintings in the dining room and on the staircase wall.

It was almost like looking at them underwater, the light from the chandelier hitting the loose rolls of canvas. I had to move my head from side to side to be able to see an entire painting. I thought of Helena refusing to have them reframed, and how stubborn a person would have to be not to have these fixed. The problem was too rampant and obvious to have been overlooked, and I sighed inwardly, remembering Finn mentioning his great-aunt's "eccentricities."

The stairs, with their heavy wooden balustrade, rose in front of me. I recalled the closed bedroom doors upstairs and how Finn had said one was the guest room that I would be free to use if I ever ended up staying the night.

It was almost as if the old Eleanor propelled me up the stairs, moving my legs up each riser. I wasn't trespassing, I assured myself. I just wanted to see which room I would use.

The door to Finn's childhood room was open. I paused outside, the sight of a duffel bag on the floor holding me back. I suppose it made sense that he would sleep in his old room when he visited, but the image of the grown man sleeping under the paper stars and planets brought a smile to my lips.

The door at the end of the hall, behind which Finn had said was the room Gigi used, was also open. I peeked inside and noticed the pink suitcase with the ballet slipper motif on the outside, and the clothes strewn around the room. I pictured Gigi racing to put on her bathing suit—probably pink—after her father told her they were going to the beach.

Not wanting to invade her privacy, I stayed on the threshold to examine the room. It was tastefully furnished with a dark wood double bed with a tall headboard, a brightly colored quilt folded neatly at the bottom. A braided rug in the same colors as the quilt covered the wide plank pine floors, and white lace curtains hung at the two corner windows.

I moved on to the guest room, satisfying myself that it was perfectly fine—if a little dated—and had its own bathroom. It was an inviting room, and if I ever needed to stay overnight, I knew I'd be comfortable.

I closed the door and headed back down the hallway, mentally preparing myself to watch *The View* or whatever weekday TV program Teri Weber was watching, but I found myself pausing in front of the remaining bedroom door. I recalled Finn telling me that it had been Bernadett's and that Helena didn't want anybody going inside. I recalled how hard Helena had been trying to get me to leave, and the part of me that couldn't resist late-night mysteries on TV couldn't help but wonder if the reason why lay beyond the closed door to her dead sister's bedroom.

Again I felt the old Eleanor pushing at me, her fingers and palms a physical force, and I found myself reaching for the door handle and turning it. I half expected to find the door locked, but the handle turned easily in my hand. Before I could stop myself, I'd pushed the door open and found myself looking inside Bernadett's bedroom.

I just stared for a long moment, wondering if perhaps somebody had already come to take away Bernadett's things, because the room was devoid of anything personal. Even the bed had been stripped of its mattress and bedclothes. But as my gaze skipped around the Spartan room, I noticed a pair of beige bedroom slippers on the rug beside the single twin bed, the hairbrush and comb sitting on top of the small dresser between two windows. An empty glass, the bottom tinged with the white crust of evaporated water, still sat on the nightstand, where it had been placed near the edge.

A small dressing table without a mirror was pushed up against the far wall. On its polished surface sat a small sweetgrass dish, a black onyx rosary coiled inside it like a snake. Behind it was another sweetgrass basket, this one shaped like a short urn and with a lid that had a small acorn-shaped knob at the center. *A secret keeper.*

I took three steps into the room, feeling a little like Alice at the rabbit hole, trying to pinpoint what was so off-kilter about the room. I spun around slowly, taking in the twin-sized plain metal bed, the simple wooden crucifix hanging over it. And then I realized. Except for the crucifix, there was nothing on the walls.

I moved closer to the wall behind the bed and could see now the telltale rectangular patterns that dotted the walls. But in the dining room and living room the nail holes had been filled so as not to draw attention. Here, the nail holes were ragged and gaping, as if the frames had been removed with brute force. As if they'd been ripped from the walls.

I rubbed the pad of my thumb over one of the spots, noticing as I did so the fresh feel of powdery plaster and paint that flecked off onto the floor and clung to my skin, as if the damage to the walls had been recent.

Wiping my hand on my skirt, I turned away from the wall. A tall antique wardrobe sat against the wall across from the bed, a gold key dangling from the keyhole. Without even thinking about what I was doing, I walked across the room and opened the door.

The heavy scent of mothballs hit me first, and I had to step back. After taking a deep breath of fresh air, I moved in to get a closer look. There were exactly four skirts, one dress, and six blouses hanging inside. I stared at them, wondering if this really was Bernadett's complete wardrobe, or if Finn had been mistaken about nothing having been touched. I looked at the floor of the wardrobe and found a single pair of low-heeled black pumps and a pair of navy blue Keds, a few grains of sand still clinging to the sides of the rubber soles.

Two small, mirrored doors sat closed above the hanging rod, and I reached up and tugged on one of the knobs. As I looked closer, I saw that a small keyhole had been placed in the mirror on one of the doors, but this lock had no key. I tugged on it harder, not really sure what I expected the doors to do. There was something about this room, something that told me before I'd even tried that the lock without a key was meant to stay locked.

"What are you doing in here?"

I stepped back quickly from the armoire, my blood lapping through my veins. Jerking around, I saw Finn standing inside the doorway, his face unreadable but his eyes dark and serious.

As if I'd just returned from a trip down the rabbit hole, I became suddenly aware of the sound of thunder outside and the lashing rain against the windows. I smelled suntan lotion and noticed that Finn wore a T-shirt and swimming trunks, his feet clad in loafers, so at least that part of him was recognizable.

I realized I was staring and that I'd pressed the heel of my hand hard against my chest as if I could slow down the thudding. "I'm sorry," I said, sounding breathless. "I was waiting for Helena to wake up and thought I'd do some exploring. I didn't mean to pry."

He stared at me for a brief second before he spoke, repeating the words he'd said the first time I'd visited the house. "This was Bernadett's room. We don't go in here."

He stood back away from the door, and I hurried past him into the hallway like a schoolgirl caught running in the hall. I didn't look at him until I'd heard the click of the door latch behind me.

"I'm sorry," I said again. "I was looking for the guest room to see where I might stay—"

He cut me off. "Aunt Helena's awake. Gigi's with her, but it's a one-way conversation, I'm afraid. I was hoping you could go down now and sit with Helena while Nurse Weber gets her lunch tray ready." After pausing for a moment, he said, "You're the only person who's elicited any kind of reaction since Helena's come home from the hospital. I think that's a good sign."

I remembered my conversation with the old woman from my last visit and wasn't exactly looking forward to a rematch. But then I thought of Eve and Glen and I found myself squaring my shoulders, knowing there were things much worse than facing an old woman who did not want me to stay.

"Of course," I said. "That's what I'm here for." I walked ahead of him down the stairs, sensing him watching me from behind.

When we reached the foyer, he said, "I enjoyed meeting your family the other day."

"No, you didn't." The words were out before I could call them back.

As if I hadn't rudely interrupted, he said, "I've met Eve before, but I don't think she remembered."

"Eve doesn't forget anything." I bit my lip, wondering where I'd left my filters. My father had taught me to be kind but to speak my mind. Maybe the salt air was reminding me of the girl my father had known.

He shook his head. "No, she probably blocked it out on purpose."

I frowned up at him. "What do you mean?"

"It was after church, when we were kids. I was with my aunts, and you and your sister were with your parents. Eve was wearing a ridiculous purple dress with lots of bows and ruffles. It was after I'd heard you play that one night—my aunt Bernadett had pointed you out to me.

"You and your family walked past us outside and I decided I wanted to say hello to you, but just as I turned, Eve stepped in front of me, blocking my way, and introduced herself. I didn't mean to be rude, but you were walking toward a group of your friends, and I wanted to reach you first." He shrugged, a boyish gesture that he wouldn't have made in one of his suits. "So I ignored her and kind of, well, shoved her aside so I could catch up to you. But I was too late. When I turned back to Eve to apologize, she looked so angry that I pretended I didn't see her and walked right past her to my aunts. I felt badly and planned to find her the next Sunday to apologize, but I didn't see you at church after that."

I didn't remember any of it, of course, except for the dress. Eve had worn it to my father's memorial service because it was new and her favorite.

"Mama stopped taking us to church after my father died, and then we moved," I said simply, forcing a smile I didn't feel. "Let's go see how your aunt and Gigi are doing."

I began to walk toward the kitchen, but his hand stopped me.

"Don't mention that you were in Bernadett's room. Aunt Helena would be upset if she knew anybody had been in there."

"Sure," I said, turning down the corridor. I heard his footsteps on the wood floor behind me as I thought about the locked doors inside the armoire and wondered if more than sentimentality was behind the reason for keeping a dead woman's bedroom door closed.

Helena

When Genevieve was born, Bernadett and I held hands over her bassinet, marveling at her tiny perfection, at her rose-white skin, and feeling grateful she had not been a boy who would have reminded us of another. Even God could not be that cruel.

We did not like the child's mother, Harper, or understand the French name she chose for the little girl. But even that could not dampen our joy at this affirmation of life, this nod from Fortune, who had finally deigned to take pity on us. At least that is what Bernadett thought. I had merely held my breath, waiting. When Genevieve got sick, I had felt the finger of God on my neck, waiting to exact due punishment. And when Bernadett died, I knew He still wasn't done with me.

I closed my eyes, listening to Genevieve's chatter. She spoke so quickly, like most Americans, so that I understood only half of what she said. But I did not need to hear all of it. Her babble was the same language of little girls all over the world, spoken through telephones and across bedrooms where another twin bed might be. It was comforting in its familiarity, even as it brought to mind the bitter winter mornings in Budapest when Bernadett and I exhaled frosty breaths into the chilly room.

My head hurt, and all I wanted to do was hold Gigi's sweet hand and sleep. I would be happy if I could die like this, to simply go to sleep in the company of a child. But I did not deserve an easy death.

"Aunt Helena? Eleanor is here," Finn's voice announced from the doorway.

Gigi jumped off the edge of the bed. "I call her Ellie. If you ask her nicely, she might let you call her that, too."

Eleanor flinched slightly when Genevieve said "Ellie," and I might have missed it if I had not been looking at her, noticing how pale she was, how round her eyes. It was almost, I thought, as if she had just seen a ghost.

"Ellie," I said, just to see her react again, but she was more prepared this time and just smiled at me. I do not know why I felt the need to press on her bruises. Maybe it was because I resented her presence as an impediment to an end to my life. Or maybe it was because I was an old woman who did not have the time to wait before I dug deep into a person's heart to see who they really were. But perhaps I was simply trying to make sure she did not have the time to dig too deeply into my own.

"You can call me Ellie, if you like," she said, as if I had been asking permission.

"No," I said. "Ellie is the name for a sweet young girl. I shall call you Eleanor." I frowned at her. "You came back."

"Yes. I said I would, and I always do as I say."

"Do you?" I asked, wondering if I had been too late, if she had already seen the dark place where my heart had once been. "That is not as much a virtue as one would think."

Finn broke in. "Gigi and I are going upstairs to change out of our swim things. I'll leave you two to sort out what you'd like to do today."

He smiled hopefully, as if he were not an investor who knew that a return on investment usually took years and not days. I simply stared back at him.

"We'll be fine," Eleanor said, as if she really believed it.

When they had gone, I turned my attention to the girl—although I suppose she was actually a woman. At ninety years old, I saw any younger woman as a mere girl. "Who called you Ellie?"

I must have caught her off guard, because she flinched. "My father."

Ah. "And he died when you were a girl."

She paused. "How did you know that?"

I sighed. "I recognize the signs."

She regarded me with pale blue eyes. "My father died when I was fourteen."

"How did he die?"

She stood and began fluffing the pillows behind my head. "He drowned in a storm. He had a shrimp boat here on Edisto."

"And your mother?"

As she reached over me, I faintly caught her scent. I had once had a keen sense of smell, but its loss had been one of the first things that told me that I was getting old. Still, every once in a while, I smelled things, detected scents that were tied to a memory like a string binding the years together. She smelled like soap, and her hair like the salt marsh, and I wondered if she had driven with her windows down. Bernadett had liked to do that, too, and if I closed my eyes I could imagine it was her leaning over me, her hair smelling like salt and sweetgrass.

"She lives in North Charleston with my sister, Eve, and Eve's husband, Glen. Eve and Glen are expecting their first child at the beginning of next year."

Her voice had tightened, and I strained my neck so I could see her face better, but she was busy pushing the curtains open farther, as if Nurse Weber had not already done so. I wanted to dig further, but she surprised me by interrupting.

"What about your parents? Did they move here from Hungary with you and your sister?"

"No," I said, wondering if I could shock her. "My father shot himself when Bernadett and I were very small."

I waited for her to comment, to extend her sympathy. Instead, she asked, "And your mother?"

"She died right before we came to America to join our older sister, Magda. She had the good sense to marry an American before the war."

She sat down again, placing her hands on her bare knees below her skirt. Her fingers were long and pale—a pianist's fingers—and her nails unvarnished. My mother would have been appalled, but I found it suited her. No perfume and no nail polish. I might have liked this girl—this woman—if I hadn't been preparing to die.

Strumming her fingers against her knees, she said, "So what would you like to do today? Finn said you enjoyed books. Perhaps I could read? And I know you enjoy music. I have a collection of classical music on my iPod and I brought my portable speakers if you'd like to listen. We could even discuss it later. I could ask for Finn to bring in a DVD player and we could watch a movie if nothing's on television. Or we could just talk." She stared expectantly at me.

I almost smiled. I sensed that she had been a caretaker before, was adept at thinking of others' needs before her own. And I also had the sense that it did not come naturally to her. She wore the role as a little girl would wear her mother's clothes, ill fitting and not her style. I suppose I recognized this in her because I had worn a similar disguise for almost seventy years.

I allowed my head to relax against the pillow, wishing Nurse Weber would come in or Finn and Gigi would return. This Eleanor was too eager to shed her own life and wear mine.

"If we talk, then we would have to decide which topics would be off-limits," I said.

She frowned, and I wanted to press my thumb against the crease between her brows as my mother had done to remind me about the wrinkles I was making.

"I would try not to ask about anything too personal, Miss Szarka. . . ."

"I was not referring to me. I thought perhaps that you had things you would not wish me to ask about."

That gave her pause. But instead of backing down, she said, "You may ask me anything you like, but I don't think that anything you have to ask me will deter me from keeping this job."

"If you need the money that much, let me give it to you and save us both a lot of bother."

Her eyes burned as she regarded me. "I work for my money, Miss Szarka, and I don't need your charity. But I do need this job, so let's try again. What would you like to do today?"

My gaze strayed to her hands, which were once again thrumming on her knees; I noticed her short nails, and I remembered what she'd said to me the last time I'd seen her, about how Chopin reminded her of her father. "Your favorite composer is Chopin?"

She nodded warily.

"Which are your favorite? The mazurkas?"

"No." She shook her head slowly. "The nocturnes."

"Oh, yes," I said. "Melancholy and passionate. Only Chopin could evoke such disparate emotions at the same time." My eyelids fluttered down over my eyes. I was still so weak and so tired, and I had grown weary of trying to convince this girl to go, to leave and not come back. Forcing my eyes open, I said, "I want you to play something for me. The Chopin Nocturne in C Minor. Number 21, posthumous. Do you know that one?"

She paused a moment before answering. "Yes," she said. "It was my father's favorite piece. I could never play it as well as he did." She swallowed, as if to erase all the words she wanted to say.

"Some find it too sad. But I like it, and I want you to play it for me. Right now. Unless you cannot because it reminds you too much of your father, and I will understand. I suppose Finn will have to find somebody else more suitable, who will do what I ask."

With the last of my energy I smiled before I closed my eyes again. I waited to hear the chair slide back and her footsteps treading slowly out of the room. Instead I felt her warm breath on my cheek, her words soft in my ear.

"If you want me to play the Chopin, then I will. That will mean, of course, that I'm here to stay and not on temporary approval. I don't know why you don't want me here, but I aim to find out. But in the meantime I will play the damned Chopin and you will eat your damned lunch and that will be the end of it."

My eyes popped open in time to watch her stand and then slide the chair closer to the bed. Only her whitened fingers on the top edge of the chair gave away her true feelings.

"I will play while you eat, and when you're done we'll discuss what you'd like to do the rest of the day. You don't have to like me and I sure as hell don't like you very much, but that's no reason why we can't be civil to each other. I need the job, and you want to make Finn happy. So here we are."

So here we are. I closed my eyes again, not because I was tired or because I wanted to block her from my sight. I closed them because she sounded so much like Bernadett that I wanted to believe that it was my sister standing so close to me, admonishing me for behaving in a manner in which our mother would not have approved.

Turning my head to the wall to hide the tears that threatened to spill from my eyes, I said, "Then go play. I want to hear Chopin."

She stayed very still for a long while, but I would not give her the satisfaction of turning around to look at her. Finally, she said, "I'm sorry about your sister. There was once a time when I would have felt the same way if Eve had died. But I do know about grief. I miss my father today as much as I did the day he died. I suppose I always will."

Her footsteps retreated, but I remained staring at the wall, wondering what she had meant by "once," and feeling an odd hope that she really would come back.

CHAPTER 11

Eleanor

I didn't see any of my surroundings as I walked toward the piano room. I stopped at the threshold and stared into the dark room and at the large black shape of the piano in the center. I flipped on the overhead chandelier, its glow reflected in the ebony sheen of the piano's top board.

I pictured the old woman lying in her bed, waiting to hear Chopin played in this dim room where only dust motes lived, performed by a girl who'd played only show tunes for nearly two decades. Helena had thought this would be my breaking point, the moment when I'd throw up my hands and go away. I knew very little about her or her reasons, but she apparently knew even less about me.

I slid onto the bench and stared down at the closed fall board, my fingers resting on top, unable to lift it. I thought of our old house near the marsh, of the music sung by the birds and insects, and the bright light that had poured inside to rest on my father and me as we sat side by side on the piano bench.

I closed my eyes for a moment, trying to remember what it had felt like to have him next to me, but all I felt was my aloneness in an unused, dark room. My eyes flickered open, and my gaze settled on the heavy drapes that either obscured the outside light or hid things inside. The question was not mine to answer, but as I stared at the thick material on the windows, I knew what had to be done.

I stood and quickly moved to the first window, pulling aside what seemed like yards of fabric to find a cord. I tugged on it, and when nothing happened, I tugged on it harder. With a slight puff of air, the cord snapped, then sagged into my hand. I tossed it behind the drape, then shoved aside one half of the window treatment and then the other.

Small clouds of dust rolled over me and into the room, making me sneeze, but I was too intent on my mission to stop. I walked quickly over to the second window and repeated the process—without breaking the cord—then stood back to admire my handiwork.

Despite the storm clouds outside and the rain pattering against the glass, the light from the floor-to-ceiling windows settled on the room with a filmy veil, lifting the shadows and illuminating the blank rectangles on the walls. From where I stood, they formed a pattern, the shape of a face with two eyes, a nose, and an unsmiling mouth. In the gloom of the day, the wall almost seemed to wear an expression of expectation.

Without thinking twice, I returned to the piano and hoisted the huge top board, struggling from the weight as I supported it with one hand while I tried to maneuver the top board prop into place. When I felt it was secure, I stepped back and stared. I seemed to be waiting either for it to begin playing by itself or for it to disintegrate into a cloud of dust like an old corpse being exposed to the sun for the first time in a thousand years.

I had no idea how much time had passed since I'd left the old woman's room, but it must have been enough to make her believe that I had left after all. I slid onto the bench again, taking my time to adjust the height and the distance between the keyboard and me. I opened the fall board and stared down at the neat rows of black and white keys before allowing my fingers to rest on top of them. I imagined I could hear their music seep up through my fingers to my veins, resonating in the place in my chest where I'd locked everything away and forgotten where I'd left the key. I pictured it as one of Dah Georgie's secret keepers, the lid bulging, the side reverberating with the music that waited inside.

My right hand found the first note at the beginning of the nocturne, then began to mimic the stroll-like tempo. *Andante sostenuto.* I hadn't played it since I was fourteen, yet I saw each stanza of music in my head, heard each note in my heart. I imagined that if I lived to be one hundred without playing it, I could still sit down at a piano and perform it from memory.

But it was more than knowing the notes. It was more about reconciling an old woman's desire to intimidate me and my own reluctance to conjure ghosts. The Eleanor whose father had wept when she played Chopin was gone forever in the way a shoreline disappears after a hurricane. The shape might still exist beneath the water, but it was gone just the same.

I spread my left hand in an octave over two E-flats, getting ready to play a Scott Joplin rag just to jar the ears of the woman who I was sure was listening intently. I paused, remembering her parting words. *Then go play. I want to hear Chopin.* The second time she'd asked me to play Chopin she hadn't specified *which* Chopin piece she wanted to hear.

With a silly grin on my face, I began playing Chopin's Polonaise in A Major, better known as his "Military" Polonaise. Hearing this piece instead of the nocturne would be the same as stepping outside during a rainstorm and finding syrup dripping from the sky.

The piece wasn't too challenging, what I used to call finger acrobatics on the keyboard, but it took all of my attention, as there were lots of racing octaves in both hands and a quick *allegro con brio* tempo. I was so attuned to the music that I was barely aware of Finn calling my name until he'd reached the side of the piano and tried it again.

"Eleanor."

I stopped in midphrase, my hands held aloft over the keyboard until I realized what I was doing and quickly placed them in my lap. He'd changed clothes and was wearing his casual uniform of khaki pants and knit golf shirt. I looked up at him expectantly.

"Aunt Helena has asked me to get you to stop and play something else. She said you'd know what she was talking about."

I frowned, pretending I didn't understand. "She asked me to play Chopin, and that was one of his polonaises."

"Yes, and Gigi and I liked it very much, but Aunt Helena says that it sounded like a child banging on the keys with a wooden bat. Nurse Weber had to give her something for her headache."

"Excuse me?" I was too stunned to get much air behind my words, and they came out more like a squeak. I might have been a little out of practice, but I certainly didn't sound as bad as she said.

As if anticipating my next words, Finn held up his hand. "I didn't say I agreed at all. In fact, my first impression remains. She just wants you to play something else. Something she said she specifically asked for."

My back stiffened. "She knows why I can't play it. She's only asking so that I'll go away."

His eyes seemed guarded. "I don't know why she's chosen to be so antagonistic toward you, but at least she's expressing some emotion—something we haven't seen since we brought her home. But you're good for her, and I know that we need you here."

It wasn't clear whom he meant by "we." I studied him carefully, seeing him for the first time as a parent who'd come close to losing a child, a child who was in her fourth year of remission—which was probably also only the fourth in a million years of worry. Grief wore many cloaks, but when I looked at Helena Szarka, I saw something more.

"You said you were the one who discovered your aunts, that Bernadett was already dead and Helena was starving to death." I frowned, trying to make the picture make sense. "Why didn't Helena call for help?"

In the murky light, his face seemed carved from stone, all marble and shadow. "She didn't want to go on without her sister."

The thumb and middle finger of my right hand began a slow half-step ascent up the keyboard, the notes ominous and lonely in the murky light. "Did she tell you that?"

He gave an almost imperceptible shake of his head. "She won't speak of it."

My fingers stalled on the keys as I recalled the stark bedroom upstairs with a door that was supposed to remain closed. "When was the last time you heard Bernadett play?"

He thought for a moment. "I'm not sure. I visited about once a week, and Bernadett would usually play for us after dinner." He began to pace between the windows, his brows furrowed. He did this at the office, too, when he was deep in thought, and his assistant, Kay, would always mutter a complaint about the antique rug. He paused for a moment to study the open drapes, as if noticing the light from the windows for the first time.

He turned and looked at me. "It was Christmas. I remember because we sang carols with Gigi and a few neighbors. I couldn't visit again until near the end of January because of several business trips. It was past Epiphany, and the tree and decorations were all up—which was unusual for the aunts. And when Gigi asked Bernadett to play, Bernadett said she couldn't play anymore. The piano was all closed up, and Gigi thought that was why.

It's funny that I hadn't thought of this before, but I don't recall her playing again after Christmas."

His eyes were guarded. "Why do you ask?"

My hands rested on the quiet keys, mute appendages that had somehow lost their voice. "I stopped playing when my father died." I paused, unsure of what I wanted to say. Finally, I said, "It just made me wonder."

A loud thumping sounded from somewhere in the house. Startled, I looked up at Finn, who didn't seem very surprised at all. A tightness had formed around his jaw.

"I'm guessing Aunt Helena coerced the nurse into letting her have her cane."

"And she's banging it on the floor?"

"Or the wall." His jaw tightened even more. "I think she's ready to hear something else."

I narrowed my eyes. "Does Gigi know chopsticks? We could do a duet."

His mouth twitched. "I don't think that's what Helena's waiting for."

"I know." I touched the fall board, ready to close it, but stopped. "Do you remember where Bernadett kept her music?"

"All over, really. Some of it's in the piano bench. But she also had piles tucked away in many of her sweetgrass baskets around the house."

I stood and moved behind the bench, then opened the lid. Three neat stacks of music sat inside, placed as precisely as chalkboard erasers on the first day of school. Being careful not to disturb the piles too much, I thumbed through the sheet music and books, recognizing many of them as old friends: Schubert, Beethoven, Mozart, Mendelssohn, and Brahms. At the bottom of the third pile was a piece of sheet music consisting of a paper cover and several loose pages inside. The word "Csárdás" was emblazoned on the front. Nothing was written in English, and I could see that the pages were very old, the right-hand corners brittle or missing in places, and I could picture long fingers turning over the page so as not to miss a note.

"Looks like an old favorite," I said, holding it up for Finn to see.

He took it from me and looked at it closely. "I know this. It's the Csárdás," he said, pronouncing it *char-dash*. "A traditional Hungarian folk song—a courting song. I remember Bernadett playing it quite a bit when I was a boy, insisting I learn to dance to it."

I bit my lip, the image of him as a little boy folk dancing too ludicrous even for my imagination. "And did you?" I managed to ask without laughing.

He looked affronted. "Yes, actually. I was quite good at it, according to both aunts. I do have Hungarian blood, you know."

Even after I'd learned that his aunts were Hungarian, I'd pictured him more like a Magyar warlord than a folk dancer. Perhaps it was possible to be both. I reached for the music, then closed the bench to sit on it again before propping the music up on the stand in front of me.

Leaning closer, I said, "Wow. This looks hard." The tempo started slowly but changed drastically throughout the six-page piece, with parts of the music nearly black with the lines from the thirty-second notes racing up and down the treble and bass clefs. I felt the hair rise on the back of my neck as I stared at the music, the notes already singing inside my head.

"It's usually played on violin, but the piano version was pretty good from what I remember. It's a fast piece," Finn said, leaning over my shoulder to study the music.

As if acting of their own accord, my fingers placed themselves on the keyboard in position and began to strike the keys. I hadn't sight-read a piece in a very long time, but I suppose it was very much like riding a bicycle, because it took me just a few stanzas to get the hang of it. At least until the tempo increased dramatically and my fingers could barely keep up. But I couldn't seem to stop myself; it was as if I'd reached the precipice of a hill I'd been climbing for a very long time, and the momentum had pushed me over the edge.

I didn't stop, Finn surprising me by turning the pages at the correct time, until I'd reached the end. I held down the sustaining pedal longer than I should have, allowing the final notes to linger in the room like guests at a party that had ended long ago.

It was only when I'd lifted my foot from the pedal that we could hear the banging coming from Helena's room. I bit my lip as I looked guiltily up at Finn. "That was terrible. If I had a cane, I think I'd bang it, too."

He surprised me by not wincing. "That was the first time you'd played that?"

I nodded.

His eyes traveled to the music propped up on the stand, then back to me. "That's remarkable."

The banging sounded again, and we both looked in the direction of the foyer. "I guess I should go see what she wants," Finn said, and I would have laughed at the trepidation in his voice if I hadn't been feeling the same way.

"I'll come, too," I said, sliding off the bench.

Moving slowly, like two schoolchildren on the way to the principal's office, we made our way through the kitchen to Helena's bedroom. Teri Weber sat on the chair by the bed knitting what looked like a sweater and looked up apologetically when we entered.

"I wanted to come and get you, but Miss Szarka insisted on using her cane." Her knitting needles continued clicking as she gave us a forced smile. She put her knitting aside, then stood over the bed, where a tray had been placed over Helena's lap. "Are you sure you're done eating? That's my grandmother's recipe for chicken soup and I'm working on a patent for it because I swear it will cure everything from depression to toe fungus and everything in between."

Helena responded by just staring at her, and then with studied movements used both hands to push away the bowl. It was the first time I'd really noticed her fingers, the swollen knuckles and the digits that no longer lay flat or straight. Our eyes met and I recalled Finn's words. *Helena became the music she played.* For the first time, I felt sympathy for this woman, understood her grief a little more.

With tightly compressed lips, Nurse Weber lifted the tray and walked out of the room to the kitchen, but Helena's eyes didn't leave mine.

"That was terrible," she said slowly, her accent more pronounced, and I wondered if this was how she betrayed her emotions, by allowing her words to slip into memories of her native tongue.

Even though I had thought and said the same thing, I felt offended. "I was sight-reading. And I'd never even heard it before—"

"Don't . . . ever . . . play . . . that . . . again." She paused after each word, as if having to translate in her head, her English fluency seeming to desert her completely.

"Aunt Helena—," Finn started.

"Never. I don't . . . want . . . to . . . hear . . . it."

I was surprised to see the start of tears in the old woman's eyes, and I realized that her reluctance to hear the song had nothing to do with the way I'd played it.

"I'm sorry," I said, looking down at my hands, unwilling to see this woman's tears.

"That song is a Hungarian national treasure, and you butchered it."

Her voice had regained control, and I looked up in surprise to see that the tears were gone. But I had seen them, had seen behind them to a heart filled with emotions I couldn't name.

"I'm sorry," I said again, jutting out my chin. "You didn't tell me which songs you *didn't* want me to play."

The light in her eyes flashed, making me wonder if she enjoyed riling me. "I am sure the list will grow longer, but please put the Csárdás at the top."

"Fine," I said stiffly. "I won't play it again, as long as you never ask me to play Chopin's Nocturne in C Minor."

Her eyes flashed again, in anger or amusement, I couldn't tell. "We will see," she said.

"Yes," I agreed. "We'll see." I moved to the door. "I need fresh air. I'm going for a walk. Be thinking about what you'd like to do when I get back."

"It is raining," she said, with a hint of triumph.

"I doubt I'll melt," I said.

I had made it to the kitchen when she called out, "The witch from Oz melted when she got wet."

I kept going toward the front door, not stopping until I'd reached the front yard, where I turned my face up to the rain and started to laugh.

CHAPTER 12

Gigi found me on the front porch in one of the rockers and handed me a large, soft towel.

"Here," she said. "Daddy said you might need this."

I looked up at her through my dripping hair and took it. "Thanks," I said, wrapping it around me and then using the corners to squeeze the ends of my hair.

She sat down in the rocking chair next to me, her bare feet barely skimming the porch. "I like to sit out here, too, when I need to work out my problems."

I was about to ask her what problems a ten-year-old could possibly have, and then I remembered. "Does it help?" I asked.

She nodded. "And so does this." She lifted her hand to show a paper towel wrapped around something the size of her fist.

"What's that?"

"Chocolate. Nurse Weber made brownies." She took one small brownie, then handed me the remaining one with the paper towel.

"You're a very smart little girl, Gigi. Has anyone ever told you that before?"

She flashed a grin that reminded me of one of her father's rare smiles. "Yes, ma'am. A couple of times at least."

I laughed, then took a bite into the brownie. "Wow. Nurse Weber sure knows her way around a kitchen."

"You should taste her chocolate chip cookies. They're a-*ma*-zing. If you want, I can go pretend that I'm sad and then she'll make some."

I would have laughed out loud, but my mouth was full of brownie. After I swallowed, I said, "That's all right. The brownie hit the spot."

She was staring at me speculatively. "You remind me a lot of Aunt Bernadett. I think that's why Aunt Helena likes you."

I almost choked on a stray brownie crumb. "I don't think she likes me very much."

"Sure she does. If she didn't, she'd just ignore you."

I stared at her for a long moment. "Did you figure that out all on your own?"

"Yes, ma'am. I guess Daddy will be figuring that out pretty soon, too. He's usually a little slower than me."

I rocked for a moment. The rain had stopped and the sun was creeping through breaks in the clouds, illuminating the weeping porch roof and the tall grasses that led down to the dock and the creek. The creek ran wide and muddy this close to the river, reminding me of the times Lucy and I would take out a johnboat after a storm and into the swollen and unpredictable water to see what secrets had been dredged from the river's bottom. I wanted to find a pirate's treasure or message in a bottle or even a skeleton, but all we'd ever found had been an old shoe and a dead snake. I grew to understand that it was the expectation of the unseen that made me want to look, and after my father died, it was the danger that attracted me. But all these years later I felt the pull of the tidal creeks and the river, letting me know that although time had altered the landscape of my life, there were some things that would never change.

I turned to Gigi. "What about me reminds you of Bernadett?"

She shrugged. "The way you talk to Aunt Helena, mostly. Everybody—not Daddy and me, of course, but pretty much everybody else—is afraid of her. But you're not. You say what you want to say. Oh, not to be hurtful. But just because it's what you feel you need to say."

She paused, probably to catch her breath. Gigi spoke so fast that I had to concentrate to make sure I hadn't missed anything.

"And I think she likes you because of the piano. The way you play it."

I studied the river below, dully shining in the struggling sunlight, keeping its secrets hidden still. "What do you mean?"

She slid from her chair, then pressed her finger gently on the button of my blouse in the middle of my chest, startling me. Her dark gray eyes stared steadily into mine. "You feel the music here, in your heart. Your fingers might be doing all of the work, but the music's here."

She stepped back and settled into her rocking chair again. "Madame LaFleur says that about dancing—so I'm not going to take all the credit for coming up with that on my own."

I was too startled to laugh. After a moment, I said, "But how could you tell? The first piece I played was a military march—one I hadn't played in years—and the second piece was, well, it was a mess."

Her bright smile illuminated her face again. "Because when you were playing *I* felt it here." She cupped both hands together and pressed them against her own chest. "That's what Madame LaFleur says is the way to tell when we're exposed to truth and beauty in art."

The heavy, dead thing in my chest stirred again like a creature startled out of hibernation. I was still trying to think of something to say when the sound of a car driving up the driveway caught our attention. I stopped rocking and stood, moving to the porch railing as I recognized the car moving slowly through ruts and puddles.

Gigi slid from her chair. "I'll go tell Daddy we've got company."

She'd already slipped inside the house before I told her not to bother, that I recognized who the visitor was and knew whom he'd come to see.

I was at the bottom of the porch steps by the time Glen had climbed from the car. "Is everything okay? Are Eve and the baby . . . ?" I felt sick, unable to finish my sentence.

He hooked his thumbs into the front pockets of his jeans. "No. Everything's fine, no need to worry about anything." He kicked a rock with the toe of his shoe and tried not to appear as uncomfortable as he looked. "Since I didn't have to work today, we all thought it might be a good idea for me to make sure everything was fine with you."

"We?" I found myself leaning toward him, an old habit I couldn't seem to stop.

"Well, your mama and Eve had voiced some concerns about you taking this job without knowing much about it, so I volunteered to drive over here to make sure you were okay."

I took a step closer. "You were worried about me?"

"Sure I am. What do we know about this guy? And he's dragging you all the way out here to a house where who knows what is going on. A person died here, remember? I wanted to make sure you were all right."

"Hello again."

We turned to see Finn emerging from the front door, his aloof, professional smile on his face.

Glen stepped forward with a proffered hand, and the two men shook. They seemed to be sizing each other up the way I'd seen stray dogs decide who would lead the pack. Glen retreated back toward me, while Finn remained on the porch, as if each was declaring territory.

"Is there anything I can help you with?" Finn asked, making me wonder if he'd heard the part in the conversation where Glen had mentioned a person dying in the house.

"Just thought I'd drive over to see how the new job was working out for Eleanor. Without a number to call, her mama and sister were getting antsy."

Finn moved farther out onto the porch and put his hands on the railing in a relaxed stance, but I could tell he was anything but. "Thanks for reminding me. I just bought an iPhone for Eleanor and added her to our plan so that she'll be reachable wherever she is. I've got it in my briefcase and will make sure she has it before she leaves tonight."

He straightened, and for a horrifying moment I thought he'd ask Glen to come inside. Instead, he turned to me. "Helena's awake and she's asking for you. She wants you to read to her now."

I raised my eyebrows. "Do I need to pick a book?"

"No. She already sent Gigi looking for the one she wants."

Facing Glen again, I said, "I'm fine, really. But thanks for making sure." I paused, wanting Finn to leave us alone for just a moment.

Finn didn't move.

Keeping my eyes on Glen, I said, "I'll call you from my phone so you'll have the number." I smiled, wanting him to know that I was glad he'd come, glad that he'd thought enough to be worried about me and wanted to check up on me. I didn't want to feel grateful, didn't want to feel the way he made me feel, but like the tides under the spell of the moon, I couldn't seem to stop.

"All right, then," he said, stepping back toward the car. "We'll see you later. Should we wait on you for dinner?"

Finn spoke. "We have dinner plans here."

Glen's mouth hardened slightly as he glanced at Finn. Turning back to me, he said, "Sure. We'll see you later, then." With a wave he climbed into his car, then turned around in the driveway and headed away faster than when he'd arrived.

I stared after him for a long time, if only to avoid meeting Finn's eyes. Without turning around, I said, "I guess I should go see if I need to help Gigi find the book for Helena."

When he didn't say anything, I faced him reluctantly, forcing myself to look at him. His eyes had darkened to the color of the storm clouds still hanging around like reluctant children at bedtime. He was watching me carefully, as if half expecting me to run down the drive after Glen. Flushing, I climbed each step deliberately to show him that I would never shame myself by falling in love with my sister's husband, or that I had once had dreams of being somebody different from who I'd turned out to be.

He stood in front of the door, barring the way, and it would have been awkward to try to walk around him, so I stopped, facing him, holding my breath while I waited for him to speak.

"You didn't ask me which book Aunt Helena wanted."

I wasn't sure what I'd been expecting him to say, but it certainly wasn't that. I frowned up at him. "No, I guess I didn't. What is it?" I asked, suddenly worried.

One corner of his mouth twitched. "*The Wizard of Oz.*"

I barked out an unladylike laugh before I could pull it back, my relief permitting me to let go. "Great," I said as he opened the front door to allow me to go inside first. "I can practice a Hungarian accent when I read the part of the wicked witch."

Finn laughed, an unfamiliar sound, as he followed me inside. I was hoping his change in mood meant that he'd forgotten how I'd leaned toward Glen like a flower toward the sun, how he'd seen me at Pete's talking to the man with the sad shoulders and defeated face. But I remembered Finn's eyes when I'd turned around and knew that he had not.

I lifted my eyes from the book and blinked at the clock on the bedside table. Although I'd seen *The Wizard of Oz* about two dozen times on television, I'd never read Frank Baum's classic. I had apparently been more drawn in than my listeners and unaware that I'd been reading for almost two hours.

Helena was propped up on her lace pillows, her mouth open in a soft snore. I took the opportunity to study her without reciprocation, noticing her still-smooth skin, the high cheekbones and finely arched brows. Her hair was a pure white now, with hints of yellow, but it was still thick and full, and I realized with some surprise that she must have once been a very beautiful woman.

But it was more than the years and her attitude toward me that made her physical beauty recede. It was as if a shadow lingered over her like the filter on a camera lens but with the opposite effect. I drew back from her, pressing against my chair. I didn't want to see too much, didn't want to see what made her frown in her sleep or understand why Bernadett had stopped playing the piano. My own shadow was long and deep, and I imagined myself sinking deep enough to drown if I stepped into someone else's.

My gaze flickered down to the foot of the bed, where Gigi had curled up on her side to listen to me read. Her narrow shoulders rose and fell in gentle sleep, and as I watched, a small smile graced her face. I knew babies smiled in their sleep but had always imagined that children past babyhood had long since forgotten how to converse with angels.

A loud snore brought my attention to Teri Weber, who'd pulled in a kitchen chair and had been furiously knitting while I read. Except now she was as prone as a person could be in a ladder-back chair, her feet straight out in front of her and her knitting draped over her lap.

Quietly, I closed the book, then spread an afghan over Gigi before removing one of the pillows behind Helena's head so that she could lie flat. As I lifted the knitting from Nurse Weber's hands to lay it on the floor beside her, I noticed for the first time the gramophone behind her.

It was shoved in a corner on top of a small table. I hadn't noticed it before because it had been blocked by the open door of the armoire where the television was kept. But when Nurse Weber had brought in her chair, she'd had to close the door.

I'd never seen a gramophone up close before, and it seemed so much larger than I'd imagined. The brass horn, meticulously polished, was about a foot and a half wide and just as tall. It sat on a rectangular wood base with a brass-and-wood crank on the side. Records in thin, yellowing sleeves were piled in a deep, round sweetgrass basket. I wanted to go through them to discover what music Helena listened to but couldn't without moving the nurse.

Unobserved, I took my time studying the room, the pale blue walls and the heavy lace curtains, which seemed from another continent, if not another era. A small dressing table cluttered with cosmetics and perfumes was pushed against the far wall, a heavy drape of purple velvet cascading from the edges of both the table and the matching stool. It was old and faded but had definitely been made for a queen.

This room was so different from Bernadett's. I wanted to know what she'd been like, if her room was an indication of her personality as Helena's was of hers. And I wondered how two such different sisters could have been as close as they were. I thought of Eve and myself, and the years between our childhood and now, and how time could sweep through our lives like a flooded river, taking all the sediment with it.

I noticed with some surprise that this room had only one piece of art on the walls, an eleven-by-fourteen-inch framed painting of Moses, its artist and time period unknown to me. Like the other paintings in the house, it hung loosely in its frame, the beauty and power of the art diminished by the uneven fall of light. I tilted my head, wondering what it was that seemed so off-kilter about the painting, why my gaze kept coming back to it as if trying to answer a repeated question.

I stretched and listened as my stomach grumbled. The smells of something cooking in the kitchen drifted to me, and I wondered who'd thought to stick something in the oven for dinner.

Tiptoeing through the room, I went into the deserted kitchen. A crumpled rectangular piece of foil lay on its back on the counter, frozen circles of what looked like marinara sauce clinging to it in spots. I sniffed the air, catching the distinctive aroma of garlic and cheese. I remembered Teri asking me earlier if I liked lasagna, but I knew she hadn't been out of the room to stick it in the oven.

Listening to the sleeping house, I slowly walked into the foyer, peeking into the dining and music rooms, both as deserted as the kitchen. I was about to make my way back to the sunroom when I decided to check to see if Finn's car was still there. I opened the front door and stopped short.

Finn sat in one of the rockers, so focused on what he was doing that he didn't immediately register that I'd come outside. He'd pulled another rocking chair in front of him, and as I watched he put a piece of paper down on the seat of the chair in front of him and made an exact diagonal crease in the paper. On the floor by his feet his BlackBerry buzzed and was summarily ignored.

"Are you making a paper airplane?"

He looked startled and then, remembering his manners, immediately stood. With a boyish smile, he said, "Guilty. I can't seem to shake the habit." As if also just becoming aware of his BlackBerry, he picked it up and, after looking at the screen, typed something into it, and then shoved it in his pocket.

"Are they still asleep?"

I eyed him suspiciously. "How did you know they were sleeping?"

"Because last time I checked, they were sound asleep. You looked like you were enjoying the story, so I didn't interrupt."

I smirked. "Thanks. And thanks for remembering to stick the lasagna in the oven."

He indicated the rocking chair next to the one he'd been sitting in, and I sat down. Tapping his long fingers on the arm of his chair, he said, "Your Hungarian accent needs work, though. Not that I can help you. I once tried to mimic Aunt Helena and I received quite a tanning, as I recall. I never tried it again."

I scooted my chair closer to the railing, then slid off my sandals to rest my feet on the slats. He eyed me for a moment, and I was about to remove my feet when he took off his own loafers and imitated me. His legs were longer than mine, and he had to move his chair back.

Grinning at him, I said, "If I knew how to use the camera on my new iPhone, I'd take a picture and e-mail it to Kay at the office."

His face sobered. "I don't think they'd like that."

That hadn't been the response I'd expected. "What do you mean?"

He stared down at the half-finished plane in his hand. "I'm the managing partner in the firm, the person the employees see on a daily basis. Their employer, the one who signs their paychecks, so to speak. It's important to maintain a certain persona so that everyone knows that the firm is doing fine and that their employment is secure. I learned that from my father, and he from his father."

I nodded, understanding, yet knowing, too, that underneath the black worsted wool was a man who wanted to prop his bare feet up on a porch railing and make paper airplanes.

We sat in silence for a long time, listening to the cicadas and night birds sing the day to sleep as the sun slowly began its descent into the creek. In the fading light, Finn returned to his paper airplane, his graceful fingers tearing and creasing and folding.

I put my feet down and scooted my chair closer so I could see better. "Who taught you to do that?"

Without looking up, he said, "My mother."

That surprised me.

He continued. "She always encouraged me to pursue whatever interested me, regardless of what my father thought. She bought me my first model airplane kit and my first how-to paper airplane book. And then she sat with me while we figured out how to make each one." He held up the creation in his hand. "Voilà!" he said, holding up a plane I couldn't identify. "A World War I Fokker Eindecker," he announced.

I felt like a little child, wanting to clap my hands. "That's amazing! And you made that with a single sheet of paper."

He nodded shyly. "Yes. If I had scissors, it would look better—a little more even. But this will do."

"Can I see it?"

He put it in my hands, and I held it up to the orange light that still clung to the sky like cotton candy. The wings and tail were so intricately folded that even if I'd unfolded it, I could never have figured out how to redo it. I looked back at Finn. "Will it fly?"

"Let's find out."

I followed him out into the wet grass, my feet quickly getting drenched. We made our way to the dock in the half-light to the place where the earth melted into the backwaters.

Finn looked down at the plane in his hand, tweaking a fold or two, seeming almost reluctant to let it go. He looked at me, his eyes serious. "My mother always told me to make a wish before launching a plane."

"Do you?" I asked quietly, the sound competing with the wing rubbing of the crickets and the cry of a black-crowned night heron.

He shook his head. "Not anymore." He turned his head toward the river. "Ready?"

I nodded. "Ready."

He drew back his arm and in a slow, steady movement set the plane aloft. We watched it as it caught the breeze, its paper wings floating delicately over the flowing water. I held my breath and found myself crossing my fingers, as if that would help it cross the creek to the tall spartina grass on the other side.

A strong wind from the direction of the ocean blew at us, making the plane wobble, as if suddenly unsure of its decision to remain aloft. It tilted to the right and then the left, the wind catching it again as it struggled to right itself, sending it crashing ignominiously into the water.

We watched as the current swept it away from us, the water cradling it until it sank from sight. We stared at the spot where it had disappeared for a long time, neither of us speaking. Finally, Finn turned to go and I followed him back to the house in silence, wondering if a wish would have kept the plane up in the air, carrying it to faraway places. And I wondered, too, what Finn had once wished for, and why he'd stopped.

The front door of the porch opened, and Gigi stood there in the puddle of light, guiding our way back to the house as the night heron called out once more, bidding us good night.

CHAPTER 13

Eve

I grunted as Eleanor moved me from my wheelchair to the passenger seat of the Volvo. Because the SUV was higher, it took a lot more out of my sister than she was used to. I was slight and kept my arms strong so I could help, which was why before now my lack of mobility had never seemed to be a problem.

After stowing the chair in the back, Eleanor climbed into the driver's seat, then turned on the air conditioner to full blast. Sweat beaded her nose and upper lip, while tendrils of hair clung to her cheek. I looked away, unprepared for the stab of guilt.

She leaned toward the air-conditioning vent. "Why can't you be like a normal person and get a handicapped ramp and van to make it easier for all of us?"

I turned my head sharply, surprised to hear her words echoing my thoughts. Since my accident, I had never heard her complain. Not once. But she'd been back to Edisto. The smell of the pluff mud and the salt air had become like wooden spoons, stirring old memories. I waited for her to say more, but she put her hand on the steering wheel and put the car into drive.

I didn't answer, perhaps because I didn't even know anymore. After the accident, I'd resisted anything that made my injuries seem permanent, any reminders that advertised the fact that I was no longer a whole person. I didn't want to drive in an equipped van or put ramps on the front of the house. My only concession was a HANDICAPPED hangtag that we used for parking—and that only because of Glen's insistence. I was easy to carry and didn't think it would be too hard to be lifted and carried the few times I ventured from the house. But even I had to admit that the pregnancy would have to change things.

After checking her side mirror twice and the rearview once—something she'd never done as a teenager—Eleanor pulled out of the doctor's office parking lot and onto Highway 17.

"I still don't understand why you changed doctors, especially for one in Mount Pleasant, when your old doctor was so close by."

I concentrated on the moving traffic around us. "My old doctor referred me to Dr. Wise."

I felt her looking at me. "A referral?"

"Yes. It seems my pregnancy is considered a high risk."

"High risk?" Her voice rose a notch. "Did you know this before?"

"Before what? Before I had unprotected sex with my husband?"

She flinched. "Before you decided to become pregnant. Didn't you discuss this with your doctor? Or with Glen?"

I tensed, prepared for battle. I wanted a child. My wanting had become a physical thing, something I carried around in my arms and curled up with at night.

"My doctor told me that if I got pregnant, she couldn't be my doctor anymore."

"What?" She jammed on the brakes, and the person behind us honked and swayed to speed past us. Glancing in her rearview mirror, Eleanor crossed two lanes and drove into a shopping center parking lot. The sickly sweet scent of barbecue from one of the restaurants filled the car, making my stomach churn.

"Why wouldn't she see you anymore?" Eleanor demanded.

I shrugged. "Apparently, anyone with a spinal cord injury above a certain nerve point—like mine—is considered high risk for pregnancy. Most doctors advise against it."

"Why?" she asked quietly.

I stared down at the small diamond of my engagement ring. "Because we run the risk of developing something called autonomic dysreflexia. Dr.

Wise gave me a lot of literature to go over so we can be informed and prepared."

I could tell she was trying to control her voice. "How serious is it?"

"In a best-case scenario, my pregnancy will be normal with no complications at all."

"And worst case?" Her tone was cold.

"It could be fatal."

She closed her eyes and didn't say anything for a long moment, but I could hear her breathing in the silence of the car. "What did Glen say?"

I looked out the side window, unable to answer her. The baby inside me was no larger than a pea, but it had already become my second chance to be the best part of me. To be the person I'd once wanted to be and who I still wanted to become.

Finally, I turned to her. "You can't tell him how serious this is. We'll have to tell him that I'm a high-risk patient so he'll know to look for the symptoms since I won't be able to feel them, but he's not to know that I could die, do you understand? And everything might be fine and I avoid any complications completely. Or I could have an AD episode and I get through it without any harm to me or the baby. But I can't have Glen worrying about this—he's got enough to worry about."

Eleanor slammed her palms on the steering wheel and threw open her door before jumping down into the parking lot. She walked away from the car to the slice of grass that separated the parked cars from the highway. Keeping her back to me, she bowed her head, but her clenched fists told me she wasn't praying.

Whipping back around, she stormed toward the car. "Why?" she shouted. "How? How could you be so stupid?"

I glanced around and saw several shoppers returning to their cars and shooting curious glances our way. Being my mother's daughter, I said, "Shut up. People are looking."

"God forbid," she muttered as she climbed back into the Volvo and slammed the door. "God forbid that perfect strangers find out what an idiot you are." She leaned forward, resting her forehead on the wooden steering wheel. "Why?" she asked again, her voice almost too quiet to hear.

I placed my hand on her arm, grasping it with my fingers and feeling the muscles underneath. "Because I wanted something that was mine. Something that would make my life a whole lot bigger than it is."

She recoiled as if I'd slapped her. She shook off my hand. "You're going to have lots of appointments over the next nine months. Are you going to make excuses to exclude Glen from all of those, too? You *are* planning on telling him eventually, right?"

"I haven't gotten that far in my thinking." I turned my head away so I could hide the gathering tears. For the first time in my life, I'd climbed a tree all on my own, without anyone prodding me. I'd wanted to feel the ride, to experience sheer and utter joy again. I was just unprepared for the crash.

"Great," she said softly as she buckled her seat belt. "Just great." She paused for a moment. "Does Mama know?"

I shook my head, still unable to look at her. "No. It would be too hard for her. And she and Glen are so happy about the baby. I don't want to take that away from them."

Eleanor leaned back against the headrest. "I'm glad you're considering Glen's and Mama's feelings about all this. But you forgot about me."

I stared hard at my younger sister, seeing the person I'd once loved more than anybody, and tried to reconcile that image with the woman she'd become. But it was like looking at an old school photograph, unable to see past the different hairstyle and childhood face to recognize yourself.

"I didn't think it would matter to you." I looked down at my hands. I was scared—I could at least admit that to myself—scared and aching for this one thing I wanted more than I'd ever wanted anything else. Scared and hurt that this one thing I wanted most in this world could be the one thing I could never have.

As I'd learned to do in the last fourteen years, I turned all of my anger and hurt on the one person I knew who would take it. "I figured you might actually be happy at the news. If I die, you'd be free."

Her face registered shock, her eyes brightening with tears. Very quietly, she said, "You can't die yet, Eve. Not before I've had enough time to make you forgive me."

I stared at her for a long time, understanding what she was saying yet unwilling to acknowledge it. It was too easy to continue with how things were instead of think about the way things could be. Forgiveness had become the door between the life I'd had before and the life I wanted. Maybe my pregnancy was a way of showing me the door. All I had to do was figure out how to open it.

I felt my false bravado evaporate like a slow leak from a balloon, and I slumped in my seat. "Promise me you won't tell them," I repeated.

Without looking at me, she nodded, then pulled out of the parking lot. We rode the rest of the way home in complete silence, both of us knowing there were no more words to say.

Eleanor

After dropping Eve off at home, I drove straight to Edisto, barely seeing the canopies of oaks as I headed down Highway 174. The feelings I had for my sister were jumbled together, like the monkeys in a barrel game we'd had as children. All the brightly colored monkeys with their curved arms tangled and entwined, so convoluted that it was almost impossible to separate them.

As children we'd played together and fought together, but we never forgot that we were sisters, bound together by blood and circumstance. When we were fighting, our mother would always remind us that one day both she and our daddy would be gone, leaving just the two of us. We loved and hated each other with the same fierceness but never lost sight of the fact that we were sisters. I sometimes wondered if the accident had been inevitable, as if the vagaries of life had decided it was time for us to pick sides.

I parked the Volvo behind Helena's Cadillac. I didn't expect to see Nurse Kester's car, because her husband drove her and dropped her off every day, but I knew she was scheduled to be there. Still, I started as I recognized the person standing on the porch, the dark wood cane held firmly at her side.

Nurse Kester fluttered behind Helena, flapping her hands. "She insisted on standing out here to greet you when you arrived. I don't think she's strong enough. . . ."

She was silenced by a look from Helena, which I, thankfully, couldn't see.

"Good morning, Miss Szarka." My voice sounded much stronger than I felt.

"You're late. Finn told me you would be here first thing."

I swallowed back the words I really wanted to say. "I'm sorry. I had to take my sister to the doctor—"

"Can't she drive herself?"

I climbed up onto the steps. "No, actually, she can't. She's in a wheelchair."

A slight rise of one of the old woman's eyebrows was the only thing that registered any emotion. "Why is she in a wheelchair?"

I paused, needing a moment to rein in my emotions before I lost this job on the second day.

"Really, Miss Szarka," Nurse Kester interrupted. "I must insist that you sit down. It's remarkable that you got this far on your own steam, but you need to do this gradually or you'll be confined to bed again." She took hold of the old woman's elbow.

Seeing my opportunity to change the subject, I climbed the remaining steps and took her other elbow, then assisted Nurse Kester in placing Helena in a rocking chair.

With an imperious stare, she turned to the nurse. "The girl is here, so you may go do something else—anything that does not involve me seeing you."

"Yes, ma'am," the nurse said with a frown before turning to me. "I'll be in the kitchen if you need anything." Behind Helena's head, she looked up to heaven as if seeking divine intervention.

I settled myself in the rocking chair next to Helena and looked out past the pecan trees and toward the creek. A mosquito landed on my leg and I slapped it, happily ending its feeding frenzy.

"The mosquitoes never bother me."

She was staring at me, as if daring me to state the obvious. *Because you're too sour tasting.* Instead I said, "Aren't you lucky?"

I had just started rocking again when she said, "Why is your sister in a wheelchair?"

I stopped, wondering how much I should say, yet also somehow knowing that she would know if I was lying. "She was in an accident when she was nineteen."

"What kind of accident?"

I sighed, feeling like a spider under a magnifying glass. "She fell from a tree." I met her eyes, knowing she wouldn't stop with the questions until she had the full story. "She climbed it on a dare."

"A dare?"

I stared at the old woman, certain she already knew. "Yes. From me. We were on the section of the old King's Highway—on Westcott Road—where two very large and very old oaks face each other across the road. I dared her that I could climb to the top of one faster than she could."

Helena leaned forward, her hands resting on the top knob of her cane. "Why?"

I'd pondered the answer to that question for nearly fourteen years. I chose the easiest one to understand. "We were both trying to show off in front of my sister's boyfriend. But it was my idea. All the worst ideas were always mine."

"So it was your fault." She settled back in her rocking chair.

I met her eyes, knowing I couldn't lie. "Yes."

She studied the water of the creek as a strong wind rippled its surface, like a woman reading tea leaves in the bottom of a cup. "When we first met, you said that you once would have grieved the loss of your sister. Is that because the guilt makes her hard to live with?"

The anger pulsed through me, my breaths coming in small gasps. But then I remembered what Eve had said to me that morning. *If I die, you'd be free.* I closed my eyes with the shame of it, recalling how for a brief moment I had thought the same thing.

"I was wrong," I said, remembering how when we were children Eve would allow me to crawl under the covers with her in a thunderstorm, and how she shared the chocolate bars my mother bought for her. And how she'd planned to learn how to sew so she could make me my outfit for my interview at Juilliard.

She gave me a hard look and I wondered if she'd read my thoughts, or if because she'd been a sister she understood what lay behind my words.

"What happened to the boyfriend?" she asked.

Helena Szarka had the unnerving habit of finding her target like a heat-seeking missile. Too wounded to move out of the way, I answered simply, "Eve married him."

Her eyebrows rose. "So he chose her over you even though she could not walk. That must have been difficult for you to live with."

Heat crept up my cheeks. I stared out at the water, unable to look at her. "Eve was . . . is very beautiful."

I felt her staring at me, but I didn't turn my head.

"And she and her husband live nearby with your mother?"

"We all live together." I faced her this time because I didn't want to simply imagine her expression of horror mixed with glee. I found myself surprised to see a fleeting glimpse of sympathy, her eyes narrowing as she studied me like a scientific specimen.

"And you probably imagine that you are still in love with him. To make this Greek tragedy more complete, I would say that he has feelings for you, too, but he is too much of a gentleman to come right out and say it. I'm just guessing, of course—too many novels, I suppose. But am I right?"

I stared at her, unable to move or utter a word. I turned my face away, toward the slope of the grassy wetland that crept down to the dock, listening as the water slapped the sides of the pilings, knowing how they felt.

"Mindenki a maga szerencséjének kovácsa." The foreign words were spoken softly, as if she hadn't expected me to hear.

"What does that mean?" I asked, not sure that I really wanted to know.

She waited for a moment. "The relationship between sisters is a little piece of heaven and hell. But we share the same soul."

I thought of Bernadett and the closed piano, all the music put away as if she hadn't expected to need it again. Desperate to deflect her attention, I asked, "Why did your sister stop playing the piano? Did something happen that made her want to stop?"

She drew a deep breath, and I waited for her to answer. Instead, she said, "I need you to gather up all of the piano music and create some sort of filing system for it. I will need to examine each sheet of music that you find so I can help you sort it into pieces you can play and those you should not attempt. A lot of them are old and fragile, so I will need you to make new covers and find a way to attach them. Perhaps you can draw? I would like any artwork reproduced on the new covers. Many are so dilapidated that a photocopier will not have anything to copy, so you will need to reproduce the covers by hand."

"Reproduce?" I thought back to my conversations with Finn regarding my job description, pretty sure that being tortured had not been included. "I'm not really creative that way. I'll be happy searching for the music but . . ."

She raised her elegant eyebrows, an expression that was becoming increasingly familiar. "If you are unwilling or unable, please let me know so I can tell Finn that you are not helping out as much as he had hoped."

I rocked in silence for a moment, wondering at what point the money I was earning would no longer be worth it. "Where is the music?" I asked, trying not to allow her to hear anything but excitement in my tone.

A satisfied smile lit her face. "All over the house, mostly stacked in Bernadett's sweetgrass baskets." She became serious for a moment. "But you are not to search in Bernadett's room. That room is closed to you."

I studied her face, remembering the locked mirrored doors and wondering if Finn had told her that he'd found me at the opened armoire.

"Do you understand?" she asked when I didn't say anything.

"Yes," I said, then swallowed. "I can get started this afternoon, if you like."

She watched me carefully as I stood, her eyes bright from the reflected sky. "Why do you want this job so badly?"

I felt a little of the old Ellie tugging at me, reminding me that I had very little to lose. "Because Eve is pregnant. And being with you is easier than being with her."

Her face was unreadable, but I remembered what she'd said earlier: *The relationship between sisters is a little piece of heaven and hell. But we share the same soul.* I'd wanted to prove her wrong, but my admission, I realized too late, had done the opposite.

As if we'd been discussing the weather, she said, "I would like fresh tomatoes on my sandwich at lunch. Please go get some at Pink's Market—they are always fresh and firm. And then we can begin gathering the music. I am afraid my sister was not very organized and it might take a while to collect it all. But we have time, do we not? I would say at least nine months."

She struggled to stand with her cane, but I did not offer assistance, nor did she ask for any. Nurse Kester came to the door and opened it, but Helena paused. She was breathing heavily, but I still would not go to her. It was as if the oppressive weight of memories and the past had pressed their hands against our throats.

"If you are quick in gathering the music, I will allow you to play the piano later."

I frowned. "Finn told me that you enjoy hearing the piano. Wouldn't I be doing you the favor by playing?"

She frowned back at me, her eyes sharp. "Do not overestimate your talent, Eleanor. God compensates those with a lack of talent with an overabundance of self-confidence."

I couldn't hit her, so I chose the next best thing. "Did you ever say that to Bernadett?"

The side of her face creased in a half grin. "Yes. Of course. She was my sister."

I watched as Nurse Kester assisted her into the house, Helena's crippled hand grasping the top of her cane. I sat down heavily in the rocking chair, bristling with anger and indignation. But I also felt energized and renewed somehow, like I'd been on a long, punishing run to clear my thoughts.

Two yellow kayaks skimmed through the water, the paddles moving in sync, and I felt myself breathing deeply in rhythm with their strokes. I'd managed to forget my worry over Eve's pregnancy, and Helena had somehow managed to get me to confess my entire past. Most of it. She'd compared it to a Greek tragedy, but she hadn't turned away in disgust, either.

I stood to go back into the house, recalling her grin as she'd turned to go, as if she'd succeeded in some mission. And as I walked to the door with a lighter step, I couldn't help but wonder if she had.

CHAPTER 14

Helena

A soft, warm breath brushed my cheek as I felt a slight pressure on the side of my bed. I opened my eyes and turned my head to see Gigi's sweet face. Her chin was cradled in the heels of her hands, her elbows digging into the mattress.

"Are you awake yet?" she asked.

I pretended to think for a moment. "I believe so, *bogárkám*."

She laughed and wrinkled her nose. "I'm not a little bug!"

I smiled at her, my aches no longer hurting so much. "I am glad to know your father is teaching you a little Hungarian." I studied her, recalling that she had not been here last night when I had gone to bed. "Is it Saturday already?"

She laughed again and jumped up on the bed, careful not to land on me. "How can you not know what day it is? I had dance camp all week and we had our big show yesterday, so that meant it was Friday. And today is Saturday because Saturday always comes after Friday."

As usual, her words were too fast for me to grasp completely, but I was able to interpret enough to know what she was saying. I lifted my arm and took my wristwatch from the nightstand and squinted at it. "It is only nine o'clock. Why are you here so early?"

Sliding off the bed, she reached for the bench at the foot of the bed and picked up two see-through plastic covers with three holes punched in the side. One was pink, the other purple. "We needed to know which color you like better."

"We?"

"Yes. Ellie and me. We're organizing all of Aunt Bernadett's piano music."

I held back a laugh. Of course Eleanor had found a way to do what I had asked but without doing what I had asked. Just like Bernadett. It was astonishing, really, how similar they were, and in more ways than I would ever tell Eleanor. I remembered what she had said about her sister Eve's accident. *All the worst ideas were always mine.* I was quite certain that Bernadett had said the same thing once, although their reasons and justifications would have been different.

Gigi saw me squinting and quickly grabbed my glasses from the night table and adjusted them on my nose. "And what do these plastic covers have to do with Bernadett's music?" I kept my voice haughty so she would know that I was displeased and pass that along to Eleanor.

The little girl seemed too excited to notice. "Nurse Weber is helping us because she's really into crafts and stuff, so Eleanor told her what we needed and this is what she brought." She wrinkled her forehead as if thinking hard. "She says they're ar-*ki*-val quality to protect the old paper. You can see through them so you know what's inside, you can slide the music out the top, and—the best part—you can decorate the cover any way you like." She smiled broadly. "Ellie said she'd take me to the store to buy the three-ring binders to put all the music in when we're done. She said I could pick the colors."

"Will they all be pink?" I asked, not as horrified at the thought as I probably should have been. One of the few blessings of age was not caring so much about how things looked.

"I told Ellie that I would keep an open mind."

As if conjured, Eleanor appeared in the doorway with my breakfast tray. "Good morning, Miss Szarka. I hope Gigi didn't wake you. I told her to be very quiet."

I watched as she placed the tray on the bench at the foot of the bed and met her insincere smile with one of my own. As she adjusted my pillows and helped me sit up, I said, "Where is Nurse Weber?"

"She's occupied making die cuts of musical notes and pianos. I told her I would be happy to bring in your breakfast."

I snorted, making sure to keep my nose wrinkled as she settled the tray on my lap. "I was quite sure that I gave you the job of organizing the music."

Still smiling, she tucked the cloth napkin into the neck of my nightgown. "Yes, you told me the job needed to be done, but I assumed by whom was being left to my discretion."

"So pink or purple, Aunt Helena?" Gigi persisted, placing the two folders between my breakfast and me. "We have two big boxes of each one, so it doesn't matter."

I reached out to stroke her fine hair, trying not to notice my ugly hands. "You pick your favorite, *bogárkám*. The music will be yours one day, so it should be your choice."

"But I dance, Aunt Helena. I don't have enough time to dance *and* play the piano, remember? Mommy said I needed to make a choice because doing both would be too time-consuming."

For Harper, I thought. It was difficult not to throw my hands in the air and say horrible things about the child's mother. My restraint over the years would make me worthy of sainthood. "It is summertime. Perhaps now, when you are not in school, you should be able to pursue other interests."

Eleanor went very still, and I wondered why until the idea came to me. "Eleanor can teach you! And by the end of summer, you should have a few elementary pieces ready for a small recital."

"I'm not a teacher—," Eleanor began.

I cut her off. "You continually tell me what you are not. If I had known that you were so reluctant to do things, I would have told Finn from the beginning that you were not suitable for a job as my companion. Perhaps he would have listened then."

I do not know why I continued to provoke her. It was clear that her motivations for staying were much stronger than her motivations for leaving. And, if I were to be honest with myself, I was no longer so sure that I wanted her to leave. It was almost as if she had given me a reason to get out of bed each morning. And her similarities to Bernadett brought back a little of my lost sister.

"But you've made it clear that my own playing is substandard. I'm surprised you want your grandniece to be exposed to it."

Touché. If anybody was keeping score, I imagined we would be tied.

"Is she eating?" Finn entered the room, dominating it without overwhelming it. I liked to think that he'd inherited the trait from my sister Magda, whose beauty and charm had been legendary. Certainly grand enough to entice a Charleston businessman in a Paris salon to marry her despite her limited knowledge of English.

But Finn possessed his own strength of bearing, born from a lifetime of suppressing his wants in favor of doing what was expected of him. It was why I had kept his boyhood room unchanged. Everyone needed to be reminded of the person he or she had once hoped to be.

"I have lost my appetite," I said, pushing away the bowl of oatmeal despite my gnawing hunger. "I asked a simple favor from Eleanor and she has refused."

I kept my face down so that I wouldn't laugh at the girl's expression.

Finn seemed genuinely concerned. "What favor, Eleanor?"

I interrupted, making my voice as old and pathetic as I could—which was not as difficult as I would have hoped. "I thought this summer would be a good time for Gigi to learn piano—when she is not at school and dance class all the time. Music was so important to Bernadett—and to me—I thought it would be a fitting tribute."

"And Eleanor said no?"

"That is not what I said," Eleanor broke in. "I simply said that I wasn't a teacher."

"But you have extensive knowledge of the piano and could certainly teach the rudiments to a beginner pupil." Finn's argument was full of reason and logic. "Unless Gigi isn't interested."

"I am! I am!" she shouted, jumping high enough that I could see her pink leggings and sandals.

"Fine," Eleanor said, and I wondered if anybody else heard the hard edge to her voice. "We'll start next week. Because this week I'll be too busy gathering music and redecorating the covers."

"Is that what Nurse Weber is doing?" Finn asked. "I wondered." He slid my oatmeal back toward me. "Now that we have that all settled, why don't you eat?"

I picked up my spoon, eagerly anticipating Eleanor's next move. I did not have long to wait. She held back as Finn and Gigi left the room, studying the single painting on the wall that I had brought down from my former bedroom.

Without turning around, she said, "When you are done with breakfast, maybe you'd like to join us at the kitchen table to help with the new covers."

I frowned. "Why would you think I would be interested in that? I can barely hold my spoon."

"True. But it's obvious you like do-it-yourself projects."

"I do not, and I have no idea what you are talking about." I took a quick bite of my oatmeal, burning my tongue, looking away to show my dismissal. My mother had used that technique, and it had always worked. But Eleanor was not as easily dissuaded.

"All of the paintings in the house—they weren't professionally framed. Did you do them all by yourself or did Bernadett help you?"

My spoon froze halfway between my bowl and my mouth. I lowered it back to the bowl, then lifted my gaze to meet hers. "When my sister and I came from Hungary, we had the artwork from our home in Budapest but very little money. We were dependent on our sister, Magda, and her husband for food and shelter. I did not want to waste money on framing when I believed it could be done with more economy."

Her defiant stare met my own and held, as if we were each daring the other to break contact first. We were saved when Finn reentered the bedroom to remove the breakfast tray. He had apparently overheard at least a part of our conversation.

"Aunt Helena, maybe we should get all the paintings reframed. I would hate to think any permanent damage is being done."

I allowed the tray to be lifted from my lap as I prayed that my breakfast would not come back. "They are fine," I said. "There is nothing to be done with them."

Finn stood in the doorway with the tray in his hand and stared at the painting of Moses. "I still say that we should at least have an art appraiser come in and give us an estimate of their worth."

I shook my head. "As I've said again and again, I do not want strangers in this house, pawing over my belongings. There will be time enough for that after I am dead."

He turned away, but not before I saw his mouth tighten. This argument was an old one, and one which I could not afford to lose.

Eleanor began to follow him out of the room until her attention was diverted by the old gramophone in the corner of my room and one of Bernadett's baskets that sat beneath it.

"I forgot about this basket. Is there more piano music in here? I've seen the records but didn't dig through them to see if there was anything else at the bottom."

Before I could reply, she'd reached into the round basket and lifted one of the records. "Are these very old?"

"Obviously." I leaned back against my pillows, watching her with mild disinterest. It was startling how easily she distracted herself from the bigger problems in her life with mundane tasks, refocusing her mind on things she could control and direct. In the end, Bernadett had been the same way, packing up her music and closing up the piano as if the rest of our world was not falling apart. As if sprinkling a little water on a house would save it from fire.

She began flipping through records, pausing over one that still had its cover. Holding it up, she read the label out loud. "The Szarka Sisters?"

"Did Finn not tell you? My sisters—Bernadett and Magda—and I were quite well-known in Hungary and had great plans for moving to America for our singing career."

Slowly, she read the small print under the title out loud. "Featuring 'All Alone' by Irving Berlin."

"That was recorded in 1937."

Eleanor looked down at the record again, as if I had spoken in Hungarian and she was attempting to translate. "You recorded an album?"

"Yes. We were quite the success in England."

She approached the bed, the record held carefully between the flattened palms of both hands. "So you sing, too."

The old pride surged back in me as the good memories resurfaced. "We were compared to the Andrews Sisters—but we were much prettier." I never would have admitted that before, but I was an old woman, and false modesty was something I had easily let go of along with my blond hair and straight fingers. "We were approached to record 'Boogie Woogie Bugle Boy of Company B'—which would have meant a new record deal and a move to America—but we had to turn it down. Bad for us but a good thing for the Andrews Sisters. But Magda got married in 1940 and her husband did not think a respectable wife should make recordings. And then there was the matter of the war."

"The war?"

I sighed. "World War II. Perhaps you have heard of it."

At least she flushed. "Yes. Of course. I studied it in school, but history wasn't my favorite subject." She tilted her head. "Is that why you had to stop—because your country was invaded by the Nazis?"

I frowned at her. "You need to go back to your history books, Eleanor.

Hungary was part of the Axis powers. We were allies with Germany. At least in the beginning." I closed my eyes, praying for patience, anticipating her next question. "No, I was not a Nazi, nor were any of my family or friends." I paused, remembering how long we had clung to our old lives in Budapest as if nothing had changed. As if we didn't know that the rest of the world was on fire. Perhaps it was human nature to attempt to avoid disaster by averting our attention to the mundane. Meeting her gaze, I said, "We were able to escape during the Nazi occupation in 1944. And then we came here."

She regarded me for a long moment, as if she knew there was more to the story, that my telling of it had been merely an accounting of the breeze before a hurricane.

"Did you ever go back? To Hungary?"

The familiar burning in the back of my throat began, and I knew I would not try to speak. I simply shook my head, the one action keeping in check years of absence, of lost friends and history, of my own past.

She focused on the record she held. "Does the gramophone still work?"

I shrugged. "It has been a while since I listened to it, but I imagine it still does. It is a portable model, one you have to wind up."

Her eyes brightened. "I'd love to hear one of your songs. Can I play it now?"

My heart seemed to shudder in my chest. Each night when I went to sleep I prayed that I would not hear my sisters' voices, afraid of what they would say to me. I could not bear to hear them now.

"I am too tired. Maybe later."

She stored the record back in the basket, trying to mask her look of disappointment. "I'm sure Gigi would love to hear it, too." She paused by the door. "Since 'All Alone' was written by Irving Berlin, I bet I could find a copy of the piano music on the Internet. If I can rework the melody into a simple piece, I could teach it to Gigi. It might be fun for her."

I wanted to protest but could not think of a reason that would make sense to her. She said good-bye as Nurse Weber came in to bathe me, but I sent her away, saying I was too tired. I lay in bed for a long time, remembering the words to the old song, recalling the day we had recorded it in the small studio in London. I longed for a cloudy memory, to be unable to remember my past. But my memories remained, like green leaves on an oak tree in the dead of winter, a fitting punishment for those of us who would prefer to forget.

Eleanor

I stood in the sunroom and looked out at the reddening sky, the hazy edges of the clouds like smudged memories. It would be full dark soon, yet I couldn't bring myself to leave. The dinner dishes had been cleared away, Teri Weber was with Helena getting her ready for bed, and Finn and Gigi were on the screened-in porch that faced the marsh playing Go Fish.

I had spent a full half hour explaining the rudiments of the game to both of them, astonished that they had never played it before. Gigi picked it up right away, but Finn took longer, analyzing it for strategy and nuances that didn't exist. I finally gave up, dealt myself out of the game, and then excused myself before I was forced to shake him.

My embarrassment over my lack of knowledge about Europe in World War II niggled at my brain, and I was determined to set things right—at least to the point where I could speak knowledgeably with Helena the next time the subject was raised. *If* she allowed the subject to be raised again. She had been flip in her comments, but I'd seen the strain in her face and the light fade from her eyes as she'd spoken.

I had left my home at seventeen because of Eve's accident, yet I'd only been less than an hour away. But Helena had left her home because of a brutal war, had traveled across an ocean to another continent and never returned to the place of her birth. My own losses had taken years—my father's death and then the accident; hers had been accomplished within the span of a few months. I wondered if one was easier than the other, if the pain of loss was the same as the pain of removing a bandage, if it hurt less if one did it quickly.

I turned on the table lamps and floor lamp between the armchairs, surprised to see that the opened book was still on the ottoman, the afghan on the back of one of the chairs still rumpled, as if the occupant had just stood and left the room.

I picked up the book, then glanced at the cover as I closed it. *The Art of Origami.* It was bound in clear wrap, indicating that it might be a library book, and when I opened up the back flap, my suspicions were confirmed. Stamped in red ink on the inside cover were the words "Charleston County Public Library," and below that was the address for the Mount Pleasant location. Stuck inside the front cover was a small receipt-like paper with the date due printed across the top: February 13, 2012.

Seeing as how the book was now almost four months overdue, I placed it on a table by the door with plans to ask Helena if she'd like for me to return it to the library. It was a small task, and certainly one that would fit under my broad job description—not to mention alleviate some of the guilt I felt in sparring with an elderly woman who'd only recently emerged from death's door, regardless of how much she encouraged it.

I focused my attention on the bookshelves that lined the doorway wall—the only solid wall without windows in the room. I'd noticed them during my brief tour of the house but hadn't yet had a chance to find out which books the two sisters had collected. I was hoping to find a Hungarian history book. If I didn't, I could always look in the public library, since it appeared I might be heading that way anyway.

I perused the shelves, sneezing several times as I removed books that looked like they hadn't been touched since they'd been placed there. There were books on the history of Edisto and Charleston, on architecture and agriculture, on gardening and sweetgrass baskets, along with stacks of old *National Geographic* magazines and issues of *Good Housekeeping*.

"Can I help you find something?"

I turned to smile at Finn. "Had enough of Go Fish?"

He ran his hand through his hair, back to front, leaving it sticking up all over. He didn't seem to be aware of what he'd done, and I was unsure if I should mention it. His hair was always so neatly combed at the office, but something about the air on Edisto seemed to change us all.

"After suffering four back-to-back defeats, I gave up. There really isn't a point to the game, is there?"

"Not at all," I said. "Next time I'll teach you the game of war. That one's even more pointless. Although I have to say that I spent hours and hours with Lucy and my sister when I was a girl playing cards. I didn't seem to think there had to be a point to our games."

He studied me with sober eyes. "I'm glad you'll be spending more time with Gigi. She needs to know someone who can teach her how to play like a child. After all she's been through, I have to remind myself sometimes that she's only ten years old."

"She's a great kid, and I enjoy spending time with her. And I don't mind teaching her how to play the piano. If she wants to pursue it after I've taught her the basics, I'd be happy to help find someone who's a much more suitable teacher."

He had the same look in his eyes that Helena had when she was ready to argue, so I turned back to the bookshelves. "I'm looking for books on Hungary. Your aunt spoke a little today about Hungary during World War II, and I'm embarrassed to say that I was clueless. I want to brush up a little on my history so I won't embarrass myself again."

He came to stand next to me, using his height to scan the highest shelves. "I really don't think you'll find anything here. They were proud of their Hungarian roots but fiercely proud of being American. They never really talked about their later years in Hungary. It was almost as if they wanted to pretend that their lives had started in 1944, when they moved here."

"But they taught you the traditional Hungarian courting dance." I looked up at him, unable to resist a smile.

"Yes, they did that. I think mostly because it was a happy memory from their own childhoods and they wanted to share that with me. Much like your piano playing, I would think."

I stared at him for a moment, then looked away, confused. My music had been the happiest part of my childhood. But I had locked it away when my father died, as if it were a part of him instead of me. It had never occurred to me that it was something to be shared or celebrated as part of my past. To me, my past was like the ocean, hiding riptides that could suck you under when you least expected it.

Eager to change the subject, I said, "Do you speak Hungarian?"

"Only a little—learned from my grandmother, Magda."

"Helena said something the other day, and she translated it for me, but I wondered if . . ." I didn't finish, realizing how what I wanted to say would be interpreted.

A corner of his mouth lifted in a half smile. "And you wondered if she might be embellishing it or telling you something else completely."

"Yeah. Something like that," I said, smiling back.

"What did it sound like?"

I bit my lip, thinking hard about the odd vowels and consonants. "Like 'Mindankee a maga shar . . .' "

"Ah, yes. *Mindenki a maga szerencséjének kovácsa*," he said, pronouncing it expertly. "I only know it because it was something my grandmother said often, usually directed at my father when he and my mother were arguing about me."

I brought my eyebrows together. "Helena said it had something to do with the relationship between sisters."

"In some ways, I suppose it can. But an exact translation is more like 'Everyone's the blacksmith of their own fate.'"

I looked outside the broad wall of windows, wondering what Helena had been trying to tell me. A flash of light arced across the sky like a silent wish, and I found myself heading for the door. "I think I saw a shooting star," I said, not waiting for Finn to follow.

We stood in the grass staring up at the summer sky littered with stars. The quarter moon hung high, a dim nightlight that allowed the stars to glow against the darkness. We stayed like that for a long time, each of us knowing that we'd missed the shooting star, but still holding out the hope that against all odds we'd see another in the same corner of the sky. As if, somehow, we both could still believe in possibilities despite all evidence to the contrary.

The music of the night marsh flooded my ears, transporting me back in time to this same place, but to a time when music filled my heart, too. Finn stood close to me, close enough that I could hear him inhaling deeply.

"'If moonlight could be heard, it would sound like that,'" he said softly.

I faced him. "Nathaniel Hawthorne, right? Daddy used to say that all the time." The memory made me smile, something I'd never managed to do before when remembering my father. I wondered what had changed. Maybe I was just growing older, the time between my childhood and now like a river heading toward the ocean, changing slowly until it was nearly unrecognizable at its end.

Finn started to say something but stopped when the back floodlight was switched on, erasing the marsh and the river and the sky in a blinding pool of light. We turned toward the sunroom and saw Teri Weber waving a can of insect spray at us.

As if on cue, I slapped at a mosquito that had landed on my arm. "I need to get going," I said. "It's getting late."

He nodded, then followed me back into the house. During the long drive home, I drove slowly with the window down, listening for the marsh music and wondering what Finn had been about to say.

CHAPTER 15

Eleanor

"Hi, Ellie."

I looked up from the smooth leather of the new client folder in which I'd been stuffing company information and the cover letter signed by Finn, "Hampton P. Beaufain." Gigi's dark gray eyes smiled at me from the edge of my desk, her father standing behind her. He was wearing another dark suit, his hair perfectly combed, his face serious. I wondered how soon after he crossed the McKinley Washington Bridge onto the mainland the transformation began, and if the mental or the physical changes were harder to accept.

I stood, aware of Kay Tetley watching from her desk. "Good morning, Genevieve. Mr. Beaufain."

Gigi smirked at my formality but didn't say anything. I looked up at Finn, surprised to see him. He was usually in his closed office when I arrived in the morning, went out with clients for lunch, and was back in his office alone or with clients when I left in the afternoon. He still brought back food from lunch on the days when I stayed at my desk—days when I came in late or left early for Eve's doctor's appointments and Wednesdays when I headed to Edisto.

"Hello, Eleanor." Finn's hands rested on Gigi's shoulders, and he wore an expression on his face that I didn't recognize. If it had been anybody else, I would have thought it was uncertainty.

He cleared his throat. "I have a favor to ask."

Gigi piped up. "I was supposed to be with Mommy this week, but my camp was canceled and she can't stay with me all day and I don't want to stay with Mrs. McKenna because all she wants to do is play bingo and watch her soaps." She rolled her eyes. "And I *need* to go shopping. Mommy was supposed to take me, but now she says she can't."

My mind backpedaled to the first part of her discourse and replayed it back in my mind at a slower speed. "Your camp was canceled?"

Finn spoke again. "It was a French immersion camp. Her mother's idea." His face remained inscrutable.

I raised my eyebrows, hoping either Gigi or Finn would explain how a French immersion camp segued into a favor.

Finn continued. "Since her mother can't take her today, I told Gigi that I could take the day off, but she says that won't work. All she'll tell me is that she needs to go shopping today for something she wants to keep secret from me, and would only discuss it with you."

"One minute," I said. Taking Gigi's hand, I began walking toward Finn's office. "We'll be right back."

He nodded, then leaned against my desk with his arms folded, the relaxed position doing nothing to soften the severity of his suit or demeanor.

Ignoring the look from Finn's secretary, I pulled Gigi into the office and shut the door. "So, what's the big secret?" I asked.

Her eyes widened, her expression more serious than I'd seen before. "Daddy's birthday is Saturday, and I need to get him a present."

"Ah," I said, straightening. "So you need somebody else to take you and your mother can't."

"Yes, ma'am. And since you're just sitting at your desk all day, I figured you'd probably have more fun shopping with me."

"And you mentioned this to your father?"

She quickly nodded. "I didn't tell him *what* I was shopping for, but I told him that I needed you to go with me."

Grinning, I led her back to her father. "I'd be happy to take Gigi today. But I've got the new client folders to put together. . . ."

"Kay will do it. Take as much time as you need, then call me on my cell when you're done. I'm going to try to cancel some appointments I have scheduled this afternoon so I can spend it with Gigi."

I glanced over at Kay, who was frowning at the little girl who had wandered over to my desk chair and was spinning it in faster and faster circles. In a lowered voice, I asked, "Are you sure that's okay? I can work on the folders when we get back, or even stay later if I—"

"I'll take care of it, Eleanor. It's more important that my daughter doesn't feel as if she's being passed around. Her mother . . ." He stopped himself. "I'd really appreciate it," he said instead.

"Should I tell Kay . . . ?"

"I'll take care of it," he said again, and I wondered if his need to be in control had been something taught to him by his father or something circumstances had made a necessity.

"All right, then." I put my hand on my chair, stilling it, then grabbed my purse from a drawer. "I'll call you when we're done."

Gigi hugged her father, receiving a kiss on her forehead. "Listen to Eleanor, Peanut, and try not to talk her ears off."

She was still giggling as we left, making a detour to the restrooms. We had to pass the accounting department along the way, and I found myself hoping that we wouldn't run into Lucy. As much as I missed our commute together and our daily conversations, I'd found myself avoiding her so that I wouldn't be tempted to explain how Finn was different on Edisto, and how he'd told me that the happiest memory of his childhood was the night he'd stood outside my house and listened to me play the piano.

Lucy was standing by the water fountain just as we reached the restroom, and after a brief hello, I made to follow Gigi. Lucy grabbed hold of my arm and held me back. "What are you doing?"

"I'm taking Fi—Mr. Beaufain's daughter to go buy a birthday present."

"Finn? You're calling him by his first name now?"

"Not here at the office," I said in a hushed voice. "But you know how it is on the island. It's a lot more casual and makes sense to call him by his first name while I'm working in his great-aunt's house."

"Um-hmm," she said, doing that neck thing that said so much more than words ever could.

"Her mother was supposed to take Gigi today but she can't, and she needs to buy a birthday present for her father, and she wanted me to take her. It's really nothing."

This time she just gave me the look she must have learned from Dah Georgie when we told her it was too hot to go looking for sweetgrass.

"Lucy, come on. You know me. And this job has become a real lifesaver for me—and not just because of the money, either." I stopped as Rich Kobylt, the human resources manager, walked past with a steaming cup of coffee. I nodded in greeting and waited until he'd passed. "Eve's pregnant."

If I'd expected her to hug me or offer words of sympathy, I would have been mistaken. All she said was "Good. Now maybe you can grow flowers in your own garden. This is a good thing for Eve and Glen." She wrinkled her forehead. "For you and Glen."

She tucked her chin into her neck like a bull getting ready to charge, and I braced myself. "You don't be needing to hang around with Mr. Beaufain, neither. You're just jumping out of the pot and into the frying pan."

"Wow, Lucy. Two clichés in the same conversation. That might be a record."

"Um-hmm. You wouldn't be sounding so defensive if you didn't know I was right."

"I'm not being defensive." I stopped, hearing myself. Gigi came out of the restroom and I sent her a grateful glance. "We've got to go. I'll talk to you later."

"You can be sure of that. Um-hmm, you can be sure of that."

I followed Gigi out the door, pretending I hadn't heard Lucy's parting words.

After I'd made sure that Gigi was buckled into the backseat—she was still too small to sit up front with the air bag—I turned to her. "So—any ideas as to what you want to get for your father?"

She looked up at the car ceiling while tapping her pink-tipped nails on the armrest. "Aunt Helena said I should get him a nice book about the stars and the sky at night. She said he used to like looking at them when he was a little boy."

I nodded. "That's an idea. How much money do you have to spend?"

She reached inside her pink beaded purse and pulled out a small envelope. "Aunt Helena had Nurse Weber put some money in here to buy something nice for my daddy. And I put all of my allowance in there, too—eleven dollars and twenty-five cents."

"Can I see?"

She handed me the envelope, and I was surprised by how thick it felt. I slid it open and looked inside. Ten brand-new and crisp fifty-dollar bills sat nestled beside two crumpled fives, a one, and a loose quarter. I looked up at Gigi in surprise. "Did she give you any idea of how much you were allowed to spend?"

She shook her head. "No, ma'am. All she said was that this would be enough to get a nice book and maybe something else."

I debated with myself about calling Lucy for her opinion, then remembered our last conversation and quickly dismissed the thought. We sat in the car for a minute in silence with the engine running and the air-conditioning blowing while I tried to figure out what to do. Eventually I turned back to Gigi.

I held up the envelope. "I'm going to hang on to this for you, all right? Now, go ahead and take off your seat belt. We're going to Market Street and then King Street. It's a bit of walking, but easier than finding parking. I've got an idea."

She grinned conspiratorially at me as she leapt from the car, my own grin softening as I recalled Lucy's words about growing flowers in my own garden. I wanted to pretend that I didn't know what she was talking about. But Lucy had known me for too long, had sat with me while we watched Dah Georgie build her baskets, asking us what kinds of baskets our lives would be. I knew what Lucy was telling me. I just wasn't ready to hear it.

Three hours later, Gigi and I had two packages stashed in the back of the Volvo. We were hot and sticky from the long walk, but I had the air-conditioning on full blast. I fished my cell phone out of my purse and dialed Finn's number.

"Finn Beaufain." His words were short and curt.

"Um, I'm sorry, Mr. Beaufain?"

There was a brief pause. "Eleanor? I'm so sorry. I'm dealing with a small crisis right now and I didn't look at my caller ID. Did you need something?"

"You, um, asked me to call you when Gigi and I were done. I fed her lunch because it took us longer than I'd anticipated."

"Thank you, Eleanor." There was another pause. "Look, I'm not going to be able to get away from the office anytime soon. Gigi is spending the night with her mother. Could you please drop her off there? Harper is home and is expecting her. Then you'll have the rest of the day off."

"Sure. Not a problem. But I can come back to the office. . . ."

"I've got everything under control. I'll see you in the morning. And please tell Gigi that I'll call her tonight before she goes to bed. I'll text you the address."

He said good-bye, and then I turned to Gigi. "Looks like there's been a change of plans. I'm going to bring you to your mother's house, all right? And your daddy promised to call before you went to bed."

I watched for any look of disappointment or reluctance, but she only smiled at me. "Thank you, Ellie. I had fun today."

My phone beeped and I looked down to see the text from Finn. I put the car in drive, meeting her eyes in the rearview mirror. "Me, too."

It was a short drive to the white single house on Queen Street. Harper Beaufain Gibbes's house was another picture-perfect example of Charleston architecture, with the side double piazzas and overabundant front garden with scents and colors vying for attention. Here again, I noticed the absence of any signs of occupancy, as if the house was merely a false front to use in a magazine spread.

I parked at the curb in front of the house and was still unbuckling my seat belt when I heard Gigi's unclasp and then felt her finger poking me in the shoulder. "Don't forget to only call me Genevieve. Mommy doesn't always have good days, and saying Gigi won't make it any better."

She regarded me with such sage and knowing eyes that I had to remind myself that she was only ten.

"Got it," I said, stepping out of the car. I followed her up the brick steps to the front door, which in any other city would be considered a side door despite the fact that it faced the street. It led onto the front piazza and the actual front door.

I rang the doorbell and waited, surprised to find myself hoping a housekeeper would answer instead of the lady of the house. I remembered what Finn had told me about her, and how she'd cut short her stay on Edisto because she'd found it lacking. Trying to push those thoughts aside, I plastered a smile on my face and waited for the front door to open.

The woman who opened the door was definitely not the housekeeper. She was tall and slender, with chestnut brown hair and bright blue eyes. Despite the fact that she was at home, she wore high heels and a pencil skirt, and a beautiful white silk blouse with a low V cinched in with a thick leather belt. This woman was the epitome of a New England yacht club member, but then again with her bone structure and elegant clothing, I would assume she hailed from anyplace that had exclusive country club memberships and boarding schools. With a start, I realized this was what my mother would have looked like if she'd married the sort of man she was supposed to instead of my father. Two months ago, I would have thought this was the kind of woman Finn Beaufain should have married. But when

I pictured him with his ruffled hair as he made a paper airplane on the porch of the Edisto house, I was no longer so sure.

"Mommy!" Gigi threw herself at the woman, confirming her identity.

Harper hesitated only a moment before placing a well-manicured hand on the small blond head of her daughter. "Genevieve, sweetheart. Don't wrinkle Mommy's skirt."

Gigi backed up, dropping her hands. As if her mother hadn't just scolded her, she grabbed my hand and pulled me forward. "This is Ellie. She's taking care of Aunt Helena and sometimes me, too."

Cool blue eyes appraised me sharply, from my shoulder-length brown hair to my simple skirt and blouse, and she didn't hide the fact that she found me lacking.

She extended her fingertips toward me. "It's a pleasure to meet you. Genevieve talks about you all the time."

Her fingertips were cool and dry, like grass that had gone too long without rain. She barely touched my fingers before withdrawing her hand.

"It's nice to meet you, too," I said. "I've enjoyed getting to know Genevieve."

"I'm sure." Turning to her daughter, she said, "Go wash your face and hands and change into a dress that's not pink, please. Your stepfather and I are having guests for dinner, and they'll be here within the hour. I'd like for you to answer the door when they arrive."

"Yes, ma'am," Gigi said, acting more subdued than I'd ever seen her. She said good-bye to me and walked sedately into the foyer.

I was in the middle of excusing myself when Gigi burst back through the door. "Ellie! What about the birthday presents? Can you wrap them?"

"Of course. I'm not sure how I'll manage the big one, but I'll think of something. And the book will be easy. You just have to make a card."

"Thanks!" She grinned at me, then disappeared inside the house.

"Is she referring to Finn's birthday?"

"Yes. I took her shopping today."

Irritation flashed across her face. "Thank God I was spared that. What did she get him?"

"A book about astronomy and a telescope." I knew better than to allow that I'd been the one to come up with the second idea.

"A telescope. Wherever did the child get the money for that?"

"From Miss Szarka. But we didn't spend that much. I have a friend from high school who has a secondhand shop on Market. Last time I was there he had a used telescope in the window and I took a chance that it would still be there."

"And it was."

"Yes."

She was looking at me now with more interest, so I took a step away to show her that I was eager to leave.

"Genevieve told me that you grew up on Edisto. Is that right?"

I nodded. "I lived there until I was seventeen, and then we moved to North Charleston, where we still live."

"I see. And where did you study piano?"

I looked up at her with surprise. "How did you know I played the piano?"

"Finn mentioned it." She looked at me expectantly.

"My father taught me."

Her brow furled. "And Finn believes that makes you good enough to teach piano to our daughter." It wasn't a question.

I flushed. "My father was a very good musician and a wonderful teacher. I feel confident I can teach the basics to Genevieve."

"Was this his idea or yours?"

I worked to keep my voice even. "Actually, it was Miss Szarka's."

She regarded me coolly. "I don't know why Finn thinks she has to learn piano—dancing is really enough."

I wanted to end this conversation, but she seemed determined to make a point. Or maybe she was just lonely and needed somebody to talk to. I opened my mouth to speak, but she continued. "Finn has some huge romantic notion about the piano. I thought it came from his aunts, who both played, but Finn told me once about how when he was a boy on Edisto he listened for hours to a perfect stranger play the piano inside a house while he stayed outside looking up at the stars. When I met him he'd made that one event into something of near mythical proportions. Which is ridiculous, really. He must have been eaten alive by mosquitoes, and how can anybody be that good that somebody would listen for hours?"

"Ridiculous," I repeated, my voice stronger than I'd meant it to be. I walked down the piazza toward the door, eager to leave. "It was nice to meet you."

"Thank you for bringing Genevieve. And I'm glad she got Finn a telescope. Maybe that will keep him busy so that he'll forget about resuming flying lessons."

I stopped to look at her. "Flying lessons?"

She waved her hand, like she was swatting away a fly. "When Genevieve was a baby, he wanted to learn how to fly, so he started taking lessons. He never finished. Every once in a while he mentions getting back to it. Luckily, he hasn't. It's not like he's a young man without responsibilities anymore." She gave a little laugh. "Men never really grow up, do they?"

"I wouldn't know," I said before turning around and walking quickly to the Volvo. I sat with the car running for a long time as I tried to erase the woman's voice from my head, unable to stop thinking about why Finn had told her about his childhood night on the marsh, and wondering what had happened to his dreams of flying.

CHAPTER 16

Eve

I met my mother's gaze over the kitchen table as yet another shouted curse followed by a clattering of metal pans came from the kitchen. I looked back at my needle, pleased to see another glimmer of the old Eleanor. Since her regular trips to Edisto, we'd begun to see glimmers more and more often.

"What is she doing in there?" Mama asked for the third time.

I glanced back at her, wondering if she was aware that she'd asked the question before. "She's making a *dobostorta*. It's a Hungarian layer cake. Apparently it's very difficult."

Another crash of pans accentuated my comment.

"I've never heard of such a thing," Mama said, leaning over her crossword puzzle again. She'd been working on it for more than an hour but had only three words penciled in so far. She needed reading glasses, but I would be the last person to suggest it.

"It's a surprise for Mr. Beaufain's birthday on Saturday. They're celebrating it out on Edisto with Mr. Beaufain's great-aunt, who's Hungarian. Eleanor thought she might appreciate a little taste of home."

I let my words trail away, aware that she wasn't listening to me anymore. A car door slammed outside and I felt the old familiar constriction around my heart, a feeling that never seemed to diminish regardless of how long we'd been married.

Glen's mouth was tight and drawn when he walked through the door, but he quickly disguised it with a smile when he spotted me at the table.

He greeted my mother and then turned his attention to me. "Hello, beautiful," he said as he bent to kiss me, his lips lingering. His hand strayed to my belly. "How are we today?"

"We're doing fine," I said. "No nausea, and Dr. Wise says everything seems to be on target."

"Dr. Wise?" he asked, pulling back a chair to sit down next to me. "I thought your doctor was Dr. Clemmens."

I focused on threading a needle so I wouldn't have to meet his eyes. "I changed doctors. I liked Dr. Clemmens, but she's starting to talk about retirement. And Laura at the fabric store swears by Dr. Wise, who's delivered her four."

I heard a sound at the kitchen door and looked up to see my sister standing in the doorway. I wasn't sure if her strangled expression was from the lie I'd just uttered or if she'd been there to see Glen's greeting kiss.

"Hello, Glen," she said. "I'm afraid dinner will be a little late tonight. I've been working on a project in the kitchen and it's taking longer than I anticipated."

"Do you need some help?" His tone was almost grudging, and I wondered if Eleanor had noticed. But she seemed distracted by the flour stuck to her blouse.

"No, thanks. I think I've got it under control now."

My mother looked up from the crossword. "Are you working at Pete's tonight? He called earlier."

Eleanor blanched. "No, I'm not. I'm not planning on working there again now that I have the job on Edisto. What did you tell him?"

"That you'd call him back. And he wanted the name of the gentleman you left with the last time you worked there. He said he'd lost the man's card but that he had a message for him."

We all looked back at Eleanor, whose cheeks had reddened, making the splotches of flour stand out even more. "Thank you, Mama. I'll call him back."

I felt Glen stiffen beside me, and I wanted to take his hand and keep him from reaching out to Eleanor. But I didn't. This wasn't my battle.

"You remember his name?" he asked, his voice hard.

Eleanor lifted her chin. "It was Mr. Beaufain. I'd had too much to drink and he offered to drive me home. He had somebody bring the car back for you the next morning, remember?"

Glen pretended to relax back into his seat, but I could still feel his tenseness. "I've only met your boss a couple of times, but he doesn't seem like the kind of person who would patronize Pete's."

Eleanor began to focus intently on cleaning out the flour and butter from beneath her fingernails. "That was the first time I'd seen him there. He said he was there for a meeting."

"A meeting? In North Charleston?"

She shrugged, but it was clear to me that she'd had the same thought. "I didn't ask—it wasn't any of my business." She turned to our mother. "Mama, I think *Wheel of Fortune* is coming on in a minute. Why don't y'all go watch it so I can set the table and get dinner ready?"

I pushed back from the table but remained there while Glen and Mama walked to the couch. Mama still walked like she was in a pageant or in a line of white-gowned debutantes, and I wondered if it was habit or defiance of her family, who'd turned their backs on her when she married Daddy. I'd always wanted to ask her if it had been worth it, but I was too afraid to hear her answer.

I waited until Eleanor returned from washing her hands and retrieving the silverware from the kitchen before I spoke. "You haven't said anything to Mama and Glen, have you? About the pregnancy being high risk?"

Eleanor paused, each hand filled with silverware. "You told me not to."

"Thank you." I looked toward the den, assuring myself that both faces were trained toward the television. "I know this is too early to be thinking about this, but I don't think I can sleep before I know I've said it."

She looked at me warily. "Said what?"

"If the baby and I survive the pregnancy, but I don't survive the delivery, would you take care of the baby as if it were your own?"

Eleanor lowered herself, straight backed, into a chair, the silverware clattering onto the table. "Nothing's going to happen to you. You're seeing the best doctor. Everything's under control."

"I know. But this pregnancy has made me start looking at things differently. We don't always get second chances, so I want to make sure that I'm doing it right this time. Like with my marriage. And you and me."

She stared down at her hands. "You and me?"

"Yeah. I'm the older sister, but I've never really been allowed to act like it."

She tilted her head. "Because that's the way you wanted it to be."

I shrugged. "Maybe. I'm still trying to figure that out. But one thing I know is that things happen out of our control. And I just want to be prepared. I need to know that you'll take of the baby."

"You know you don't need to ask me that."

"I need to hear you say it."

Her eyes remained fixed on mine. "Of course I will. I'm your sister."

We froze, both of us remembering the last time she'd said those words. I'd just started scaling the large oak tree on Westcott Road and had almost reached the same height Eleanor had in the tree opposite. I was horribly afraid of falling, as afraid as I always was when I was goaded into one of Eleanor's escapades. I'd been laughing at Glen, who stood in the road looking up at us with a worried expression, before I'd turned to Eleanor. *If I get hurt, will you take care of me?*

Neither one of us spoke for a long moment, as Pat Sajak's voice filled the background, the sound of canned laughter floating toward us. "Thank you," I said, keeping my gaze on my hands as I smoothed down my skirt. "But I won't give you Glen."

It was the one thing we never spoke of, the pink elephant that we tiptoed around. Her eyes widened in surprise, looking at me as if I didn't know my own breathing, or the sound of her footsteps on the front porch late at night. I waved my hand at her as she struggled for words, trying to spare us both.

"He's never been yours, and whether or not I'm still here, he never will be." I forced myself to meet her gaze. "I'm not trying to be cruel. But you and Glen are too different; you want different things. Your infatuation has grown simply because it's the one thing you can't have—like a child crying for the moon. Once you got him, your disappointment would kill you both."

She stood suddenly, hitting the table. "I have never . . ."

"I know there has been no infidelity. We wouldn't be having this conversation if there had been. But that's not who you are, and it's not who Glen is. And even if he were free, he wouldn't make you happy. His dreams are too grounded, like mine. That's why our marriage has survived. You need to find somebody whose dreams match your own. Somebody who's not afraid to touch the sun."

Without a word, she stood, then retreated into the kitchen, where she turned on the sink full force so I wouldn't hear her cry.

Eleanor

It was still early morning when I reached Luna Point on Saturday. I was eager to get there before Finn and Gigi, and I also wanted to leave home before I had to face Eve again.

I parked in the driveway and then unloaded the cake and presents onto the porch before I fumbled in my purse for the house key Finn had given me. Teri Weber was in the kitchen replacing the drawer liners. All of the silverware, china, and glassware were laid out on towels on the counter, and Teri stood on a step stool, her head inside one of the cabinets.

"Where should I put the birthday cake?" I asked.

Teri poked her head out of the cabinet. "I made room in the fridge. I hope you don't mind, but I made a breakfast casserole."

"That's great. Thank you. Did you add paprika to it? According to Helena, Hungarians like paprika on everything."

"No," Teri said with a wry grin. "But I can always sprinkle some on top of her serving." She opened the door to the refrigerator and I slid the *dobostorta* cake onto the top shelf. Then I returned to the porch to bring in the gifts. I'd given up trying to wrap the telescope and had ended up just tying a large red bow on it. Luckily, the book on astronomy had been easier. After I'd hidden both gifts in the piano room, I took the book I'd bought for myself while we were shopping at Blue Bicycle Books on King Street into the sunroom.

I'd just settled into a chair to read when I heard the unmistakable thumping of Helena's cane on the wall. Knowing that if she'd wanted Teri she would have just called out, I assumed the summons was for me.

With my book in hand, I made my way to Helena's bedroom. She was propped up on her ruffled pillows, a white lace bed jacket tied with a satin bow at her neck. Teri was in the process of placing a breakfast tray on her lap despite Helena's protests.

"I am not hungry. Are you trying to make me fat?"

I looked at Helena, seeing that she wore a little blush and lipstick and her eyelashes were darkened with mascara, a pale reminder of the beauty she'd once been. This woman propped up like a doll seemed so different from the gray, frail old lady I'd first met. This new person wasn't exactly what I would call a beacon of hope and optimism, but she was a much-improved version of the woman who'd planned to die alongside her sister.

"You look very pretty this morning, Miss Szarka."

She frowned but I could tell she was pleased. "Hrumph. I am just old. Nurse Weber insisted on the makeup since it was Finn's birthday. I told her it would be like draping tinsel on a dead Christmas tree. But she would not listen to me."

Teri shook her head as she tucked a napkin under Helena's chin. "Are you up to feeding yourself this morning?"

Helena's dark blue eyes met mine. "I want Eleanor to do it."

Not wanting to give her the satisfaction of protesting, I set my book on the bedside table and took my place on the chair drawn up to the side of the bed. "Do you want butter on your toast?"

"Just a little. It is that low-fat rubbish that Nurse Weber insists on, and I do not want it to ruin the taste of the bread."

I did as she asked and broke the bread in half, placing it on the tray in front of her. I filled the spoon with oatmeal and held it to her mouth, and she ate it slowly and thoroughly. As I prepared the next spoonful, I said, "It's amazing how you can find the strength to grab a cane and bang it against the wall, but you can't hold a small spoon."

Her eyes flashed but not with irritation. She chewed and swallowed the next bite. "What book are you reading?"

"It's a book on the history of Hungary. Our conversation the other day piqued my curiosity, and when I was at the bookstore looking for Finn's birthday present, I picked it up. I'm still in the Magyar period in the first century, so don't spoil the ending for me."

She raised her eyebrows as she tried to suppress a smile. "I would not dream of it. I am old but not that old. When you get to the nineteenth century, I might know more."

I handed her a piece of toast and waited while she ate it. "Gigi had money left over from the envelope you gave her. I've given it to Nurse Weber to put away for you. It was quite a bit of money."

"In Hungary we celebrated name days—an old Catholic tradition—as much as birthdays, but here we only celebrate the birthdays. Since I missed Finn's name day, I thought I might be allowed to be more extravagant."

I nodded as I scooped up the rest of the oatmeal onto the spoon. "Do you have a gift for Finn that you'd like me to wrap?"

She leaned back against her pillow. "I was not planning on wrapping it, but if you insist . . ."

I suppressed a sigh. "Tell me where it is and I'll take care of it before they get here—which should be any minute."

"It is under my bed. Not the most clever place to hide it, but I did not think that Finn would be hunting for gifts."

The mental image made me laugh out loud, granting me a startled look from Helena. I knelt beside the bed and pulled out an approximately twelve-inch-square package wrapped in brown paper and masking tape. I sat down in the chair and carefully unstuck some of the tape so I could slide out the framed object inside. I let the paper fall to the floor as I held the black frame in my outstretched arms.

It was an old record album cover, in the colors and style of the early 1940s. "The Szarka Sisters" was written at the top in a large, red bold font. It was like I was looking at a Clairol ad from the last century. One of the women was a redhead, the other two blond, all with shiny hair and porcelain skin. I peered closely at the tallest blond, recognizing the blue eyes and perfect nose. Even the aristocratic lift of the eyebrows had been captured perfectly in this rendering of Helena Szarka and her two sisters. All three women had large, almond-shaped eyes, hinting of perhaps a bit more than a drop of Gypsy blood.

I looked up at Helena.

"I think Finn will love this. Which one is his grandmother?"

"The redhead, Magda. She was the real beauty. And she and Bernadett had all the charm."

If she'd been wanting me to refute her comments, she was disappointed. Instead, with only a hint of sarcasm, I said, "Then you must have had all the musical talent."

"Most of it. But not all," she said matter-of-factly. "We could all sing and play piano. But I was better at it than they were."

"So you were the reason for the Szarka Sisters' success."

"I did not say that. It takes three voices to sing in three-part harmony, after all. But Bernadette had the best voice—like that of an angel. She wrote music, too. Not that she would ever allow us to record one of her songs. She was much too shy for that.

"Magda was the brains of the operation, as they say. She was the one who talked her way into a recording session in London. She was so persistent, I think the poor man just gave in so she would not pester him again." A soft smile crossed her face. "She had the sort of beauty that would make the earth spin a little slower. On her sixteenth birthday our mother took us to dinner at the New York Palace Café in Budapest."

"New York Palace? That doesn't sound very Hungarian."

"It was very Hungarian, I assure you. It was commissioned by the New York Insurance Company for their offices, but it was designed and built by the best Hungarian craftsman. The café was on the ground floor and open to everyone. You've never seen such beauty—everything was marble, bronze, silk, crystal, and velvet. A mix of Italian Renaissance and baroque styles if you can imagine such a thing. I remember being a little afraid of the sixteen devilish fauns that decorated the outside windows, and completely awed by the beautiful paintings and frescoes on the ceilings and walls inside. I have never seen anything like it here in America."

"It sounds lovely," I said, easily picturing the three beautiful Szarka sisters in such a setting.

"It was," Helena said, her voice wistful. "And by the time we left, Magda had three marriage proposals and another gentleman had paid our bill."

I raised an eyebrow, wondering how much was true.

"It is all fact, I assure you. Men were gentlemen in those days. But it took a gentleman from Charleston to turn Magda's head. Finn looks a great deal like his grandfather, so you can imagine how handsome he was."

I thought of Finn at the office and how I didn't think I'd ever realized what he looked like beyond the austere suits. And when I'd seen him that night at Pete's Bar, he'd seemed almost intimidating. But when I pictured him here, on the island, I could definitely see what Magda must have seen in his grandfather.

Eager to change the conversation, I said, "Did you live near the Danube?"

"Not too far—up Castle Hill on Uri Utca. It was an easy ride up the steep slope on the Siklo, which I believe in English is called a funicular railway. We lived on the Buda side. Did you learn that yet? That Budapest is actually two cities, Buda and Pest, that are separated by the Danube?" She didn't wait for me to answer. Her face was animated as if she were no longer sitting in her bedroom on Edisto Island but in a place that had lived only in her memories for a very long time. "We lived in a small house on a cobblestone street, over a bakery where my mother worked. We could not see the river from our house, but on very warm days, we could smell it. And sometimes, on very still nights, we could hear the boats."

She closed her eyes and I watched as they moved under the paper-thin lids.

"Bernadett and I shared a room, but Magda, because she was the eldest, had her own tiny room in the attic. She did not care that it was so small, because she did not have to share. But even when Magda married and moved to America, Bernadett and I chose to stay together. It is that way with sisters, is it not?"

I answered without hesitation. "Yes. Eve and I shared a room our whole lives. Even when we had a three-bedroom home, we chose to share."

"Until her marriage."

I looked at her sharply. "Yes. Even after her accident, we shared. It was easier to take care of her that way."

"I am sure." She studied the framed record cover for a moment. "You being nosy with the record albums made me think of this. Thank you."

I was unsure what I was supposed to say with an insult and a thank-you thrown so close together. I remained quiet. Reaching up a gnarled finger, she brushed the tip against the faces of her two sisters. "It is hard to believe that I am the only one left. Sometimes at night, I awaken and feel as if I am in our old bedroom in Budapest again. And that all I have to do is reach out and touch my sister."

I picked up the loose wrapping from the floor and settled the frame inside. "Maybe it's the river. Maybe living on the Edisto River reminds you of home."

She shook her head. "I think that is why my brother-in-law thought Bernadett and I would be happy here, because of the river. But they are very different." She met my eyes. "They call it the Blue Danube because of Strauss's waltz. Did you know that? It is really quite brown. But in my dreams I always picture it blue." She frowned and began plucking at her bedclothes. "And I hear my sisters, their voices, and I think that they are still here. Like they have never left me."

All good-bye ain't gone. I felt the breath blow into me, bringing me back to the day of the sunbaked dirt road and the white wooden church near the marsh. I looked at Helena, and she was looking back at me as if I'd spoken out loud.

I took a deep breath. "I made a *dobostorta* for Finn. Will he know what it is?"

"You made one? By yourself?"

I nodded. "I like to bake. In the back of the Hungarian history book there's a section on Hungarian food. I'd like to try *Duna kavics* next. That means 'Danube pebbles.' "

"Really?"

I flushed, realizing that I probably hadn't needed to translate for her.

Without waiting for me to respond, she said, "Those would be easier than a *dobostorta*. There are so many layers, and all the fillings must be perfect—not too thin or too thick. My mother would sometimes start one, then have to throw it away and start again. Which is not a good thing when one is baking for other people to earn money for food and shoes." She tilted her chin up. "You went to a lot of trouble for Finn's birthday."

She held my gaze for a long moment as I flushed again, realizing her implication. Leaning forward, she asked, "Have you ever made something so complicated for your brother-in-law? What is his name?"

"Glen," I choked out, wondering which comment was constricting my throat. "And no. Eve makes his birthday cakes. I'll help if she needs it, but she rarely asks."

"When is his birthday?" she asked.

"November. November fifth."

"It will be interesting to see if you make another *dobostorta* for him."

"Did somebody mention a *dobostorta*?" Finn entered the room, Gigi racing past him to Helena's bed.

I stood quickly, holding Finn's gift behind my back while he pretended he hadn't noticed. I backed slowly toward the door, grateful for their interruption and wondering how much of the conversation he had overheard.

"It's a surprise," I said, making it to the doorway. I paused, remembering my phone call with Pete the night before. Juggling the frame with one arm, I reached into the pocket of my skirt and drew out a piece of paper before handing it to him.

"Pete from Pete's Bar called my house looking for you. He'd lost your business card but wanted to talk to you. I didn't feel I should give him your contact information, so I wrote down his instead. He said the man looking for your aunt had been in once—right after you were there—but hadn't been back since. He said to call him if you needed anything else."

His jaw tightened, noticeable only because I was watching him closely as I recalled what Helena had said about me making the cake for his birthday. And asking if I would do the same for Glen.

Finn slid the note unopened into the pocket of his pants.

"Why is somebody at a bar looking for me?" Helena's imperious tone cut through the silence.

I saw the tic in his jaw as he regarded his aunt. "Not you," he said. "Bernadett. Before she died, she asked me to meet with someone—she didn't give me his name—at Pete's Bar. She didn't explain what it was about but said that it was important to her that I meet this person. But the date of the meeting was the Thursday after she died, and . . ." He paused. "I was hoping the man would come back so I could find out why she'd wanted me to meet with him."

"Daddy!"

We both jerked around to see Gigi leaning over Helena while the older woman seemed to gasp for air. Nurse Weber, alerted by Gigi's shout, ran past me. I took the little girl's hand and retreated into the kitchen.

I listened to Teri's gentle voice. "It's all right, Miss Szarka. You just got a little excited. I'm going to give you something to settle you and I'm going to sit right here while you rest. You're going to be fine. I just need you to breathe in and breathe out."

We sat down at the table, the gift hidden on my lap, and waited until Finn left Helena's bedroom, closing the door behind him. He stood next to the table without sitting. "She'll be fine," he said. "Just too much stimulation."

"I'm sorry," I said. "Everything was fine up until you arrived; otherwise . . ."

"It's not your fault. It's nobody's fault. And Teri said all she needs is a bit of rest right now. We can have my surprise birthday celebration when she wakes up." He smiled weakly, the effort completely for Gigi's benefit.

"I'd better go wrap your present, then." I stayed where I was, hoping he'd get the hint and leave so I could stand.

"She did want me to tell you something."

All moisture left my mouth as I recalled the conversation I'd been having with Helena when Finn arrived. "What was it?"

"That if she's dying, she wants you to play the Chopin Nocturne in C Minor."

I put my hand over my mouth, not sure if she'd want me to laugh or cry. Finn reached his hand out for Gigi and led her from the room. I stayed where I was for a long time, grateful that Helena couldn't be too close to death's door if she was still trying to antagonize me, and wondering, too, what I had said that had made her think she was dying.

CHAPTER 17

Helena

I awoke to find Gigi sleeping on the foot of my bed, and Eleanor curled up like a cat asleep in the chair, *The History of Hungary* splayed across the arm. I studied her, noticing how she frowned in her sleep, and wondering what she was dreaming about. I doubted she would remember upon waking; people like Eleanor refused to admit they still dreamed.

I noticed the rectangular folding table that Nurse Weber had set up for my medications and a few of the tools of her trade. She had decorated it with a square lace cloth she had made and had organized my medications in a flat basket. But sometime while I'd slept, somebody had placed my small Herend porcelain rooster on the tray, its broken plumed tail turned away from me so I wouldn't have to look at it. My breath caught as I regarded it, unwelcome memories flooding my heart like the marsh at high tide. I assumed Eleanor had put it there, as she was so fond of meddling with other people's things.

Turning my head, I saw Finn in the doorway, watching Eleanor as I had. I continued to regard him until he noticed me. As always, his expression remained inscrutable. He'd always been good at keeping secrets. Just like Magda.

"Are you feeling better now?" he whispered as he sat on the edge of the bed, careful not to disturb the little girl, and took my hand.

I snatched my hand away, irritated at being treated like an invalid. It still amazed me sometimes when I caught sight of myself in a mirror. I would be startled to see the stranger there, as if still expecting to see my blond hair and tight skin, my hands with long, straight fingers. Age was a thief, an insidious one who instead of robbing you at night while you slept took all of your possessions one by one and forced you to watch.

"I am fine. And I am certainly well enough to join you all in the dining room for your birthday celebration. I hope Eleanor respected my wishes and set the table in there?"

"Yes, she did, and Nurse Weber added a few decorations—a hand-painted banner and balloons. I know you won't like them, but please pretend that you do, as both women put a lot of effort into it. And personally, I like the transformation."

I raised an eyebrow, trying to pinpoint exactly what had changed in Finn in the last month. His hair was lighter from spending more time on the beach with Gigi, but there was something more, too. It was as if the shutters on a window had suddenly been thrown open. He was still his grandfather's grandson, but I was beginning to see more Magda in him, too. For the most part, that was a very good thing.

"If you wish. I am good at pretending."

He reached over and plucked the Herend rooster off the table and held it loosely in his hands, turning it over and running his index finger over the broken part. "I've been meaning to ask you something. About Bernadett. To see if maybe you had any idea about the man I was supposed to meet with."

I shrugged, keeping the movement casual. "You remember how Bernadett was—always involved in one cause or another. It was hard to keep them all straight. I am sure it involved giving a good deal of money to a charity, and she either wanted your approval or, if the sum was very large, your assistance. You should see the mail we get still, all for Bernadett, and most for causes I have never heard of."

Finn looked up, his eyes hopeful. "Have you saved them?"

"Of course not. I throw them away without opening them. I have my own causes to which I like to contribute."

He thought for a moment. "If you receive any more solicitations, could you please save them for me? I'd really like to know what that meeting at that awful bar was all about. When Bernadett called me, she left a message with Kay, my secretary, who put it on the calendar. I didn't even think to call back and ask her about it. And then . . ."

"And then she died."

"Yes," he said. "And then she died." Our eyes met and held for a long moment as we each remembered events we'd rather not and secrets we'd prefer to keep.

Eleanor stirred and I turned toward her, wondering how long she'd been watching us and listening. Her gaze fell to the rooster Finn still held.

She sat up, alert. "I hope you don't mind. I found the rooster in the sunroom while looking for more piano music. It was pushed back on a shelf and I thought it too beautiful to be hidden—even with its broken tail. I saw that it was made in Hungary and thought that you might enjoy having it in here."

I reached for it and Finn placed it in my hand, a jolt of memory like electricity shooting up my arm.

Eleanor continued. "Your childhood home must have been lovely with so many paintings and treasures like this. I'm sure it was difficult bringing them to America, but how nice it must be to have a piece of home with you."

I focused on drawing deep breaths as Nurse Weber had shown me. She had explained that it was the short breaths that had deprived my head of the oxygen it needed and caused my earlier episode.

"Yes," I finally managed. "Just like home." I examined the rooster in my hand, the fine fishnet pattern on its tail, the delicate face, remembering it on the small table in the entranceway of the tiny house in Budapest. "It was a wedding gift to my parents. My mother—my *anyukám*—was very proud of it."

"How did it get broken?"

Breathe in, breathe out. "It was my fault. I could sometimes be very clumsy. I bumped into the table and it fell to the floor. *Anyukám* was dead by then, but I could still sense her disappointment in me for breaking such a treasure."

I closed my eyes, the memory so sharp it could still make me bleed. I wanted to tell this girl about that night, longed to tell her about how the rooster had come to be broken. *It was pitch-black because I was told I could not turn on any lights. The Americans had started bombing the city and the Nazis were flooding in from where they'd been encamped in the countryside. And I was rushing, moving so fast that I could barely catch my breath, trying to move our suitcases toward the back door. When I'd heard the crash I knew what it was, and I spent precious minutes searching for it on my hands and knees before I found it and shoved it into my coat pocket. It stayed there until I had disembarked from the ship in New York. I had shoved my hand into the pocket and cut my thumb on the sharp edge. It had bled and bled as if to empty all of my Hungarian blood into the harbor, to cleanse me of my sins. If it could only have been that easy.*

But of course, I could not tell her. Pulling at this one secret, like pulling a single loose thread on a tapestry, would unravel it all.

My finger rubbed the top of my thumb, and I almost expected to see blood. I refocused my attention on the girl. "I want to hear Debussy later. I hope you can play something without making the poor man turn in his grave."

I watched her back stiffen as she and Finn exchanged a look. "I will certainly try," she said. "But only if you think my time wouldn't be better spent sorting through all of the sheet music."

"I'll let you decide after dinner and birthday cake. I hope your baking is better than your piano playing."

"Me, too," she said, with no hint of animosity.

She stooped and picked up the basket of records, and it was then that I noticed that the gramophone case was missing.

"I put it on the screened porch," Finn said, answering my unspoken question. "I thought we'd listen to your records after dinner."

No, I wanted to say. *No, because I am afraid—afraid I will hear the recrimination and accusation in their voices regardless of what words they are singing.*

"I will see if I am up to it," I said. "Please tell Nurse Weber to come help me out of bed and I will join you in the dining room."

Finn gently shook Gigi awake and led her from the room. But Eleanor held back, looking at the broken rooster. "Do you have the other half of the tail? It's a clean break, and I bet if I glued it you couldn't even tell."

I shook my head. "No. It has been gone for a very long time."

She nodded briefly, then left the room before I could tell her that there were some things that, once broken, could never be repaired.

Eleanor

The late-afternoon sunlight slanted in through the windows in the dining room. I'd thrown open the drapes to allow in the light, illuminating the antique wallpaper and gleaming wood floors. The medieval-garbed subjects of the two large oil paintings on the wall opposite the buffet stared down their long noses at us as we filled our plates with fried chicken, black-eyed peas, and corn on the cob.

Helena sat at one end of the table and Finn at the other, while Gigi and I sat on one side facing Teri. She'd been reluctant to join us, but after I'd pointed out that I was an employee, too, she'd graciously accepted the invitation to sit down to eat.

I noticed how Finn kept an eye on Gigi's plate, making sure she got a little of everything and twice the helping of vegetables. Despite several warnings from her father, she ate quickly, shoveling in forkfuls of food and then gulping down organic milk.

"Is there a fire I'm unaware of?" Finn finally asked.

Gigi placed her knife and fork across her empty plate. "I want you to open your birthday presents. You're going to be *so* surprised."

He glanced toward the buffet, where Helena's gift and the book were neatly wrapped with paper and ribbon.

"There's *more*," Gigi said. "But it was hard to wrap, so Ellie just stuck a bow on it."

I smiled, then stood. "I'll go ahead and clear the table, and on my way back I'll bring in Gigi's present."

Gigi bounced up and down in her seat. "Hurry!"

Teri and I brought the dishes to the kitchen, and then I ducked into the piano room for the telescope. With as much fanfare as I could muster, I brought it in and set it in front of Finn's chair.

"Are you surprised?" Gigi shouted, jumping up from her chair. "It was Ellie's idea."

He regarded me with cool gray eyes. "Really?"

"You mentioned to me how you used to have one, but that somewhere along the way you lost track of it. I thought that you might like to have one again. And Gigi agreed."

Embarrassed, I turned toward the buffet to collect the other two gifts, then placed them on the table in front of Finn. He was still looking at me closely, and I found myself unable to meet his eyes.

"Thank you for helping Gigi shop. It's perfect." He opened his arms for Gigi to step into them, then kissed her forehead. "I've been wanting to get another one for a while now, but life kept getting in the way."

"It's not brand-new," Gigi announced, "but who in their right mind would spend all that money on a brand-new one when this is just as good?" She was quoting me verbatim, making me cringe.

Finn held her at arm's length. "Did you figure that out all by yourself?"

"Sort of?" she said with a smile, glancing up at me.

"We figured it out together," I said. "I don't think NASA would have any use for it, but for recreational star viewing here on Edisto, it should be perfect."

"Can we use it tonight?" Gigi asked, jumping up and down and making the glasses shake on the table.

"Absolutely," Finn answered. "The sky is clear, so it should be a good night for it. We can do that while we listen to Aunt Helena's records."

I was aware of the old woman watching us closely, and I thought she might have flinched.

Gigi shoved the astronomy book at her father. "Open this one next. I picked it out."

Finn took his time opening and examining Gigi's handmade card, despite her impatient hopping up and down, then quickly unwrapped the book on basic astronomy with the appropriate appreciative comments. He'd barely finished speaking before Gigi shoved the other gift toward him. "And this is from Aunt Helena."

He glanced up at his aunt, who shrugged with one shoulder as if the gift were just a trifling matter. Slowly, he untied the ribbon and slid his fingers beneath the tape, unveiling the back of the frame. After lifting it from the paper, he flipped it over and laid it on the table.

He stared at the framed album cover, a soft smile lifting his lips. "I like it. Very much." He stood and kissed his aunt on her cheek. "Thank you, Aunt Helena." He sat down again, staring at the photo of his grandmother and two great-aunts.

"You can hang it in your office," Gigi commented.

I thought of his office filled with antiques and computer monitors, and the serious man who inhabited it, and then regarded the framed photo of three beautiful Hungarian singers and I almost laughed. It would have been like hanging a poster of dogs playing poker next to the Mona Lisa in the Louvre.

"You're right, Peanut." Finn sounded as surprised as I was to hear him say it. "I think on the wall between the two windows behind my desk would be perfect. What do you think?"

"Perfect," she said. "Don't you think so, Ellie?"

"I think so," I said slowly. "Maybe it's time the office sees your other side."

He looked almost annoyed. "My 'other side'?"

Gigi and I shared a look.

Before I could formulate an appropriate answer, she said, "Madame LaFleur would say that you're more of a classical ballet dancer instead of a jazz dancer. But sometimes all you have to do is change costumes to become something different." She smiled matter-of-factly before turning to me. "Can we have cake now?"

"After your medicine," Finn said, scraping his chair away from the table and standing. Although he was wearing casual pants and a golf shirt, his face was the one he wore to the office, and it occurred to me that regardless of who he wanted to be, his daughter's illness would always dictate his choice of dance.

Gigi groaned, dragging her feet as she followed her father to the kitchen. I waited for them to be done and then shooed everyone, including Helena, onto the screened porch so I could bring out the cake. Teri had brought the candles, and after the two of us agreed that we had no idea if Finn was turning thirty-four or thirty-five, she stuck three candles in the middle, then lit them.

We began singing "Happy Birthday" before we'd left the kitchen and were quickly joined by Gigi and Helena, who, despite her age, still had a strong contralto voice. I set the cake down on the wrought-iron table in front of him.

"Three candles?" he remarked. "I'm much older than that, I can assure you."

"One for the past, one for the present, and one for the future," I explained.

Helena leaned forward, her eyes reflecting the light from the candles. "There should be more than three," she said.

Finn's eyebrows lifted. "Two for the future? For the road not taken as well as the well-trod path?"

She shook her head, her eyes focused on the candles. "Two for the past. For the one we wish we had and for the one we have to live with."

Finn stared at his great-aunt for a long moment and then blew out the candles, all extinguishing at the same moment as if an unseen hand had suddenly closed a door.

❧

I stood in the grass outside the screened porch, the long blades tickling my legs. The sound of the old gramophone scratched out its music, a ribbon of sound that wove itself like a river into the night.

We'd listened to the Szarka Sisters album only once and not more—at Helena's insistence—and their voices had been pure and clear, their harmonies as if sung by a single voice. Now we were listening to an old Bing Crosby album, one of his earliest. There was something about the music of the early forties that made one nostalgic for another time.

Helena had retired to her room and Teri rocked in one of the rockers, a sleeping Gigi on her lap. Teri's head bobbed as she tried to stay awake.

I glanced over at Finn, who was fitting a lens onto the telescope. "Should I wake Gigi? She was so excited about seeing the stars."

"It's past her bedtime and it's important that she gets her sleep. I'll make sure that she gets a chance tomorrow night. We'll just start a little earlier." He peered into the eyepiece, then made another adjustment. "It's better to wait until full dark, but not necessary."

He moved his hands toward the stand and began to turn a knob, raising the telescope. "We should get a good view of Ursa Major—Big Bear." He paused, studying the sky. "The best time to view the constellation in the Northern Hemisphere is in April, but we'll still get a good view—and of Ursa Minor, too." He looked through the lens again and began to move it slowly to the right. "I'm assuming you know the Big Dipper?"

"Of course. And the Little Dipper. But I'm afraid that's where my knowledge of astronomy ends."

He lifted his eyes away from the telescope to give me an amused look. After returning to his perusal of the sky, he said, "The handle of the Big Dipper is the Big Bear's tail, and the dipper's cup is the bear's flank."

Stepping back, he said, "Here, it's your turn."

I moved up to the telescope, lifting my hands to the wide neck to steady myself, but Finn grabbed them before I could touch the cool metal. It was the first time he'd touched me, and the warmth of his skin startled me, as if I'd dipped my fingers into sand and found water instead.

Our eyes met for a brief moment before he released my hands. "Try not to touch the telescope. It took a while to get it in the precise spot."

I nodded, not trusting my voice to speak, and pressed my eye against the eyepiece. I felt momentarily dizzy as I tried to reconcile how close the constellation suddenly seemed, as if I'd been propelled into space and was floating weightless amid the moon and stars. "They look so close," I said, resisting the temptation to stretch out my fingers to see if I could touch them.

"I have the lens set so that you can see the whole thing. With a stronger lens we could focus on individual stars, but I thought we'd start with this."

I blinked my eye carefully, as if I were afraid the whole bright expanse of stars would disappear. But they were still there, waiting for me. "Tell me what I'm looking at. I'm guessing you probably didn't need the beginner's astronomy book."

"A refresher couldn't hurt," he said diplomatically. He moved closer, close enough that I could hear him breathing, feel his warm breath on the back of my neck. "Do you see the Big Dipper?"

It took me only a moment to hone in on the familiar group of stars I'd once proudly pointed out to my father. "Yes, I've got it."

"Follow the two stars at the end of the cup upward, and the next bright star you'll run into is Polaris, which is part of the Little Dipper."

"The North Star," I said quietly, remembering another quiet night like this with Eve and my father on his boat listening to him explain the stars to us and their importance to sailors.

I heard the smile in Finn's voice. "So you do know more about astronomy than you think." He stepped closer, his voice very close to my ear, as if he was trying to see exactly what I was seeing. "The distance to Polaris is about five times the angle between the two stars at the end of the cup of the Big Dipper. Because they're so useful in finding the North Star, these two stars are known as the Pointer Stars."

He gently touched my shoulder. "Step back for a minute. I want to see if I can get closer to the North Star."

I did as he asked, watching as he reached into a small box of lenses that had come with the telescope. Because I was preoccupied with what he was doing, his question came as a surprise, which was probably intentional.

"How is your sister?"

"Eve? Oh, you mean with the pregnancy? She's doing fine."

He nodded absently, moving the telescope slightly to the left. "I remember how sick Harper was the whole nine months with Peanut. It was exhausting for both of us." He tilted his head to give me a wry smile.

"No, nothing like that. So far, anyway. It's still early. But thanks for asking."

He straightened and focused his attention on me. "It's just that I know how much she depends on you, and I wanted to make sure that I wasn't making more demands on your time right now than you're able to give."

"Thank you, but I'm managing fine. Glen will be taking Eve to some of her doctor's appointments, which will be a big help, and he's been doing the grocery shopping since I started working here."

His eyes seemed to glow in the moonlight, as if they held answers to questions I wasn't ready to ask. "Glen—that's your brother-in-law, right? The one who came to check up on you on your first day here."

I was glad it was too dark for him to see my reddening cheeks. "Yes. He feels he needs to be the man of the house, since it's only him with us three women." My attempt to lighten the mood failed.

"I see," he said, making it clear that he didn't. He placed his eye over the eyepiece, keeping both eyes open as he'd instructed me to do. "It just seemed to me that his concern for you went a little overboard." He paused. "And that you didn't seem to mind."

The air seemed too thin, my lungs unable to gather enough oxygen. I saw spots that mingled with the stars in the black sky and felt as if all of my deepest secrets had been laid out across the universe for the world to see.

"He's Eve's husband," I managed.

"I know," he said matter-of-factly. He stepped back from the telescope and motioned for me to come forward again. "Here's a better look at Polaris."

I stumbled, my feet feeling numb, but Finn caught my arm and positioned me in front of the telescope. I leaned forward and looked through the eyepiece. The North Star seemed huge, filling the lens with bright light.

He stood behind me. "If you can spot Polaris in the sky, you can always tell which way is north, and the angle of Polaris above the horizon tells you your latitude on earth. That's why the North Star has always been important for sailors. It was the star that brought them home."

I stepped back and looked up at him, wondering if he was still talking about the stars. The record had stopped, the scratching bump of the needle a steady percussion beneath the wings of the chirping insects and the night birds that flitted invisibly across the marsh toward the river.

"I need to go," I said, my voice breathless. "It's late." I didn't move, and neither did he.

"I was hoping you'd play the piano. Aunt Helena wanted to hear Debussy."

I began walking back toward the sanctuary of the screened porch. "I'll play for her when I come on Wednesday."

I'd made it to the porch when he called out, "Thank you for the birthday cake. It wasn't as bad as Aunt Helena said it was."

I pressed my forehead against the wooden frame of the door, surprised to find myself smiling. "That's a relief," I said. "Good night, Finn."

"Good night, Eleanor."

I let the screen door shut softly behind me, closing out the night and the bright star that guided lost souls toward home.

CHAPTER 18

Eleanor

It was barely ten thirty in the morning, but Glen's car was at the curb when I pulled up. I quickly jumped out of the car, a sick feeling in my stomach, hearing Eve's voice repeating itself over and over in my head. *If I die, you'd be free.*

The door opened and Glen met me on the porch. Trying to quell my panic, I asked, "Why are you home? Is Eve all right?"

"She's just resting on the couch. She seemed real tired this morning when I left. It was slow at work, so I decided to take an extended lunch break. What are you doing home?"

"I'm heading out to Edisto later, but Mr. Beaufain said I could take the rest of the morning off, too, when I told him I was going to the library first to return a book and pick up a few new ones for his great-aunt."

I sank down on the porch swing with relief. "I think it's natural for pregnancy to zap a lot of energy."

"That's what her doctor said."

I glanced over at him, trying not to show my surprise. "Her doctor?"

"I called Dr. Wise. I wanted to make sure that I didn't need to bring her in or anything."

I bit my lip to hold back from blurting out more than I should. It was Eve's life, Eve's pregnancy, and not mine.

He continued. "She had me take Eve's temperature, and that was normal." Glen sat down next to me, rubbing his palms down the thighs of his pants. "I don't know how I'm going to get through nine months of this."

I studied his face, still seeing the boy I'd fallen in love with all those years ago. But something was different, too. Somehow his jawline didn't seem right, his nose not as straight, and his hair too dark. I pulled back with alarm as I realized I was comparing him to Finn.

"Are you all right?"

His concern made it worse. "I'm fine." I forced a smile. "You're really happy about the baby, aren't you?"

He nodded without hesitation. "Yes. I hope—"

An image of Helena, all alone in her house by the river, loomed in my mind, yet instead of her face I saw my own. I cut him off, not wanting to hear the rest of what he wanted to say, knowing it would lead me to the same dead end I'd been circling for years. "I know how much Eve wants the baby, too. Being wanted is a great place for a child to start out."

"I still care for you—"

I held up my hand. "Don't. Don't say it. You and Eve have your life together, and I'm finding my own."

He reached over to tuck a strand of hair behind my ear. I wanted to lean into him, to allow him to make all the hurt go away as if I were still a teenager waylaying him on his way to pick up Eve for a date. I'd steal a single kiss as if that might make me happy until the next time. It seemed to me as if I were still waiting, and for the first time I couldn't think of what I'd been waiting for.

I jumped off the swing. "Is Mama dressed and ready? I called to tell her I was taking her to the library."

Glen looked at me oddly. "She's in the den, watching television. I wasn't aware that she was a big reader."

I walked toward the door, remembering to keep my tread light so I wouldn't awaken Eve. "She used to be, when my father was alive. When she became a single mother, it was a little hard for her to find the time. They have magazines, too—anything would be better than her sitting in front of the television set all day."

A wide smile split his face.

"What's so funny?"

"Remember that time you stole Mr. Grund's television set so you and Eve could watch the premier of *The X Files*?"

"I didn't steal it; I borrowed it. Ours was broken and Eve didn't want to miss the beginning of the series. And I would have gotten away with it if Eve hadn't taken her time raiding their refrigerator."

"Because you told her to raid it. She wanted to leave as soon as the TV set was back on the stand."

I clamped down on the inside of my cheek to stop smiling. Our mother had been livid—not that I'd taken the neighbor's television but that I'd involved Eve in another episode of misbehavior. "Yeah, well, she didn't have to do it just because I said so."

He leaned back in the swing, placing his left arm over the back so that his gold wedding ring caught the sunlight. "You were the one bright spot for her. I don't think she thought she had a choice to say no."

I was about to ask him what he meant, but my mother came through the door. "Are you ready? I've been waiting all morning."

I looked at my mother, the woman who'd once been so perfectly groomed, and wondered when she'd begun to wear sensible shoes and think that a housedress was acceptable to wear out in public. At least her hair was clean and brushed and she'd applied lipstick—the same shade of coral she'd worn ever since I could remember.

She looked behind me, her face lighting up when she spotted the Volvo. "It will be so nice to drive in a new car again."

I said good-bye to Glen, then opened the door for my mother before climbing in behind the steering wheel. "I know it's a bit of a drive, but we're going to the Mount Pleasant branch. The book I have to renew came from there."

She just nodded, clutching her purse on her lap like I used to when I rode the bus to work. Her hands reminded me of Helena's, with the swollen joints and curled fingers, and I wondered absently if a lifetime of insensitivity could be a precursor to arthritis.

I glanced in the backseat to where I'd tossed *The Art of Origami*. I'd forgotten to ask Helena if she wanted it returned, so I'd decided to renew it. I needed to visit the library anyway, hoping to find some kind of travel guides or coffee table books on Hungary to give me a better visual of a country I'd known very little about a mere month before. I also wanted to find a few books to read to Helena, and I knew just where to look.

While searching for piano music, I'd found a hidden trove of well-read historical romance novels. They'd been tucked behind literary classics on bookshelves as well as under some of the sheet music in Bernadett's baskets. I thought they might have belonged to Bernadett until I'd noticed the penciled-in HS on the inside covers. I'd laughed outright at the thought of Helena reading the books in secret and then hiding them from her sister. I thought of Bernadett's austere bedroom and the type of person who would have lived in such a place and felt a tinge of sympathy for Helena.

I glanced at my mother in the bright light, realizing it had been a while since I'd seen her in broad daylight. The fine lines around her eyes had become etched wrinkles, although her chin and neck were still firm. If she'd married the kind of man her family had expected her to instead of an Edisto shrimper, she would have been able to take care of herself better, been able to afford a good colorist and regular facials. But even the blue of her eyes seemed to have faded, as if her stolen dreams had leached the colors from her face.

I looked back at the road, eager to avert my thoughts. "I'm glad it's a long drive, Mama. We haven't spent a lot of time together since I started working for Miss Szarka."

She sent me a perfunctory smile, then seemed to mull over something in her mind. Finally, she said, "I didn't want you to take that job, Eleanor, you know that."

Not again. "I know you had objections, based on something you read in the paper, and gossip from an old friend who's lonely now that both of her children have moved out. But it's all been fine."

"I know, but remember that I've known the Szarka sisters for years. There was always something odd about those two women."

"They're from another country, Mama. And they're different—not odd. Even as a child I knew the difference." I couldn't believe I was defending Helena. I wondered if I should tell her—to get brownie points. Or if she'd even care.

"I cleaned for them once. Did I tell you?"

I whipped around to stare at her. "No. You didn't."

She clutched her handbag tighter. "It was a long time ago, when your father was still alive. We needed the money. When your father sold his second boat I thought it was to help with household expenses. But he bought that piano for you instead." She waved her hand at me. "I'm not blaming you, or him. The local shrimping industry was just about dead, anyway. Eve needed new costumes for two big pageants in the spring, and you needed new school shoes—not to mention Christmas presents. The Szarkas were throwing their big Christmas party that they had every year and were looking for people to come in and clean before and after and to help at the party. It was good money, but I didn't tell anyone except for your father." She leaned closer to me. "And don't tell Eve, either."

I rolled my eyes. "It's okay that I know you cleaned somebody else's house for money, but not Eve?"

Her chin wobbled a bit. "She's always needed to be protected. But you . . ." She shrugged. "Even as a child, you seemed able to take care of yourself. That the outside world didn't matter as long as you had your father and your music. I think that grounded you in ways that Eve's beauty and talents couldn't. That's why I always made a big deal out of her. Somebody had to even the playing field."

I had to focus on my driving so that I wouldn't plow into anything. If she'd always felt this way, this was the first I'd ever heard of it. Is that what happened as a mother grew older? She saw her children as adults she could confide in, despite how painful or revealing the subject matter? It seemed, almost, that because I was an adult I'd suddenly ceased to be her child.

I looked down at my white knuckles on the steering wheel, all the old anger and hurt close to the surface, like I'd been underwater for so long that my lungs would burst from holding in all that air. *What about after Daddy died? Who was there to protect me?*

I wasn't interested in rehashing the past, which would never change, so I attempted to return the conversation to a safer place. "You didn't think to mention that you'd worked for the Szarkas when I told you about the job offer?"

Her lips pressed together. "No. It was humiliating, and it still is. I'm only mentioning it now to tell you why I know things aren't all right in that house and that you need to keep your guard up."

"Well, you haven't told me anything other than that they were different from everybody else, which makes sense since they're not from here."

She shook her head, her brows puckered together. "It was just odd—all those paintings hanging on the walls and all the drapes shut. They were nice paintings, too—old ones, and probably quite valuable. I grew up with nice art, so I can recognize the real thing when I see it."

"They brought it from their home in Hungary—most people do bring along their possessions when they move. There's nothing odd about that."

"I didn't think so at first, either, until I got in a conversation with the older one—Miss Helena—after I saw an old photograph of her and Miss Bernadett and the oldest sister, who was already dead by then. I told her they looked like the Gabor sisters. They were Hungarian, too, and all three were movie stars here in the States.

"But Miss Helena just shook her head and seemed angry, saying that she and Bernadett hadn't relied on rich husbands to get them out of Hungary, nor were they raised with a lot of money, and that they were expected to work for a living."

"That all makes sense to me," I said, flicking on the blinker to turn onto Anna Knapp Boulevard.

I felt my mother staring at me, and I didn't need to look at her to see her disappointment in my inability to think things through. "It didn't make sense, then, if they didn't come from a lot of money, that they would have all that expensive art."

I pulled into a parking spot at the library but sat there for a moment with the engine idling, wondering why I felt so unnerved, as if my mother's words had unlocked a box of my own unasked questions. "The three sisters recorded an album. That must have brought in a lot of money."

She unsnapped her seat belt. "I remember that. Bernadett would play it over and over on her gramophone until Helena took it away from her. I told her I didn't know that they were famous, and she said that they weren't, that they'd only recorded the one album. I'm sure it's not like it is today, where you can retire on just one album."

"Well," I said, turning off the ignition and opening my door. "They could have inherited the paintings from a relative, or they could be worthless. Helena's never had them appraised. Maybe she knows they're not worth anything but is too proud to admit it."

Mama rubbed her hands up and down her arms as if she were chilled. "There was something about Helena that I didn't like. Something secretive. And so protective of her younger sister, who was still so frail. Like Audrey Hepburn, who never recovered her health, either, after surviving near starvation during the war. I saw that on the Biography Channel not too long ago," she said, nodding once as if to punctuate the veracity of her statement. "Anyway, I did like to hear her play the piano. I know your father said you were the best, but I think she was even better."

I swallowed at the implied insult. "Bernadett?"

"No, Helena. Even I could tell her music was special. I'm guessing she doesn't play too much anymore. As far back as that Christmas, she was complaining about how much it hurt her fingers to play—because of the arthritis."

I leaned back against my seat, recalling Helena's knotted fingers and wondering when she'd finally stopped playing—not because she chose to but because she had to. It made me a little ashamed to recall how reluctant I'd been to play for her, how selfish. Even in the last months of Bernadett's life, there had been no piano music. A silent house for a musician would be a kind of death. I clenched my eyes shut, my internal voice shouting at me, *Yes, it is.*

I realized my mother was speaking, and I concentrated on listening to what she was saying.

"I saw Mrs. Reed again at the craft store yesterday while I was picking up some beading for Eve. When I told her that you were working for Helena Szarka, she told me something she'd read in the local paper. She said they didn't do an autopsy on Bernadett. And everybody knows that when somebody dies at home they do an autopsy. She said Mr. Beaufain's father was good friends with the Charleston County coroner and maybe did the family a favor. I don't like you being with those people, Eleanor. You are known by the company you keep."

"What is that supposed to mean, and why are you telling me all this now?"

She tucked her chin into her neck in an attempt to appear affronted. "I told you when you first got the job offer that all wasn't right in that house. I didn't say any more because I knew you weren't ready to listen. And maybe you're still not. But I am your mother and I would be neglecting my responsibilities if I didn't tell you what I thought."

I focused on breathing slowly to control my anger. "Bernadett Szarka was eighty-eight years old, Mama. It's not unusual for people of that age to die."

"I know. It just seemed odd. And that Mr. Beaufain—he's from a good family, and that little girl is just precious, but there was a lot of ugliness surrounding his divorce. Something not very nice about his wife."

"Really, Mama? You know his ex-wife?"

"No, of course not. And I don't mean to sound like a gossip, but Mrs. Reed's cousin is a dental hygienist in the office where all three of them are patients. Again, I don't usually listen to idle chatter, but you're in contact with these people and I thought you should know."

I stared at her, torn between asking for more information and wanting to be the adult and discourage gossip. Either way, I needed to be a better monitor of the sources of information my mother had access to.

"I've only met her once, so I really couldn't say."

"Well, the circumstances surrounding the divorce were very ugly."

Unable to resist, I asked, "How ugly?"

"Haven't you wondered why the father has custody instead of the mother? That never happens unless they can prove that the father would be a better parent."

"Mama, I don't think we should be talking about—"

"The little girl got really sick—cancer, I think—and her mother couldn't deal with it. She took up with another man and moved out of the country for a little bit, only came back when it looked like the girl—Gigi, is it?—would survive."

"It was leukemia," I said softly.

"Well, from that one time I met her, it seems like she turned out all right despite all that."

"Yes," I said, exiting the car and then moving to the passenger side to open my mother's door. "She's a terrific kid, thanks mostly to her father. I think he's doing a great job. You should see her room—it's the kind of room I used to dream about."

She'd turned and sat on the edge of the seat, looking up at me. "I remember you telling your father exactly what you wanted. I used to cut out pictures in magazines when I thought it looked like what you'd been talking about and stored them in a box for when we'd have the money. I think I still have them somewhere."

While I tried to think of something to say, she reached into her handbag and held up a small gold tube. "Here, take this."

I looked down at my mother's tube of coral lipstick. "Why?"

She exhaled with exasperation. "Even the most beautiful women can always benefit from a little bit of color. I don't know why you've always shied away from makeup. You don't need a lot, but maybe a touch of powder and mascara would really enhance your natural features. They're really quite lovely, you know. You take after your father's side, and all the women in his family were always late bloomers."

She stood while I just stared blankly at the tube of lipstick that had somehow ended up in my hand, wondering if it had been the first time my mother—even in an indirect way—had called me beautiful, and why it suddenly meant so much to me.

Leaning down toward the side-view mirror, I smoothed the lipstick over my lips and grudgingly admired the results.

We walked into the library and I settled my mother in the periodical section, while I made a beeline for the racks of paperback romances. I picked out one, then added a second for my mother. Then I found the history section, where I discovered several books on Hungary, waffling between two of them before finally settling on one that focused on the two world wars and the years behind the Iron Curtain. After a quick visit to the library's reference computer, I found a photography book that featured Eastern European cities and had a photograph of the Buda Castle in Budapest on the cover.

Feeling satisfied, I made my way to the checkout desk, where an attractive woman in her mid-forties with short, curly dark hair sat behind a computer. A name tag in the shape of a tiara, complete with rhinestones, had the name WANDA JEWELL stamped on it. She was muttering under her breath as I approached, her fingers flying over the keyboard until she gave a final loud thump to the return key before focusing her attention on me.

"Sorry about that. It just makes me so angry when people can't return their books on time. It's not like we hide the due date from them or anything."

My smile faded slightly. "Yes, um, I'd like to check out a few books, and I have one to renew as well."

She smiled expectantly, and I slid the new books toward her. "I have a library card, but I haven't used it in a while."

Her smile dimmed perceptibly as I pulled the card from my wallet. Wanda took it, then typed something into the computer. "Is all of your information still current?"

"Yes, it is."

Wanda glanced at the line of library patrons that was forming behind me. "You know, you could have gone online and done this at home."

The overdue book I still clutched in my hand seemed to grow heavier, and I considered taking it back without renewing it. But when Wanda handed over my newly checked-out books to me, I slid *The Art of Origami* to her. "This is an elderly friend's book who has recently suffered a death in the family. I was hoping I could renew this for her."

Wanda removed the small receipt from the inside cover, and I watched as her eyes widened. "This book is almost four months overdue."

I glanced at the people lined up behind me and smiled. "I know. I was just hoping to do this as a favor, considering the circumstances. . . ."

My voice trailed off as she started typing into the computer again. She leaned forward to read something before fishing for the reading glasses that hung on a chain around her neck and sticking them on her nose.

"Bernadett Szarka?" she asked.

"Yes," I blurted out, not sure why I'd been thinking it had been Helena's book.

She peered at me from over her reading glasses. "I'll waive the fine because of the extenuating circumstances." She was silent for a moment as she read from her screen. "This is interesting. Apparently your friend ordered a few books from another library as an interlibrary loan, but she didn't want to be notified. She left very explicit instructions not to be called, but that she would be in to pick up the books."

I leaned over the counter. "When was this?"

Wanda lifted her index finger and dragged it along the screen. "January. I don't know why she didn't renew the origami book when she was here then, since she probably would have known by then that she wouldn't be done with it by the due date. That would have saved us all a lot of trouble." She tapped her finger on the screen. "She has an address on Edisto. You could have gone to any of the Charleston County library branches to renew this, you know."

I glanced blankly at her, unable to find the courage to tell her that I didn't know because I rarely used the library anymore. There simply weren't enough hours in the day. Instead, I said, "Do you still have the books on hold?"

"I'll have to go check. Usually we return unclaimed books within thirty days, but we've been dealing with a lot of part-time help, so things have been overlooked. I'll go see."

There was an audible sigh from the woman standing directly behind me, and I sent her another apologetic smile.

Ms. Jewell reappeared from the back holding two books rubber-banded together with a piece of paper with Bernadett's name written across it in bold black letters. I had no intention of telling the librarian that the person she'd been holding the books for had died nearly two months before. I figured I'd just take them home, see if Helena wanted to read them, then bring them back, except I wouldn't drive all the way to Mount Pleasant to return them. Surely somebody had mentioned that to Bernadett. There was even a library in Edisto. It made no sense that she would have driven all this way.

Wanda dropped the books on the desk in front of me. "Do you have Miss Szarka's library card?"

I quickly slid mine over to her. "Use mine."

She took the card and added Bernadett's books to my account. As I took the proffered books, she said, "Please tell Miss Szarka that if she wants to keep books for such a long time, she might consider purchasing them. We have a lot of fine bookstores in the area—including a very nice one right on Edisto." She smiled broadly. "Have a nice day."

"Thanks. And you, too."

I found my mother poring over a current issue of *Charleston* magazine. "Did you find anything you wanted to check out?" On my walk over to her, I'd already decided that if she did, I was sending her through the line by herself.

"No, not really," she said as she stood, giving the magazine a final, lingering glance.

"That's all right," I said as I led her toward the door. "I got a book for you that I think you might like."

I handed her one of the romance novels.

"Eleanor! You know I don't read this kind of thing." She quickly pressed the book, cover first, into her chest. "What if somebody sees?"

"Nobody knows you here, Mama, and nobody would care, anyway."

She scowled, but instead of giving the novel back to me, she stuck it in her purse.

When I opened the back door of the car to toss the books onto the backseat, the rubber band snapped on Bernadett's books, spilling them onto the floor. I bent to pick them up, then froze as I read the two titles. *Great Art of the Eighteenth and Nineteenth Centuries* and *The Dutch Masters*. A cool hand seemed to brush the back of my neck, as if somebody was leaning close to whisper in my ear. I replaced the books on the seat, then quickly slid behind the wheel.

My mother started reading her book on the way home, leaving me with more time than I wanted to picture her cutting out pictures from magazines for a girlhood room I would never have, and to ponder all the reasons why Bernadett would have ordered those particular books, and why she hadn't wanted Helena to know.

CHAPTER 19

The early-morning air held a coolness despite its being summer, and I had the sunroof of the Volvo opened to the sky. The drive down Highway 174 was one filled with color and light, passing the local restaurants and produce stands and the myriad white wooden churches that dotted the island. Growing up here, I'd never appreciated the beauty of the old highway, of the canopies of oaks that cast light and shadow over the road, and the way the road stretched over the winding creeks and marsh. You could smell the pluff mud through the open windows of the car as soon as you crossed the bridge over the Dawho River, a scent you never forgot no matter how hard you didn't want to remember.

I recalled Eve and Lucy and me on our bicycles on the same road, without shoes or helmets or anything that would distract us from feeling the wind in our hair or going as fast as we could. I was always in the lead, always determined to go faster, to turn sharper. Even in those days before my daddy died, my need to agitate my senses always pushed at my back.

Although it was the middle of the week, Gigi accompanied me. Her head was tilted back so she could watch the passing limbs of the trees, her mouth open as if she was surprised that there was a world above her that she'd never suspected, as if no one had ever shown her before.

The canceled French immersion camp had apparently been a two-week deal, and Harper had already made plans during the second week that she couldn't rearrange, so Finn had been left to juggle his work and Gigi. I hadn't waited for him to ask me to help, volunteering to bring Gigi with me to Edisto. Although I enjoyed her company, I would be lying by saying I didn't have ulterior motives—she was a lovely buffer between Helena and me. At the very least, it would give me the perfect opportunity to start her piano lessons.

As we neared the single sweetgrass basket stand on Edisto, I slowed to see if I recognized the woman seated to the side of the hut. Dah Georgie was long gone, as were all of the Edisto basket makers Lucy and I had known, and I knew that the women who infrequently inhabited this stand came all the way from Charleston. Still, I slowed, belatedly realizing the face I'd been wanting to see was the face of the woman from my dreams.

"Can we stop?" Gigi's voice piped up from the backseat.

"Sure." With a glance in the rearview mirror, I made a quick U-turn in the middle of the road, then drove up onto the grass near the basket stand.

The woman was humming a song I recognized, having heard Dah Georgie sing it many times. "Take Me to the Water" was used at riverside baptisms in Lucy's family. It seemed their baptisms were more authentic than ours at the Presbyterian church, but I'd never mentioned that to my mother, knowing I'd probably have received a stiff punishment for even broaching the subject. But I still loved the song, and it was the words "take me to the water" that I heard when I thought of the myriad creeks and waterways of my childhood. It made my exile easier to accept, somehow, as if all I needed to do was find a boat and put it on a river to take me home.

Gigi held my hand as we approached the woman, who looked up and smiled at us, revealing bright white teeth with a gold tooth on the bottom. Her hair was steel gray threaded through with thin reeds of black, the pattern resembling those of some of her baskets. She wore a blue-and-white-checkered dress that threatened the integrity of the buttons holding the front together over her voluminous chest. We greeted each other while Gigi looked at the baskets. She stood on tiptoes to see the ones on the higher shelves, then squatted to see those closer to the ground, taking her time to examine each one carefully with her fingers.

I opened my mouth to tell her to look without touching, but the basket weaver put her hand on my arm. "It be okay," she said, nodding in Gigi's direction. "The milk still dry on her face."

Gigi frowned up at me. "What does that mean?"

"It means you're young. But you still need to be careful."

"I know," she said, sounding impatient. "She's got almost as many baskets as Aunt Bernadett," she said, running her fingers along the edge of a large tomb-shaped basket with a lid.

The old woman laughed, her fingers not pausing in her work. She was at the beginning stage of a basket, making the bottom, just past the seven rows of palmetto strips where she'd begun to weave in the sweetgrass. Dah Georgie had taught me that from this stage any basket of any design could be made, and it was up to the weaver to decide. Each strand, each leaf, would determine how it would look, making it impossible to go back and start again without unraveling the whole thing.

I watched her for a moment, relishing the power she held in her hands, and wondering what it would be like to start from scratch again, to determine the size and shape of your life with the benefit of hindsight.

Gigi was still staring at the large oval-shaped basket with a lid. "I could fit in that, don't you think, Ellie?"

The old woman leaned over to see what Gigi was looking at. "That one called the Escape Hatch."

Gigi tilted her head to the side. "Do they all have names?"

"Most. Some of the old designs, their names be forgotten with the names of the sweetgrass maker who make them."

I watched as she slowly turned the round bottom of the unmade basket, the skin of her hands dark and worn like old leather. "Do you know what you're making yet?"

She looked up at me and I saw that one of her eyes was cloudy with a cataract, but it didn't seem to be slowing her down, as her nimble fingers manipulated her sewing bone and the grass as if they had eyes of their own. "Not yet. I feel the grass first, let it warm in my hands and let it tell me what it want to be. Sometimes you got to bend it and twist it and pull it hard before it knows."

"What's this one called?"

We looked at Gigi, who gingerly held a shallow basket with a narrow base and opening but with a wider middle. The handle was two to three times the height of the basket, with delicate loops and swirls decorating the sides.

"That an old one. They use it for an egg basket, but the pattern called Path of Tears."

Gigi frowned, then delicately set it back on the shelf before picking up another. This one had no handle or lid and was wider on the bottom than at the top. "What about this one?"

The woman squinted for a moment. "Dreams of Rivers."

I walked over to Gigi and she placed it in my hands. I felt the smooth, tightly woven grass tucked into the tightly wound palmetto frond binding. "How much for this one?"

"Are you going to buy it?" Gigi asked.

"For Helena," I said before the thought had completely formed in my head.

"Because of the name?"

I looked down at this wise child, once again amazed that she was only ten. "Yes. She told me that she used to live by the Danube River when she was a girl. And now she lives by the Edisto River. I think she might appreciate the name."

"And she doesn't have any of her own baskets—they're all Aunt Bernadett's. Aunt Helena needs one by her bed, I think, to put her glasses and her watch and the TV controls in, even though she's always asking me to turn it on and off and change the channels because she can't figure it out."

I smiled. "It's settled, then." I handed the basket to her while I reached for my wallet. The price was high, as I had predicted for a piece of handcrafted artwork, but I paid it with just a little bargaining down, since that was expected. I had a little more spending money, thanks to Finn's generosity, and even though I couldn't quite believe I was buying something for Helena, the basket with the name Dreams of Rivers had to belong to her.

Gigi was uncharacteristically silent as we made our way to the house, the basket held carefully on her lap. I drove extra slowly past the pecan tree orchard, thinking maybe she needed more time to get all her words together.

She finally spoke as I put the car in park. "There's another basket."

I looked at her in the rearview mirror. "Another basket?" I had no idea where this was leading.

"Remember how Aunt Helena wanted us to gather all the music from Aunt Bernadett's baskets and we've been working on putting them together in those pink binders that we bought even though I tried to find another color that I liked as much?"

I shifted in my seat and turned to face her, giving me a moment to process the subject of her sentence. "Yes. I was hoping that since you're here today we can work on that project a little after we have your first piano lesson."

She looked at me earnestly. "Yes, ma'am. We can do that. But first I was wondering if we should go get that other basket."

"You mean another basket with music in it? You know where there's another one?"

Gigi nodded. "Yes. But I don't know if there's music in it. I was too afraid to look inside."

I shifted uncomfortably in my seat. "Where did you find this basket?"

She looked down at her hands. Almost mumbling, she said, "In Aunt Bernadett's room."

Oh. I waited for her to continue.

"I know I'm not supposed to go in there, but sometimes when I'm here with my daddy and you're not here and Aunt Helena is sleeping and Daddy's busy on his computer or phone, I get bored and I'm not supposed to leave the house by myself so I sometimes walk around the house looking for something to do."

I remembered doing the exact same thing, and the temptation of a closed door to a room I was told to stay out of. With a neutral voice, I said, "So you went into Aunt Bernadett's room and saw the basket."

She bit her lower lip.

"Where was the basket?" I prodded.

"Under her bed," she said very quietly.

As somebody who'd been caught inside the armoire, I wasn't about to castigate her for looking under the bed. "Is it still there?" I asked.

She shook her head.

When nothing else seemed forthcoming, I asked, "Do you know where it is?"

She nodded her head. "It's under my bed."

"At the Edisto house?" I asked hopefully.

"No." Her voice sounded very small. "At my other house. I took it to look inside, but then my daddy called for me and I got scared so I stuck it in my bag to hide it and then I brought it home with me, but then I felt guilty about it so I just hid it under my bed."

I sighed heavily. "All right. So all you need to do is bring it with you when you come on Saturday and then put it back."

"I thought of that, too, but then I thought that maybe Aunt Helena doesn't know about that basket and would like to know what's inside it and maybe there's music in there that needs to go in the binders and we'd be doing her a favor by looking inside of it."

I paused for a moment to process what she was saying. "Yes, it's certainly possible that there's music we need in that basket, and that the basket was simply overlooked at some point or even accidentally shoved under the bed. I'm even thinking that Helena forgot there were a few baskets in Bernadett's room, since she told us not to go in there." I paused, thinking. "If you like, I can come over tomorrow after work and we can look in it together and then replace it when we come back on Saturday."

She grinned broadly. "I knew you'd figure it out. Thank you."

"You're welcome," I said as I climbed out of the car, eager to get to the house before I changed my mind and headed back to Charleston to find out what might be in Bernadett's basket.

Nurse Kester was in the kitchen making photocopies of the more intact pieces of sheet music using the small copier Finn had brought from his office. The kitchen table was littered with die cuts, glue, and the purple see-through pocket folders. She looked up apologetically when we came through the doorway.

"Nurse Weber said that if I got caught up I could work on the music. Miss Szarka is resting right now and there's nothing on television, so I figured why not?"

"Thank you," I said, placing the Dreams of Rivers basket on the table. "I was hoping to use the piano, but I don't want to disturb Miss Szarka."

Nurse Kester shook her head. "Don't worry about that. There are pocket doors that separate the music room from the hallway. There's some good, sound construction in this house—which is why it's been here for so long—and she won't be able to hear anything back in her room."

"Great. Then we'll go ahead and get started. Could you please let us know when she awakens?"

Gigi skipped to the music room—a good sign that she hadn't been coerced, I thought—and I followed her, gently sliding closed the pocket doors behind us. They were two inches thick of solid wood and I knew Nurse Kester had been right.

The curtains remained opened, the room now filled with light. None of the portraits were in direct sunlight, and the woman in the long red velvet dress on the wall facing the piano seemed to glow in her newfound view of the world.

I sat on the edge of the piano bench and motioned for Gigi to come sit beside me. I pointed to the M in the "Mason & Hamlin" written on the fall board. With my index finger, I slid it from the letter down to the keys, finding the white key directly to the left of the two black keys. "This is middle C. You should always position your bench so that you can sit right in front of this key. That's a good starting place so that you can reach the entire keyboard."

"Kind of like first position in ballet. Every step and position starts from there."

"Exactly," I said, making a mental note to use as many dance correlations as I could think of. "Before we start learning how to read music, I want you to get comfortable with your fingers on the keys." I paused, hearing my words echo my father's the first time he'd sat me on the piano bench. I'd been five and had grown tired of waiting to play myself and had simply crawled up to sit next to him. He'd had an electric keyboard at the time, but within a year my father had bought the Mason & Hamlin.

"Put your right hand up here on the keyboard with your thumb on middle C."

"When do I get to use the pedals?"

I bit back a smile. "You have to wait for a while before we get to that. Using the pedals is like being put in pointe shoes. You'd hurt yourself if you tried it too early."

Her eyes widened in surprise. "You can get hurt playing the piano?"

"Only if your aunt Helena is here with her cane," I muttered.

I showed Gigi how to keep her wrists lifted and to round her fingers so the tips hit the keys. She was an avid pupil and listened carefully without growing frustrated. But by the end of half an hour we were both ready for a break.

Gigi slid off the bench. "I want you to play now."

"I don't think—"

"Madame LaFleur always dances for us when we've worked really hard. Unless you don't think you can. Aunt Helena says that the reason why you won't play for her is because you really don't know how and that the songs you played that first time you were here were the only songs you knew and that you've played them so many times that they sound like they come from a can."

I looked at her steadily, unraveling her words to the starting place to make sure my anger was directed at the right person. "Did she, now?" I asked, standing up and moving to the edge of the room, where the stacks of music we'd been gathering lay sorted in their various piles. "Do you remember where we put the Debussy?"

Gigi skipped over to a pile beneath the portrait of the woman in the red dress. "You said you were putting all the composers who weren't Beethoven, Mozart, or Chopin in this pile."

"I did?" I asked, not remembering the reasoning behind my methodology. I did remember, however, the general ill will I'd felt toward my assignment and the woman who'd issued it, which most likely had a lot to do with the incomprehension of my organizational edict.

I squatted down and began thumbing through the sheet music, having remembered seeing a copy of "Clair de Lune" that was not in a book. I was halfway through the pile when I found it. I held it up like a prize. "I think you'll like this one," I said.

I placed it on the music stand, then made a grand show of sitting in front of middle C and adjusting the bench accordingly. I studied the music for a long time, my fingers seeming to remember the notes in the way a memory is resurrected by a forgotten scent. I loved Debussy and this piece in particular for the sheer beauty of it; the brightness of the melody mixed with sensuality made this piece and all of his music a joy to listen to and to play. It had been the first composition I'd learned on my own, and the first time I'd ever seen my father cry. It had embarrassed him, and he'd swiped at his cheeks with the back of his weathered hand and pretended he had something in his eye.

"I hope you'll like it, Gigi. Claude Debussy was known as the founder of musical Impressionism—although he always disputed that. I'm not sure if there's a correlation to dancing Impressionism, but maybe you're familiar with the paintings."

She stared at me blankly, corroborating my suspicion that I was not a born teacher.

"All right, then," I said, placing my hands over the keys. "I'll probably make some mistakes, but try to enjoy the music. In fact, I'm not even going to tell you to watch my fingers or anything like that because I'm not sure I'll do it correctly."

Gigi sat down on the small love seat, her feet barely brushing the floor. "Stop making excuses and just play."

I didn't bother to ask if she'd come up with that on her own. I'd never met Madame LaFleur, but from what I'd learned of her, it sounded like something she would have said.

I let my hands fall on the first chords, delicate and hesitant, like diving underwater, where light and sound wavered. And then I forgot where I was and who was listening and why I was playing. I *saw* the music, felt it as one feels a boat one is navigating, the sways and swells, the ripples of excitement. I forgot everything, losing myself as completely as if I'd started to follow a new river whose creeks and bends were unfamiliar to me.

I lifted my hands from the keyboard after the final chord, the notes staying in the air as if they knew I didn't want to let them go. And then I let my foot slide from the pedal, allowing the music to fade completely.

Gigi moved from the love seat to slide next to me and pressed her hand over her heart. "I heard it here," she said.

Before I could respond, the telltale thump of a cane sounded behind me. I stood quickly and faced Helena. "I hope I didn't disturb your rest."

Her eyes held a light in them that I hadn't seen before. "That wasn't horrible."

I remembered that Gigi was in the room and had to bite my tongue so I wouldn't say the first thing that came to mind. "Does that mean Mr. Debussy isn't turning over in his grave right now?"

Ignoring my question, she said, "Why did you stop?"

I started to say, *Because the song was over,* but I knew that wasn't what she meant. I considered my answer only for a brief moment. "Because my father died."

She regarded me intently, the light in her eyes seeming to grow brighter. "And he did not want you to play anymore after he died?"

I stared back at her, unable to answer. I had never been asked that before, even by myself. I blinked hard, determined that I wouldn't shed tears in front of Helena. Swallowing thickly, I said, "It was too painful. He taught me how to play, and without him I didn't see a purpose to it."

Her gaze was relentless. "And so you honor him by dismissing the music he taught you?" She waved her hand at me as if to reject anything else I might want to say. "You want to tell me that you did it for love." She leaned closer to me, her hand gripping the top of her cane. "But that can be a very selfish thing. Maybe you were afraid that you really were not as good as he said you were. It does not matter. We all say we do things for love. But even love has its price. Be careful what you are willing to pay. It might cost you more than you could ever imagine."

I was shaking, shaking with anger and frustration and the horrible knowledge that part of what she'd said had nudged at the truth. And I wanted to hurt her as much as she'd hurt me. I threw back my shoulders. "Why did Bernadett stop?"

Her expression never changed except for the raising of a single elegant eyebrow. Her voice was calm when she spoke. "I would like to have another piece of the leftover *dobostorta*. You and Gigi may have one, too, and join me out on the screened porch."

She turned and began to make her regal, yet slow, exit from the room, her hand trembling on her cane the only evidence that she was as shaken as I was.

I had nothing left in my arsenal, so I blurted out, "So the cake wasn't so bad, was it?"

"I never said that," she said without turning around.

Gigi tried to hide her laughter beneath the palm of her hand, while I stared after Helena's retreating back trying to decide if she was the cruelest person I'd ever met or simply the most observant.

CHAPTER 20

Eve

At the sound of Eleanor's footsteps clambering down the stairs, I quickly slid the beautiful burgundy wool gabardine fabric under the yards of tulle I'd been buried under for nearly a week. Since Mama's unexpected meeting with Mrs. Reed at the fabric store, she'd not only rediscovered an old friendship, which—thankfully—took her undivided focus off me, but also brought an unexpected opportunity in the form of Mrs. Reed's granddaughters and their heavy involvement in a dance academy.

Mama had been embarrassed when I'd asked her to call her old friend and ask who was making their costumes for the various shows. As I'd explained to her, opportunities sometimes arrived when you weren't even looking for them. Like when you're standing in front of rolls of fabric in a fabric store or lying broken on a dirt road staring up at the sky through the gnarled arms of an oak tree.

"Are you ready to go?" Eleanor asked, dangling her car keys.

I spotted a piece of the burgundy and quickly leaned over to fiddle with the sewing machine while using the other hand to hide the wool. It hadn't taken me long to figure out that I needed to use the old pattern we'd bought all those years ago and make Eleanor a suit. I think I'd decided to do it even before I'd found the material on sale in a color I knew would look beautiful on my sister. If I could see my child as a second chance, then I could see this suit as my penance. Each stitch, each hour a letting go, a saying good-bye to anger and to old dreams that had never really been mine.

"I'm ready," I said, placing my purse in my lap as Eleanor wheeled me to the door.

As she headed the car toward Charleston, I said, "I'd like to send a thank-you note to Mr. Beaufain. He's been more than generous in allowing you time off for my appointments, and now for maternity clothes shopping."

"Believe me, he knows he's getting a bargain with all the time I spend with his aunt. She's not the easiest person to get along with." Her mouth hardened. "Besides, it's only for a few hours. Glen said he could come pick you up around eleven thirty, right?"

I nodded. "Unless you wanted to grab lunch; then I can call him to come a little later."

She looked startled at my suggestion but quickly composed herself. "I'll probably take lunch at my desk to catch up on the work I'm missing this morning." She waved her hand at me, as if to dismiss further conversation on the subject, and I wondered when she'd started doing that. "Finn usually brings me lunch when I come in late."

I raised my eyebrows, trying to think of why somebody like Mr. Beaufain would bring lunch to an assistant. "Still, I'd like to send a note. Do you know his home address?"

I was amused to see her blushing. "Yes. I'm actually heading there this afternoon after work. To see Gigi," she added hastily.

She pulled into the parking lot behind Beaufain & Associates, right next to a beater car that could belong to only one person.

"Is that Lucy Coakley's Buick? I swear I remember her daddy driving that car fifteen years ago."

"The one and only," she said as she popped open the tailgate on the Volvo to retrieve my wheelchair. "Do you want to go inside and say hi?"

"Maybe when we're finished, if there's time." I had no intention of laying eyes on Lucy again if I could help it. I hadn't spoken to her since my wedding to Glen. Or, more accurately, since the day before my wedding, when she'd shown up at my house to ask me what I was doing. I'd known exactly what I was doing, even then. But I'd been unable to explain to Lucy that my reasons had nothing to do with spite, regardless of what she thought. Mama had wanted me to be a senator's wife or a movie star, but my own aspirations had been closer to the ground. And [illegible]ized that in Glen when I'd first seen him, knew his dreams had nothing to do with chasing stars.

"You do know there are easier and cheaper places to shop than King Street, right?" Eleanor asked as she worked the wheelchair over a curb, her voice having an edge to it that she seemed to have brought back from yesterday's trip to Edisto.

"I know. But I just got paid for three Junior Miss gowns and I have a meeting scheduled with the dance academy Mrs. Reed's granddaughters are enrolled in, so things are looking up." I smiled hopefully. "It's just that it's been so long since I've been downtown, and I need to see what non-mall stores have in their windows for inspiration for the dance costumes I need to create. A lot of the stores are running sales now, too, so if I can find some good deals on a few maternity outfits, it's a win-win."

Eleanor didn't say anything, neither agreeing nor disagreeing. I'd grown used to this neutrality over the years, but it still seemed as unnatural to me as the Eleanor Murray I'd grown up with driving the speed limit in a Volvo.

I continued. "If you change your mind about lunch, I was hoping we might go to Carolina's. It's been far too long since I've been there."

She remained silent and I thought she might not have heard me.

"It's where we met Glen, remember?" I prompted.

"I remember." Her voice was flat, and she was walking so fast that my chair was bouncing all over the uneven sidewalk, making me thankful for my seat belt.

I put my hand on hers. "Stop."

She stopped abruptly, my body jerking forward. I looked around to see if anybody had noticed before turning to look at Eleanor. "What's got into you? You've been carrying a chip on your shoulder since you got back from Edisto."

I could see her deliberating on how much she should tell me. Finally, she said, "It's that woman. Helena. She said something that upset me, that's all."

"What could she have possibly said that would affect you so much?"

She bit her bottom lip, just as she'd done as a child. "She told me that I stopped playing the piano after Daddy died because I was selfish." She swallowed. "That I was afraid of failure."

I remembered very little of those dark days before they found my father's boat, except for Mama's blank face and the police chief bringing a cold and shivering Eleanor home from her vigil on the dock. And I remembered the absence of music, the silence of the house, as if it had already begun its mourning. "Then why did you stop?"

Her eyes were empty as she stared back at me, as if the library of understanding she'd built up over the years had been suddenly scattered to the wind.

"I don't know," she said with a vicious tug on my wheelchair that sent me swaying sideways.

"We were talking about Carolina's," Eleanor said after we'd gone about half a block, eager to pretend that our previous conversation hadn't happened, that the world still revolved in the direction with which she'd grown familiar. "It's where Daddy asked Mama to marry him."

"I'd forgotten that," I said. I'd spent years listening to my mother talk about her glory days as a Charleston debutante and how she'd disappointed her family to marry my father. "I suppose there really is something special about those round booths in the front of the restaurant."

"More likely there's something special in what they serve from the bar," Eleanor said, a welcome hint of amusement in her voice. She was silent for a moment as she made the turn from Broad Street to King. "I remember how shy you were being, hardly saying a word, and trying not to let anybody notice how you were staring at those boys in their Citadel uniforms at the other booth."

"If I was being quiet, it was probably because I was keeping a tally in my head of how much money we were spending. I only had twenty dollars in my purse, my entire paycheck from working the cosmetics counter at Gwynn's."

She pushed me in silence, then paused in front of the window at Berlin's. "Then next time we go to Carolina's, my treat."

I shook my head. "Oh, no need for that. You always paid your way by adding the excitement factor." I'd grown up thinking that Eleanor's misadventures were part of what I was supposed to forget. Instead, as the years progressed, I'd found myself thinking about them more often, considering them the parts of my growing-up years that I most wanted to remember.

Our gazes met in the reflection from the store window. "Like stealing Mr. Grund's TV?" she asked as a corner of her mouth reluctantly lifted.

"Actually, I was thinking about that evening at Carolina's. I didn't know until later that nobody had given you those dresses. To think I met my future husband in a stolen dress."

She sounded offended. "It wasn't stolen—it was borrowed. Mama's cousin had no idea they'd even left her closet."

"Until she saw us at Carolina's."

A snort of laughter escaped from Eleanor's mouth. "I shouldn't have done it. Relationships with Mama's family were strained enough, and that was pretty much the end of it."

"But you were the one who dared me to go talk to those boys." I stared at the red spaghetti-strapped dress in the store window without really seeing it. "It used to drive Mama crazy, the way I'd let you drag me into trouble."

We were both silent as we thought about our last adventure and the consequences neither of us could have foreseen. Turning my chair, she said, "Let's go in here. They're bound to have a maternity section, and if not, maybe some loose-fitting tops."

She pushed me into the store as if that could silence the memories of two sisters who'd somehow grown to think that the long arms of the past were too short to reach them.

Eleanor

It was nearly eleven o'clock before we emerged from the third store, a small assortment of shopping bags dangling from the chair and me and resting in Eve's lap—all proudly purchased on sale and under the budget Eve had allotted. I also had a phone full of photos for Eve's burgeoning costume designs.

I'd given Eve my phone to call Glen to let him know that she was ready to be picked up, when I heard my name. I turned and spotted Finn walking toward us, the sun glinting off his hair, its brightness at odds with the black suit. He carried a bag from Sugar Snap Pea Children's Boutique.

"I hope I didn't miss Gigi's birthday," I said, indicating the bag.

"No. Not quite. It's four years of remission as of today. We celebrate it like another birthday."

His grin at his daughter's success spread a fissure of warmth through my chest. "That's wonderful. Let me guess—whatever you bought is pink."

He laughed. "How did you guess?" Turning his attention to Eve, he said, "It's good to see you again, Mrs. Hamilton."

I was impressed that he'd remembered her name, but then I imagined that was something that had been ingrained in him since birth.

"Please. Call me Eve."

"All right. But only if you call me Finn."

Eve smiled brightly, her confinement to a wheelchair having done nothing to diminish her beauty. But Finn only gave her a glancing smile before refocusing his attention on me.

"We've been doing a little maternity shopping for Eve," I said.

"I can see that." He looked down at his watch. "I have a lunch appointment at one, but maybe I can interest you both in some coffee?"

Before I could say no, Eve was already redialing Glen. While it rang, she said, "That would be lovely. Let me just tell Glen that he can pick me up at noon. Where do you suggest we go?"

"How about the City Lights Café? It's just around the corner on Market."

I tried to catch Eve's attention, but she was too busy answering Finn's questions regarding her health and the baby's. Reluctantly, I began to push the wheelchair at a quick pace, eager to get through what promised to be a very awkward hour.

Luckily, we'd missed the morning rush and it was too early for the lunch rush, which made it easier for us to navigate the wheelchair through the narrow café to a table near the back. I stayed with Eve while Finn went up to the bar to place our orders.

"Is 'Finn' a nickname?"

Eve's question brought my attention back from studying the bohemian crowd around me. I looked at her in surprise. "I suppose so. The name on all of his correspondence is Hampton P. Beaufain. I have no idea where the Finn comes from."

She propped her elbow on the wooden table and tapped her fingertips on her chin. "I bet the P is for Phineas. You should ask."

I leaned closer so I wouldn't be overheard. "No. He's either Mr. Beaufain at work or Finn when we're on Edisto. I don't need to know more than that."

Eve raised her eyebrows but was prohibited from saying anything else by Finn's appearing at the table with an iced latte for me, a black coffee for him, and an iced water with lemon for Eve.

Finn took a sip from his steaming coffee, not even flinching at the temperature as he swallowed. "Eleanor, I was hoping to get the chance to talk about something that's come up."

I kept my face neutral while I secretly prayed that whatever he had to tell me didn't involve spending more time with Helena.

He placed his cup on the table. "I have to go to New York on business for a few days. I'd like you to take Gigi to Edisto after work today and stay there while I'm gone."

I wasn't sure if I completely disguised my dismay, but I was too busy trying to think of an excuse. "But my job—"

"I'll tell Kay to take care of any of your work projects. Gigi is good for Helena. And both Gigi and Helena enjoy your company."

I coughed, my last sip of latte not going down the way it was supposed to. When I'd recovered, I said, "You're joking about the Helena part, right?"

His eyes were cool and assessing. "You remind her of Bernadett."

I almost choked again. "I thought she liked her sister."

Finn kept back a smile. "Bernadett had a way of taking care of things, whether or not she wanted to do them. Like you do." For Eve's benefit, he added, "She and my aunt Helena have had their differences. She's got Eleanor reorganizing all the music in the house and putting it in binders as well as teaching my daughter how to play piano. I don't particularly think that your sister had this in mind when she started this job."

Eve sipped her water. "So how else does Eleanor remind Helena of her sister?"

He put his fingers around his cup but didn't lift it to his lips. "Bernadett worked hard taking care of others, almost to the exclusion of everything else. She was really driven, really devoted to all of her causes. Almost like somebody who was paying off a debt."

"Or atoning for past sins," Eve said as she took another sip of her water.

I looked down at my lap, unable to look at either one of them. "Or maybe you've seen too many movies."

Ignoring me, Eve asked, "Was either of them ever married?"

"No. Maybe that's why they were so close—because it was only the two of them for so long. My grandmother married and moved away to Charleston." Finn thought for a moment and grimaced, although he didn't say anything.

"What?" Eve prompted.

"I was just thinking about something Helena said to me at my wedding. Something about how she was happy I was marrying my true love even though she'd lost her chance. I've never really thought about it until now."

I thought of the album cover, remembering how the Szarka sisters looked like models. "They were so beautiful. I can't imagine it would have been that difficult to find husbands."

"I think my grandparents tried by introducing them to friends and business associates as soon as they arrived in Charleston. But Helena and Bernadett were more interested in making a new home on Edisto and getting involved in their church and causes."

"As if they were both atoning for past sins," I said, mimicking Eve's words but seeing Bernadett's sparse room. And the locked door inside the armoire.

Finn took a sip of his coffee, the unusual color of his eyes shifting like that of the river at dusk. "I think she sees herself in you, too. Gigi told me about you playing Debussy."

I closed my eyes, hoping she hadn't replayed the entire scene blow by blow.

"Did you play 'Clair de Lune'?" Eve asked. "You always made me cry when you played that."

I looked up at her, surprised at her admission. "Yes. Debussy's always been one of my favorite composers."

"Next to Chopin," she added, taking a sip of her water.

I stared hard at her. "How did you know that?"

It was her turn to look surprised. "Because you're my sister."

The relationship between sisters is a little piece of heaven and hell. But we share the same soul. Helena's words came back to me like a cold blast of wind, making me shift uncomfortably in my seat.

I realized that Finn was watching us with interest, and I quickly looked at my watch. "We need to be going. Where did you say Glen is picking you up?"

"Here." She turned her head to look out the large front window. "Actually, I think that's him at the curb."

Finn took charge of Eve's wheelchair while I cleared the table, then followed them out onto the sidewalk. Glen jumped out of the car, then ran around to the passenger side.

"I would have come inside, but I'm parked illegally."

He approached Finn and the two men shook hands. Finn was taller, and while both were of a similar slim build, Finn's shoulders were broader, his stance more powerful-looking despite Glen's military bearing. I stopped myself, wondering why I was comparing the two.

Glen lifted Eve out of the chair and settled her in the car while Finn stored the chair in the trunk.

"You didn't have to do that," Glen said to Finn, his words sounding more aggressive than I think he wanted them to.

"It's no problem. You needed to take care of your wife."

Glen's eyes narrowed almost imperceptibly.

Finn continued speaking as if he hadn't noticed. "And the baby, of course. You must be really excited about becoming a father. It's one of the best things in a man's life. Just be prepared for your wife and child to occupy all your spare time and energy."

"I'm prepared to deal with the demands of fatherhood," Glen said stiffly. "I'm thinking it'll all be good."

Finn nodded. "Absolutely. We all think that. But I know some men who were knocked off their feet when the realization set in, that's all. Me, too. But you'll find that there's nothing else in the world more important than your baby and wife—so much so that you really won't miss the other stuff."

Glen was actively frowning now. "I'm not sure I get your meaning, sir. But I'll tell you now that I'm prepared to be a good father to my baby."

Finn's eyebrows rose.

"And a good husband to my wife," Glen added, flushing.

Finn smiled, then waved at Eve. "It was good seeing you both. Enjoy the rest of your day."

Finn stood next to me as their car pulled away from the curb and headed down the street. Before I could stop myself, I blurted out, "Why did you do that?"

He didn't pretend not to know what I was talking about. "I just keep remembering how he came out to Luna Point to check on you on his day off, leaving his wife at home. I thought that he needed a little reminding of his priorities."

"He doesn't need you or anybody else to remind him. He's got a lot on his plate—going to school while working full-time, a wife in a wheelchair, a baby on the way, and a complicated pregnancy—" I stopped, realizing I'd said too much.

I began walking quickly. "I've got to get to work. I've been gone too long as it is."

He caught up to me in two quick strides, easily keeping up despite my almost-jogging pace. "What's complicated about the pregnancy?"

"Forget I said anything. It has nothing to do with you."

I kept walking, but his hand grabbed my elbow, making me stop. His face was very close to mine, his unusual gray eyes darkening, but I didn't step back. It took him a moment to speak, as if he were discarding the first thoughts that came to mind. "Because you're working two jobs for me, and Helena and Gigi have come to depend on you. I figure somebody needs to be looking out for you, too."

I bit my lip, trying to stifle the sudden urge to cry. Not since my father's death had anybody cared enough to look after me. "I've got to get back to work," I said.

Neither one of us moved, but he didn't look away. "Maybe Eve's right. What are you trying to atone for?"

We continued staring at each other while passersby walked around us. Finally, I pulled away and began walking quickly again toward the office, hoping he wouldn't follow me. And half hoping he would.

CHAPTER 21

Finn was still in his office when I turned off my computer and slipped away from my desk as inconspicuously as I could. I was about as eager to continue our earlier conversation as I was to run into him at his house while picking up Gigi. His last words had dogged me all afternoon like a persistent sand fly. *What are you trying to atone for?*

The housekeeper, Mrs. McKenna, answered the front door at Finn's house, followed by the clattering sound of Gigi running down the steps to greet me. After hugging me with her usual exuberance, she stepped back and I looked down at the source of all the clattering. Her small feet were encased in shiny black shoes with pink grosgrain ribbons tied in enormous bows.

Mrs. McKenna shook her head with a smile as she closed the door. "Her dance instructor told her that her old tap shoes were too small and she needed new ones."

"I've grown a whole half size!" Gigi announced jubilantly.

I hugged her back, wondering how long it had taken her. "Congratulations!" I said, admiring the shoes. "But why are you wearing them in the house?"

"That's the first thing I asked," Mrs. McKenna replied good-naturedly. "Seeing as how I'm the one in charge of polishing the floors."

Gigi grabbed my hand and began tugging me toward the stairs. "Daddy said I needed to pack, but I've already filled one suitcase and I'm wondering if I need another."

My eyes met Mrs. McKenna's. The older woman shrugged. "I offered to help, but she's very independent." We shared a smile before I turned back toward the stairs to run after Gigi, who'd already made it to the top.

A large suitcase lay open on her bedroom floor. From what I could see, there were a number of bathing suits, shoes, shorts, skirts, and sundresses—mostly pink—haphazardly thrown inside. Most of her dresser drawers, with a few exceptions, were pulled open, with various items of clothing hanging out of them. Her closet door was ajar, but I resisted the temptation to look inside, knowing I'd be compelled to clean it up.

I stood surveying the mess with my hands on my hips. "Your daddy did say three days, right? Not three weeks?"

"Silly!" she said, tossing a ball of pink socks at me. "I just like to make sure I have everything I need. If we go to the beach in the morning and then in the afternoon, I'll need two different bathing suits because putting on a cold, wet one is gross, and then I'll need clothes to wear in the afternoon, and if we go somewhere at night—like the movies or something—I might need something else, and every outfit has to have a pair of shoes. I'm pretty sure I need everything in there."

I peered at the pile of shoes that lay next to the full suitcase. "Maybe I can help you start over from the beginning," I said, calculating how much time I'd have before Finn got home.

She collapsed in a heap on the floor, making me wonder if she should be taking drama lessons on top of dance and piano. "All right," she said with an exaggerated sigh.

I sat down on the carpet next to the suitcase and began taking everything out. "Let's start with a nightgown and your underclothes for four days—I always like to add an extra day's worth of clothes just in case."

I lifted out what appeared to be a dance recital costume and held it up to Gigi. "Why did you pack this?"

"To show Aunt Helena. She missed my last recital."

I looked down at the yellow and purple tutu with a sequined heart on the bodice, fluffy purple feathers on the shoulder straps. The seams were uneven, the sequins were missing in spots where they'd easily fallen off, and the hem at the leg holes was half pulled out.

"I'm sure your daddy has a photo of you wearing this. And if not, I'll take one. It's a lot easier packing a picture than a bulky costume."

Gigi jumped up. "He's got one on the table next to his bed. I'll go get it now."

"Not yet," I said, holding her back. "Let's focus on sorting through this now, and when we're done you can go get it."

I pulled out another stack of clothes, this batch including a purple velvet dress, and set it on the floor next to the tutu. "Sit down, sweetheart. This might take a while."

With another sigh, she sat down cross-legged next to me and began to sort through enough clothes to get her through until the end of the year.

She looked horrified as I packed the last pairs of shoes inside the suitcase. "Only three?"

"Actually four, if you count your tap shoes."

"I was thinking of leaving them here. They'll probably give Aunt Helena one of her headaches."

I made a mental note to throw them in the suitcase when Gigi wasn't looking—assuming I could pry them from her feet.

Her face became very serious. "What about Aunt Bernadett's basket?"

"It's still under your bed?"

She nodded.

"Can I see it?"

Pulling herself up to her knees, she shuffled over to her bed, then crawled halfway under before she started scooting backward. I moved toward the bed and tugged on her ankles to help her out.

"Thanks," she said, blowing rug fuzz from her lips.

We both looked down at the sweetgrass basket on the floor by the bed. It was an escape hatch with a lid, the small knob at the top shaped like an acorn. *A secret keeper.* I lifted the basket onto the bed, surprised at how light it was.

"You didn't peek inside even once?"

She shook her head. "No, ma'am. I'm afraid of ghosts."

I looked at her sharply. "Ghosts?"

"If Aunt Bernadett was mad at me for looking into her basket, I didn't want her to come back to let me know."

I diplomatically didn't point out that exploring Bernadett's room would probably have been enough to arouse an angry spirit.

We sat on the bed with the basket between us. I rubbed my palms on my skirt. "Okay, then. We're looking for sheet music because Helena asked us to. If that's not what's in here, we'll put it all back under Bernadett's bed like it never left. All right?"

She nodded vigorously, as somebody who'd just dumped a problem onto somebody else's shoulders.

I leaned over and very slowly lifted the lid, using it to shield the contents just in case there was something Gigi shouldn't see. I hesitated, feeling like Pandora opening her forbidden box and letting loose all the evil in the world. With a deep breath, I looked inside, then placed the lid on the bed beside me.

"Is it music?" she asked, her eyes wide.

I shook my head. "No, it's not." I picked up the lid from the bed, prepared to put it back on the basket, but her hand stopped me.

"Don't you think we should at least see what's there? Even if it's not music, there might be something in there that Aunt Helena would like to have. Something that might remind her of Aunt Bernadett and make her happy again."

I couldn't imagine the old woman having ever been happy, but I understood Gigi's point. Still, I wasn't completely convinced. "Maybe we should give Helena the basket so she can go through it on her own."

Gigi's pale eyebrows knitted together. "But what if there's something that might not be nice? Like a letter to their other sister saying that Bernadett didn't like Helena or something like that that could hurt her feelings and make Aunt Helena feel even more sad? Wouldn't it be better if we looked through the stuff first to make sure none of it hurts her feelings?"

I chewed on my lip, weighing what I thought were Gigi's legitimate concerns with what could be considered an invasion of privacy. I wanted to think of Helena as strong enough to withstand anything, good or bad, but all I could think about was how Finn had found her after Bernadett's death, unwilling to go on living. What if something in this basket would send her back to that dark place? Or what if something inside would bring her peace?

"All right," I said. "We'll look through it first. And if we don't find anything objectionable, I want you to come straight with Aunt Helena and tell her how you came to find the basket."

Her shoulders curled forward, making her appear even smaller than she was. "Yes, ma'am," she said quietly.

Slowly, I moved aside the lid again and we both stared inside.

"What's that?" she asked.

"I'm not sure," I said, peering closely at the contents. The bottom of the basket was filled with what appeared to be old photographs and a single book. Nestled on top was a small silver box, so tarnished it was almost black. Four tiny legs protruded from the bottom, and a small clasp held the hinged lid closed. I lifted it out and held it in my open hands for us both to see.

"It looks like there's writing on the top," Gigi said, leaning close enough that I could smell her shampoo.

"Do you have a tissue?"

She jumped up, then quickly returned from the adjoining bathroom, a handful of tissues in her hand.

Folding them into a fat square, I began rubbing. When I was done, I sat back in disappointment, staring at the engraved words.

Az Isteni Megváltó Leányai

"What does it say?" Gigi asked.

"It's in Hungarian, I think." Gingerly using my thumbnail, I flicked open the lid.

I felt Gigi's warm breath on my cheek as she leaned over to see inside the box. "Is it a necklace?"

I lifted up the black onyx beads, a gold crucifix dangling from the end of the circle. "It's a rosary. Have you never seen one before?"

"Not this one. But Aunt Bernadett used to walk around with a red one all the time saying prayers."

"Was she Catholic?"

Gigi shrugged, reminding me that I was talking to a ten-year-old. "I don't know. She and Aunt Helena would go to church with us when we were visiting, but I don't think it was their church because they always went to another church for Christmas and Easter."

I remembered the two women bringing Finn to the Edisto Presbyterian Church when we were children, although the Catholic mission church of St. Frederick and St. Stephen was just down the road. I could well imagine Finn's father demanding his son be taken to the Presbyterian church, regardless of the aunts' faith.

I carefully replaced the heavy beads in the silver box and latched the lid. The basket seemed laced with a sense of desolation, either projected from my own emotions or simply because of the fact that it had been forgotten under the bed of a dead woman.

Placing the box next to me, I reached inside the basket and pulled out a small, white, leather-bound book.

"It looks like a Bible," Gigi said in a hushed voice, as if she, too, breathed in the sad air that rose from the basket like dust from an old tomb.

"It is," I said, holding it up where we could both read the words HOLY BIBLE embossed on the front in gold. "At least it's in English."

I opened up the front cover and paused at the inscription inside, written in a beautiful slanted cursive.

To my sister Bernadett on the occasion of my wedding,
October 12, 1940
Magda Katherina Beaufain

"And so is the inscription," I added, although mostly for my benefit, as Gigi had already started peering into the basket again. "I wonder if Bernadett was a bridesmaid. Maybe this is what she carried during the ceremony."

I glanced up to see Gigi with both hands inside the basket. "Hang on," I said, wanting her to wait so we didn't miss anything. With a reluctant sigh, she sat back while I continued to examine the Bible. The spine was worn and creased, the gold that had once edged the pages long disintegrated, leaving only flecks. Two ribbon bookmarks, a red and a black one, were stuck inside a single page. I carefully tugged on them, then slid my finger inside the pages where they'd been and opened the Bible to the book of Matthew. In black ink, a single verse had been underlined.

> In Rama was there a voice heard, lamentation, and weeping, and great mourning, Rachel weeping for her children, and would not be comforted, because they are no more.

A cold chill enveloped me as I read the words. I thumbed through the Bible, noticing creased pages and other signs of wear, but nowhere else did I find a verse that had been marked.

"Can we see the rest now?" Gigi asked impatiently.

I'd almost forgotten she was there. The Bible verse rested heavily on my heart, its meaning unclear but its importance signified by the heavy black marks under each word.

"Sure," I said, laying the Bible next to the silver box. Together we looked at the loose photographs in no apparent order or importance. But I could see they were old, as all were in black-and-white, many with the scalloped edges that can be found only on older photographs.

There were about thirty photographs, and Gigi and I carefully lifted them one by one from the basket and spread them over the top of the bed.

"This looks like the ladies in the picture Aunt Helena gave to Daddy for his birthday."

I picked up the photo Gigi indicated. "I think you're right. This might be Magda's wedding—she was the oldest sister."

"Older than Aunt Helena?" Her mouth formed a perfect O of astonishment.

"We were all young once, Gigi."

We examined what appeared to be a wedding photo, considering the bouquets the women were holding and the small veil on the hat of the tall middle woman. "They're all really pretty. I like their costumes," Gigi said.

I smiled at her assessment. "They are very beautiful. But those aren't costumes—that's how women dressed in the 1930s and early forties."

All of the women were dressed in suits—Magda's the only one in white—with exaggerated shoulders and butterfly sleeves, and tight bodices that emphasized their tiny waists. The skirts came to below their knees, and their feet were covered in T-strapped heels. The men wore black tails with white waistcoats and striped trousers, a single white carnation blossoming on their lapels.

There were several pictures of the wedding, including photos of an older woman I assumed was the girls' mother—a kinder, gentler version of Helena—as well as a tall, dignified gentleman that could only have been Finn's grandfather. He was tall and broad shouldered, with fair hair and expressive eyes, and it was clear why Magda's head had been so easily turned.

"Who's this?"

I turned to look at the photograph Gigi held in her outstretched hand. I took it and gently held it as if it were a fragile butterfly. The subject was a young man leaning against a tree with one leg bent, the booted foot resting on the trunk. He wore a uniform—what could have been a gray or green jacket with a wide black belt and inch-wide strips of fabric buttoned onto each shoulder. A patch of an eagle with outstretched wings sat above the right breast pocket.

The boy—he looked too young to be called a man or to be wearing a uniform—had white-blond hair and large light eyes. His nose was crooked, as if it had been broken at least once, but it did nothing to hide the shy, sweet smile. His hair seemed lifted off his forehead, and he had a hat tucked under one arm as if he'd just swept it off to be able to feel the breeze. But the smile was all for the photographer, his eyes full of secrets.

"I don't know," I said, turning the photograph over in my hand. Written in a feminine cursive with a pencil across the back were the words *Gunter Richter.* I turned it around again to stare in the boy's face and said the name out loud. "Gunter Richter."

"That's a funny name. Is it Hungarian?"

I shook my head. "I'm not sure. I don't think so. It sounds more German to me." I studied the uniform, wishing I could place it.

The grandfather clock from downstairs chimed. I glanced at my watch, appalled to see how late it was. I quickly started placing everything back in the basket, wishing I'd had more time to go through all the photographs. "We've got to get on the road." I placed the lid on the basket, then went over to Gigi's suitcase and closed it easily since there was about one-third of what had been in there previously. "Let's not give Mrs. McKenna a heart attack and try to make your room look a little less like a disaster zone."

We both began darting around the room, tucking clothes into drawers and forcing them shut. All of the extra shoes I put in a neat pile in the closet and shut the door with a promise to myself that I would straighten it all properly another time.

When it all looked passable, I grabbed the suitcase. "If you could carry the basket, I think we're good to go."

"I need to go to the bathroom."

Resisting the need to sigh heavily, I put down the suitcase. "All right, but please hurry. I don't like driving over the bridge after dark."

She rushed to her connecting bathroom and slammed the door, only to open it right away. "Don't forget the photo of me in my dance recital costume. My daddy's room is at the end of the hall and the picture's on the table next to the bed."

Before I could protest, she'd slammed the door again. Feeling a little like I had when I'd entered Bernadett's room at the Edisto house, I made my way out into the hallway toward the room at the end of the hall.

Thankfully, the door was wide open and I breezed through it as if walking into Finn's bedroom was the same as walking into his office.

I'd made it only halfway inside before I stopped. The middle of the room was dominated by an enormous dark wood sleigh bed with a gold brocade bedspread and at least a dozen throw pillows artfully arranged on top. I assumed Mrs. McKenna had made the bed because I couldn't imagine Finn expending energy in that direction.

Like the rest of the house—with the exception of Gigi's room, which held more personality than most people I'd met—this room seemed torn right out of an interior design magazine. The furniture, fabrics, and color palette were exquisite—and completely cold. I couldn't imagine Gigi jumping on top of the bed or whipping aside the heavy draperies to hide during a game of hide-and-go-seek.

I looked up toward the ceiling, wondering what was missing, and I found myself grinning when it occurred to me. There wasn't a model airplane, paper planet, or moon-phase chart anywhere on the ceiling or any of the four walls. I couldn't help but think that their additions could only add to the beauty of the room.

My mind's eye formed a picture of Harper Beaufain Gibbes, with her perfect bone structure and elegant limbs, and I knew this was her bedroom regardless of who had slept in it before or who still did.

I heard a door shut somewhere in the house and figured Gigi must be ready. Quickly, I moved to the side of the bed, my eyes scanning the scattering of framed photographs that sat on the large round skirted table. I pulled a crimson tassel on the bedside lamp to see better and I found the costume picture immediately. But as I leaned forward to pick it up, I knocked over a simple acrylic frame that had been decorated with pink sequins. As I straightened it, I made the mistake of looking at the photograph.

It was a picture of an impossibly small Gigi in a hospital bed surrounded by nurses and doctors and Finn. All—including her father—were wearing pink head scarves and holding pink balloons with the number six printed on them. A large banner behind her bed read HAPPY 6TH BIRTHDAY, PEANUT!

Gigi wore the broad grin I'd become familiar with, and I wondered if she'd been born with such a propensity for joy or if it had been God's recompense for a childhood interrupted.

But it was Finn's image in the picture that captured my attention. Even with the silly pink head scarf, I could see his serious eyes and the tautness in his jaw. I couldn't imagine what he was going through or thinking when that photo was taken, but the fact that he wore a pink scarf over his head and willingly subjected himself to a photograph told me more about the man than I'd learned in nearly two years of working for him.

"Can I help you find something?"

I startled at the sound of Finn's voice, enough so that I shook the table and knocked over several more frames. I cringed, realizing this was the second time he'd caught me in a place I wasn't supposed to be.

I began scrambling to replace the fallen frames into their upright positions but ended up knocking more over in my nervous haste. "I'm sorry," I said. "Gigi asked me to come in here and get the photograph of her in her dance recital costume to show Helena because she'd originally packed the costume in her overflowing suitcase but there really wasn't any room for it, and I thought . . ."

"Stop," he said, and I felt his hand on my arm. "You're starting to talk like Gigi and I'm finding it a little unnerving coming from a non-ten-year-old."

I stopped, listening as one more frame fell onto the glass-topped surface. Slowly, I raised my eyes to his, surprised to see a hint of amusement in them. "Sorry," I said again.

"Please stop apologizing. That's almost as irritating as the nonstop chattering." He pried the acrylic frame from my frozen fingers and replaced it without incident on top of the table. "I don't think that was the photograph you were looking for."

I took a deep breath, trying to pretend that everything was normal and that I wasn't standing next to Finn Beaufain's bed with the man himself very close to me, his gray eyes studying me and seeing more than I wanted him to. I took a step back, bumping the table. The answering sound of falling frames told me without turning around that I had probably knocked over the rest of the pictures.

"I'm sor—" I stopped, heat rushing to my cheeks. I quickly searched for something else to say. "We weren't expecting you home."

"Obviously."

I shook my head. "That's not what I meant." I stopped for a moment, remembering the basket and the real reason why we were running behind. "I need to show you something." I hadn't quite figured out how Gigi and I were going to explain how we'd come across the basket, but he didn't have to know about it right now. I just needed to know what was written on top of the silver box, and who Gunter Richter was.

He looked alarmed. "Is it Gigi?"

"No. Not at all. It's something we found in Helena's house. We're just not sure if we should show it to Helena or not."

He glanced at the antique carriage clock that sat on the Georgian mantel of the fireplace across from the bed. "Can it wait? My plane to New York leaves in less than three hours and I haven't packed yet."

I began a hasty retreat to the door, eager to leave. "Yes. Of course. I'm sorry." The word was out before I could call it back. Our eyes met, and I knew we were both thinking about his last words to me earlier that afternoon. *What are you trying to atone for?*

"Have a good trip," I said, grabbing the photograph of Gigi in her costume before turning on my heel and practically running to Gigi's bedroom.

On the way to North Charleston to pick up a few days' worth of clothes and my toothbrush and during the forty-five-minute drive out to Edisto, Gigi kept up a constant chatter, including two quick phone calls to her father on my cell phone. I listened to her babble with only half an ear, murmuring a "yes" or a "no" at the appropriate times, my mind occupied with the images of a serious Charleston businessman wearing a pink scarf on his head and of a young soldier with a smile full of secrets.

CHAPTER 22

Helena

I dreamed that I was walking across the beautiful Chain Bridge over the Danube, the four crouching stone lions that guarded the bridge seeming to watch me. I could feel the chill, damp air and hear the sounds from the boats beneath. I was like a ghost, part of the scene but unable to interact with the world around me. I wondered if death would be like this, moving endlessly in a shadow world, searching for what would not be found. Or if my dream merely echoed my life.

I looked down into the murky brown of the river and watched as a single drop of water became a gushing torrent of bright blue until the entire river had turned the color of his eyes. I wanted to clap my ghost hands in delight, to shout that Strauss had not been wrong after all. But someone called my name, and I looked up, hoping and praying it would be him, finally coming for me, his last words still lingering in the shriveled organ that had once been my heart. *I will come back for you.*

Instead I saw the white ceiling of my room and Nurse Kester leaning over my bed, and for a brief moment I imagined her eyes were a deep, bright blue.

"Are you all right?" she asked, a worried frown wrinkling her face. "You were talking in your sleep."

"What did I say?" I asked, although I already knew.

"I'm not sure. It wasn't in English."

I closed my eyes and turned to face the wall. "I wish to go back to sleep now."

The infernal woman would not be deterred. "You need to eat your breakfast. And Eleanor and Gigi arrived last night after you retired. They can't wait to see you."

I wanted to laugh at her exaggeration. At least half of what she said was true. I turned over, trying to give her my most put-out expression, but was secretly pleased that they were there. I had been looking forward to having the two of them to myself for three days. Gigi, because she filled the old house with joy and laughter and made my old bones move easier. And Eleanor because of the way she had played the Debussy piece.

It had not been horrible. It had been brilliant, despite the obvious fact that she was unprepared and not properly trained. She had played the way I once had, before my fingers had betrayed me and my heart had forgotten the music. But it went beyond the notes and the unschooled and rusty mechanics. The poignancy of her musical expression had told me something about her, something she was not even aware of. Yet still, she was holding something back, something precious to her that she did not want to share. It was the one thing that separated good musicians from great musicians.

I sighed heavily. "I suppose I should eat, then, to build up my endurance. They are here through Sunday." She helped sit me up, propping pillows behind my back. "I am tired of this room and this house. I think it is time that I venture out."

The nurse smiled. "I think you're ready—although we'll have to take it easy. It hasn't been that long since you were in the hospital."

I waved my hand, dismissing her concern. "I am fine. I think I will ask Eleanor to take me on a drive. Perhaps to the beach."

I stared with what I hoped was my most imperious look. At least she knew me well enough not to continue with her efforts to dissuade me. Instead she said, "I'm sure Eleanor will enjoy that."

I looked at her sharply to see if she meant it, but her expression showed bland innocence. "I am hungry now. Please tell me my breakfast is ready."

The nurse moved to the door. "Yes, of course. I'll be right back. It's your favorite—oatmeal."

I was in the middle of voicing my disapproval when she turned back.

"I almost forgot. You had a visitor yesterday while you were napping. It slipped my mind until this morning. Actually, he was here to see Bernadett, but when I told him she had passed, he asked to speak with another member of the family."

My neck stiffened. "Who was it?"

"He said his name was Jacob Isaacson. But he left a card." She reached into the pocket of her pants and pulled out a white card and handed it to me. Before I could complain about not being able to read it, she reached for my glasses on the bedside table and placed them on my nose.

Jacob B. Isaacson
Isaacson & Sons
European Fine Art, Antiques

The bottom of the card listed an Atlanta address. To hide my shaking hand, I placed the card on the bedside table, then let my hand fall to my side. "Did he say what he wanted?"

"No. But he said he was in town through the weekend. He said you could call the cell number on the card."

I waved my hand. "I am sure it is because he heard of my paintings. He wants to see if he can take advantage of an old woman. If he comes back, please tell him that they are not for sale. I hope you did not give him our unlisted number. I do not like to be disturbed."

She gave me the blank look used by those who are dependent on others for their livelihoods and meant to mask thoughts or feelings that might offend. I knew it well, having once relied on it.

"Yes, Miss Szarka. And can I send Gigi and Eleanor in?"

"I suppose so. As long as it does not delay my breakfast."

She had barely moved into the kitchen before they appeared in the doorway, Gigi's smile more authentic than Eleanor's—as if that should surprise me.

"Good morning, Aunt Helena!" A yellow shopping bag flopped against Gigi's leg as she raced toward me to give me a hug and kiss.

Eleanor was more sedate in her approach, her smile not yet wavering. She carried three large books and a smaller one, on top of which was a small open sweetgrass basket, placing them all on the floor when she sat down. "Good morning, Miss Szarka. I hope you slept well."

I recalled my dream, and the image of the blue Danube and the pair of eyes in the same shade, and almost said yes. "No. When you get to be my age, a good sleep is an impossibility. Something is always hurting and it is too much trouble to bother with changing position. Besides, something else will find a way to start hurting, so what is the point?"

Gigi moved to the other side of the bed so Nurse Kester could place my meal tray on my lap.

"Yum, oatmeal," Eleanor said, giving an exaggerated sniff. "Your favorite."

I frowned at her, but before I could ask her to feed me, she said, "If you're strong enough to feed yourself, then Nurse Kester thinks you're strong enough to go for a drive to the beach. Or a walk to the dock. Or even a visit to church. Your pick."

Nurse Kester tucked a napkin into the neck of my nightgown and then left the room, walking faster than necessary. With as much dignity as I could, I picked up the spoon and took a bite. Glancing at Gigi, I asked, "What is in the bag?"

"Yesterday was my four-year-remission birthday. So Daddy bought me this." She turned the bag upside down and something that resembled pink stuffed animals with ribbons tumbled onto the bedclothes. "It's a mobile of the planets! They're soft and smushy and pink, so Daddy knew it had to be mine, and we both agreed that my room at home had plenty enough pink in it, so we thought that maybe we could hang it in my room here to make it more like home when I come to stay with you."

I nodded, then took another bite of oatmeal so that I wouldn't have to respond. I was still busy translating what she had said.

"Ellie brought you a gift, too, although it's a just-because gift and not a birthday or remission birthday or anything else. . . ."

Eleanor retrieved the basket, stood, and put a soft hand on Gigi's arm. As she placed the basket on the night table, she said, "We spotted this at the sweetgrass stand on Highway One-seventy-four and thought you might like it to put your glasses and watch in while you sleep."

"It's called Dreams of Rivers. That's what the basket-maker lady told us." Gigi gently lifted the glasses from my nose and placed them in the basket along with a pen and notepad and a small tube of hand lotion I kept by the bed. I thought she was done when she spotted the business card and stuck it inside, too, where it disappeared into the bottom of the basket. "Perfect!" she said.

"The name of it made me think of you," Eleanor said quietly.

Our eyes met, and I wanted to ask her how she had known, how she had seen the two rivers that always flowed through my dreams. But I suppose I already knew, had probably known since I had first heard her playing the piano. She reminded me of Bernadett in many ways, but she reminded me of myself even more. Perhaps my constant irritation with her was simply directed at a younger version of myself intent on making the same mistakes.

"Thank you," I said. "It is lovely. And so useful, too," I added for Gigi's benefit. I glanced at Eleanor. "Have you brought books to read to me?"

She smiled tightly as she picked up the three larger books she'd set on the floor. "Actually, I think these were for Bernadett, but I thought I'd show them to you first and you can decide if we want to keep them or not."

The hair rose on my arms, as if someone had just walked over my grave. "How do you know they were for her?" I asked, concentrating on my oatmeal, unable to see the titles on the spines because Gigi had removed my glasses.

"I found the first book, *The Art of Origami*, in the sunroom and saw that it was long overdue. I threw it in the back of my car to return it but kept forgetting to ask you, so instead I went to renew it. While I was there, the librarian told me that Bernadett had requested an interlibrary loan and that the books were still waiting for her. So I brought them home, just in case you were interested in them, too. If you don't want any of these books, I'd be more than happy to take another trip to the library tomorrow and return them and pick up something else."

She dropped the origami book on the bench, then held up two more books, the front covers facing me, and I had to squint to see the words. "What are their titles?" I asked, almost sick with impatience, as if she held a communication from beyond the grave from my sister. I dropped my spoon in the bowl and pushed it away from me.

"*Great Art of the Eighteenth and Nineteenth Centuries* and *The Dutch Masters*." She wrinkled her nose. "Probably not great reading-out-loud material."

I stared at the books as time seemed to stop and I was back in our kitchen in Budapest, at the time when we did not have money for heated water. I sat in a cold tin washtub next to the oven as my mother poured icy-cold water over my head. I remembered that now, remembered it because Eleanor's words cut into my flesh in much the same way.

The girl was watching me closely, as if to measure my reaction. I kept my face calm as I flicked my hand in the air. "Bernadett always had the oddest reading tastes. I suppose I should keep them since you went to all that trouble. I might enjoy looking at the pictures."

If she was disappointed by my reaction, she did not say anything. Instead, she placed the books on the bench at the foot of the bed. "Just in case you *did* need reading material, I brought another book for you, too." She reached down to the floor again and held up a paperback novel, a man with a woman wearing a gown from a previous century wrapped in a passionate embrace on the cover. "I saw that you already had several books by this author, so I thought you might enjoy her latest."

Her eyes seemed to challenge me to deny that I knew anything about those books, but I would not give her the satisfaction of telling her that I had been embarrassed to let my sister know what I was reading—my good and dutiful sister who volunteered at church and taught Sunday school. But I had once known the girl with the romantic heart and sweet singing voice who loved a pretty pair of shoes as much as she loved a God she thought she knew. I suppose that the masks we choose to wear can sometimes become permanent if we are not careful.

"How kind," I said coolly. "Unfortunately, the print in those books is usually too small for me to read, so you will have to read it out loud to me. I hope that certain scenes will not cause you too much embarrassment. Especially since you are an unmarried woman."

"Not at all," she said, her tone matching mine. "You'll just have to let me know when you want me to skip over certain parts, seeing as how you're also an unmarried woman." She smiled sweetly and placed the novel on top of the art books.

Touché. It took all of my strength not to give in to the temptation to throw my head back and laugh. I did not want her to know that her words had reached their target, and besides, it would have hurt my neck too much.

"I want you to play for me again today. Perhaps after Gigi's lesson. After supper I would like to go for a drive with the windows down. And then after we put Gigi to bed, we can sit in the sunroom and you can read to me."

Eleanor slapped her palms against the tops of her legs. "Glad to see you have your day planned. That's a good sign."

I looked up at her sharply. "A good sign of what? That I'm not planning on dying today?"

She flushed, then sent a glance over to Gigi, who was busy studying the origami book. "No. Of course not. I meant it's a good sign that you want to get out and do things. That means you're moving forward."

"And you know so much about that."

She stood very still, her eyes flashing. "You know nothing about me. Please don't pretend that you do, and just let me do my job."

"I know a lot more than you would like to think. You and I are not that different. Except I have had more years on this earth to dwell on my mistakes. And you are still young enough to wrongly believe that your mistakes are permanent."

Her chest rose and fell in an attempt to dispel her anger, or maybe she was simply trying to decide who would get in the last word or if she should just leave. I was not surprised when she chose the former.

"Those art books—did you know that Bernadett went all the way to the Mount Pleasant Library and ordered them to be sent there? And she left instructions that they would be held for her until she came to collect them—that under no circumstances should anybody call this house to let her know they were in, because I'm assuming she didn't want you to know about them. I can't imagine why she'd be so secretive. Can you?"

Our eyes remained locked for a long moment. "It is of no consequence, is it? Bernadett is dead. Her wishes need no longer be understood."

Her expression softened. "Maybe Finn should know. Maybe Bernadett had unfinished business that should be taken care of."

Her words lacked malice, which made it clear to me that she was more concerned about my dead sister and her legacy than about shining a light into the dark corners of my past.

"Do not concern Finn with such trivial matters. He has plenty to keep him busy." I indicated sweet Gigi, praying that for once God would forgive me.

Eleanor nodded. "All right. I'll go tell Nurse Kester that you're finished with your breakfast, then start with Gigi's piano lesson."

"I would like to hear Mendelssohn. I am especially partial to his *Songs Without Words*."

Eleanor's eyes lit with interest. "Are you familiar with the Venetian gondola songs?"

"Not really. I never played them. My mother considered them too foreign."

"Good. Then those are the ones I'll play. Maybe that way you'll be less critical." Eleanor reached for Gigi's hand and began walking out of the room.

I waited until they were both out of sight before I allowed myself to smile.

Eleanor

"I am more than capable of driving my own car." Helena stood by the side of her Cadillac, stamping her cane into the sandy ground.

Nurse Kester had already gone home and Nurse Weber hadn't yet arrived, so I had no one except Gigi to help me coerce the old woman into the passenger seat of the Volvo. And it was a good thing that Gigi was there, or I might have resorted to foul language or just thrown my hands in the air and stormed into the house. It was startling to realize how much the presence of a child could make adults act more like adults.

"Aunt Helena, you get to sit up front. And the seats have air conditioners or heaters for your bottom in case you're hot or cold." Gigi smiled encouragingly up at her great-great-aunt but was rewarded with only a softening of the old lady's frown.

"I would like to drive. I always have and see no reason why I should stop now. Besides, I have more years of experience than Eleanor." She looked at me smugly, as if daring me to argue that point.

I refused to take this on a personal level—I didn't have the energy. So I tried another tactic. "I already called Finn and he said absolutely not. Especially not with Gigi in the car."

Helena stayed where she was, her hand tightly grasping the top of her cane. "He is not here. And he will not know unless somebody tells him."

I resisted the impulse to roll my eyes. "I know you didn't just ask Gigi and me to lie to her father." I took a step toward her, an idea forming in my head as I recalled her sneaking second helpings of cake and ice cream at Finn's birthday party, away from the watchful eyes of her nurse. "Let's compromise. We'll take the Cadillac, but I'll drive. And after we drive to wherever you want to go, we'll stop by Island Video and Ice Cream for a treat. We'll eat it there so Nurse Weber will have no idea what you've been up to."

A bright gleam formed in her eyes. "I suppose that will work. But next time, I drive."

I didn't say anything as I led her around to the passenger side, then helped her in. Gigi climbed into the enormous backseat and buckled her seat belt.

I started the engine, then turned to Helena. "Where to?"

"To see Magda."

I looked at her closely, wondering if I had heard her correctly. "Your sister Magda?"

"Do you know of another? Of course my sister."

I continued to stare at her, needing more direction.

She looked at me with exasperation. "I am not suggesting we go ghost hunting, or that I have become unhinged, if that is what you think. I would like to visit her grave."

I hid my sigh of relief as I put the car in drive. I drove slowly down the long driveway, admiring the way the late-afternoon sun wove through the branches of the pecan trees and shot arcs of light through to Steamboat Creek. "I wasn't aware she was buried on Edisto."

"She loved it here, even though she lived in Charleston. That is why she requested to be buried here. Finn's father had a box of Hungarian soil shipped to us here to be buried with her."

I paused at the end of the drive onto Steamboat Landing Road. "At the Catholic church?"

"No. She is at the Presbyterian cemetery. Magda converted when she married Finn's grandfather. I am just glad our mother was not there to witness it. She was very Catholic and wanted at least one of her daughters to be a nun."

"But you and Bernadett remained Catholic?"

She twisted in her seat to look at me more closely. "Why would you assume we remained Catholic?"

I thought of the crucifix in Bernadett's room and the rosary found in the basket under her bed and knew I couldn't tell Helena about either of them. "Gigi mentioned that you and your sister would go to another church on Christmas and Easter, so I just assumed. If you'd like, I'd be happy to take you to Mass on Sunday."

"Perhaps. Although God and I have not been on good terms for a long time."

I stared straight ahead through the windshield, unwilling to dig any deeper. I was here as an employee and not as a confidante and friend. Borrowing her darkness would not lighten my own.

I stopped at the intersection with Highway 174 and then turned right. "I remember you and Bernadett at the Presbyterian church with Finn when we were children. We were always late and had to sit in the back because Eve took too long getting dressed, but the three of you were in the front pew without fail."

Helena actually chuckled, the sound so rare it startled me. "Bernadett made us get there twenty minutes early, regardless of which church we attended. Before the Catholic mission was started here on Edisto, we would have to drive all the way into Charleston to attend Mass. There are so many churches here on Edisto that I would tell her that we could just pick one, but she insisted." Her voice grew softer. "She was always very strict about doing the right thing."

We'd reached the Presbyterian church, with its bright white clapboards and steeple, the green shutters making it look like we'd accidentally stepped into New England. But the palmettos and Spanish moss were easy reminders of where we were.

The church was deserted as I parked beside the cemetery and helped Helena out of the car. I knew she wouldn't ask, so I took her elbow and pretended that she wasn't leaning on me as heavily as she was. She had her cane, but it seemed to me that she might need a walker. I would not, under any circumstances, be the one to suggest it to her.

She was unusually subdued as she indicated our direction through the old cemetery, through the blackened tombstones and mausoleums, many of the markers leaning toward each other like gossiping old women. I knew the church building was almost two hundred years old, but the congregation and cemetery went back further than that, as evidenced by the familiar names on the ancient tombstones of the founding families of the island: Whaley, McConkey, Pope, Bailey. There were even a good number of Murrays, perhaps more prosperous branches of my own family tree.

"Is Bernadett buried near Magda?" I asked, watching as Gigi trailed her fingers along an old stone on which the writing was no longer visible. I had the brief thought that I should not have brought her here to this place of death, that I was tempting a fate that had already spared her once.

Helena paused for a moment before answering. "No," she said softly. "I have her with me."

Confused, I turned to her and then realized what she was telling me. "She was cremated?"

Helena nodded.

"Oh," I said, surprised. "I didn't think Catholics—"

"It was my decision in the end," she said, cutting off my question. "She wanted to return to Hungary. I have hopes that one day she will."

We'd stopped and I realized that we were in a section with newer graves, where the inscriptions were still legible and time had not yet painted the passage of years on them. I looked down at the marble stone and read the inscription:

IN MEMORY OF
MAGDA KATHERINA BEAUFAIN
1920–1988
BELOVED WIFE, MOTHER & SISTER

Engraved on the top of the tombstone were three beautiful tulips in different stages of blooming.

"Why the tulip?" I asked.

She gave an irritated shake of her head. "You apparently have not been reading your Hungarian history books. The tulip is the national flower of Hungary. And I am hoping you can at least determine why there are three."

I didn't dignify her comment with an answer. Instead, I said, "I do know that in Hungary the tradition is to put the last name first. But not on Magda's tombstone."

Helena shook her head. "William—Finn's grandfather—would not have allowed that. But he agreed about the tulips." She frowned. "I always bring her flowers when I visit. If tulips are not in season, I bring another flower—as long as they are red. I cannot believe that I forgot."

She seemed genuinely upset, and I put a steadying hand on her arm. "It's all right. I'll be happy to bring you back tomorrow, or I can come back by myself. Just let me know in the morning."

Helena gave me a grateful look. I didn't expect words of gratitude; her look was enough.

"Why red?" I asked.

She gave a little shrug. "Red tulips are used to symbolize Hungary more than other colors. Did you know we even have two separate words in Hungarian for different shades of red? They are considered completely different colors."

"Interesting," I said, looking up and realizing that we were alone. "Where's Gigi?" I glanced around the deserted cemetery. I was only mildly concerned, having often wandered this same cemetery with Lucy and Eve as a child. I looked for a flash of pink amid the dark green and brown of the cemetery foliage, and when I didn't see any I called her name.

Her response came from a distance, but I knew where she'd gone. It was a place where all curious Edisto children found themselves at one time or another. I looked at Helena. "Are you okay to walk a little more? Otherwise, I can take you back to the car and turn the air conditioner on while I go get Gigi."

She gave me a haughty glance as her answer, and I took hold of her arm again. We made our way to the old section of the cemetery behind the church, where a large stone mausoleum sat nestled between an iron fence and thick green foliage.

The name J. B. LEGARE was set in bold-lettered relief above the doorless opening. I knew the missing door was part of an island legend, a legend about how one of the crypt's internees had been mistakenly buried alive and found on the floor inside the door years later when the crypt was reopened for another burial. Afterward, the door wouldn't stay closed, so it had simply been removed. I'd be lying if I said I hadn't prowled the cemetery at night with Lucy and Eve to see if I could hear ghostly moans. But I had no intention of mentioning any of that to an impressionable Gigi.

"Gigi?" I called again.

Her head popped out of the opening. "There's a mommy and a daddy and a little boy in here, and the little boy was only six years old when he died. His parents must have been very sad."

She said this matter-of-factly, as if her expression of grief had nothing to do with her at all.

I looked at the dates on the three headstones that were part of the far wall of the crypt. "His mother died when he was three, and then his father died two years after he did. How very tragic."

"Daddy says that happened a lot a long time ago when they didn't have medicines or shots or clean hands. Or chemotherapy," she added cheerfully, the long word slipping so easily from her young mouth.

"They say the father died of a broken heart," Helena said.

"Do they have medicine for that now?" Gigi asked, her upturned eyes reflecting the dappled light.

"No," answered Helena. "I do not think they will ever find a cure. Perhaps time. But I have always thought that those who did not have long to grieve were the fortunate ones."

I thought of the young soldier with the blond hair and the enigmatic smile. "Have you ever been in love?"

Her gaze remained focused on the stone pediment. "Yes. Once. A very long time ago."

"Did you get married?" Gigi asked with the enthusiasm of one who sees weddings only as an occasion to wear a long, beautiful white gown.

"No. We planned to marry after the war."

I held her arm tighter, feeling her wilt like a tulip in the heat.

"And you, Eleanor. Have you ever truly been in love?"

I thought of Glen and all the feelings I had ever had for him, but I was no longer sure of their label. "I don't know," I said, looking away.

"Things do not always work out as we have planned, do they? Sometimes the hardest thing is not to just survive the grief, but to step around it and move on. It helps if your suitcases are not so full." She took a deep breath. "I am ready for my ice cream now."

She pulled away from me and began her slow progress back to the car. I stayed where I was, watching her and the small figure of Gigi staying close, wondering if Helena had been talking about herself or about me.

I followed them out of the cemetery as the setting sun sent shadow arms between the stones, embracing those who no longer had the choice to move on.

CHAPTER 23

Eleanor

I sat at my desk, occasionally glancing up to see if Finn was off the phone or away from his computer, or to see any movement away from either that would indicate that he wasn't actually working and I could interrupt. The tarnished silver box that Gigi and I had found in the sweetgrass basket nearly three weeks before sat in the bottom of my purse wrapped in a dish-cloth. The fact that it was hidden from view did nothing to make me forget that it was there.

Because there'd been no music found in the basket, Gigi had returned it to where she'd found it, just as we'd agreed. But the image of the soldier's face haunted me, and I could not forget him. Nor could I forget my conversation with Helena in the cemetery about love and grief, and I remembered something she'd said to me when we'd first met. *Have you ever known grieving that ends only when your own heart stops beating?*

I had thought at the time that she was speaking only about Bernadett, but now I wasn't so sure. I had felt the frailness of her bones under my fingers and seen the paleness of her skin as we'd walked in the cemetery, and I knew that whatever the items in the basket might mean, she was not yet strong enough to see them.

But, true to form, I couldn't let it go. For weeks I had tossed and turned at night, seeing the boy's face and recalling the Bible verse verbatim. *In Rama was there a voice heard, lamentation, and weeping, and great mourning, Rachel weeping for her children, and would not be comforted, because they are no more.*

I'd wake up, drenched in sweat, imagining the old Gullah woman sitting in the dark watching me, watching and waiting for me to understand something that was as evasive as capturing moonlight in my hand.

Finally, Finn stood and walked over to his coffeemaker, but just as I started to stand, his secretary, Kay, also stood, with a stack of papers, and entered his office after a brief knock. She sent me a smug look before closing the door behind her.

The phone on my desk rang and I picked it up.

"It's me, Lucy. Do you have plans for lunch?"

"No, but I have work—"

"No excuses, Eleanor. You've avoided me long enough. We're going to Fast and French. I'll meet you out front at noon."

I took a deep breath, knowing she would come in and drag me out if I stood her up. "Sure. See you then."

"And you might want a little heads-up. The ex–Mrs. Beaufain just stormed the building. She should be hitting your desk at about t minus five seconds. She doesn't look happy. Good luck."

The phone went dead. I looked up at the commotion in the reception area as Ellen Ward, the receptionist, ran into the back-office area, trying to catch up to a fast-moving Harper Beaufain Gibbes dressed in head-to-toe navy blue Chanel. If I thought I could get away with it without being noticed, I would have taken a photo with my iPhone to show Eve for costume ideas.

But then I saw a dejected-looking Gigi trailing behind her mother, her face streaked with tears. Thinking only of the little girl, I walked quickly over to her and scooped her up in my arms. I had never held her, and although I knew she was small for her age, I was still surprised by how light she felt in my arms. She nestled her face into my neck, where I could feel each shuddering breath.

"Put her down." I recognized the voice from the only other time I'd spoken with Gigi's mother. It was one I wouldn't forget.

"No," I said without thinking. All I knew was that Gigi was now clinging to me like a baby monkey, her fingers clutching my shoulders so tightly that I knew she'd leave marks.

"How dare you? I am her mother and I am telling you to put her down."

"Harper. Always a pleasure. I don't believe you're the one in charge here."

She whipped around to stare up into the very angry eyes of her ex-husband. "She is *my* child," Harper said, her skin darkening but making her no less attractive.

"Actually," Finn said with a wry smile, "from what I recall of high school biology, she's my child, too."

It was the first time I'd seen them together, and even I had to admit that they must have once made a very beautiful couple. Just like the house in which they'd lived together, where everything seemed almost too perfect.

Finn continued, his darkening eyes belying his calm voice. "And last time I checked, I had full custody, which means I'm in charge. Why are you here, and why is Gigi upset?" He touched Gigi's head, as if to let her know he was near, but she remained clinging to me.

I wondered if Finn had called her Gigi in front of her mother on purpose.

With her lips clenched together, Harper yanked a wrinkled piece of paper from her handbag and threw it at Finn. "Because of this."

Finn unraveled the paper and stared at it with a blank expression for a few moments. "What is it?"

"It's a drawing Genevieve made for me. It's disgusting."

Finn lowered the piece of paper. "There is nothing *disgusting* about this. And please watch what you say in front of our daughter."

"She needs to hear it. She needs to learn what's appropriate and what's not, and apparently with the ragtag crew you've set up to watch her this summer, she's being exposed to unsavory things."

Harper didn't look at me, but I knew to whom she was referring.

Finn's voice deepened into something closely resembling a growl. "I'm not going to repeat myself. Watch what you say in front of Gigi, or I will throw you over my shoulder and physically remove you from the premises."

I almost laughed out loud at the mental image, but the weeping child in my arms held me back.

Harper stiffened. "You can at least tell me what that's all about," she said, indicating the drawing.

"I have no idea, except that it shows our daughter has a drawing talent we hadn't known about and that she has a very clever imagination."

Harper narrowed her eyes. "You must be joking. It's a picture of a cemetery. A *cemetery*. How would she even know about such a place?"

My throat seemed to shrink. "May I see it, please?"

I could tell that Harper was about to object, but Finn ignored her and held it up for me to see. Finn was right about Gigi's drawing talent. Although it was not true art in any sense of the word, she had an amazing eye for detail and color, and the subjects in her colored-pencil drawing were easily recognizable. But it was the subjects that I focused on simply because they were so odd.

The mausoleum we'd visited while at the Presbyterian cemetery was cleanly drawn, complete with the green forest behind it and the large, bold letters J. B. LEGARE. The walls of the structure weren't colored in a solid color like most children would have done, but in varying shades of brown.

It wasn't even the figure of the Gullah woman from the basket stand sitting in the middle of the doorway that made my heart shudder. She wore the same blue-and-white-checkered dress she'd been wearing when we stopped by her stand and bought the Dreams of Rivers basket. The woman's voluminous chest was accurately portrayed to the point where the buttons were pulling apart in the middle, where dark skin showed through the breaks in the fabric. She was holding a pretty good representation of a newly started basket, the fronds sticking out from the round bottom like the sun's rays.

It was the words written in a childish hand in blue letters across the sky that caught my attention as I read them over and over. *All good-bye ain't gone.*

My eyes met Finn's. Regardless of what he interpreted the drawing to be and my own interpretation of it, we were of like mind. Gigi had drawn this because she was ten years old and was borrowing from things she'd seen and heard in her short life. Unfortunately, she'd chosen to share it with her mother.

"Do you see what I mean?" Harper spit out. "Look at her . . ." She struggled to find a word other than "breasts." "Her chest. It's grotesque. And who taught Genevieve to speak in ungrammatical English?" Her voice rose to an even higher pitch. "And who is that woman? Certainly nobody I've introduced her to."

Something pulsed in Finn's jaw. He reached for Gigi and she slid into his arms. Looking at his ex-wife, he said, "I need you to leave now, before I say something we'll both regret. Gigi can stay with me."

Harper looked surprised, as if she'd been expecting Finn to side with her about the appropriateness of the drawing. "You're not going to punish her?"

I understood now why Finn had asked to hold the child. Otherwise, I think he might have been forced to resort to the physical removal he had threatened earlier.

"Of course not. It's a beautiful, artistic drawing, made by my daughter. I think I might even frame it and put it on my desk to look at every day. That's how much I love it. And if you can't see any of that, then you need to resign your position on the board of the Gibbes Museum of Art."

I thought Harper might actually stamp her foot. "This is my child, and I will not have her raised like a . . . a . . . a street child."

It was so absurd that if it had come from anybody else, I would have laughed.

Finn deserved an award for how calm he remained. But then I was reminded that this was his office, and all these people worked for him. He was in control, as always, and I wondered if he ever got tired of it.

With precise and deliberate words, he said, "Despite who is raising her, Gigi has become a loving, smart, charming, and polite little person, and if you'd ever take the time to get to know her instead of projecting who you'd like her to be, you'd see that."

Harper's chin shook, but ever cognizant of how things looked, she kept her voice low. "I am her mother. I *know* who my child is, and it is my job to make sure she is raised properly."

Finn's eyes turned frosty. "It's a little late to remember you're her mother."

Harper drew back as if struck, and that's when it occurred to me and apparently Finn that Gigi was listening to every word. Finn set Gigi down next to me and, after a brief pat to her head, said to Harper, "Let's continue this in private, please."

He began stalking toward his office, anticipating that Harper would follow, which, after a brief hesitation, she did. As soon as the door closed behind them, Gigi sighed, then hiccupped. I sat down at my desk and pulled her into my lap.

"I think your picture is lovely. I'd love for you to make one for me. But only if you want to."

She gave me a wobbly smile, and it hurt to know that anybody would ever wound this child with words. "What does 'grotesque' mean?"

"It means your mother doesn't recognize true art or beauty when she sees it." I stopped, forcing myself to remember that I was talking about Gigi's mother. I tucked a piece of fine white-blond hair behind her delicate ear. "Sometimes when people are unhappy but don't know why, it makes them angry, and sometimes they turn that anger on innocent people. You just have to remember that their hurtful words aren't about you at all."

Gigi rested her head on my shoulder. "Why is Mommy unhappy?"

I shook my head. "I don't know. Unfortunately, it makes it hard for her to appreciate her perfect, sweet, and talented daughter."

She lifted her head, a deep furrow between her brows. "When will she be ready to see me like that?" Her expression lacked any guile, her gray eyes wide and innocent.

I recalled the conversation on the way to the library that I'd had with my own mother, when she'd told me that it was my independence that had made her focus on Eve during our growing-up years, and not any lack on my part. I was still trying to digest it, not to forgive or explain it, but simply to excise the part of me that believed I would never be good enough.

"I don't know, sweetie. Time is a funny thing. It can take some people a whole lifetime before they realize they've been playing tug-of-war all by themselves."

She stared blankly at me.

"I'm trying to say that it takes some people a very long time to realize something they thought was true isn't true anymore. And maybe never was." I stopped, aware that I was no longer thinking about Harper.

Taking a deep breath, I asked, "The words at the top of the picture—where have you heard them before?"

She shrugged. "I don't know. Maybe the basket lady said it."

Gooseflesh erupted on my arms as I realized that I would have remembered it if I'd heard it again. "Maybe," I said, eager to stop this conversation so I wouldn't have to think of other explanations.

We both looked up to see Kay standing by the desk and holding out a wrapped candy bar. "I figure I don't really need this but thought Gigi might like it."

The little girl's eyes lit up and I gave Kay a grateful smile. Whatever misgivings or suspicions she might harbor toward me, I knew that we were in accord concerning this child.

"Thank you, Mrs. Tetley," Gigi said, already opening the wrapper.

At that moment, Finn's office door was thrown open and Harper stormed through it, heading toward my desk. Her frown softened as she regarded her daughter, who had already managed to smear chocolate over her mouth.

"Your father wants to keep you for the rest of the day and possibly tonight, too. Is that all right?" She actually looked as if she wanted Gigi to say no.

Gigi just nodded.

Harper forced a smile. "All right. Just please try and remember your manners." Bending down, she gave Gigi a kiss on the top of her head.

She turned cold eyes to me. "Finn assures me that you are more than capable of taking care of Genevieve, and although I distrust many of his instincts in other areas, on matters pertaining to our daughter I do not." She moved her gaze to Gigi, who had stopped eating and was solemnly staring up at her mother. "Just . . ." She stopped. "Please be extra careful with her."

With a brief touch to her daughter's head, she turned on her Louboutin heels and walked quickly out of the office. I stared after her, realizing something about Harper Beaufain Gibbes that she probably didn't even know about herself. She was afraid. Afraid of loving her child too much. As if she kept her at arm's length so the thought of losing her wouldn't hurt so much. I almost felt sorry for her.

"Eleanor?"

Finn stood by my desk where Kay had been. "Can I see you in my office, please? Kay can keep an eye on Gigi."

Kay was already walking toward us, her hand outstretched. "I'll take her to the kitchen to see if we can find some milk to wash down that candy bar."

"Organic, if you can find it," Finn called out to her.

He motioned for me to go ahead of him, then indicated one of the chairs opposite his desk. He remained standing. "Do you have anything pressing this afternoon?" he asked.

"No. Actually, I'm pretty caught up. I do have a lunch date with Lucy in accounting, but if you need me to watch Gigi . . ."

He shook his head. "I don't want to impose on your position here any more than I already have. But I would like to ask a favor."

I raised my eyebrows.

"Gigi needs to have more fun. Personally, I can't imagine there's too much fun in French immersion camps and the like. I was hoping that maybe you and I could take her down to Edisto this afternoon to go kayaking. She's never been. Since you grew up there, I'm assuming you know the creeks pretty well."

"Yes, of course. And I'd love to, but you only need one person to paddle a kayak. You wouldn't really need me." I wasn't sure why I was trying to talk him out of his invitation, because my heart had jumped at his first mention of kayaking.

"Well." He paused. "That's the problem. I've never been. Not once. And despite summers spent on Edisto, if you put me in a kayak and told me to paddle, you'd never see us again."

I remembered once more the lonely little boy with the paper airplanes, and despite all the reasons I could think of why I should not be spending so much time with Finn Beaufain, I couldn't make myself say no.

"I suppose I could. I left a bathing suit and shorts at the house, so I wouldn't need to go home to change first, and if it's okay with your aunt, maybe I'll spend the night since tomorrow is Saturday." I paused. "You do have a kayak, right?"

"Two. They're in the shed. They've never been used. Aunt Bernadett gave them to me on my twelfth birthday, but my father insisted that he accompany me when I went."

"Why two?"

"So I could invite friends to go with me."

I had no response to that at all.

"If they've been stored in a covered shed all these years, they should still be seaworthy. If they sink, we can just swim to shore."

He gave me that blank look again that strongly resembled his daughter's when I'd been explaining the vagaries of human nature to her. I stared at him in astonishment. "You don't know how to swim?"

"I was never given the opportunity when I was a boy, and when I got older it was too embarrassing to admit to anybody. I just stayed out of the water. Gigi took lessons when she was a baby, but we had to stop when . . ."

He didn't finish because he didn't need to.

I thought for a moment. "I'm really not comfortable going with two nonswimmers. But if I suggest bringing another experienced kayaker, we could take both kayaks."

"Do you know somebody you could ask?"

"Yes. But I'm going to have to pull some strings to get her excused from work." I smiled up at him while he stared back at me, confused.

"Lucy Coakley in accounting. I'm sure she'd love to play hooky for a day."

He was already reaching for his phone, his movements more relaxed and almost boy-like. It seemed that the little boy still lived inside the man, waiting for the right moment to reappear.

After a brief conversation with Rich Kobylt in human resources, he hung up the phone. "She'll be on her way shortly. In the meantime, I believe you wanted to speak with me?"

I remembered the silver box, still lying wrapped inside my purse, and felt a stirring of guilt. "How did you know?"

He leaned against his desk, his arms crossed over his chest. "I saw you watching me."

He said nothing more but continued to regard me with his dark gray eyes. Eager to hide from his scrutiny, I said, "I have something to show you. I'll be right back."

I grabbed the box right away but pretended to rummage under my desk for an extra moment until I composed myself. I walked calmly back to his office and placed the wrapped box on the desk in front of him.

"Gigi found it in one of the sweetgrass baskets while looking for Bernadett's sheet music."

I held my breath, praying that he wouldn't ask for specifics. I'd already told Gigi that I was going to show her father the box and that I would tell the truth about exactly *where* she'd found it if he asked.

"What is it?" he asked, slowly unwrapping it.

I released my breath. "It's a box with a rosary inside."

The cloth fell to the desk. Finn lifted the lid and looked inside briefly before examining the lid again. "This is Hungarian," he said, indicating the inscription on top.

"I figured as much. I was hoping you could tell me what it says."

He raised his eyebrows. "Why?"

I wasn't really sure except that I'd found it in the same basket with the Bible and its marked verse and the photograph of the boy soldier. I wanted to know why they were all saved together. And by whom. "Just curious, I guess."

He lowered his gaze to examine the inscription again. "Curiosity killed the cat, you know."

I reached for the box, flustered. "I'm sorry. You're right. I'm being nosy. I'll just put it back where we found it."

He held the box beyond my grasp. "Why didn't you show this to Helena? Her Hungarian is much better than mine."

His eyes stared steadily into mine, and I knew I needed to be as honest as I could. "Because she's more fragile than she'd like us to believe. There's something in her past that won't let her go. I didn't know if this would press on an old bruise or not, so I thought I'd ask you first. If you'll give it back to me, I'll go put it where I found it and forget about it."

He gave me a look that told me he didn't believe that last part any more than I did. "One of the words is 'daughters.' I have no idea what the rest is. But I could find out, if you like. Without telling Helena."

I took a deep breath, pleased at having somehow managed to solicit Finn's help without getting Gigi into trouble. "Thank you. I appreciate it."

I looked up to see Lucy walking toward us from the reception area, her forehead creased. I was glad I hadn't brought my cell phone into Finn's office with me, as I was sure she'd called me fifty times before making her way across the building.

I stood and smiled at Lucy to reassure her while I spoke to Finn. "Lucy's going to have to know that you don't know how to swim. Are you okay with that?"

A deep chuckle came from his throat, surprising me. "Should I be ashamed?"

Turning to face him, I said, "No, but your father should. And maybe even your aunt Helena. It's time we set this right."

The light appeared in his eyes, and I saw that boy on the riverbank again, tossing his paper plane high into the air, hoping to catch the wind. "Be gentle with me," he said.

My face flamed just as Lucy reached Finn's office, making her give me a wide-eyed look that was something between confusion and amusement.

As Finn explained to Lucy what he wanted to do, my mind wandered back to the rivers and creeks of my childhood, my heart lightening. Before we left the office, Finn took the silver box and rewrapped it, then placed it in his briefcase. Thoughts of the unknown engraving and its connection to a lonely, bitter woman followed me out into the Charleston sunshine.

CHAPTER 24

Eleanor

Lucy and I walked down the dock at Luna Point holding the four life jackets we'd borrowed from various Coakley relatives, including one small enough for Gigi. Finn and his daughter waited at the end of the dock next to the two kayaks, both in mint condition despite being two decades old. Finn wore shorts and dock shoes, a baseball hat and sunglasses. Gigi had on a similar outfit, but in varying shades of pink. Even her dock shoes were pink patent leather.

"That man is *fine*," Lucy said under her breath.

Despite the fact that I'd been thinking the same thing, I turned to her. "He's our *boss*. Please try and remember that. Besides, you've spent a lot of time warning me away from him."

"That's before I saw how much he loves his little girl. Any man that can love a child like that is good people."

"That's all well and good, but I'm not interested in any kind of relationship with Finn Beaufain other than boss-employee."

"Um-hmm," she said. I didn't look at her because I knew she was doing her chin-wag thing that punctuated all of her arguments.

Gigi jumped up and down when she saw us, and Finn smiled, doing nothing to lessen Lucy's original assessment. Lucy handed him the small jacket intended for Gigi and he knelt in front of his daughter to put it on her.

"Thanks again, Lucy, for doing this," he said. "I really appreciate it."

"Don't thank me, Mr. Beaufain. It's not every day I get an extra paid vacation day so I can go kayaking in Edisto. If I was talking to anybody but you, I'd say something was very wrong here." She moved closer to where Finn was trying to fasten Gigi's jacket. "Maybe you better let me do that. This is a life jacket, not a straitjacket. The clips go in the front."

Finn stepped back, his hands thrown up in surrender, surprising us with a loud laugh. Even Gigi seemed unfamiliar with such a sound coming from her father. "You're the expert here, so whatever you say."

Without looking up, Lucy said, "Eleanor, why don't you help Mr. Beaufain with his jacket?"

I stared hard at her, but she wouldn't look up at me. I waited for Finn to protest, but when he said nothing, I knew I had no choice. I picked up one of the adult life jackets and held it up. "I'm guessing you can figure out where your arms go?"

"I might," he said, grinning as he turned his back to me to slip both arms into the jacket. Facing me again, he said, "But I might need help fastening it."

My cheeks heated as I moved to stand directly in front of him, close enough that I could smell his aftershave and the scent of his skin. I resisted the urge to breathe in deeply and instead focused on tightening the straps and fastening the clips without meeting his eyes.

"Are you sure they're tight enough?" he asked.

I looked up into dark gray eyes that seemed to be laughing at me.

Without evading his gaze, I said, "If they're not, I guess we'll find out when you go overboard."

After Lucy and I put on our own jackets, we turned our attention to the kayaks and put the first one in the water. I was about to suggest that I go with Gigi when Finn said, "I'd like Gigi to go with the better swimmer, if that's okay."

"That would be me," Lucy said without any hint of the broad lie she'd just uttered. I glared at Lucy, but she just smiled innocently back at me. We were both strong swimmers, but there'd never been a race I'd allowed her to win, and I could always swim farther and longer than any of our friends.

"That settles it, then," Finn said. "Thank you, Lucy."

Lucy ignored me as she stepped into the first kayak while I held on to it.

Then I lifted Gigi to put her on the board in front of Lucy, feeling surprised again at how light she was. The little girl grinned up at me, her pink sunglasses reflecting the sun. I reached over to wipe a smear of sunscreen off her nose, then handed her her paddle. "Remember to scoop and pull just like I showed you, and Lucy likes it when you just skim the surface of the water and throw the water in her face with the paddle."

Without waiting to see Lucy's reaction, I moved up on the dock, where Finn had already placed our kayak in the water. "Our turn," he said with a broad grin, and I wondered if he and Lucy were somehow in cahoots.

"You go first," I said. "Just go slowly—step into the middle, then sit down quickly in the rear seat. Try to keep a low center of gravity so it won't rock too much."

"What happens if I rock it too much?" His voice was innocent, but he couldn't hide his boyish grin.

"Then you'll go overboard and we'll find out if I did a good enough job fastening your life jacket."

Squatting and placing a hand on the dock while I held on to the kayak, he stepped in with an athlete's grace, as if he'd done it hundreds of times before, and sat down, barely moving the kayak.

"Are you sure you haven't done this before?" I asked.

He held up three fingers. "Never. Scout's honor."

"You were a Boy Scout?"

"Just for a couple of years. Until the first camping trip and my father wouldn't allow me to go. I figured there was no point in being a Scout unless I was allowed to commune with nature."

His voice had a wistfulness to it, reminding me of the sound of the migrating birds in the fall, their mournful call always making me think they were begging to remain.

"Well," I said, settling myself into the kayak, "I suppose it's never too late to learn."

He stretched his legs out on either side of me, and I deliberately focused my attention on my paddle so I wouldn't have to think about how close they were, or how close Finn sat behind me.

"Do you need instructions on how to paddle?" I asked without turning around.

"I think I can manage," he said, giving a deep shove with his paddle, propelling us into the waters of Steamboat Creek.

"Go left," I shouted so Lucy could hear. "Let's head to Russell Creek."

I turned to watch Lucy struggling to navigate the two-person kayak as Gigi valiantly tried to help. I didn't hide my laugh as Gigi swept her paddle over the surface of the water in a near-perfect trajectory toward Lucy's head. Their kayak pulled up beside ours and Lucy shook her head, showering all of us with the water and making Gigi squeal with delight.

I felt a surge of power as Finn began paddling. "Aren't you going to help?" he asked.

Lifting my paddle out of the water and laying it across the kayak, I said, "Apparently I don't need to. Especially since Lucy's struggling to keep up."

Lucy, her hair and face drenched, was indeed struggling to keep up with our kayak. Feeling no pity for my friend, who'd rigged the seating arrangement and was responsible for the fact that Finn's legs were now pressed against mine, I shouted, "Let's race!"

She glared at me as Finn and I pulled forward, easily leaving them behind. My muscles moved beneath my skin as I dug my paddle into each side, imagining my father behind me as the wind kissed my face. I looked around me as we approached Russell Creek and slowed down, waiting for Lucy and Gigi to catch up. Nothing had changed in this corner of the world. The view from the creek—of the docks and houses and approaching marshes—had not changed; the sun still hung in the same sky. If I didn't look down to see my longer legs and the jagged scar on my finger, I could almost imagine I was thirteen years old again, racing the tide through the creeks and marshes with Eve and Lucy.

I breathed in deeply, smelling the familiar scent of the marsh, the scent that always reminded me of home. I wanted so badly to believe that I was that same thirteen-year-old girl with dreams of Juilliard who did not yet know grief.

"What are you thinking about?"

Finn's voice brought me back to the present. I looked behind me, my surprised expression reflected in his sunglasses. Still lost in my thoughts, I didn't take the time to filter my response. "My childhood. How absolutely happy I once was."

We'd both lifted our oars from the water, and we allowed ourselves to rock on the current. "And you're not anymore?"

I opened my mouth to reply, realizing that I didn't know what to say. The answer should have been easy. I considered my life over the last few months, the months since I'd met Helena and Gigi. I wasn't even sure if I'd been *unhappy* before; I just knew that something had changed.

"Yes. No. I mean, I don't know. I haven't thought about it in a very long time."

We watched as a great egret settled on the creek bank, its eyes regally surveying its domain as its ancestors had probably done for hundreds of years. Finn spoke softly, his words brushing the back of my neck. "I've found that you can't measure happiness the way you measure yards in a race. You just learn to recognize it when it arrives so you can enjoy it while it lasts."

I looked down at my hands as they gripped the paddle, my knuckles white, and wondered why his words made me so angry, why I found myself wishing someone had thought to teach them to me before my years of aimless wanting. I had a brief flash of memory, of me lying faceup on Westcott Road, while words I still did not understand were whispered in my ear. I felt unsettled, as if I'd just stepped on an escalator that had suddenly stopped.

Desperate to lighten my mood, I asked, "Did Gigi teach you that, or did you come up with it all by yourself?"

He chuckled, and I felt the rumbling in my own chest. "I figured it out because of her, but, no, the words are my own."

I wanted to see his face but was glad he couldn't see mine. Lucy and Gigi's kayak was slowly approaching, and Gigi's high voice carried like musical notes on the breeze. "Is she going to be okay?" I asked quietly, wondering where the words had come from.

"We don't know. Four years of remission is great; five years will be even better. But it can still come back at any time, even in adulthood, as the same cancer or a different one. Or not at all."

"Does she know?" I could hear Gigi's giggle as she splashed Lucy again, and then more laughter as she tried to apologize.

"Yes. She asked me and I felt I owed it to her to tell her the truth."

Their kayak pulled up alongside ours just as the giant egret spread its wide wings and flew over us, its long, yellow beak leading the way. Gigi tilted her head back and stared at it, her mouth open in awe. She watched it until it had made its way across the creek, soaring over the marsh grass until it disappeared from sight.

"Did you see that, Ellie? Wasn't it beautiful?"

I was about to tell her that I'd seen millions of egrets, so many that I barely noticed them anymore. But then I realized that she'd probably seen a few, too, but was still mesmerized by their grace and beauty.

"Yes, Gigi. It was beautiful. It's a great egret, did you know that?"

She shook her head.

"It's part of the heron family and is the biggest. They're very brave. Sometimes you can find them perched on top of alligators."

Her mouth formed a perfect O. "Really?"

I nodded. "Yep."

"And Eleanor would probably do the same thing," Lucy interjected, her face, hair, and shirt completely soaked.

"Did you fall in and not tell us?" I asked, eager to deflect where I was sure Lucy was trying to turn the conversation.

"What do you mean?" Gigi asked.

"This girl was fearless. Once, when she was mad at her sister, she hid under the kayak until Eve and her boyfriend got in—I swear Eleanor held her breath for five whole minutes, and who knows what else was swimming with her in the creek—and then she flipped it."

I felt Finn's gaze on me, but I didn't look behind me.

"I was young and not very bright at the time."

Lucy snorted. "What about all those other times? Like when you tried to make your own bungee cord out of rope and jump off the new Dawho Bridge? Thank goodness I told my daddy and he put a stop to it. You would have yanked your whole leg off. Or worse."

I glared at Lucy, willing her to stop, but she appeared to be enjoying herself.

"And remember all those red ants you collected to put in Mrs. Anderson's desk on Friday morning so we could have a long weekend?"

"Really, Lucy, I don't think you dredging up my past is something Mr. Beaufain or Gigi needs to hear."

"I disagree," Finn said from behind me, and I heard the smile in his voice. "We really had no idea about the real Eleanor Murray."

Lucy slowly moved her head from side to side. "Um-hmm-hmm. That girl was like a cat with nine lives. I think she's used about eight of them by now."

I dug my paddle into the water and pulled hard. "Come on—let's go see if we can find a dolphin."

"Or maybe an alligator," Finn said from behind me as he joined his paddling with mine, the sound of splashing water mixing with his soft laughter. "I'd like to see Eleanor trying to perch on top of it."

We spent about two hours on the water, returning to the dock at Luna Point only when Finn thought Gigi was getting too fatigued and despite her adamant protests. Lucy and Gigi were desperate to use the bathroom, so Finn and I were left with bringing the kayaks out of the water and laying them out on the dock to dry.

"That was fun. Thank you," Finn said when we were finished.

Never easy with compliments, I fumbled with the life jackets, spreading them wider on the dock so they looked like bright orange birds in flight. "I had fun, too. But you really need to thank Lucy. We couldn't have done it without her."

He didn't say anything, and I was forced to look up at him. He was grinning broadly. "So all those things Lucy said about you—were they true?"

I grimaced. "Guilty as charged."

"I never would have suspected." His smile faded. "What changed? Your father's death?"

I hugged my arms around me and breathed in the scent of sun-heated marsh grass. "No. I was always a little hellion—since I could walk, I'm told. I'm guessing it was to gain some attention from my mother. It got worse after my daddy died. I just remember . . ." I stopped, not really sure I understood what I wanted to say.

"You remember what?"

His eyes met mine, calming me, and my thoughts became clear. "I was numb. My daddy was gone, and I couldn't play the piano anymore. I felt so desperate just to . . . feel. It was almost as if physical pain was all that could shake me out of my stupor."

"Did it?"

"No." I didn't drop my gaze. "Not until I almost killed my sister."

He didn't react but kept his cool gray eyes on me.

I kept talking; it was suddenly important that he know everything. "I dared her into doing something stupid, and she did it. And she fell and broke her back. It's why she's in a wheelchair."

"Did you push her? Or threaten her?"

"No, of course not—"

"Then I can't see how it was your fault."

"You don't understand," I said, flustered. "I knew she would climb the tree as high as she could because Glen was there, watching. She wanted him to think she wasn't afraid, but I knew she was. And . . ." I stopped, unable to admit to him something I'd never even admitted to myself.

"And what?"

I shook my head. "I'm not the person you think I am."

He took a step toward me. "Of course you are. Why else would I allow Gigi to spend so much time with you? Or put my aunt Helena in your care? We've all made mistakes, Eleanor. It's moving beyond them that makes us the people we are."

My cell phone rang just as he took another step toward me. I quickly took it out of the pocket of my shorts and saw with some alarm that it was Glen.

"This is Eleanor." I waited for Glen's voice.

"Eleanor? This is your mother. I'm on Glen's phone."

The hairs on the back of my neck stood at attention. "Is everything all right?"

"We're at the hospital, but everything is just fine."

"What? Why are you at the hospital?" Finn touched my arm, as if to remind me that I wasn't alone.

"Eve had an episode and her doctor wanted her to come to the hospital so she could check her out. She's fine now."

"What do you mean, 'an episode'? And which hospital? I'm on Edisto but I can be in Charleston within the hour—"

"No, there's no need for you to come. That's why Glen had me call you. He's with Eve and the doctor, and everything is fine. We were just afraid that if you called the house and nobody answered you'd get worried."

"I need to be there," I insisted.

"No, you don't. The doctor has explained everything to us and it's all fine. Glen and Eve don't need you to come."

"But . . ." Tears of frustration welled in my eyes.

"I know you want to think that Glen needs your help. But he doesn't. He's her husband, Eleanor. Let them be."

I looked at Finn, realizing that he was standing close enough to hear the entire conversation.

"We'll call you once we get back home. I've got to go now." Without waiting for me to say good-bye, my mother ended the call.

I stared down at the phone for a long moment before Finn took it from my hand. "She's right, you know," he said gently.

My gaze whipped up to meet his as feelings of hurt and betrayal and utter loss poured through me like batter hitting a hot skillet. "You don't understand."

I turned around and almost ran down the dock toward the house just as the first stars of the evening appeared in the sky, as if to guide my way.

CHAPTER 25

Eve

I sat on the sofa, my legs resting on Glen's lap, while I hand stitched the lapels of Eleanor's jacket. I could have used the sewing machine, but I wanted to know each stitch, wanted to ensure that it fanned out perfectly behind her neck; I wanted her to feel the love and care that had gone into making this suit for her, regardless of where she would wear it.

Headlights illuminated the wall over the television set, and the three of us turned to see Eleanor's white Volvo pulling up in front of the house.

"I thought you called her," Glen said.

"I did," my mother replied. "I told her that everything was fine, that she didn't need to come."

I tucked the jacket behind me before placing my hand on Glen's arm while we listened to the sound of a key in the latch. Eleanor stood inside the doorway, her hair disheveled as if she'd been in the wind, her nose and cheeks tinted pink by the sun. Her eyes were wide and sparkling, filled with too many emotions for me to recognize. Except for the hurt. I was way too familiar with that one. I had also never seen her look so beautiful.

Mama put the television on mute, then stood and walked toward Eleanor. "I told you that we were fine. I hate that you came all this way."

Ignoring our mother, Eleanor closed the door and came to stand in front of me. "She said you were in the hospital." Her gaze flickered over me as if to make sure that I was still whole, finally settling on the very small swell of my abdomen. "Is everything really all right?"

Glen gently lifted my legs off him and placed them on the sofa so he could stand. "We're fine. Really. I'm sorry you had to drive all this way for nothing."

She fumbled for words while she stared at him with reproach. "I . . . she's my sister. I was worried."

"I know. But I was there, and everything was taken care of. I can handle this, Eleanor. Regardless of what you and Eve might think."

Her eyes met mine in an unspoken question.

"I told them about the AD. I had to. Dr. Wise said I needed to, just in case you weren't here when I needed emergency care, or I didn't recognize the symptoms. I can't always feel when things aren't right because of my paralysis, and Dr. Wise said it would be best if somebody was able to monitor me at all times." She glanced up at her husband. "The doctor made me see how stupid I was being."

Glen began walking to the kitchen. "I need a beer."

"Get one for me, too," Eleanor said, surprising us all. I hadn't seen her drink a beer since she was seventeen, riding shotgun in Rocky Cooper's truck.

Mama sat down on the love seat and patted the spot next to her. "You can sit here, Eleanor."

My sister accepted the beer from Glen and took a long drink. "I'm exhausted. I think I'll just go upstairs and go to bed."

Glen and Mama exchanged a look, while I kept my gaze focused on my sister. "Because we weren't expecting you back until tomorrow night, we were using your room to paint the new baby furniture."

"New baby furniture?" she repeated.

"Yes. A crib and a changing table. And a rocker. Glen found them at a flea market for practically nothing—and the crib is almost brand-new. I just wanted everything to be like new, so Glen said he'd paint everything."

She stared at me for a moment, then took another swig from her beer. "Is the paint dry enough that I can climb over it to get to my bed?"

"Should be," Glen said, ignoring her sarcasm.

Eleanor turned to regard Glen more closely, studying him as if she'd never seen him before, and perhaps she hadn't. At least not this Glen, who'd suddenly discovered that just because you'd always thought something was true didn't always mean that it was. I'd only recently begun to recognize the same look in my own reflection.

Glen sat down again, sliding under my legs and resting his free hand on my knees. A look of disappointment crossed Eleanor's face, as if she'd hoped that Glen would pull her aside to tell her that everything wasn't all right and that he'd needed her to be there with him while he'd been driving me to the hospital. But Glen simply put the beer bottle to his lips and patted my knees.

"Will Mr. Beaufain be expecting you back at Edisto tomorrow?" Mama asked.

Eleanor frowned. "Probably, since it's Saturday. I didn't think to ask. Why?"

"He called here earlier, wanting to know if we'd seen you."

She flushed. "I didn't pick up. I needed time to think. I'll send a text before I go to bed."

"What did you need to think about?" I asked, having noticed the way the color on her cheeks deepened when Mama mentioned Mr. Beaufain's name.

Her eyes focused on Glen's hands on my legs. "About happiness. Something he said about learning to recognize it when we find it so we can enjoy it while it lasts."

The room was silent for a moment, the muted mouths of the actors on the television screen moving in pantomime. Finally, my mother spoke. "He's a very smart man."

We all turned to look at my mother, who seemed uncomfortable with the attention. I recalled how she had once been, when our father was alive. How she'd always been dressed immaculately, with hair meticulously styled and makeup expertly applied, as if my father would have noticed and loved her less if she hadn't made the effort. Her widow's weeds had been the gradual shedding of all the things she'd once taken pride in: her glossy hair and beautiful face. Gone, too, were her inexpensive clothes, which with her needle and thread she had always managed to make look like runway couture. I figured she knew a thing or two about how fleeting happiness could be; she had taught us that it happened only once and could all be taken away with an ocean's wave across a bow or a fall from a tree.

Eleanor wandered into the kitchen, tossing her beer bottle into the recycling bin with a clang. She returned to the den and stood there motionless for a long moment, as if wondering where she was and what she was supposed to be doing. Finally, she headed toward the stairs.

"Good night," she said softly as she began to climb, her tread hesitant, as if she was no longer sure where she was, as if the stars that guided her had illuminated the wrong path.

Eleanor

The week following the kayaking trip in Edisto, Finn was gone to New York and Gigi stayed with her mother. I missed Gigi, and if I wanted to admit it to myself, I missed Finn and his cool, assessing gray eyes, which always made me want to tell him everything without holding back, regardless of how much I regretted it afterward. But I didn't want to see him, didn't want to resurrect our conversation about happiness and my failure to attain it.

I spent my time with Helena reading, walking with her around the property, and driving her to get ice cream. We bought red tulips and brought them to Magda's grave, and we even ventured to the local library. We were both happy to find her romance novels in large print so that I was no longer forced to paraphrase certain parts when I read aloud to her.

I played the piano for her, but only after a long argument about what she wanted to hear versus what I was willing to play. I found myself not really caring anymore what I played, but we both enjoyed our arguments too much to stop.

On Saturday afternoon while Helena rested, I ensconced myself in one of the deep armchairs with a history book on Hungary, eager to read more and impress Helena with my knowledge of all things Hungarian. Nurse Kester had left to run errands, so when the doorbell rang, I had to sprint for the door to make sure the noise wouldn't disturb Helena.

The man in his mid-thirties standing on the front porch at a respectful distance wore an expensive-looking suit with a rumpled tie and scuffed shoes. It made me think that he had a wife at home who knew how to dress him, but it was obvious that the man had other things on his mind.

He had solemn, dark eyes that creased at the corners when he smiled, as if he smiled often, and beautiful wavy black hair that most women would envy. He regarded me with some surprise.

"May I help you?" I asked.

He withdrew a white business card from his jacket. "I hope so. I'm Jacob Isaacson. My family owns an art and antique dealership in Atlanta. I was in town a few weeks ago and stopped by to see Bernadett Szarka but was told that she had passed. My sympathies."

"Thank you," I said. "I never knew her, but I'm working for her sister as a kind of companion. I will be happy to convey your sympathies."

He looked uncomfortable. "Actually, I left my card the last time I came, hoping Miss Szarka—Helena Szarka—would contact me."

"Regarding . . . ?" I prompted.

"Some of her paintings. Bernadett contacted me prior to her death about one in particular, and I was hoping that her sister would allow me to see it."

"To buy? As far as I understand, Helena isn't interested in selling any of her paintings."

"I'm afraid you might be mistaken, Miss . . . ?"

"Murray. I'm Eleanor Murray. And, no, Helena has been quite adamant that she is not interested in anyone seeing her paintings, much less selling them."

He reached into his jacket pocket again and drew out two sheets of white printer paper folded in quarters. "After I heard from Bernadett, I did some research. Over the years, Helena Szarka has sold quite a few paintings."

I took the papers, which showed small black-and-white photos of various paintings, listing the title, artist, and date sold. I wanted to tell him that he must be mistaken, but all the blank spots on the walls, the rectangles where the paint was darker, kept me silent.

I looked back at Mr. Isaacson. "What exactly did Bernadett want to show you?"

He looked contrite. "I don't feel at liberty to discuss this with you since you're not a family member. I hope you understand. But perhaps if you could tell Miss Szarka that I'm here?"

I handed the papers back to him. "She's resting, I'm afraid, but I'd be happy to give her your card."

It looked like he wanted to argue, but I stood firm, with the door partially closed behind me. I wasn't afraid of him; I was afraid of what the pictures of the sold paintings and the art books that Bernadett had wanted to keep from Helena might mean. A cold chill blew at the back of my neck as I stood in the doorway. It took all the control I had not to slam the door in Mr. Isaacson's face.

"Well, then, if you could just let her know that I stopped by again. I'm staying in Charleston through the weekend. That's my cell number on the front of the card. Please ask her to call me day or evening—I'll be available."

His gaze flickered above my head, as if he were trying to see into the hall behind me. I took a step forward, bringing the door with me as I wondered why I was trying to protect Helena. And from what.

"I'll do that," I said. "Have a good day." I stayed where I was until he was safely inside his car and backing out of the driveway. Then I moved back into the foyer and closed the door, my head down as I read the business card.

Jacob B. Isaacson
Isaacson & Sons
European Fine Art, Antiques

"Who was that?"

Helena's voice startled me enough that I dropped the card. We both watched as it slid beneath the hall chest, out of sight.

"Leave it," she said, gripping the head of her cane tightly as she turned toward the music room.

"But you don't know who it was—"

"It is that man who is wanting to see my paintings. I am not interested. It is because of people like him that I have an unlisted number."

"He said Bernadett called him—that's why he was here."

She didn't stop her slow progress across the hall. "And Bernadett is dead, so there is no reason for him to return."

Confused and not a little annoyed, I followed her. "Don't you think you should see him? You don't even know what he wants. What if he's the man Bernadett wanted Finn to meet?" I rushed so that I stood in front of her, blocking her way into the music room. "I can have Finn call him to see—"

"No." She didn't shout the word, but she didn't need to. She stopped, and I could hear her rapid breathing.

I put my hand on her elbow. "Are you okay?"

She shook her head, as if speaking would be too much effort. After a moment, she raised her eyes to meet mine. "I want you to play for me."

I allowed my hand to fall from her arm as she moved into the room and settled herself onto the love seat. With a voice that shook only a little, she said, "Today is Bernadett's birthday. I would like you to play Brahms. He was her favorite."

"The waltzes?"

"I suppose. I would suggest his Hungarian dances, but they might prove to be too difficult for you. The waltzes are overdone, but Bernadett loved them. To play and to listen. And to dance. She loved to dance. She was so light on her feet and so tiny. Bernadett never lacked for partners when we would go to dances." She stared wistfully out the window, seeing a world that I could not. "Magda and I would tease her that the reason she liked to waltz was so everybody could see her dress and the way the skirt would twirl with her." She smiled at a memory, for a brief moment transforming her face into that of a beautiful young woman.

I could not see the Bernadett that Helena was talking about. All I could see was the sparse room and the handful of hanging clothes and two pairs of shoes in the armoire.

"All right," I said, moving to the stacks of music lining the room. There were fewer piles now, as I'd managed to place quite a few in the pink binders.

"I'm going to put all the waltzes in the same notebook so that they're easier to find instead of organizing them by composer. I've got them all stacked somewhere—"

"You did not ask me if that is how I would like you to do it," Helena interjected.

"No, I didn't. But you also didn't tell me how you *would* like to organize them, either. I figured I couldn't wait for the small window of opportunity when you're awake to find out how you'd like it done. After you fire me, you can redo it all."

I didn't look up from my perusal of the piles, as I could well imagine her tightened lips and wobbling chin as she decided whether to laugh or put me in my place.

"That could be a problem. I do not believe that Finn would allow me to fire you now."

I straightened, holding up the small coverless book of Brahms waltzes, pretending I hadn't heard her. "Opus thirty-nine. Any particular one you would like to hear?"

"Number four in E minor. It was Bernadett's favorite of all the waltzes. She had a heavy touch on the keyboard, which made that particular one more fun to play but more difficult to listen to.

"And pretending that something is not there will not make it go away, Eleanor. My eyesight is bad, but I am not blind."

I knew she was no longer talking about the music.

I sat down on the piano bench, taking my time adjusting it so my back could remain turned toward Helena. "If you'd like me to make an appointment to have your eyes examined, please let me know. And remind me not to get any more romance novels for you at the library."

"You're worried about your brother-in-law and your feelings for him. Have you ever considered that the reason why you remain infatuated is because it is safer for you? There is no risk in wanting something you can never have."

I stilled, clutching the music book and staring at the keyboard, the black and white keys blurring together as I struggled to keep my anger in check. "And you know so much about these things because you're ninety years old and have never been married."

I heard her sharp intake of breath and used her silence to place the Brahms book up on the music stand.

"I was in love once."

I turned around slowly to face her. "Yes. You told me."

"He was the love of my life, and I remember how it was when he looked at me and how I felt when I looked at him. It is something that is hard to forget."

"But you never married. So what happened?"

Her gaze remained steady. "He never came back for me after the war."

I didn't say that I was sorry, couldn't say it. Not because I wasn't—I was. But because no words could soften the raw grief I heard in the old woman's voice. Saying that I was sorry would be like trying to stop an incoming wave with my hand.

"Play," she commanded. "Number four."

Turning back around to face the music stand, I reached up and opened the book, the pages opening easily to waltz number four. As I spread the pages wide, a small photograph that had been stuck inside the binding fell from its spot and fluttered into my lap.

I picked it up and studied it, recognizing a young, blond Bernadett in the photo but not the serious dark-haired man beside her. They were in what appeared to be an outdoor café, sitting close to each other. She was smiling broadly and leaning toward him, her blond hair spilling onto his dark shirt, her hand resting possessively on his arm.

Despite his smile, the man regarded the photographer with serious dark eyes, his black hair and mustache making him appear very Hemingway-esque. He was attractive in a way that intelligent men often are, with an air of knowledge and self-possession about them. *Like Finn.* I brushed the thought away and turned back to Helena.

"This fell from the book. I think the woman is Bernadett—do you know who the man is?"

I stood and brought the photograph to her and placed it in her open palm.

She didn't say anything at first, and then, "This was stuck in the music?"

"Yes. On the same page as the E minor waltz."

"Of course," she said, not bothering to explain to me why that made sense to her.

"Is that Bernadett?"

She nodded, her face losing color. "Yes. And that is her Benjamin. Benjamin Lantos." Her hand began to shake. "He had two left feet and could not dance. But Bernadett loved him anyway. After she met Benjamin, she never even looked at another man." With a low voice, she added, "I wish she had never met him."

"Why?" I asked, startled at her vehemence.

As if I had not spoken, she said, "When Magda died, her husband gave us all of her old photographs—the ones she brought from Hungary. There were not very many, but they were special to us—like this one. Bernadett always said she would put them in an album for me, but she was always too busy with all of her charities. I wonder where the rest of them are."

I stared down at the photograph, not willing to meet her eyes. I would have to tell Finn about the basket and the rest of its contents and let him decide what we should do.

Trying to assuage my guilt, I said, "I can find a frame for it and put it on your nightstand, if you like."

"Yes. Thank you. I would like that very much."

I left the photograph with her and returned to the piano bench. I picked up the book and shook it to see if anything else fell out of it, then returned it to its perch. I placed my hands on the keyboard as my eyes scanned the music, each note playing in my head. I lifted my foot over the pedal in preparation, then stopped, the thought that had been swirling in my subconscious finally demanding to be brought to the surface.

Turning around one more time to face her, I said, "The man you said was the love of your life—what was his name?"

Her eyes softened, again reminding me of the beauty she had once been.

"His name was Gunter. Gunter Richter."

CHAPTER 26

Helena

"I will come back for you."

The night lit up again as the American bombers swept over the city, bombs and leaflets falling into the Danube and in the streets, the percussion of sound echoing in our ears.

"Do not leave me, Gunter. I am so afraid."

He slipped the small parcel into my hands. "Do not lose this. This is safe passage for you and Bernadett." He squeezed my hands together over the package and kissed them. "My brave Helena. You can do this. And when it is all over, we will be together again."

His eyes reflected the burning fires on the bridges that crossed the river, the smoke and flames reaching up to a heaven that no longer seemed to be watching. "I am afraid," I said again, no longer wanting to be brave. I was tired of being brave, of pretending that all was fine, tired of the persistent hunger, of the constant vigilance.

He took my hand and led me back to the farmer's truck, where Bernadett lay in a feverish sleep. "You are saving her life. Do you understand this? You are doing this for her."

"But what about—?"

He took my head in his hands, his lips brushing mine. "They will be safe. I promise. And when this is over I will come back for you."

"Miss Szarka?" Eleanor's voice broke through my dream.

I jerked awake to the sound of the Szarka Sisters singing "Time Waits for No One." The words squeezed my heart, making it hard to breathe, the crackling of the gramophone reminding me too much of that long-ago night when fire and sound erupted in the sky, rending my life forever into two parts—the time before and the time after.

"Miss Szarka?" she asked again, her hand on my shoulder.

I blinked up at her. "Turn that off. Magda had a difficult time staying in tune, and it is plainly clear in that song."

Eleanor moved to the gramophone and lifted the needle. "I was going to ask if you were okay, but I can see you're in fighting form."

I frowned at her as she sat down again in Bernadett's chair and picked up the book she'd been reading. It was the book from the library about eighteenth- and nineteenth-century art, one of the books that Bernadett had not wanted me to see. I was about to suggest that Eleanor read to me from one of the novels we had just selected from the library when she looked up.

"I'm curious about something," she said.

"Curiosity . . ."

"I know. It killed the cat. Finn already pointed that out to me. But it's my nature to ask questions, and I figure you can always refuse to answer."

I sighed to show my disinterest, all the time aware of the book in her lap.

"You've told me a little about your life in Budapest, growing up with your sisters and your mother in a tiny house near the river. My mother—who I told you once helped at one of your Christmas parties—said that when she referred to you and your sisters as just like the Gabors, you got angry. You said something like you and your sisters weren't raised with a lot of money and worked for a living so you didn't need to rely on wealthy husbands to save you."

"Your mother has a very good memory."

"You have no idea." She rolled her eyes, then looked back at me expectantly.

"I was a very hard worker. I sang in cafés at night to earn money when our mother got sick and could not bake anymore. Somebody had to support our family. Bernadett was too busy trying to save the world and teaching music to orphaned children for free." I narrowed my eyes at her. "But you have not asked a question, so I do not know how you want me to answer."

"Well, I guess I'm wondering where all of your paintings came from."

Breathe in. Breathe out. I focused on the simple function so that I would not pass out again. But perhaps it would have been easier to hold my breath and wait for the darkness to take me.

"Do I ask you where you buy your unfashionable clothes?"

"No, but if you did I'd tell you. I'd like to think that we knew each other well enough by now to ask each other questions, as well as be comfortable enough to refuse to answer."

I narrowed my eyes. "That man who came today—he told you to ask about my paintings."

"No. The only thing he asked me to do was to extend his sympathies regarding Bernadett's death and to ask you to call him." She patted the open page in her lap. "I've been reading this book and I've recognized several of the artists as the artists of a few of the paintings in your house. While you were sleeping, I took the liberty of studying the signatures at the bottom just to make sure."

She continued. "I'm not an art expert, but I would think that if one Breitner was sold at auction for over one hundred thousand dollars, the rest of his work would probably be valuable as well."

"Most likely," I said, not willing to give any more away than I had to, but knowing that Eleanor was like a termite, unable to resist until she'd poked a hole into my foundation. "What do you think?"

"I thought that perhaps you'd inherited the paintings from a relative, or that they were worthless. I know now that they aren't worthless. Mr. Isaacson mentioned that you've sold several through the years that have brought in decent money. So that leaves me with my other theory. That you could have inherited them from a relative."

I stared hard at her, willing her to stop now. "Yes," I said. "They could have been."

"I guess I was wondering why you won't allow Finn to have them appraised. There are such things as hurricanes and house fires."

When she realized that I was not planning on saying more, she leaned forward, her elbows pressing into the book. "Why did Bernadett want to keep this book from you? It's not like there's any love scenes in it or anything." She grinned, referring to the spicy romances we had been checking out from the library.

I did not return her smile. "Perhaps we should get a Ouija board and you can ask her. My sister always thought like a child, never worrying about where the money would come from for food or a new dress. She had a large, compassionate heart, and if she had a meal or a pengö to spend, she would share it with those who had nothing. I loved my sister, but she was not an easy person to live with. So, no, I do not know the reasons why she did the things she did. You will have to ask her directly."

We both turned at the sound of car doors slamming outside. Eleanor stood and moved to the window. "Nurse Kester is in the kitchen, so I have no idea . . ." The loud squeal of laughter echoed in the night air. Turning to me, she said, "I didn't think Finn and Gigi were supposed to be here until tomorrow."

I watched as she smoothed down her hair and skirt, the color in her cheeks pinking. "Perhaps Finn could not stay away for another day."

The color in her cheeks deepened. Sticking out her chin, she said, "I doubt your company is enough to get him to drive all the way here after dark."

"Exactly," I said, enjoying her flustered look.

We heard the front door open and then, "Aunt Helena! Ellie! Come quick—you don't want to miss this!"

I began the long process of moving myself to the edge of my seat in preparation to stand. Eleanor stood in front of me. "Just give me your hands and I'll pull. It'll get you out of your chair ten minutes faster."

Not in the mood to argue, because what she said was mostly true, I stretched out my arms and she managed to lift me by my elbows.

"Hurry!" Gigi called, her voice this time accompanied by running feet followed by her head peeking into the room. "Aren't you coming?"

She stopped and watched our slow progress, with me leaning on both my cane and Eleanor's arm. "You need one of those mini-scooters, Aunt Helena, like you see on TV."

I took another step. "I could not do that, darling girl. Because then people would think that I was old."

I heard Eleanor snort through her nose at Gigi's expression, the little girl trying to determine if pointing out the obvious might be rude.

Gigi began walking backward in front of us, moving her hand like a man guiding an airplane on the runway.

"Why are we racing through the house at such breakneck speed?" Eleanor asked.

Oblivious to sarcasm as the young often are, Gigi replied, "It's Aunt Bernadett's night-blooming cereus. And if we don't hurry it'll be gone."

I stumbled with my cane, remembering how adamant Bernadett had been about finding this one species of cereus, the *Selenicereus grandiflorus,* and waiting all year for it to bloom. I had forgotten it in the months since her death. It usually bloomed in late spring or early summer, and I could not help but wonder if it had waited for me to be ready to see it.

"Surely it won't stop blooming in the time it takes us to get there," Eleanor said.

Gigi's eyes widened. "It could. Daddy said so."

As if conjured, Finn emerged in the foyer from the front door. "Do you need help?"

"I told her she needs a scooter," Gigi said. "Then we wouldn't have to wait for another year before the flower bloomed again. But then Aunt Helena would be afraid people would think she's old."

Both Eleanor and I laughed while Finn just looked confused.

When we neared the porch steps, Finn's arm replaced my cane.

"What do you mean you have to wait another year?" Eleanor asked.

"It only blooms one night a year," Gigi said, running down the steps. "And only for a little while. So you *really* need to hurry."

"I am," I said, truly trying to make my old legs move faster.

Bernadett had planted the cactus twenty years ago after reading about it in a novel. Always the romantic, she had written to nurseries around the country until she found one who would ship the plant to her. They did not last long, and she had ordered a new one every three years or so, planting it in a small rock garden near the pecan orchard with a direct view of the creek.

I had once asked her why she went to so much trouble over a plant that bloomed only once a year. She had looked at me oddly, as if I should have known the answer. "Because sometimes that is all we have," she had answered. I did not want to embarrass myself by asking her what she had meant.

Gigi ran ahead, the glow from the porch light and the full moon lighting her way through the alley of old pecan trees, until she stopped, her pale pink dress like a beacon for those of us in the dark.

"It's beautiful," she said, her voice full of awe.

We made our way to stand behind her as she squatted down in front of the large white flower. We needed no light to see it; the petals reflected the moonlight as if according to some prearranged plan. It was only a single bloom, creeping up between the stones and its waxy vine. Silky flowers gathered together on top like a tulip, and behind those were spiky petals resembling a starburst. It was unique and brilliant and magical, but I still could not understand why Bernadett had needed it here in her garden.

"By dawn, it will have already started to wither," I said, already feeling its loss.

No one said anything for moment. Then, in a hushed voice, Gigi said, "But it was worth it."

Finn laid his hand gently on her head, while I turned to meet Eleanor's gaze, as if neither one of us could fathom the wisdom of a child.

Nurse Kester came out from the house. "Miss Szarka, it's time to get you ready for bed."

I said good night and allowed the nurse to lead me slowly back into the house, still seeing the bright white bloom in my mind's eye, and imagining it was Bernadett's voice telling me that it was worth it.

Eleanor

I sat on the piano bench with a pencil in my hand and a blank spiral music book propped up on the music stand. I was tapping out the melody for the Csárdás in an effort to transpose it into a simple version for Gigi to learn.

"Sounds beautiful," Finn said from the doorway.

"I'm sure," I said, placing the pencil down on the piano. "Is Gigi all tucked in?"

"Yes. And she wanted you to go up and say good night to her, but she was already passed out by the time I left her room."

I smiled awkwardly, suddenly aware that he and I were alone. Finn had sent Nurse Kester home for the night since we would all be there, and both Helena and Gigi were asleep.

"Well, then, I guess I should head back, then, since you're here."

"You don't have to go." His words hung in the silent house like a question. "Unless you have to."

I thought of the baby furniture that sat pushed against the wall in my tiny bedroom at home, and the pull of the creek and the marsh tugged at me like a small child at her mother's hem.

"I don't want to intrude on your time with Gigi and Helena."

He leaned against the doorframe. "We enjoy your company. It's not an intrusion at all."

I studied his eyes, trying to see behind them, but they remained inscrutable.

"All right, I'll stay. Thank you."

"Thank *you*," he said. "Now I won't have to bear the brunt of Helena's tongue all by myself tomorrow."

"Right. Like she's ever said a cross word to you."

He gave me an uncharacteristic shrug. "Yeah, I know. I just said that to make you feel better."

We laughed, and the awkwardness was dispelled.

Straightening, he said, "I brought back the silver box you gave me."

I looked up hopefully. "Did you find a translation?"

"Yes. I'm not exactly sure what it means, but the exact translation is 'Daughters of the Divine Redeemer.'"

"Sounds like a convent or something."

"That's what I thought, too. I looked it up and found that's exactly what it was."

"Was?"

He nodded. "The motherhouse for the order was in Budapest before the war. It's no longer there. I went online to see if I could find out more. The motherhouse is now in Odenburg, about two and a half hours away from Budapest. The congregation has about three hundred sisters, and they're still very active—conducting schools of all kinds and caring for the sick. Things nuns normally do."

I thought for a moment. "I wonder if they were forced to move by the Communists after World War II."

He raised his eyebrows. "You've been reading your history books."

I smiled smugly. "Yes, I have. I'm trying to get Helena to like me."

"Oh, I wouldn't worry about that. She likes you just fine."

I rolled my eyes.

"Actually," he continued, "the last mention of the motherhouse in Budapest that I could find was from 1944."

"The year of the Nazi occupation."

"Right. So if they were forced to move or close, that would have been a reason. Up until March of that year, Hungary was allied with Germany. From what little Helena and Bernadett told me, people's lives in the capital remained pretty much the same until the occupation."

"Even for the Jews?"

"If I recall correctly from my own high school history classes, they weren't forced into ghettos or deported, but most lost their jobs and livelihoods, and many of the young people were forced into labor camps even before the occupation. It's why many Jews went into hiding. They realized it was just a matter of time." He paused. "Neither one of the aunts really liked to talk about that period in their lives, so I'm a little ashamed that I don't know more."

"I haven't read the World War II section of the book yet—trying to save the most interesting part for last, I guess. I started with the really old history—the warlord period—and then I skipped to the Communist years and modern day since that was more current. When I was done with that, I was going to go back to the World War II history." I sent him a sheepish look. "I'm afraid I was never much of a history buff."

"But you'd study Hungarian history to make an old woman happy."

"I don't think that's possible." I tapped my fingers on the keyboard, making one of the notes sound. "I'm just wondering why Bernadett would have that box, and why she'd hide it away."

Finn's brow wrinkled. "I thought you said it belonged to Helena."

I closed my eyes, wishing—as usual—that I could call back words. "To be honest, I'm not sure whom it belongs to. We found the basket with the box inside it under Bernadett's bed."

"We?"

Realizing that I needed to be completely honest, I said, "Actually, Gigi. Please don't be angry with her. She was bored one day and exploring the house, and she found the basket under Bernadett's bed. To her credit, she didn't look inside until after she'd told me about it and I decided we should see if it held any of Bernadett's music."

"And you found the box instead."

"Along with a few other items that I wanted to ask you about. I don't know their significance, so I don't know if we should bury it back under Bernadett's bed or show it to Helena."

He didn't say anything for a moment, and then, "Thank you."

"For what?"

"For your kindness. To Gigi and Helena. For considering their feelings."

Embarrassed, I looked away. "Anybody would have done it."

"No. Not really." He straightened. "Is the basket back in Bernadett's room?"

"Yes."

"Then let's go put back the silver box and see what else is in there."

I felt as if an enormous weight had been lifted from my shoulders, and we climbed the stairs. I retrieved the basket from under the bed while Finn went into his room to get the silver box. We sat on the floor, as if neither one of us wanted to be reminded why the bed frame was starkly empty. As I'd done before with Gigi, I sat like Pandora before the basket and lifted the lid.

As Finn examined the Bible, I took out the photos and spread them on the floor between us, spotting a few that I hadn't had the time to examine before. I attempted to group all the wedding photos together, and then the random ones of Helena and her two sisters and mother. Finn was already looking at those by the time I moved to the remaining photographs that were too disparate to be grouped—unlabeled pictures of buildings and scenery and people I could not name.

As I was stacking a small group of photos, I realized that two of the photos were stuck together with some sort of adhesive, the front of one attached to the back of another. Very carefully I pried them apart, the yellowed tape coming away easily and making me think that the photo had once been taped to a wall.

It was a photo of a baby propped up in an old-fashioned stroller staring at the camera with an openmouthed grin. Two feminine hands could be seen on the stroller's handle, the arms covered in long black sleeves, but the woman's face wasn't visible. I turned the photograph over, disappointed to find nothing written on the back.

"Do you know who this is?" I asked, holding it up for Finn to see.

"I have no idea. Is there nothing on the back?"

I shook my head. "No." My gaze fell on the photograph of the soldier. I picked it up again and looked into those wide eyes, wondering what he was trying to say to me.

"Who's that?" Finn asked.

"I think this was the love of Helena's life. She told me his name was Gunter Richter, and that name is written on the back."

He took the photo and flipped it over before studying the front for a long moment. "Helena said that he was the love of her life?"

I nodded. "She told me that they had plans to marry after the war but that he never came back for her."

He held up the photograph in front of me. "And this is the man?"

"I don't know for sure. I just assumed."

Finn was looking at me oddly, as if I'd just told him that the sky and ocean had switched places. "What's wrong?" I asked.

"Don't you recognize this uniform?"

I shook my head, trying not to look as ignorant as I felt.

"It's a German army uniform from World War II." He paused as if to let his words sink in. "So if you're correct, then my aunt was in love with a German soldier."

CHAPTER 27

Eleanor

The following weekend, I sat in the sunroom with a book from the stack of new ones I'd selected from our last visit to the library. These books focused on Hungary during the war years, the years Helena and Bernadett knew well yet would not speak of. And the more I read about the deprivations and death tolls, the more I began to understand why.

In the middle of the stack was an old booklet that I'd found stuck between two larger books and that I'd added as an afterthought: *The Catholic Church and the Holocaust in Hungary*. At the time, I'd been thinking about the silver box from the Daughters of the Divine Redeemer and how they'd disappeared from Budapest in 1944. I didn't know what I expected to find in the obscure booklet. All I knew was that for somebody who had never made higher than a C in history, I was now burning with curiosity.

I looked up as Finn walked in, smelling of soap, his hair still damp from his recent shower. He'd spent most of the afternoon at the beach with Gigi in exchange for leaving her at home with Nurse Weber this evening. She'd been promised a nonending marathon of Disney princess movies—something Nurse Weber said she was looking forward to, as her own daughter was now in college and long past the Disney stage.

I'd been invited to go with them to the beach, but I'd had to point out that my job was to be with Helena, who had a list of things she wanted me to do. Secretly, I'd been glad. Spending time with Finn at the beach would mean that every time I saw him at the office, I'd most likely be picturing him with his shirt off.

"Are you ready?" he asked, straightening his cuffs.

"Yes," I said, noticing his clothing for the first time. "Your suit is gray."

"It is," he said slowly. "Is that a problem? The Waterfront restaurant isn't really fancy, but I could find a tux if you think it's necessary."

"No, I meant your suit isn't black. I didn't think you owned one in any other color."

He frowned at me. "My father and grandfather always wore black suits and built a successful business."

"Sure—but I bet it wasn't because they looked like funeral directors."

Still frowning, he said, "Have you been talking with Gigi? She said I looked like the character Gru from *Despicable Me*."

"She's a very observant girl," I said, repressing a smile. "So you bought a new suit based on that?"

"Actually, I bought it last year. Just haven't worn it yet."

"Well, it looks very nice," I said, noticing how the shade brought out the color of his eyes.

"Thank you for noticing," he said quietly.

"You're welcome," I said. I placed the book on the ottoman in front of me and stood, taking my time smoothing down the skirt of my dress. It belonged to Eve, who'd practically threatened me if I didn't wear it tonight. It was a soft, sapphire blue knit with a wrap top and wide belt that flattered any figure. I loved the way the skirt swished against my legs, and the way the shade of blue brought out the color in my eyes. All the reasons why I wanted to refuse Eve's offer. But it's very hard to argue with a woman in a wheelchair.

Finn and I were taking Helena to dinner, ostensibly to celebrate her Hungarian name day, but in reality to talk about her past. I hadn't expected Finn to be so eager to delve into a part of Helena's life that nobody seemed to know anything about. But when I'd placed Gunter's photo back in the basket and suggested we replace everything under the bed, he'd touched my hand to stop me. His eyes had been shuttered as he'd regarded me, and it had suddenly occurred to me that this wasn't the first time he'd seen the basket. And that there was something he wasn't telling me.

Now, as he stood in the sunroom looking at me with serious gray eyes, his body moving with restless anticipation, I knew that I'd been right.

"I like your dress."

I flushed, embarrassed that he'd noticed the dress, but flattered, too. "I borrowed it from Eve. She wore it for her engagement party, but we're about the same size and she's saved it all these years and thought it would work for tonight and because I don't really have any dresses and it didn't need alterations, I thought I might as well . . ."

He held up his hand. "Stop. Please. Maybe it's not such a good idea for you to be hanging around Gigi so much." His lips twitched into a half smile. "You look beautiful tonight. And it's okay to accept a compliment."

I opened my mouth to say more, then closed it and just said, "Thank you."

"She's ready!" Gigi shouted from the front of the house.

I picked up the gift bag from the end table and preceded Finn from the room.

I almost didn't recognize the woman standing in the foyer. Helena's white hair had been brushed until it shone and was coiled in an elegant French twist at the back of her head. Her blue eyes were accentuated with a tasteful application of eye shadow and mascara, her cheeks and lips delicately colored with rouge and lipstick. She wore an old-fashioned green floral silk dress that still managed to look regal, despite the low hem and sensible pumps on her feet.

"You look wonderful," I said, meaning it. She had come such a long way in the three months since I'd first met her, a bedridden and wan old woman. She'd managed to transform herself into this person who bore a strong resemblance to the beautiful young woman she'd been.

"And you do not look too terrible, either, Eleanor." She waved her free hand as if to signal an end to all compliments for the evening. Turning to Finn, she said, "I am starving. I suppose if you had asked, you would know that I eat at five o'clock and then you would not have made the reservation for the ungodly time of six o'clock."

"Yes, Aunt Helena," Finn said graciously. "I'll remember that for next time."

Her eyes were bright like a little girl's as Finn escorted her to his car and settled her into the passenger seat.

I hugged Gigi good-bye, suspicious that there weren't more protestations, despite the promise of Disney movies.

"We'll be fine," Teri Weber said, waving me through the front door. "We're going to make a sparkly tiara and my world-famous brownies, so don't worry about us getting bored."

"I won't," I said, the door closing before the last word had left my mouth.

The Waterfront restaurant was located on Jungle Road on Edisto Beach, almost on the elbow where the island jutted out into the Atlantic. Although the food was excellent, the Waterfront wasn't a jacket-required eatery, but Finn's suggestion that we take Helena to Charleston and one of its myriad high-end restaurants had been quickly dismissed by both Helena and me because of the long drive for Helena.

We were seated at a table near the front of the restaurant where we could see the toy-sized lighthouse through one of the large windows. We looked conspicuous in our dresses and suit compared to the groups of tourists and locals in shorts and T-shirts, but Helena's only request was that wherever we went to eat wasn't far and that they served fried food and had dessert. After a quick glance at the menu, I realized we'd come to the right place.

Our waitress was a college-aged girl name Jenn who took our drink orders with a promise to return soon to take our dinner orders. While we waited, Helena looked pointedly at the gift bag I'd brought and had placed on the extra chair.

"Are you going to wait until dessert to allow me to open my presents?" she asked.

"Of course not," I said. "Unless you don't plan to eat your vegetables, and then I'll have to reconsider."

Finn picked up the bag and placed it in front of Helena. "I must confess that my gift to you was Eleanor's idea and that she wrapped it."

"This should be interesting," she said with one raised eyebrow. "I wonder if it is one of those romance novels she always insists on reading to me."

I glared at her as she reached into the tissue. I'd wrapped everything lightly so she wouldn't have any problem opening her gifts. "That one's very fragile," I said, sitting on the edge of my seat, ready to assist as I watched her lift out the present.

She sat it on the table in front of her and began to peel back the tissue to reveal the blue-and-white Herend rooster. It was the same design pattern as the broken one she had at home except this one was blue and stood in a different pose so that they could be placed together as a set. It had its glazed head down, as if pecking for corn.

She didn't say anything for a long moment, and I thought that I'd made a terrible mistake.

"I broke the other one," she said quietly, her eyes focused on the china bird in her hand. "I knocked it over by accident."

"Yes, you told me. I'm not suggesting that this should replace the broken one, but it would be a nice companion for it."

Her eyes met mine, but I was aware that she was no longer seeing me, or Finn, or anything else that we could see, too. "It was so dark that night. Inside the house. I had been forbidden to turn on lights. The Americans were bombing us—bombs and leaflets. But it should not have happened that night. Of all nights it should not have been that night."

Before I could ask her why, Jenn returned to our table with our sweet tea and a scotch and soda for Finn. Helena seemed to recall where she was again and sat back in her chair. "And because I could not see, that is how I broke it. *Anyukám*'s favorite possession and I broke it." She smiled at Finn. "She would be very pleased to see this new friend for it. Thank you, darling. And thank you, Eleanor."

I wanted to hear more, and I knew that Finn did, too, but it was clear that Helena had moved on from the dark house and the bombs and a broken piece of china.

We ordered our food, and then Helena reached into the bag again and withdrew the tissue-wrapped framed photograph of Bernadett with Benjamin at the café. I remembered how her hand had shaken when I'd shown it to her but how she'd seemed grateful when I suggested framing it for her bedside table. Remembering the look on her face when she'd unwrapped the rooster, I was no longer sure I'd done the right thing.

The tissue fell away to the floor, but nobody reached to retrieve it. Helena's face paled slightly, her lips opening as if she wanted to speak to the subjects in the photo, words she'd been wanting to say for a very long time.

She began to look around as if searching for the tissue, and then simply placed the frame against her chest, the photo side pressed against the silk of her dress.

"What is it, Aunt Helena?" Finn asked gently.

She seemed reluctant to show him, as if she'd suddenly realized why we were here, as if showing Finn the photograph would be like opening a book to chapter one.

After a brief hesitation, she placed the frame on the table so Finn could see. "Eleanor found this photo in one of Bernadett's music books. It is Bernadett and her Benjamin."

He studied it for a moment, then raised his gaze back to Helena. "Who was Benjamin?"

Slowly meeting his eyes, she said, "It does not matter now, does it? It is too late to do anything to change everything that has happened."

Finn took her weathered hand in his own strong one, and something passed between them that sent a cool shiver across my skin, something dark and unspoken and not completely understood.

"For Gigi," Finn said quietly. "And for me. We should know." From the look they shared, it became apparent to me that he was no longer speaking only of the distant past.

Very carefully, Helena lifted her iced tea glass and took a sip from her straw. "You are planning for me to die soon?"

Despite the lightness of her tone, Finn winced. "No, Aunt Helena. Gigi is already planning what shade of pink you'll wear to her wedding, which is a long way off." He smiled softly. "But you and I both know that life has its own current, and we can't hold it back."

She placed her hand on top of Finn's and squeezed, and I knew they were both thinking of a childhood cancer that lurked like a monster in a child's closet.

"Who was Benjamin?" he asked again.

After settling back in her chair, Helena took a deep breath. "Bernadett never wanted to speak of him after . . ." She gave a small shrug. "But I suppose it does not matter now. The dead cannot hurt us, can they?"

"I don't know," he answered. "Can they?"

Her chest rose and fell, and I glanced at Finn, wondering at the edge in his voice, wanting to remind him that she was an old woman.

"He was a Jewish resistance fighter."

Finn sat back in his chair, his face contemplative. "And he and Aunt Bernadett . . . ?"

"They were in love. It sounds so simple now, but back then it was not. He was a Jew, working with the underground resistance, smuggling medicine and food to his people, who were hidden throughout the city. And she was a Catholic, teaching music to orphaned and handicapped children at a local convent. They were doomed before it began."

I looked at her. "Is that why you told me that you wished they'd never met?"

Her lips moved; too many words stored in her heart seemed to be rushing forward at the same time. But she stopped them at the last moment, as if realizing those words were her last safety net, and to cut one loose would allow them all to spill out. "No, Eleanor. There were many, many more reasons."

"And Gunter," Finn said. "Did he know Benjamin?"

Her eyes widened. "How do you know about Gunter?"

Finn and I exchanged a glance. "Eleanor and Gigi found a photo of him while searching for Bernadett's music. Eleanor said that you told her that Gunter was the love of your life."

She looked down at her clasped hands. "Yes. He was. There could never be another love for me. It is why I never married. Why I never wanted to."

Finn waited for her to say more, but I knew she would give him only what he asked.

"Did Benjamin and Gunter know each other?"

Her eyes were hard as she stared back at him. "They met. Once. Maybe twice."

"And did Gunter know who Benjamin was?" Finn pressed on.

I placed a hand on his arm, wondering how he could not see the weariness in Helena's eyes or the way her ruined fingers had begun to pluck at the skin of her hands.

"We did not speak of it," she said. "Gunter and I spoke only of his family in Lindau, in the Bavarian Alps on Lake Constance, where from his bedroom window he could see snow on the tips of the distant mountains even in the summer. Of how his father was a butcher with a shop on the main street in town." Her face softened. "We spoke of how Gunter would open his own shop in America when the war was over, or we could live in Lindau and watch the moon rise over the lake." The last word cracked in half, as if spilling all of her lost hopes. "We spoke of the children we would have and what we would name them. We did not speak of the horror around us."

Jenn appeared at the table with a basket of hush puppies and our salads, but nobody picked up a fork or lifted a napkin.

Eager to change the direction of the conversation, I said, "It must have been very difficult for you to be so close to your sister, but for you to be in love with two men who in another time might have been friends but could not be then."

Her lips lifted in a soft smile. "Bernadett said the same thing. I think about that sometimes now, what it would have been like if we had all come to America after the war. If we all could have been a family. And I think, yes, it could have been." Helena stared down into her salad, and I watched as she breathed in and out, and then I imagined I could hear the sound of a book being shut.

"I am feeling ill. I am so sorry, but you must take me home now. Perhaps we can bring our food home for later."

Finn placed his hand gently on her arm. "I'm sorry, Aunt Helena. I didn't mean to upset you. We won't talk about the past anymore tonight. I promise. We'll talk about Gigi and make plans to change her favorite color."

Helena looked at Finn, and a weak smile of determination lit her face. "All right. But let us go ahead and order dessert now so they can wrap it up and we can bring it home."

The rest of the meal was subdued, each of us buried in our own thoughts, my own occupied with the unspoken question that hovered between Finn and Helena. Our short drive home was mostly silent, except for the crinkling of paper take-out bags and the sound old memories make as they slip back and forth behind your eyes.

Nurse Weber and Gigi were surprised to see us home so early, and Gigi might have even been a little disappointed since she was only in the middle of *Beauty and the Beast* and the brownies were still in the oven. I was happy to see rhinestones drying in glue on two tiaras on the kitchen table.

I gathered my things, preparing to leave, and then went in search of Finn. After looking around the house and porches, I found him on the dock with his telescope, looking up at the night sky.

He looked at me in surprise as I approached. "I'm sorry about dinner. I didn't mean to upset Helena."

"It's not my place to voice my opinion regarding your behavior toward your family members. I'm only an employee."

His face was in shadow, but I felt him watching me. "Is that how you really feel, Eleanor?"

My heart thudded loudly. "Yes," I said, afraid to answer any other way.

He went back to his telescope, looking into the eyepiece. "Did you know that the earth isn't perfectly round? It makes the earth wobble like a spinning top as it rotates around its axis. That means that in about fourteen thousand years Vega will be the North Star, and fourteen thousand years after that, Polaris will be the North Star again."

He straightened. "I find it reassuring that no matter what, there will always be a North Star to guide us."

I stepped closer and moved up to the telescope to look into the eyepiece. The bright light of the stars filled the space, the sound of the rushing creek beneath our feet at odds with my proximity to the stars. I was suspended in time, it seemed, floating somewhere between the earth and the sky, where all possibilities seemed endless.

I looked up from the telescope and found Finn standing very close to me. I didn't move back. "Why wouldn't you back off with your questions? Couldn't you tell that Helena was getting upset?"

His eyes glittered. "Because I was the one who found them. Bernadett was dead, and Helena was eager to join her. And I don't know why, and nobody will tell me, and I can't just let it go." He paused. "We're both like that, aren't we?"

I thought of all the unanswered questions I'd asked my father since his death, unable to take silence for an answer. "A bit," I said. I tilted my head back so I could look into his face. "Bernadett stopped playing the piano a few months before she died."

He didn't say anything, as if he knew what I was going to say next.

"Why did you stop taking flying lessons?"

"Because Gigi got sick."

"Exactly. I'm thinking something happened with Bernadett, too. Maybe it's the romantic in me, but what if she heard from Benjamin after all these years?"

He was silent for a long moment. "I never took you for a romantic."

"I used to be. A long, long time ago." I paused. "Now that Gigi's better, why aren't you taking flying lessons again?"

I felt his eyes on my face, blending with the light from the moon and the stars. "Because I've forgotten why I wanted to fly."

He kissed me then, our bodies touching only with our lips. His were soft and warm and tasted of a summer night, and I didn't want him to stop.

I smelled his scent, as if just realizing whom I was kissing, and I pulled back, my hand flying to my mouth. "Oh," I said stupidly, staring at him. "Oh," I said again, backing away and trying to put as much distance between us as I could, the odd feeling of having been unfaithful to something or someone pinching at my heart.

"Good night, Finn," I said, turning around and walking quickly down the dock. The current pushed at the boards, making me sway, and I looked up at the stars to steady me, imagining the earth wobbling on its axis as two stars switched places in the heavens.

CHAPTER 28

Eve

I pushed back from the kitchen table and held up the jacket to Eleanor's suit. It had taken me longer than I'd expected, but I'd needed it to be perfect. I'd hand sewn the lining and the hems and inserted darts in the exact places to accentuate her tiny waist. I was glad that Mama had suggested I measure myself for it before I'd even started, because my pregnant body had already disguised my previous proportions completely.

A car door shut outside, announcing Eleanor's arrival, but I didn't bother to hide her new suit. It was Tuesday, and I'd made sure that I would be alone with my sister. I took my time folding the skirt and the jacket and placed them on the table as I listened to the sound of her slowly climbing the front steps and then the jangle of her keys in the front door.

She stopped when she spotted me. She looked at the quiet TV and the empty kitchen before turning her gaze back to me. "Where're Glen and Mama? You shouldn't be alone."

"I knew you were on your way, and I've got the phone right here." I patted the phone on the table next to the suit, which she hadn't noticed yet. "Mrs. Reed picked Mama up about an hour ago to shop for fabric. Looks like Mama and I are designing recital costumes for Mrs. Reed's granddaughters. And," I added with a big smile, "thanks to your suggestion and

Mr. Beaufain's introduction, Mama has an appointment with Madame LaFleur next week to talk about recital costumes for Gigi's dance academy."

She slid into the chair opposite me and dropped her purse on the floor. "That's really great—but what does Mr. Beaufain have to do with it?"

"When I sent him that thank-you note to thank him for allowing you the flexibility to take care of me, he called me."

"He called *you*?"

"Yes. He wanted to let me know that he appreciated everything you'd done for his family, and also gave me his cell number so that if I ever needed anything I could call him directly."

Eleanor stared at me as if I'd suddenly started speaking another language.

I continued. "You must have mentioned something about Mama and me making costumes at some point, because he asked me if I'd ever designed anything in pink with lots of sequins and tulle. And that's all it took."

"I had no idea. . . ." She stopped, and I watched as she raised her hand to her lips.

Ah. Studying her closely, I said, "He's a very nice man. And not too hard on the eyes, either."

She quickly lowered her hand, as if she'd been caught doing something she shouldn't have. "He's my boss," she said, her tone not very convincing. "Which makes your comment very inappropriate."

I smirked. "And you've always been such a stickler for what's appropriate in relationships."

"Stop," she said, her eyes serious.

I touched her hand and she looked at me with surprise, reminding us both of how little physical contact we'd had over the years, except for the necessary care of a woman in a wheelchair. "I'm sorry," I said, meaning it. "You make yourself such an easy target sometimes."

She pulled her arm away. "No, I don't. I'm just trying to make it through each day."

I slipped into the unfamiliar role of older sister and found that if I spent a little time altering it, it would fit. "How's that working for you? When you were younger and people would ask you what you wanted to do when you grew up, you used to say go to Juilliard and play in Carnegie Hall. I don't think that's the same as 'making it through the day.'"

She stood. "I didn't come home from a long day at work to listen to this." Snatching up her purse, she headed toward the stairs. "I was going to wait and have dinner here, but I'm going to head straight out to Edisto. I'll be there all week."

I watched her retreat. "I liked the Ellie you used to be, and I wish she'd come back. It's my fault you changed, and I don't know what I can do to bring her back."

She stopped with her hand on the banister but didn't turn around. "What are you talking about? Nothing is your fault."

I continued, speaking quickly before she changed her mind about listening. "After my accident, when everything was so crazy, it made sense that you would take care of me. Mama was half-crazed with grief and there was nobody else, so you stepped in. And we let you. You wanted to wait on me and serve me from some false sense of guilt, and I let you. I let you not because I thought you deserved it, but because I was so angry with myself for doing something so stupid that I'd break my back, and I wanted to blame somebody, so I blamed you. And you let me."

She was shaking her head as she faced me. "I wanted to help you; I wanted you to get better. I didn't want Mama to cry anymore, and I was the only person here to do it."

"No," I said softly. "Glen was there, too. But you insisted on playing the martyr, and we let you. And we let you believe that my accident was your fault. But it was wrong of us. I see that now. My pregnancy has allowed me to see my life from a whole new perspective. It's my second chance, and I want you to have one, too. Because my accident wasn't your fault. It was mine. But you think you need my forgiveness, so I forgive you. There, I said it. You're forgiven." I took a deep breath, knowing that my next words would sting. "I'm the paralyzed one, Eleanor. Not you. So stop acting like you are."

"How dare you?" she said, marching toward me. "How dare you presume to know everything about me!"

I didn't flinch as she approached. "But I do. Since the moment Daddy placed you in my arms, I have known you. And studied you. And wanted to be you. You were always so brave—and not just all the crazy physical stuff you did, but the way you always said what you meant, and never hesitated to ask questions. Didn't you ever wonder why Lucy and I always tagged along and tried to do what you were doing? We wanted to be just like you. Maybe I still do."

Eleanor just stood there, shaking her head, as if the mere act could negate everything I'd said. But I had to make sure she understood. "Do you want to know where Glen is now?"

She stilled and looked at me suspiciously. "Where is he? Is he all right?"

"He's fine." I paused. "He's out with a Realtor looking for a house for us and the baby."

She slid back down into the chair she'd just vacated. "A house?"

I nodded. "Just something small—probably a two bedroom—and close by Mama. And a garage. We'll want to use that as my workroom, and a place where customers can come and be fitted for their costumes."

She frowned. "But how can you afford it?"

"Glen's boss quit, and because he's so near to getting his business degree, they decided to go ahead and allow him to be the operating manager for three of the metropolitan-area rental agencies, and when he gets his degree next spring, they'll make him the official manager."

Her smile was tentative. "That's great, but when did this all happen?"

"We found out about the promotion last week, but we've been talking about the house ever since we found out I was pregnant. We just didn't expect to be able to afford it so soon."

"Last week? But nobody said anything to me."

I held her gaze for a moment, hoping I wouldn't have to point out the obvious.

She lowered her eyes, finally noticing the neatly folded burgundy suit on the table in front of her. Her fingers brushed the soft wool, then withdrew just like she was a child caught reaching for a gift that wasn't hers. "What's this?"

"It's your Juilliard interview suit."

She looked at me and then back at the suit.

"I promised that I would make it for you."

"When I was fourteen," she said softly as her hands smoothed over the fabric.

"Do you want to try it on? I had Mama help me with the measurements, so it should fit just right, but it might need a few tweaks."

She stood and held up the pencil skirt with the small pleated flounce at the back split. "It's just like on the pattern cover," she said, her voice almost reverential. She placed the skirt over a chair, then picked up the jacket, holding it up to the light and seeing the tiny hand stitches and flared collar. Without further prompting, she slid her arms into the jacket and buttoned it, then stood the collar up at the back to frame her face. Just as I'd predicted, she looked stunning.

"It fits perfectly," she said, her face unsmiling.

"What's wrong?" I asked. "Don't you like it?"

She carefully slid her arms from the sleeves, then laid the jacket on top of the skirt. "It's beautiful, but I'm never going to an audition at Juilliard."

I rolled my wheelchair over to her so I could look her in the eyes and make her understand why I'd made the suit. "It doesn't matter if you never go to New York or set foot inside Carnegie Hall. It doesn't even matter if you never wear the suit." I took her hand again and looked up into her face, hoping to see understanding. "I want you to hang it in your closet as a reminder that you *could* do all of those things, that you are smart, and strong, and beautiful, and brave. And that's never changed."

Her chin dropped to her chest. "You're wrong, you know. About everything. You don't really know the person I am."

"I'm your sister," I said.

She closed her eyes as if summoning strength, and when she opened them again, her eyes were bleak. "The day of your accident—I knew you were scared. I knew you didn't want to climb that tree. But Glen was there and we were so eager to show off to him. So I egged you on, trying to get you to admit that you were scared. But you wouldn't. No matter how much I teased and tried to get you to climb back down, you wouldn't. I always admired that about you, you know. Your ability to get what you wanted at any cost. I hated you a little for it, too."

She held her hands out, palms up, as if to show me she was playing her last hand. "Right before you fell, Glen was looking at you and telling you to be careful, and I saw that he loved you, knew then that he always had even if he didn't realize it. I hated you so much right then. So much that I closed my eyes and wished with all my heart that you'd fall and die. And then you fell."

She grabbed her purse and ran out of the house, leaving the beautiful suit behind. I'd wanted to point out that she'd almost died, too, trying to get to me as quickly as she could. But it wouldn't have mattered. The truth had become like the scent of a moonflower, easily erased by the wind of hindsight and guilt.

I watched her go, hearing the old Gullah woman in my head again for the first time since the accident. *All shut-eye ain't sleep; all good-bye ain't gone.*

I'd finally come to understand what she'd meant, and I wondered how long it would be until Eleanor did, too.

Eleanor

I sat curled up in Bernadett's armchair in the sunroom at Luna Point, trying to focus on the art book about artists of the eighteenth and nineteenth centuries that Bernadett had reserved. It was due on Saturday, and since it didn't seem that Helena had any interest in it, I figured I should look at it one more time before it went back to the library.

I was having a hard time concentrating, my mind wandering to my sister's words and my own confession, and to the previous weekend, when Finn had kissed me out on the dock. I didn't want to dwell on any of it, having long since learned that the past couldn't be changed no matter how much we looked back. Yet I still found myself touching my lips and remembering the kiss, wondering at its implications. Wondering, too, why I wished I hadn't backed away.

Happily, Finn was in New York all week, and although it also meant that Gigi was with Harper, I was glad I didn't have to face him every morning in the office.

Nurse Weber stuck her head into the sunroom. "I just put the broccoli casserole in the oven, and now I'm going to the grocery store. I should be back before it has to come out, but listen for the bing of the timer just in case. I'll be back in about an hour."

I waved her off and returned to the book, skimming through the text and slowly thumbing through the pages. I lifted my head for a moment, listening to see if I'd heard Helena or just imagined it, then turned the page, a photograph capturing my attention. I started, recognizing one of the paintings in a photo that took up one third of the right-hand page.

I flipped on the floor lamp behind me and held up the page, the glossiness of the paper reflecting the light and making it hard to see. Impatient, I stood and moved toward the window to see it in better light. It was an oil painting from the eighteenth-century Dutch painter Pieter van der Werff depicting a woman sitting at her dressing table, leaning toward her mirror. She looked at the viewer from the reflected glass as she fastened a necklace, the color of the ruby matching the red of her long velvet dress, which billowed around the bottom of the painting like a crimson dust cloud.

I stared at it on the page for a long time, trying to tell myself that it couldn't be the same painting that I stared at every time I sat down to play the piano. Using my finger to mark the page, I made my way to the music room. After flipping on all of the lights and pulling back the drapes as far as they would go, I moved toward the painting, my suspicions confirmed before I was halfway across the room.

Squinting, I read the artist's name scrawled in gold paint in the bottom right of the canvas. I could see the brushstrokes in the paint and the hardened tips of color in the drapes of red velvet fabric. Even the woman's expression, of wariness and welcome, was exact. If this was a reproduction, it was a very good one.

I scanned down the page to read the caption: *Portrait of Woman with Ruby Necklace, 1712. Believed to be one of the premier examples of the aim of Dutch painters to employ words with their images to transfer knowledge and information about the world, and cannot be taken in from a single viewing point.*

I looked up at the portrait on the wall, trying to interpret what I'd just read with what I was seeing, but all I could see was a painting of a beautiful woman in a red gown. My gaze flickered through more description and then stopped on the final line: *From the Reichmann Family Collection. Believed lost in the bombing of Budapest, July 1944.*

The words began to jump under my eyes until I realized that my whole body was shaking. I made it to the love seat and sat down, forcing my arms to remain steady so I could read and reread the last two lines over and over to make sure I had them right. *From the Reichmann Family Collection. Believed lost in the bombing of Budapest, July 1944.*

Could Helena be related to the Reichmann family somehow? And why was the painting believed lost when it was hanging on the wall in an old house on Edisto Island? I frowned, my mind jumping from one possible answer to the next, but none of them resolving all the questions. Such as why Bernadett had requested this book from the library and why she hadn't wanted Helena to see it.

My gaze traveled to the wall across the room, to the other portraits hanging there, the overhead lights emphasizing the waves in the unstretched canvases. Helena had framed them herself and had not wanted anyone to come in and appraise them, despite Finn's repeated requests.

Yet she had sold several of them over the years, according to Jacob Isaacson—an assertion that seemed to be confirmed by the blank spots on the walls.

Jacob Isaacson. As an art dealer, he could probably answer some of my questions. And maybe even some I was afraid to ask. I thought for a moment about calling Finn first, and just as quickly dismissed it. What I'd just discovered had nothing to do with my job. And if I did find something, I wanted Helena to be the one to tell him.

Placing the library receipt in the book as a bookmark, I left the art book on the piano bench and moved into the foyer. He'd given me a business card for Helena, with his phone number for her to call, and I remembered it falling to the floor and slipping under the small space between the bottom of the small hall chest and the floor.

After removing the lamp from the table, I braced myself against the solid piece of furniture and managed to slide it until I spotted the small white rectangle lying faceup, waiting to be found.

I picked up the card and replaced the furniture, knowing that if Helena saw it she would know immediately what I'd been looking for. Then I returned to the music room, where I'd left my phone, and called the number before I could talk myself out of it.

He picked up on the third ring. "Jacob Isaacson."

"Mr. Isaacson, this is Eleanor Murray. We met a couple of weeks ago, when you came to Edisto. I work for Helena Szarka."

"Yes, of course. And please call me Jacob." From his excited tone, I knew that I had his full attention.

"I, um, wanted to talk with you, because when you were here, you mentioned a particular painting that Bernadett wanted you to see. I was hoping you could give me a little more information."

There was a brief pause. "Eleanor, as eager as I am to discuss this subject further, I hesitate since you're not a member of the family—"

"I understand," I said, cutting him off. "And I'm not expecting you to give me any more details than you feel comfortable revealing. I just need to know a couple of things. So that . . ." I paused, no longer sure of my motive. "So I can put my mind at rest."

"All right," he said, excitement and trepidation wrapped around each other in the two simple words.

I took a deep breath. "Are you familiar with Pieter van der Werff's *Portrait of Woman with Ruby Necklace*?"

There was a brief silence on the other end of the phone, filled with hushed anticipation. "Yes. I'm very familiar with it."

"Is that the painting Bernadett wished to discuss with you?"

Instead of answering my question directly, he asked, "Have you seen it?"

I thought for a moment. "I saw it in an art book. The caption says that it was lost during the bombing of Budapest during the war."

"Yes," he said slowly. "I know."

"Who were the Reichmanns?"

"They were a wealthy Jewish family who lived in Budapest before the war. They were bankers, at least until the Horthy regime allied with Germany and Jews were no longer allowed to be anything but menial workers."

"Do you know what happened to them?" I closed my eyes, wanting to block out the images from the history books I'd been reading, images of skeletal humans in rags, and piles of empty shoes.

"They were put on a train and sent to Auschwitz. All of them died there—the mother, father, three children, grandparents; they all died. Except for the youngest, a daughter, Sarah, who was hidden by neighbors when the Nazis came." There was a brief pause, and I imagined the somber young man measuring his words. "Sarah Reichmann was my grandmother."

I felt pressure on my chest, as if I was lying beneath a wall of stone, and I realized that I had stopped breathing. I recalled Nurse Weber's words to Helena. *Breathe in, breathe out.*

"I'm sorry," I said, knowing how inadequately stupid those two words were.

"Did you know, Eleanor, that during the war the Nazis confiscated the personal property of the Jews they forced into ghettos and then sent to the camps? All across Europe, they took jewelry and silver and fine art. Some of it has been recovered, but so much of it is lost now to the survivors. Sold privately over the years, and hanging in homes where most people don't realize that the painting is more than a lovely portrait of a landscape. Or a beautiful woman. They don't see the blood of six million Jews. They don't think to look, or if they know, they look the other way."

Breathe in, breathe out.

"Are you there?" he said, his voice sounding very far away.

"Yes. I'm here. I need to call you back. I need to speak with Miss Szarka again."

"I understand. And Miss Murray—Eleanor. It's not about the money. It's never been about the money."

We said good-bye and I ended the call, my phone frozen in my hand. A cloud crossed over the sun outside, darkening the corners of the room as if trying to hide all the secrets that had gathered there, unseen, for too many years.

CHAPTER 29

Eleanor

I sat on the piano bench staring at the painting of the woman in the red dress, wondering how many people had seen it in the years it had hung there. *Sold privately over the years, and hanging in homes where most people don't realize that the painting is more than a lovely portrait of a landscape. Or a beautiful woman. They don't see the blood of six million Jews. They don't think to look, or if they know, they look the other way.*

I heard the thump of Helena's cane banging on the wall, but I still couldn't move. I felt chilled to my core, reminding me of the only other time I'd felt this kind of inertia. It had been the night the storm took my father away from me, and all I could do was sit on the dock and stare out through the pouring rain, thinking that if I just looked hard enough, I'd spot his boat.

The thumping came again, and I willed myself to move, wishing for a star to lead the way, to tell me what I was supposed to say to this woman whom I thought I knew, and, if I was honest with myself, had grown to like. I considered calling Finn in New York, but I couldn't let go of the thought that there was some other explanation besides the obvious, that Helena was innocent of any wrongdoing and there was another reason why art that had once belonged to a prominent Jewish family was hanging on Helena's wall. And why she'd lied and said she had brought all the paintings from their little house in Budapest.

Slowly, I walked toward Helena's bedroom. She sat up in bed, her cane held aloft as if she was preparing to bang it against the wall again. I stared at her, half daring her to do it while I watched. She lowered the cane and let it rest against her night table.

"Where have you been? I woke up and called for you and for Nurse Weber and nobody answered. I thought I had been left alone to fend for myself." She gave me a petulant smile. "The housekeeper has moved my Herend roosters where I cannot see them. I need you to move them back to the little table by my bed so I can enjoy them."

I was glad she was doing all the talking and giving me orders. It gave me a reason to move my limbs and kept me silent while I tried to think of a way to ask a ninety-year-old woman why she had a painting that didn't belong to her, and why she'd lied to me about where it came from. I wanted to know the truth, but more important, Finn *needed* to know the truth. If he didn't already.

I picked up the two roosters from the dressing table and moved them closer to Helena, where she almost purred with satisfaction at seeing her two treasures again.

I stared at the broken tail of the orange rooster, my mind's eye flickering like an old movie, trying to guess the plot before it happened. "Helena, remember how you told Finn and me about how you broke the rooster?"

"Yes, of course. I was clumsy. I am sure you find that hard to believe."

I didn't rouse to her distractive bait, and for the first time I saw a glint of wariness in her eyes.

"You said it was the night the Americans bombed Budapest. I read in one of my books that they did it to convince the Hungarian government to stop the deportations of Jews that had started in March."

"Yes, but I did not know that then. I was too busy trying to earn money for food for my sister and myself. We tried not to involve ourselves in politics."

"You told me before that you sang in cafés to earn money for food. Is that how you met Gunter?"

A secret smile touched her lips. *He was the love of my life.* "Yes. The Germans were encamped outside of the city, but when they had leave they would come into Budapest. Gunter came to my café every night he could and sat at one of the front tables. It took him nearly a month before he said anything to me. And then it was only to ask me if I was thirsty. He told me I was too thin and bought me dinner. He would not allow any of the men to say anything he considered too rude. Gunter was only a butcher's son, but he was a gentleman."

I looked into her face, trying to see what I needed to know. "Did it bother you that he was a German soldier?"

The wariness returned to her eyes. "I did not see him that way. I only saw him as the young man who brought me flowers and spoke to me of the life we would have. The war did not exist for us."

"But I imagine it did for Bernadett." I waited for that to sink in. "Did Bernadett ever join you in singing for the soldiers?"

Gnarled fingers started picking at her bedclothes. "She was very shy and did not like to perform in front of others. But no, she did not join me. She could not."

"Because of Benjamin?"

Her hands stilled and she sent me an odd smile. "Yes, I suppose you could say that." She sighed. "They were difficult times for everybody. I did not care who I sang for, or who gave me money. You would understand if you knew what it is to do without, and the things that you would do to be safe, or to have food in your belly. It is a choice we sometimes have to make."

I reached over and picked up the broken rooster again. I rubbed my thumb over the rough stub where the tail had once been, wondering what it had been like for her. For Bernadett. To know how fragile life could be. "I'm curious about something."

She tilted her head back, narrowing her eyes. "And all of my warnings about the curious cat have not stopped you with your questions."

"No. Not yet. My sister, Eve, told me it was one of my good qualities."

"And when have you ever listened to your sister?"

"Not often enough, apparently," I said, knowing I never would have admitted such a thing to Eve. "And you could always ask me to stop." I wasn't sure why I'd said that. Maybe because a part of me didn't really want to know. Or maybe because I'd always sensed something in Helena, a darkness she tried to hide from the outside world. A darkness she wanted to shed. Maybe it was this last thing that made me ask Helena if she wanted me to stop.

She didn't say anything.

I continued. "I suppose it's because I've been reading all of those history books that I'm so intrigued. Especially since you were *there*. I have a firsthand witness to what I'm reading about now."

"A witness?" Her hands stilled on the bedclothes.

"Yes. To the bombing and your escape. It couldn't have been easy to get out of Hungary. It had pulled away from Germany and was looking to ally itself with the Allied forces. So Germany invaded Hungary, and all the countries surrounding it were already under German control. I can't imagine they would have allowed just anybody to walk across the border."

"You have a strange way of asking questions, Eleanor. You say you are curious and are going to ask a question, and then you do not. Instead you tell me things I already know."

I pressed my thumb hard against the stubbed tail, hard enough that I broke the skin and made it bleed. "I'm just trying to help you with your memory. Trying to set the mood, so to speak, and the scene, so you can picture that night and tell me what you saw. You can tell me how you and Bernadett escaped during the Nazi occupation with a broken china rooster and a collection of valuable paintings that came from your tiny house."

Her gaze turned steely, but I wouldn't look away. Nor did she ask me to stop.

"Did you escape before or after the bombing? I'm trying to picture you and Bernadett with all these rolled-up paintings stuffed under your coats, trying to cross the border without being stopped, and I can't. Did Gunter help? Or Benjamin? I'm hoping you do a better job than my imagination in telling me how you managed it."

"I would like some water, please," she said, her feeble voice at odds with the feisty woman I'd just been speaking with.

I got up and went to the kitchen and returned with a glass. I put it in her hands and sat down again. "If you'd rather rest now, we can stop."

Her eyes met mine and she lifted her chin. "I am not so old that I need to rest all the time."

I leaned back in my chair. "So how did you leave the country?"

She stared into her water for a long moment, and when she looked up at me again, her eyes seemed to be warring with light and shadow. "By vegetable truck," she said, her mouth twisted in a crooked smile.

"A vegetable truck?"

"I do not know what Gunter promised the farmer, but he got us a truck. We could not leave on foot. Bernadett was ill—too ill to walk."

"What was wrong with her?"

The glass in her hands shook. I reached over and held it to her lips, then placed it on the bedside table. "She had been ill for nearly a year. She would divide her food rations with the children at the convent where she taught music, and she was too thin. She had colds and coughs constantly so that she never regained her strength before the next ailment. This last was typhus. Gunter was able to give us some medicine for her, and food, but we knew that would not last. She needed penicillin. Everyone knew that the war was over for the Germans, and they were becoming desperate. And the Russians were eager to take over when the Germans left. So Gunter and I made plans for Bernadett and me to escape."

"And you made plans to meet and marry after the war."

"Yes," she said. "He promised to come back to me." Her voice broke, and I had to look away.

I wanted to ask her about the paintings, ask her if the truck made it easier to conceal rolled-up canvases. But her story made me pause. It made me picture my own sister, starving and sick, whose only hope was me getting her to safety. I leaned closer. "Where were you trying to go?"

"America eventually. Magda's husband had booked us passage from England—a prospect that terrified me. The German U-boats were everywhere, and even though the Allies had invaded France the previous month, I was afraid to cross the channel, much less the Atlantic Ocean. But there was no other way. First we had to get to Switzerland for medical care. If Bernadett died, I did not care what happened to me, so I did not dwell on anything after Switzerland. There would be time to think about it later."

"And Bernadett—what did she think?"

Helena turned toward the window, to allow light on her face or to hide from me; I couldn't tell which.

"She was delirious with fever. It was a good thing that she could not fight me. She would not have gone."

"Why? Surely she knew how desperate the situation was."

Helena continued to look out her window, seeing sights too large for my own imagination. "There were some she would not leave."

"Benjamin? Could he not go with her?"

She looked at me then, her face contorted with grief, and I waited again for her to ask me to stop. And still she did not. It was almost as if she'd been waiting all these years to tell someone.

"Benjamin?" she echoed. "No, she would not have wanted to leave without him, just as I know he would not have left with her. It was the children. The children in the convent where she worked. She would not have left them. But I told her that I would take care of things, as I always did. And she believed me."

I sat up, remembering the silver box. "The convent where Bernadett taught the children—was that at the motherhouse of the Daughters of the Divine Redeemer?"

She looked at me with only mild surprise, as if her thoughts were turned so far inward that she could not focus on anything else. "Yes. That was it."

"Would you like more water?" I asked.

She didn't answer right away. Then she blinked as if she'd just realized I had spoken. "Yes. Please."

I lifted the glass to her lips. "And so Gunter got you a vegetable truck. Did he drive you all the way to Switzerland?"

"He would have if I had asked, but it was too dangerous for him. Dangerous for us, too, but more so for him since he was a soldier and he would have been shot for desertion. I had to do it on my own. Gunter arranged papers and passes for us, and train tickets through Austria, but he could not go with us." She studied her hands as if she were surprised that they were hers, surprised not to see the smooth skin and straight fingers of a young woman.

I, too, saw the young woman, determined to save her sister. Despite the danger and uncertainty and threat of losing her own life. I thought of Eve, saw her fall from the tree again, felt the need to get to her as quickly as I could. I could still feel the rough tree bark slipping through my hands, slicing my finger, and the pain as my skull hit the hard-packed dirt of the road. I had thought of that moment many times in the years since, and not once had I considered reacting differently.

"Have you ever told Finn your story?"

She shook her head. "I have never spoken of it. Even to Bernadett. It is not something we wished to remember."

"But you made it. With a broken rooster and a collection of oil paintings." I waited for her to speak again, my words suspended in the air between us, a hole into which we both could fall. When she didn't say anything, I said, "You were very brave. I don't know if I could have done what you did."

"She was my sister," she said, the words simple yet filled with meaning. Her gaze swept past me to the window again. "We gave away one of the paintings to the farmer near Bern who fed us and let us sleep in his barn for three days. He and his wife were very kind and did not ask questions. The wife made chicken soup for Bernadett and gave her medicine. I do not know if Bernadett would have made it if we had not stopped there on our way to the train station in Bern."

"It was a small price to pay, then. To give them a valuable painting in return for Bernadett's life."

"Yes. It was." Her gaze met mine, the old arrogance back in them as she regarded me. "There are some things in life for which the cost cannot be measured. Even if it means paying for it for the rest of your life."

The hair rose on the back of my neck as our gazes met. "Did you know the Reichmanns? They were a wealthy family in Budapest before the war."

Her expression didn't falter. "No. I am not familiar with the name. Should I be?"

"I don't know," I said, suddenly unsure of what I needed to know. Or why I needed to know it.

I stood. "I want to show you a picture I found in one of the library books about art—one of Bernadett's books."

"Could we not listen to music instead? I am in the mood for some Schubert. And I see you are just about finished organizing the music. I would like for you to show me what you have done and where you intend to file all of the books. Perhaps I can help you."

I wanted to say yes and forget about the art book and my conversation with Jacob Isaacson. Forget about the Reichmanns and their stolen art and a painting that had been misplaced by history. But I could not. I knew what guilt without forgiveness did to a soul, and Helena was running out of time.

"Maybe later. Let me show you the book first."

Her eyes showed no alarm as I walked from the room. Or maybe I mistook the lack of alarm for resignation.

I paused in the entranceway to the music room, taking in the tall windows, the stacks of music against the walls, and the beautiful piano. I thought of the music I'd played there and the way that Helena would sit with her eyes closed and a smile on her lips as she tried to disguise the fact that what I played wasn't too horrible to listen to. And I thought of the simple songs I'd taught to Gigi and how Finn would sometimes slip into the back of the room when I played as if I wouldn't notice. As I went to where I'd left the book, I couldn't help but wonder if I would ever see the room the same way again. Or if I'd ever be allowed back in it.

My phone rang, jarring my thoughts. For a horrified moment, I thought it was Jacob Isaacson, calling to see if I'd spoken to Helena yet. I fumbled for the phone in my pocket and saw that it was a Charleston number I didn't recognize. "Hello?"

"Hello, Eleanor? This is Harper Gibbes, Genevieve's mother."

"Yes, hello."

"I'm sorry to bother you, but my daughter told me you were on Edisto babysitting that horrid old aunt of Finn's, so I figured you'd need a reprieve."

"Um, she's not—"

She didn't wait for me to finish. "Genevieve says she's bored to death and wants to go to Edisto. She has no camps this week, so I have no objection, and neither does Finn. There's just the matter of getting her there."

My eyes fell on the painting of the woman in red velvet. "I'd be happy to come pick her up. I just have to wait until the nurse returns from the grocery store and then I can leave. Tell Gigi—Genevieve that I'll be there within the hour."

"Thank you, Eleanor. I'll be sure to tell Finn how amenable you've been so he can put a bonus in your paycheck. We'll see you in an hour, then."

She ended the call before I could say good-bye.

I wasn't sure if I was more disappointed or relieved at having to postpone my confrontation with Helena. Leaving the art book where it was, I made my way back to Helena's room to tell her the change of plans.

She lay on her back with her hands folded on her chest in a pose one sees on medieval crypts. The bedcovers rose and fell in a steady rhythm designed to feign sleep, and as I approached she let out a small sigh, then turned her face toward the window.

I leaned down to whisper in her ear. "We're not done with our conversation, Helena. And you can't sleep forever."

I slipped out of her room, passing Teri Weber on the way in, and climbed into the Volvo. Absently, I rubbed the cut on my thumb from the broken tail of the rooster, thinking about something Helena had said about choices and what people would do to survive.

CHAPTER 30

Eleanor

Gigi's small suitcase was already packed and waiting by the door when I arrived, dashing through the rain to the covered piazza, the front door thrown open before I could ring the bell. I heard the tap of high heels and waited for Harper to appear behind her daughter in the doorway.

Harper's hair and makeup were perfect, as were her slim ankle pants and crisp blouse. I tried to remember the last time I'd looked in a mirror, realizing with some horror that it had been that morning when I'd brushed my teeth.

"Thank you so much for doing this, Eleanor. Finn's actually finished a bit early and will be returning from New York this evening. He'll probably drive right out to Edisto, regardless of the hour." She shook her head and rolled her eyes to the ceiling. "I'll never understand his love for that place."

I bit my lip to prevent myself from saying what I wanted. "It's not a problem, and it's always more fun when Genevieve's around."

The little girl beamed up at me, then turned to her mother and threw her arms around Harper's slim hips. "I love you, Mommy." She kept her face tilted toward her mother, waiting.

A smile softened Harper's angular face as she leaned down and kissed

Gigi's cheek. "You behave and don't talk everybody's ears off. We'll go shopping for new school shoes next week."

"Can they be pink?"

Harper actually laughed. "You know your school doesn't allow that." She bent to straighten the pink floral headband in Gigi's fine hair. In a conspiratorial tone, she added, "But maybe we can find a way to stick a pink ribbon in the laces."

"Thanks, Mommy," Gigi said, giving her mother a final squeeze before racing down the piazza toward the car.

I picked up the suitcase. "You have my cell number if you need me."

Harper nodded, a wistful look on her face as she watched Gigi disappear. "Yes, thanks." She turned back to me. "She had a little cough this morning, but she seems to be totally fine now. Just keep an eye out for any other symptoms."

"I will," I promised, wondering what it must be like to interpret every cold symptom or ache or pain or even allergy as a potential precursor to a relapse.

"And drive carefully," she added almost absently. "All those cruise-ship tourists are like palmetto bugs scurrying across the road and just begging to get hit."

"I always do," I said, repeating the same thing I told Finn every time he watched me drive away with his little girl.

I waited until Gigi had buckled her seat belt before putting the car in drive and heading down Queen Street. It was nearly five o'clock, so the cruise-ship passengers had mostly disappeared from the streets and sidewalks back into their mother ships—what Rich Kobylt at the office called the massive cruise liners—so now it was mostly rush-hour traffic as I headed out of the downtown area. Traffic seemed heavier than usual owing to the steady drizzle that burst into a heavy downpour at regular intervals.

Gigi started chattering as soon as we reached the first stop sign. "I got a birthday invitation from my best friend, Teensy Olsen. People always get our names confused because she's really tall, but they call her Teensy anyway probably because she was tiny when she was a baby, but aren't all babies? Anyway, Teensy's been my best friend since kindergarten, although there was that time in second grade when she didn't invite me to her ice-skating party. . . ."

I nodded and interjected syllables here and there, trying to concentrate on seeing the road with my wipers at full throttle. The driver behind me honked—obviously a Charleston transplant—because it took too long for me to turn right on Broad Street as I waited for an opening.

". . . I just have no idea what to wear to a boy-girl party since I go to an all-girls school so I don't get to hang out with boys too much unless you count my daddy since he's a boy but not really. . . ."

I took the right and headed down Broad toward Lockwood and Highway 17, the rain so heavy now that I could barely see in front of the car. The obnoxious person behind me swerved around to cut in front and I saw the Fulton County, Georgia, license plate. *Atlanta.* "Figures," I said under my breath as he sped away.

". . . I'd wear jeans but I don't have a pair since my mommy doesn't think they send the right message and I'm kind of okay with that because I have never seen a pair of pink jeans and I wouldn't want a pair unless they could be pink . . ."

The light on Lockwood turned yellow and I slowed to a stop while the three people in front of me sped through it. The younger me would have joined them, but then again the younger me wouldn't have been driving a Volvo or have Gigi Beaufain in the backseat.

". . . and since you're so good at picking out birthday presents, I was really hoping you could go with Mommy and me to get one for Teensy because Mommy always gets the kind of present *she* would have liked as a little girl instead of what my friends would like and I don't want to hurt her feelings so maybe if you and I both said we didn't like something . . ."

The light for my lane turned green and I slowly depressed the accelerator, not always trusting myself with the V8 engine and erring on the side of caution. The sound of a car horn being held longer than necessary carried through the noise of my wipers, and I wondered absently if the obnoxious driver from Atlanta had somehow managed to circle around to antagonize me again.

Gigi asked me something and I turned my head slightly to ask her to repeat the question. The earth seemed to pause in its rotation, the rain frozen in midair, as I spotted the dark blue sedan, its headlights on, barreling toward us. A graduation hat tassel swayed from the rearview mirror, twisting, twisting. Gigi's scream mixed with that of screeching tires and shattered glass and the sickening crunch of metal against metal. I jerked to the side, my arms reaching toward her, her mother's voice coming from inside my head—*Please be extra careful with her.* Something hit me in the head, the pain so sudden that I was aware of it only as an afterthought, and then I was no longer aware of anything at all.

I was up in a tree and I looked across the road to see Eve, but it wasn't Eve at all. It was my father, wearing his overalls and hat and beard, just as I remembered. He was far away, but I could see his eyes, and they were disappointed eyes. He didn't open his mouth, but I heard the words he was saying to me, except they were Helena's words. *And so you honor him by dismissing the music he taught you?*

I tried to speak, to tell him that he was wrong, but no words came out. I looked down, expecting to see Eve but instead seeing only the rain-soaked asphalt of Lockwood Boulevard, the blue and red reflections of the emergency vehicles' lights shimmering on the ground.

I was not in a tree at all, but hovering over my corner of the world. *I've been here before.* The words threaded through me like sunlight through fog, illuminating and warming.

A fireman pried the rear door off the Volvo and carefully leaned inside, and I was behind him, a passive bystander once again. Blood stained Gigi's white-blond hair, her pink shirt and shorts, ran down her legs and into her pink sandals. Rain poured down on her, diluting red blood to pink.

But she had cancer, I said, my words falling unheard with the rain, as if having survived one tragedy should make her immune to another. *It was worth it.* The words were in my head as I looked down to see a night-blooming cereus sprouting from the asphalt, its edges already starting to wilt. I stared at it, wanting to let it know that there were other flowers to put in my garden.

And then I was staring at my own body, laid on a gurney, a long gash on my forehead oozing blood as one of the paramedics pressed on my chest and forced air into my lungs. I turned away, and I was now on a dock that stretched far out into the ocean. And at the very end, my father stood, waiting for me. I knew it was him; I knew from the shape of his shoulders and the beard that would tickle my cheek when he kissed me.

I began to run toward him, but it was a dream-run, where the harder you tried to move your legs, the slower they became. When I looked again at the end of the dock, my father was walking away. Somebody else was there, somebody taller and younger, but I couldn't see his face.

All shut-eye ain't sleep; all good-bye ain't gone.

I turned abruptly at the woman's voice in my ear, expecting to see the old Gullah woman. Instead I saw Bernadett and Magda leaning over Gigi like guardian angels as her gurney was rolled into the ambulance.

You ready?

The Gullah woman held out a secret keeper toward me, the lid sealing the top. I didn't recognize the pattern, an irregular zigzag of loops and lines that reversed on themselves and then simply stopped, the pattern unfinished. A vessel that could pour out or keep in. I looked in her wide eyes and knew she was handing me my life, the lid hiding what was to come.

What if it hurts? My head shouted the words.

What if it don't? She smiled, her teeth shining light into the darkness.

I reached for the basket and I was floating toward my body, where the paramedic was leaning back on his heels and shaking his head.

I opened my mouth and sucked in a deep breath, feeling the cool, wet rain on my skin, hearing the startled shout from the paramedic. The pain came next, but I welcomed it as a reminder that I could still feel.

When I awoke, my head throbbed and a thick bandage covered most of my forehead. I was disoriented at first, wondering where I was and why Glen was sitting in a chair by my bed. And then I remembered.

I struggled to sit up, but Glen gently held me down. "It's okay, Eleanor. You're okay. It's going to be okay."

"Where's Gigi?"

"At Children's Hospital."

"And Finn?"

"He's with her." He paused. "She's hurt pretty bad."

He didn't look away, but I knew he was holding something back.

"What aren't you telling me? Please, Glen. What aren't you telling me?" My head throbbed, but the feeling of panic over Gigi overpowered the pain.

"You need to keep calm. . . ."

"I need to know about Gigi. And if you won't tell me, I will yank these tubes out of me and go find out myself."

A shadow of a smile crossed his face before he turned serious again. "She's had severe head trauma. There's swelling on the brain." He swallowed. "They've put her in a medically induced coma to see if they can get the swelling down."

The white fluorescent light above me seemed to intensify, increasing the pain in my head, pressing on my heart, and I had the image of Gigi looking at the night-blooming cereus and saying it was worth it. I struggled to sit up again. "Oh, God. No. No. I was driving, Glen. I was driving and we got hit. . . ."

He put a hand on my arm and made me lie down again. "I know, Eleanor. We all know. It wasn't your fault. Some idiot ran the red light and couldn't stop because of the rain. Finn told me to make sure you knew that. You did nothing wrong. Nothing. And she's hanging in there—no change, which means she's not improving yet, but she's also not getting any worse. Finn said he'd keep us posted so you won't worry."

"How long has it been?"

"Almost a whole day. It's almost four o'clock in the afternoon. They gave you some painkillers that made you sleep. You need to rest."

I shook my head, feeling as if my brain was sloshing from side to side. "I've got to see her." I struggled to sit up again, but Glen held me back.

"You can't do anything for her right now. But you can take care of yourself so you can be strong for her. And for Finn." He'd said Finn's name with a forced reluctance, as if from an old habit instead of any real resentment.

I closed my eyes briefly. "How soon can I get out of here?"

"Probably tomorrow. All your vitals are fine and you don't have any broken bones. Just a nasty cut on your forehead from the air bag. They're just keeping you for observation, really. Your heart stopped." His eyes met mine. "Like before. When you fell from the tree."

"I remember . . . ," I said slowly, seeing my father on the dock again, and Magda and Bernadett. "Glen?"

He leaned closer. "Yes?"

My head throbbed as thoughts moved in and out of my consciousness, and I reached to grab hold of one before I forgot it. "Do you believe in second chances?" I closed my eyes, the pain in my head too intense for me to think clearly or to even understand what I was asking. "Or do you think we only have one shot at happiness and we'd better milk it while we have it because when it's gone it's all over?"

He sat back, his slender hands spread wide on his thighs. "I think both. I think it's what you make of it, like a choice. You can choose to move on or you can choose to dig in your heels. Why?"

Because I died again yesterday, and then I woke up because I think I've been given another chance. I shook my head, no longer sure. "Why are you here? Where are Mama and Eve?"

"Eve wanted to come, but her doctor said no—too many germs and your condition wasn't critical. Your mother can't drive and somebody needed to stay with Eve. So Eve sent me. Don't worry—I wanted to come. Make sure you were all right and drive you home when they're ready to release you." He indicated the table next to the bed. "Eve asked me to bring you that. She actually made me come home and get it after we knew you were okay."

I looked at my bedside table, where instead of flowers sat a Piggly Wiggly grocery bag. "What is it?"

"I don't know. Eve just told me to give it to you."

I looked into his eyes and for the first time saw only my sister's husband, an old friend, a person I'd grown comfortable with. Eve had been right when she'd said that we would never have made it together, that we were too different. I tried to picture him flying airplanes, or climbing a tree to bring me down, but I could not.

"Thank you," I said, indicating the bag but meaning so much more. I shifted myself into a sitting position, pausing for a moment to quell the rising nausea, so I could open the bag. Glen unknotted the handles and pulled it open, and I leaned forward, realizing as soon as I did that I didn't need to take anything out to know what it was.

"What is it?" he asked.

"It's something Eve made for me," I said as I reached in and pulled out the burgundy wool jacket and rubbed it against my cheek. There was no note, but I didn't need one. In the special way between sisters, we didn't always need words to communicate. But I remembered what she'd said when she'd given me the suit, right before I'd told her that I'd wanted her to die. *You are smart, and strong, and beautiful, and brave. And that's never changed.*

"Is it clothing?" Glen asked.

"Sort of. More like a suit of armor and Superwoman costume done up in wool gabardine." I pressed the fabric against my head as if it could take the pain away, then placed the jacket back inside the bag and knotted the ties closed. "Can you push the nurse's button, please? I need to get out of here."

"I guess I can't convince you to stay a little longer—just to make sure?"

"No. And if you could just drive me to Children's Hospital, you can drop me off—I can take a taxi home or ask Lucy to come get me."

"Don't even think of calling Lucy or a taxi. Call me. And I could stay if you need me to," he said, his expression earnest.

"Thanks, but no. Eve needs you at home."

His look was unconvinced, but he pushed the nurse's button anyway while I remembered a secret keeper basket with an unfinished pattern and wondered what was beneath the lid.

CHAPTER 31

Eleanor

The Medical University of South Carolina Children's Hospital was one of the best in the country. I kept repeating that to myself on the short drive between hospitals, my mind busy with images of a little girl who'd fought cancer and won a reprieve, and praying that she'd inherited the courage of her aunt who'd taken her sister across war-torn Europe and an entire ocean to save her life.

Glen insisted he would come with me to make sure I didn't pass out in the middle of the parking garage, his tight lips a silent reproach for checking myself out of the hospital before the doctors thought it wise. He'd barely slid into a space before I'd thrown open my door, then immediately misjudged the distance and stumbled onto the pavement, spilling my purse and its contents.

Glen lifted me gently, then put my belongings back into my purse. "You've just been in a serious accident and have been given painkillers. Stop trying to act like you're the old Ellie."

I stared at him, blinking at him through a haze of pain and old memories, recalling what Eve had said the last time we'd spoken. *I liked the Ellie you used to be, and I wish she'd come back.*

"Maybe it wouldn't be such a bad thing to bring her back." I indicated the Piggly Wiggly bag with the suit inside that I'd left on the seat. "Can you bring that, please?"

He sent me a questioning look but did as I asked. I didn't bother to explain, knowing that Eve would have understood and that was enough. Clutching the bag was like having my sister with me, the sister who believed me to be strong and brave. It didn't take my fear away, but it made me calmer, more centered. As if all the emotions swirling around inside me had been reined in and gathered together in a single manageable pile.

We walked as quickly as we could to the hospital entrance. I hated hospitals. Hated the antiseptic smells and the fake cheery smiles and patterned scrubs. I hated them mostly because they reminded me of my numerous trips to fix broken bones and twisted limbs—both mine and Eve's—and withstanding my mother's disapproving looks and reproachful sighs for me getting Eve involved in another one of my adventures.

"I can stay," Glen repeated.

"I know, and I appreciate the offer. I do. But I want you to go home to Eve. There's nothing you can do here. I still have my cell phone and I promise to call if I need anything, or need you to come pick me up—or I can always take a taxi."

"Don't you dare. Call me first."

We were directed to a waiting area with brightly painted orange and yellow walls, the colors blurring as I scanned the empty orange chairs for Finn. Two women, both knitting, sat chatting quietly in one corner. The only other occupied chair was filled by a man I didn't at first recognize.

The man stood. "Eleanor?"

Finn? His sunken eyes reminded me of those of the homeless men I sometimes saw in Marion Square. He was in his shirtsleeves, without a tie, and he looked like a little boy, utterly lost and lonely. Without thinking, I slid into his arms, allowing him to bury his face in my neck.

I looked up in time to see Glen give me a gentle smile and a wave before leaving.

Finn and I held each other for a long moment without speaking, until he released me. Taking my hand, he led us to two chairs covered in bright orange fabric. I appreciated the idea of the crayon-hued walls and furnishings in an attempt to comfort the children with the familiar. But for the adults, no bright colors or cheery smiles could do anything to make us forget that we were in a place where sick and hurt children were brought to be put back together.

"How is she?" I asked, holding my breath for the answer.

He gently touched the white bandage on my forehead. "You shouldn't have come. You're hurt."

"How could I not?" I felt the press of tears behind my eyes that I'd promised myself I wouldn't shed in front of him. "It was my fault. It was raining so hard that it was difficult to see. I should have known to pull over and wait until it stopped. Or gone a different way—it's such a bad intersection—"

He put a finger on my lips. "Stop. You did nothing wrong. It was an accident, nothing more. I don't want to hear another word about it being your fault."

I felt a tear wind its way down my cheek, and I brushed it away, wishing he hadn't seen it. "How is she?" I asked again, trying not to think of all the reasons he hadn't already answered me. "Can I see her?"

He looked down at our entwined hands. "She's still in ICU, and they're only allowing in immediate family members. Harper's with her now. I had to step away to call her husband—he's in London. And let others know . . ."

He clenched his jaw, working hard to regain control, to find territory he recognized. "She's . . . so small. Even with the side air bag . . ." He didn't continue, and I willed him to cry, knowing, too, that he wouldn't. He would have been taught that along with the proper way to address a senator and how making paper airplanes and camping outside were endeavors meant for other boys.

I'd given up trying to hold back the tears, and I had to let go of Finn to reach into my purse for the wad of Kleenexes that I'd learned from my mother to always have on hand. For the first time I appreciated her words of wisdom.

"She is small. But Gigi has the strongest spirit of anybody I've ever met. If anybody can get through this, it's her. I think she inherited it from her aunt Helena."

A dark shadow passed behind his eyes, and an icy wave shuddered through my veins. "Don't say that, Eleanor. Don't say that Gigi is anything like Helena."

Sharp pins pricked my skin, as if I were freezing from the inside out. "What do you mean?"

"There are things about Helena . . . things you don't know." He looked away, but not before I saw his eyes shutting me out. "Something dark. I don't want to think Gigi has any of that in her. Not when we need to focus on the positive."

I thought of the painting in the music room and the Reichmann family. *What does he know?* I found myself pulling back from him, unable to meet his eyes, unable to forget his barrage of questions at the Waterfront restaurant. Unable to forget how the old woman's hands shook as she'd held the Herend rooster.

I recognized the cool, controlled voice when he spoke again. "I need to ask a favor."

"Anything," I said without thinking. Just like the old Ellie would have.

The two women in the waiting area stood, leaving their knitting on their chairs, and left the room, saying something about the cafeteria downstairs. We watched them until they were gone.

Finn continued. "Helena doesn't know yet—about Gigi. I can't leave the hospital, but I don't want to tell her over the phone."

"And you want me to tell her."

He nodded. "Yes. I have a car and driver standing by outside that you can use. He can take you to your house first if you need to pick up some things, and then take you to Edisto."

"Do you think telling Helena is wise? The whole reason I'm even in her life is because she broke down after her sister's death. Maybe she's not strong enough to know about Gigi." My throat choked on Gigi's name, even my words rejecting the thought of Gigi being hurt.

Finn stood and walked away from me as if to study the abstract painting on the wall, a painting that looked like melted crayons had exploded on the canvas. "There was more to her breakdown than just Bernadett's death."

I recalled my mother saying something about gossip on the island after Bernadett had died, how there hadn't been an autopsy or a funeral announcement in the paper. About how family connections had kept details from the public. Yet all I could picture in my mind's eye was a feverish Bernadett being smuggled out of Budapest during a bombing raid, and then through Europe, to save her life.

"What?" I asked, afraid I already knew.

He turned to face me. "Bernadett killed herself."

My wound began to throb even more, as if some unseen hand had pressed on it. "Why?"

"I don't know."

I walked to where he stood, looking into his eyes to see if he was telling me the truth. But his eyes remained dark and shuttered, leaving my question unanswered.

"I'll tell her," I said. "For you."

He pulled me into his arms, and I thought I felt his lips on the top of my head. "Thank you."

We both looked up, then stepped back as Harper walked in. She wore the same clothes she'd worn the last time I'd seen her, when I'd gone to pick up Gigi at her house, but her hair was undone, her mascara smeared under her eyes, her pants and blouse rumpled. As I watched, she used the heel of her hand to dry her cheek.

I went to my purse and pulled out a clean Kleenex and handed it to her. She looked at it with surprise before taking it. "Thank you," she said. She paused, and I waited for her to speak again, to accuse me of being responsible for hurting Gigi. But I was prepared, clinging to the ghost of the old Ellie, waiting to resurrect her.

But any fire that Harper possessed was extinguished beneath a pile of guilt and anguish. She loved her daughter. I knew that. She'd simply been too selfish to show it, and now it might be too late. She regarded me with haunted eyes. "She had on her seat belt, right? And was in the backseat?"

"Yes. Always."

She closed her eyes and took a deep, shuddering breath. "I know. It's just . . . It's just that I always need a reason. . . ." Her voice faded away, her confession halted when she realized whom she was speaking to, afraid to admit to me that it was hard living in a world where there aren't always reasons.

I moved to gather my purse and grocery bag to leave, but Harper held me back with a hand on my arm. "Gigi gave me this right before you picked her up today." She reached into her purse and pulled out a folded picture. I froze, remembering the last time Gigi had drawn something for her mother.

She handed it to me and I opened it. I recognized me first, most likely due to the navy shorts and striped shirt the woman wore in the picture. Except in this rendition I also wore a beautiful set of wings that arched over my back. I held hands with a small blond girl dressed all in pink with a wide, beautiful, red-crayoned smile. The background was filled with swirls of black, depicting night, and a large moon hovered in the top right corner near two angels—a redheaded one and a blond one—flying up near the stars. On the ground in front of us was a large, waxy-white flower, a night-blooming cereus, its petals like sunbursts.

I wanted to cry and laugh simultaneously, but mostly I wanted to thank the little girl who'd drawn it.

"Do you know what it means?" Harper asked.

"I'm not sure." My mind skipped over the events after the accident, like a stone across water, settling on the memory of the old Gullah woman and my father. I studied the picture. "I think it means that saying good-bye to someone doesn't mean they're gone from your life forever." I touched the flower with my finger, feeling the wax of the crayon, its bloom as large as my crayoned head. "And that when all you're given is one night to bloom, you should go for it."

I looked up and met the eyes of a woman trying to make sense of a universe that sometimes made no sense at all.

I folded up the picture and handed it back to Harper. "Thank you for showing it to me."

She shook her head. "I want you to keep it. And we can ask her about it when she wakes up."

I smiled and nodded quickly, eager to leave before the dam holding back the tears broke. I was glad I couldn't see Gigi in ICU. Because I didn't want to think of her that way; I wanted to think of her as the little girl in pink holding the hand of an angel while two more watched over her.

"I'll go now and tell Helena. Please keep me posted."

"Thank you," Finn said. And as Harper began to sob, he gathered her in his arms and I turned away, gathered my belongings, and left. The car was waiting where Finn had said it would be, and I climbed into the back.

I was grateful for the throbbing in my head that wouldn't let me sleep, allowing me time to resurrect old prayers I hadn't uttered in more than seventeen years and to wonder why an old woman who had been through so much would suddenly decide to end her life.

CHAPTER 32

Eleanor

It was after midnight by the time the car dropped me off at Luna Point. I had fallen into a fitful doze despite my headache, and dreamed of trees and angels and my father. I dropped my overnight bag and the Piggly Wiggly bag with my purse in the foyer, then walked through the sleeping house to the sunroom.

I threw open the door into the summer night and stepped out into a dark where not even the stars dared to show their light. The night sounds of the marsh and the smells of water and summer grass brought the old Ellie back to me in waves, the girl with the brave heart and fearless soul. I needed her now, more than ever. If I was going to be any use to Gigi and Finn, and even Helena, I needed Ellie to move back permanently. I felt her hovering, waiting for me to bring her back.

There is no risk in wanting something you can never have. Helena's words no longer made me angry, just ashamed. Ashamed that my father knew what I'd become, the father who'd risked his life on runs where other shrimpers wouldn't because he believed in the dreams he had for our family. Because he believed I was good enough to go to Juilliard. Because he loved us. The only risks I'd taken since the day he'd died were simply stupid stunts to make me feel again. I'd been asleep all these years but hadn't known it. *All shut-eye ain't sleep.*

"Come back to us, Gigi," I whispered to the moonless night, hoping her angels would take the message to her. I needed her to come back so I could thank her for teaching me so much. I thought of her short life and her health struggles, but I knew that even if her life was short, she would say it had all been worth it. She lived each day with both eyes wide and an open heart, and I needed her to wake up so I could tell her she was right.

I retreated back into the sunroom, closing the night behind me. I was too wound up to go to sleep, knowing that when Helena woke I'd need to tell her about the accident. All she knew now was that Finn had called to tell her that we'd be staying in Charleston for the night. I hoped the half-truth had at least granted the old woman a night of restful sleep.

I sat down in one of the armchairs and picked up the television remote, then put it down again. I was in no mood for the late-night television of old reruns and white-toothed men shouting at me to buy food choppers and exercise machines. I wanted to call Finn, but I didn't want to wake him just in case he'd managed to fall asleep. I had no claims to him or his daughter, but I could no longer deny that I wanted to.

My gaze fell on the stack of unread library books by the chair. I picked through the thick history books, pausing at the small booklet I'd shoved at the last minute into my stack. *The Catholic Church and the Holocaust in Hungary.* I was more interested in it since finding out the name of the convent where Bernadett had taught, but I selected it now mostly because it was short enough to hold my attention when my thoughts threatened to veer off in dangerous directions.

I fanned through the booklet, noting that it consisted of very little narrative and seemed to be just a listing of various Catholic institutions in Hungary during World War II. The words "Divine Redeemer" caught my attention, and I quickly flipped back pages until I saw the words again. The bold-faced header for the short paragraph that followed read: "Motherhouse of the Daughters of the Divine Redeemer." Then, beneath it:

The motherhouse sheltered 150 children in secret, mostly Jewish but many physically and mentally handicapped, relying on the underground resistance movement to supply them with food and medicine. In July 1944, following information supplied by an informant, the Nazis raided the home and took all of the children, including many of the Sisters who chose to stay with them. They were deported to Auschwitz. All believed to have perished.

I stared at the words, all of my exhaustion vanished. My head throbbed harder, yet the pain seemed far away, disconnected from me somehow. The words moved on the page in front of me, twisting and turning, shifting positions like pieces in a puzzle. A puzzle in which the edges had suddenly formed, making the rest easier to place. *July 1944. All believed to have perished.*

My mind jumped and leaped, then turned back again like a winding path around the truth. I ran through old conversations with Helena and Finn, about the night Helena left Budapest, about Gunter and Benjamin. About Helena and Bernadett's trek to Switzerland and their tiny house above the bakery where they grew up. Yet nothing seemed connected except for the July date in 1944 and the convent where Bernadett worked. *And the paintings.* The paintings had come with them from Hungary, and at least one of them had belonged to a family who had also all perished in Auschwitz except for little Sarah Reichmann.

The booklet slid from my fingers to my lap, and I let it fall to the floor. The throbbing in my head became real again, intensified by my growing sense of confusion and grief. Gigi lay in a coma, and I needed to break the news to Helena, an old woman who'd wanted to die following the death of her sister. *Bernadett killed herself.* It was as if all these pieces were like strings of yarn rolled in a tight ball. And at the center was an old woman with plenty of secrets.

I dug in my purse for the pain pills I'd brought from the hospital but tossed them aside. I needed to have all my wits about me. Instead I took two extra-strength Advil that I found floating in the bottom of the inside pocket of my purse, then lay back against the chair and closed my eyes.

Helena

I dreamed again that the Danube was blue, and that I walked along the bridge with my arms linked with Magda's and Bernadett's. We were young again, with smooth skin and bright hair, and it seemed as if war and death and separation were very, very far away. Then the sky darkened, the bombs falling like rain, and I watched as the water turned red.

"Helena?"

It was Eleanor. It must have been early morning, and the sun broke through the sides of the curtains. When had she started calling me Helena? I didn't mind it, I decided. I blinked my eyes to focus them and then felt her slide my eyeglasses onto my nose. I saw the bandage on her forehead, and I suddenly knew why the river in my dream had turned red. "Where is Gigi?"

The look in her eyes answered my question. She moved forward and took my hand, her skin as cold as my own. "We were in an accident yesterday, on our way here. A driver ran a red light. . . ." She stopped, knowing that the details didn't matter. None of the details would alter the end result.

She continued. "She's in the hospital. She has swelling on the brain, and they've had to put her into a coma. If the swelling comes down, she has a good chance of a complete recovery. But we won't know for a few days. Finn and Harper are with her."

An icy cold settled around my heart, oddly soothing me so that I could no longer feel it beating in my chest. I expressed no emotion as I looked at Eleanor's wounded face, the tear streaks she had tried to brush away, the light that had dimmed in her eyes. It is hard to feign surprise when the news has been expected for a long time, a patient panther waiting to pounce.

Her expression changed and I realized she thought I was in shock, had not comprehended her words. Impatiently, I pulled my hand away. "I am hungry. Is Nurse Kester making my breakfast?"

Eleanor drew back. "Didn't you hear me? Gigi is in the hospital. She could die."

"I heard you. I am not deaf. But I am hungry." I could not stomach food, but I wanted her to leave before I was forced to tell her how it was all my fault, that I had been waiting all these years for God to exact his punishment on me: an eye for an eye, a tooth for a tooth. A child for a child. I wanted to tell her how I had not wanted to love Gigi as much as I did, how I held back at first to protect her. And when she'd recovered from her cancer, I had felt the finger of God pass over me. But He had merely been waiting. "God giveth, and God taketh away," I said, hoping she'd understand.

"Do you not care?" she asked, her voice quiet and incredulous.

I leaned back against my pillows, resigned now that I knew my fate. *"Mindenki a maga szerencséjének kovácsa,"* I whispered to the dark corners of my room and the ghosts who hovered there.

"Everyone's the blacksmith of their own fate," she translated, saying each word slowly as if one of them would hold the answer to why I could not cry over my sweet Gigi.

Her shoulders were rounded, her palms flat against her pants, reminding me of the girl I'd first met—the odd mixture of defeated posture and fierce eyes. Even then, I had seen the hint of who she truly was, but I could see now that her true spirit had almost completely reemerged. I knew that if she sat down at the piano and played now, the music would be pure and exquisite and would make me weep for all the sorrows of the world. And if Gigi were here, she'd press her small hands against her heart.

"I don't understand," she said, her voice tinted with anger and confusion. "How could this be Gigi's fault?"

I shook my head. "Not Gigi's. Mine."

Her light blue eyes stared at me without really seeing me, and I could almost picture the pages of the history books she'd been reading flipping through her mind, the things Finn and I had told her, trying to draw conclusions to a story to which she did not want to know the end.

She straightened, her eyes widening, our gazes meeting in a battle of wills neither of us wanted to lose. I felt the bonds of my web snapping strand by strand, and I flailed desperately, trying to hold on to what was left. And I did it with the only weapon I still had left.

"How is Eve? Is her pregnancy going well?"

Eleanor didn't answer, but I had not expected her to. I continued. "I have a question for you—something that has been running around in my brain all these months." I pretended to gather my thoughts for a moment. "Now that you have feelings for Finn—and do not say that you do not—do you no longer wish that she would die?"

She jerked out of her chair. "I never said that."

"You did not have to. I had two sisters, remember. I would think it odd to go through life with a sister without having had that thought at least once. Love and hate are merely two sides of the same coin."

Eleanor stormed to the door, but until she left this house I knew that I had not yet won. She stopped, then slowly turned around, and one more strand popped, the sound as it hit the wall and slithered away loud in my ears.

"Is that what this is about? Misplaced guilt over Bernadett's death? I know she killed herself—Finn told me. And you wanted to die—but not because you couldn't live without her. It was because you couldn't live with the knowledge of *why*."

"How dare you?" I said in the feeble voice I used when I wanted to get my way. "I am an old woman. . . ."

"Yes, you are. Which is why, I would think, you would not want to die with whatever guilt you have hanging over you. And I can't stop thinking how, after all of this time we've been together and I've been digging into your past, you haven't once asked me to stop. Not once. I never stopped digging because I couldn't help but wonder if you've been hoping all this time that you would be forced to tell your story."

"None of this has anything to do with you." Even I could tell that my voice had weakened, that my protestations weren't real.

"I suppose in the beginning it didn't. I was simply curious and digging up your secrets meant I didn't need to dwell too much on my own. And your antagonism toward me from the beginning encouraged me."

She bit her lip, something I recognized as a sign that she was measuring her words. But I already knew what she was going to say before she had even uttered the first word.

"It is my business now. Because of Finn, and because of that sweet little girl whom I've grown to love as if she were my own who is fighting for her life. How will Finn feel when I tell him that he could have just called you and told you on the phone, since you don't apparently care about what happens to Gigi? I know that's not true." She pressed her hand against her heart, reminding me of Gigi. "I know you love her, and I just want to understand how something that happened in your past could come to this. I need to know. . . ." She stopped, her eyes widening, like a person seeing the stars for the first time. "I need to know because for a long time I could see myself in your place sixty years from now—guilt ridden and lonely."

I wanted to yell at her, to tell her she was wrong and insulting and that she had no idea what she was talking about. But I had seen it, too, and knew that she was very, very right.

Eleanor took a deep breath, and I felt her weariness. "Whatever happened to you and Bernadett is part of your family's legacy. Something to pass on to Finn and Gigi. Good or bad. You *survived*, Helena. When so many did not. I don't know what it is to have my home invaded by a foreign army, or to have bombs falling on my roof while I'm trying to save a dying sister. I cannot and will not judge you for whatever choices you've made. Maybe you just need to be forgiven."

"Is that all I need?" I asked, my words bitter-tasting. "Did your sister forgive you?"

After a moment she nodded. "Yes."

"But have you forgiven your sister?"

She stared at me, not comprehending.

"Forgiveness works both ways. It will not be finished between you two until you both are at peace with choices you've made that hurt the other, regardless of your intent."

"And for you and Bernadett, you think it's too late. But what if it's not?"

"And what if it is?"

Eleanor returned to the chair by the side of my bed and took my hands in hers again. "How will you know unless you try?"

The last strand popped, and I was suspended, it seemed, as if I hadn't been the one holding on to them all of these years, but they had been clinging to me. A relic of my Catholic school education emerged from my mouth. *"Veritas vos liberabit."* I smiled at her confusion. It was not as easy as I had once hoped to stump Miss Eleanor Murray, but I had finally managed it. "I should have assumed your American education neglected to teach you Latin. It translates to 'The truth shall set you free.'"

"Something like that," she said, her eyes grave, and I found myself wishing that I had married after all, that I'd had a child, and that she'd been a daughter just like Eleanor. But wishes are only food for small children and fools.

"All right," I said.

She leaned back, her expression wary. "All right, what?"

"I will start at the beginning of my story. But what will you give me in return?"

"I'm not sure what you mean."

"You expect me to tell you all my secrets, yet you still hold back your own."

"I don't have any secrets. Not anymore."

"We all have secrets."

She began to protest. "I don't know—"

"Will you play the Chopin for me? The Nocturne in C Minor that was your father's favorite?"

"I don't think—"

I cut her off. "Everything has its price. You just have to decide if what you want is worth what you need to give up. And perhaps you will find that there are also things you have held on to that need letting go."

She stared at me in horror, and I wanted to laugh, feeling for just one moment that I had won after all. But she was the daughter I had never had, and of course I knew that she would not declare defeat so close to the finish line.

"All right. I'll play it." She sat still, as if waiting for me to make the first move.

"You go first," I said, our eyes meeting in an unspoken challenge.

"All right," she said again, and I knew that I had won. Or maybe I had lost after all.

CHAPTER 33

Eleanor

I took my time hunting for the music, even though I knew exactly where it had been filed, and even though I knew every note from memory. It was a mournful piece, full of loss and longing and too many memories of my father. Thinking of Gigi would make it even more difficult.

And so you honor him by dismissing the music he taught you. Helena's words haunted me, as did the memory of my father in the moments after the car crash. He'd been wanting to say something, but no matter how hard I tried to reach him, I couldn't. Maybe because I already knew what he'd wanted to say to me.

My phone buzzed and I eagerly read the screen. It was a text from Finn. "Still stable. Nothing's changed. Will keep you posted." It was the fourth I'd received so far that day, in addition to three phone calls. And each time, I held my breath until I no longer thought that I could remember to breathe on my own. I read the text out loud, hoping to get a reaction from Helena.

Helena sat perched on the love seat, freshly dressed, her hair brushed, and said nothing. A cup of tea sat on the small table beside her, the steam catching the light from the windows. We'd both walked past the painting of the woman in the red dress without comment, the pink elephant waiting its turn.

"Do you want me to correct your mistakes while you are playing or wait until you are finished?"

Ignoring her, I placed the music on the stand and raised the fall board before adjusting the bench. It was too close up, the edge of the bench matching up to the edge of the keyboard. It was where Gigi sat when I worked with her on her lessons, her short legs unable to reach the pedals.

Swallowing thickly, I sat down, determined to remember the Gigi swinging her legs from the piano bench instead of the girl I had seen pulled from the car wreckage. I opened the music and studied it, the melody plucking like harp strings on my heart. After a deep breath, I began to play the first notes, stumbling over the keys, my fingers as stiff as twisted twigs of driftwood. I lifted my hands from the keyboard and stared at the raised fall board, waiting for Helena to say something. When she didn't, I lowered my hands and played the first note again. And then I stopped.

Don't see the notes. See the music. See the story it is telling you. Allow the music to change you. Allow it to give you the courage to do whatever you need to do. My father's voice was so real that it was almost as if he were sitting on the bench next to me, his beard tickling my cheek. I'd forgotten those words, just as I'd forgotten how it felt to play with my heart instead of my hands. How it felt to be the Ellie of the brave heart and fearless soul. "I remember," I whispered quietly to the black and white keys and to my fingers, which sat poised like hands in prayer.

I folded the music and put it on the floor. Then I closed my eyes to see the music and allowed my fingers to play the first notes. The piece was one of Chopin's lesser-known nocturnes, published after his death. Maybe that's why it had been my father's favorite, and my own—a piece of music we shared with the composer and only a small number of people. The music became a river, and I a boat, winding my way through tidal creeks and marshes, following the current toward the river and out to the ocean. Yet the music took unexpected turns and I followed it through the waterways of my childhood, going against the current in places, drifting aimlessly in others. It was a journey filled with sadness and joy, life and death. Mournful yet uplifting, ultimately conquering. Each note a strand of time, a piece of sweetgrass woven into a basket.

The last notes faded and my hands fell to my sides. I was breathing heavily, my cheeks wet. I waited for Helena to tell me that it hadn't been horrible. Or that it had. It no longer mattered to me what she thought.

"They killed the children first," she said. Her voice was strong, resonating in the nearly empty room, the woman in red staring at us in silent accusation.

I turned around to face her. "What?"

"We had an agreement. You play the nocturne, and I tell you my story. So I am going to start where it starts. Where it ends. With the children. With Bernadett's son."

Helena

I crawled into the back of the truck, the odor of rotting vegetables mixing with the smell of fear and the sickly-sweet scent of fever. I pressed the cool rag against Bernadett's forehead, and I felt her turn to me in the darkness.

"Where are we?" She moved as if to sit up, but I knew she did not have the strength to do it on her own.

"Do not worry. I will take care of you." I tried to hide the urgency in my voice, to mask my panic at the growing sound of running feet passing us on the old cobblestones of the street. A window shattered nearby, and the smell of spoiled fish spilled out into the night.

She moaned and I pressed my eyes shut. The distant sound of a bomb vibrated the night air, sending a faint tremor through the truck. "What is that?" she asked, her words slurred.

"It is nothing to worry about." I pressed the pill Gunter had given me on her tongue, then brought water to her lips. "Drink this, and you will sleep."

"Where is Samuel?"

"He is safe at the convent. Gunter has promised to keep him and the children safe."

"Take me there. You said we would go to him."

"They have bombed the bridges, and it would take all night to get to him. People and soldiers are everywhere, clogging the streets. We will have to come back for him. When it is safe we will come back." It wasn't the plan at all, but I wanted her to go to sleep with the knowledge that we could come back.

"You promised. . . ." Bernadett's head lolled back in my arms as sleep overtook her, and I was spared from uttering one more lie. We had planned to bring Samuel. But the Americans and their bombs had changed everything. Gunter had told me that the Nazis were flooding the city, shooting innocent civilians, blocking those trying to flee. It might already be too late for us, and we could not waste the precious time it

would take us to get to the motherhouse on the Pest side of the river. I wanted to argue with him, but I knew that he was right. They were looking for Bernadett already, and it was simply a matter of time.

I wiped away the hair that stuck to her forehead. "It is better this way," I whispered to my sleeping sister. "He is only a baby, and he will be safe. We can move faster, and we will not have to worry about him getting your sickness." I closed my eyes, hoping I was telling her the truth.

I reached into the small bag of Bernadett's possessions and found the small silver box that had been gifted to her from the motherhouse for her service to the children there. I pulled out the rosary and wrapped it around Bernadett's clenched hands, a talisman against evil.

Sliding from the truck, I reached for Gunter, smelling his sweat and the wool of his uniform. A woman holding a child's hand ran past us, bumping into Gunter and pressing him against me.

"Do not be afraid, my love. When we are old we will look back and laugh at how difficult things once were." He paused. "I have wrapped the paintings inside maps, just in case. But if anyone should get close enough, tell them that the paintings are from St. Stephen's Basilica and you are taking them to hide them from the Russians."

"Who will believe that? The Russians are not here."

He lowered his voice. "They will be. We cannot fight everyone on all fronts. The Führer knows this, and things here will get even more difficult. I will rest better knowing you are safe."

"The paintings—are they really from St. Stephen's?"

He kissed me gently. "Do not worry yourself. They are our insurance. They are what paid for your passes and train tickets. My commanding officer ordered me to get them out of Hungary, and so I am. It is not up to us to question this gift."

"It is not a gift," I said. I took out the folded piece of paper and held it for a moment before pressing it into his hands, feeling like St. Peter and waiting for the cock to crow. "It is something awful I cannot name."

He took the paper and shoved it into his jacket pocket. "The children will be safe, I promise you. I will give the sisters advance warning, and the children will be hidden. And that will be the end of it. After tonight Hungary's regent cannot afford the wrath of the United States and must stop the deportations here in Hungary. It is the beginning of the end."

"And when this is over, you will find me, and you will bring Samuel to us."

He held me close. "Yes. I promise."

"And you will tell Benjamin?"

He tensed. "Benjamin is gone."

"Gone?" My unease at his words mixed with relief.

"He was caught coming from a safe house with forged papers and documents. They have taken him away."

"What shall I tell Bernadett?"

"She does not need to know. Tell her that Benjamin will find her after the war."

"Do you really believe that?"

Gunter did not answer, and my twenty-two-year-old self refused to see what lay behind his silence. I did not want to think of Benjamin being taken to the Danube and shot. I only wanted to think of him as the man who had brought danger to my doorstep, had involved my sister, with her blond, bright hair, in traveling with supplies to the labor camps outside Budapest and returning with contraband letters. My beautiful sister, who was so shy and allowed me to make all of her decisions for her and take care of her, had become another person for Benjamin. She showed no fear delivering messages or running the supplies to the camps. It was at the labor camps where the typhus had found her.

Yet Benjamin was Samuel's father, too—Samuel, my darling nephew with the dark hair and laughing eyes whom we had been forced to hide both before he was born and now after. The sisters at the convent were happy to pretend that he was just another child Bernadett spent time with.

Gunter took my arm and gently led me to the driver's seat, and I felt his urgency, his nervousness that all of our plans would go awry because of all nights the Americans had chosen to come tonight. He did not need to tell me that we would not have another chance. "I have covered the top half of your headlights to make it harder for the planes to see you. And I have marked your map so that you are traveling away from their targets, north through the countryside. And if you are stopped by soldiers, show them your passes. I have secured for you the highest clearance."

He kissed me one last time. "Godspeed, my love. I will find you. When all of this is over, I will come back for you."

He closed the door and I started the engine. I did not look back as I headed toward the darkness of the suburban forests, exiting through the medieval town gates to plunge into the foothills. It was military territory, where vehicles could be stopped for any reason or no reason at all, but I had run out of choices. The distant fires burning buildings along the Danube flamed in the rearview mirror as I drove away, the road like scissors neatly clipping my life into the time before and the time after.

Eleanor

"The note you put into Gunter's pocket, what was it?" I felt sick—sick with exhaustion and worry over Gigi, and sick with the knowledge of a harrowing night that had happened nearly seventy years before, yet still echoed in the walls around me and in the heart of an old woman.

Helena's face betrayed no emotion, and I wondered if she'd had the long trip through the dark forests of Hungary to teach her how. "It was the name of the convent and their address." She closed her eyes. "We had it all planned, you see. Gunter would warn them in advance so they could hide. I had no choice. The Gestapo knew about Bernadett, that she'd been working with the underground. They had been following her, so it was simply a matter of time before they knocked on our door in the middle of the night and dragged her from her bed.

"She could not afford to be in a prison camp. She had been sick and weak since Samuel's birth, giving her food rations to the children. She would not have survived. I had no choice. And Samuel, we were supposed to pick him up that night, but we could not because they had bombed the bridges. With the confusion in the streets, and the Nazis flooding into the city, it would have taken hours to get to him, and we could not afford the time. They knew who Bernadett was. We had a much better chance if we were stopped and questioned out in the countryside, where they did not know who she was."

I continued to stare at the woman across the room from me, her face becoming older as she spoke. The words from the small booklet swam in my mind, the words in their black-and-white hygienic way telling about the children from the convent. About the informant and the subsequent raid. *They were deported to Auschwitz. All believed to have perished.* And I remembered the Bible I'd found in the basket beneath Bernadett's bed.

"In Rama was there a voice heard, lamentation, and weeping, and great mourning, Rachel weeping for her children, and would not be comforted, because they are no more," I quoted, my voice quiet, as if I was afraid to speak louder and have my words absorbed into the room, soiling the room forever. I'd never been able to remember Bible verses in Sunday school, but I remembered this one as if it had been burned into my brain.

Her voice was hoarse. "Where did you see that?"

"In a Bible hidden in Bernadett's room. I didn't understand why that was the only verse marked. But now I do."

"She made me mark it. She put the pen in my hand and made me mark it." She raised desolate eyes to mine. "All of these years I kept the secret, and then . . ." Her voice trailed away.

I swallowed, finding it hard to ask my next question. "Did Gunter not reach the convent in time?"

She shook her head. "I do not know. I will never know what really happened. The war, with all of its uncertainty—it was foolish of us to believe we could follow a plan." Her eyes bore into mine. "But in my heart, I know with all certainty that Gunter tried to save them. He was a good man. He loved children, and he loved hearing me talk about Samuel. Gunter told me that he would want a son just like him." Her voice wilted to a near whisper. "He would have saved them if he could have."

I sat down next to her, afraid to touch her, afraid that she would break. "Is that why Bernadett killed herself? Because she found out about the children?" Something Helena had said to me when we first met came back to me. *Have you ever known grieving that ends only when your own heart stops beating?* I did know, and I understood.

I touched her softly on the hand, and then tentatively, slowly, I reached my arms around her in a gentle hug, the human need to touch and be touched overwhelming.

She stiffened at first, then bent her face into my shoulder and began to cry. I closed my eyes, remembering when Eve and I were small, how even after a fight I'd climb into her bed and she'd put her arm around me, words unnecessary, and that had been enough. When had we lost that? When had we both allowed ourselves to pull away, separating two halves of the same soul?

Helena pulled back, using a tissue she kept in the wrist of her sleeve to dry her face and wipe her nose. Without looking at me she said, "I do not want to be inside anymore. I need fresh air."

I wanted to tell her that she wasn't done, that there was so much more to her story. But what she'd already said sat heavily on my heart, a riptide that threatened to drag us both out to sea.

Helena struggled to stand, pushing away my attempts to help her. "Call Nurse Weber. I want her to take me to the dock so I can see the river."

I didn't tell her that it was too warm outside or that the grass was still too wet with dew for her to walk on. I couldn't. "I'll let her know. I'll go set up two chairs in the shade."

"I want to be alone," she said, her eyes cold as they met mine.

"I'm not judging you," I said, wanting to tell her that all I saw was her courage. And her fear. And her inability to forgive herself.

She raised silent eyebrows.

"I told Eve that I had wanted her to die. That I *willed* her to die. And she forgave me. But I see now that I need to forgive myself, or the past will never let me go. Can you see that, Helena? Can you see that you don't need Bernadett's forgiveness? She wasn't there to make the tough decisions you had to make. But you were, and you made them, and you've lived with the consequences all of these years. You need to forgive yourself for any mistakes you might have made along the way, or you will never rest."

She shook her head. "I'm too old for forgiveness. All that is left for me is my punishment."

She made her way slowly from the room and I watched her leave, my gaze slowly traveling to the painting of the woman in red velvet. I wanted to cry, needed to cry for Gigi and the lost children, and for Samuel and Bernadett, and for an old woman who'd never been allowed to forgive or forget.

CHAPTER 34

Eleanor

For two days, Helena and I existed in a kind of limbo, fitfully sleeping, barely eating, and waiting for the phone to ring. Her story remained unfinished, neither of us willing to immerse ourselves in more darkness. We danced around each other like two prizefighters, each no longer sure what the prize would be if we won. And so we waited.

I spoke to Finn briefly throughout the day, the news never changing. Gigi was neither getting better nor getting worse, which, in the absence of an immediate recovery, was the best news we could expect.

On the third day, I heard the approach of a car on the drive outside. I ran to the door, my stomach climbing into my throat, wondering if Finn had come to tell me bad news in person.

I stood on the steps, watching with surprise as Glen's car pulled up, Eve in the passenger seat. The car stopped and I ran down the steps to Eve's side of the car, where she was already opening the door.

She looked up at me, her smile hesitant. "I hope it's okay that I'm here. I didn't want to call first and have you tell me no."

I stared at my sister, seeing the small swell of her belly and the new fullness to her cheeks, my mind trying to process all the reasons she would be there.

When I still didn't respond, she said, "Your phone calls have been so short and I know how worried you are about Gigi. I thought you could use a little moral support."

"I don't. I mean . . ." I stopped, feeling the press of tears in the back of my throat, and watched as Glen lifted Eve's wheelchair from the trunk, then moved it up to the porch. "Of course it's all right." I swallowed, feeling like a drowning victim being tossed a life ring. "I'm glad you're here."

Glen lifted Eve from the car and placed her in the wheelchair. "I don't want to be in the way, so I'm just delivering her. I'll be back in a few hours to pick her up."

I smiled my gratitude. "Thanks, Glen. Thank you both." I hadn't realized how alone I'd been in the last few days since Helena shared her story, how much I wanted to reach out in mutual consolation with as much fervor as she pushed me away.

Glenn took a grocery bag out of the backseat and handed it to Eve before kissing her and saying good-bye to both of us. Neither of us spoke until the car had disappeared.

Eve was looking at my forehead, where I'd left off the bandage, tired of trying to scratch through layers of gauze. The stitches were still visible under the ointment, the skin around it angry and red. "That's going to leave a scar."

I barked out a laugh, the sound coming from the scared, dark corner of my heart. It felt so good for things to be normal between us again. "Yeah, probably."

"What's with the bag?" I asked her as I wheeled her into the foyer.

"A present. For you and Gigi."

I stopped and moved in front of her, watching as she took out two pink T-shirts from the bag. She handed the first one to me, and I held it up to see the front. The edges of the sleeves and collar had been embellished with soft white lace, the hem embroidered with blue thread to make it look like waves. And stitched across the front of the shirt, in large, quilted letters, were the words BIG GEECHEE GIRL, Lucy's nickname for me when we were children and I'd wanted so badly to be a part of her Gullah family. Being called a Geechee girl was as close as I'd come.

I laughed. "It's adorable. Thank you."

With a searching look, Eve handed me the second shirt. I held it up, seeing how tiny it seemed against mine. The two shirts were identical, from the lace to the blue embroidery, but the letters on this one read LITTLE GEECHEE GIRL.

"Remember a million years ago when Lucy gave us T-shirts with GEECHEE GIRL on them? I had this idea of how cute you and Gigi would look, running around Edisto with matching shirts. I just guessed on the size. I knew yours, of course, but I've only seen Gigi once, and I remember how small she is. . . ."

I pressed the shirt to my mouth, stifling the sobs that had lingered there for days, tears for Gigi, and Samuel, and all those lost to Helena. Then Eve's touch on my hand was like a talisman from my past, reminding me that I wasn't alone anymore. The sobs came from deep within me, pouring out all the years of keeping the hurt inside, making room for something new, a simultaneous hollowing out and filling up. I knelt on the floor next to Eve's chair and cried while she stroked my cheek and smoothed the hair away from my face, saying the little words our mother had once said to us when she rocked us to sleep, little words lost in the years between then and now.

When I was done, I sat back and looked at my sister with swollen eyes. "It's going to be okay, right?"

"I can't promise you anything except that I'll be here."

She took my hand and squeezed. Glancing around the foyer at the warped paintings and odd rectangles of color, she said, "I've always wanted to know what it looked like inside. It's a little . . . eccentric."

I smiled carefully. "You have no idea."

"Is she awake? Helena?"

I sat back on my heels. "Why?"

"You talk so much about her, I figured it was time I finally met her. I've made sure to gird my loins first."

I sniffed, wiping my nose against the back of my hand. "She's actually been pretty docile, which worries me. She's in the sunroom." I stood and took a deep breath. "Be gentle with her. She's been carrying some pretty large burdens."

"Haven't we all?" Eve said quietly as I moved behind her chair and pushed her toward the sunroom.

Helena sat in the armchair that had been hers, staring at the bend of the property where creek met river, the current wide and fast. There was no book in her lap, and the television was off. But the framed photo of Gigi in her ballet recital costume lay faceup on the side table as if it had just been placed there. Helena didn't look up when we entered.

"Helena? Miss Szarka? I've brought somebody to meet you."

She didn't turn around.

"It's my sister, Eve."

Eve moved forward. "I'm so sorry about Gigi. My mama and I have been praying every day for her, and we added her name to the prayer list at church." She smiled at the old woman, a trick that had never failed to garner notice. "It's nice to finally meet you, Miss Szarka. Eleanor has told me so much about you."

That seemed to rouse her, and she turned her head slowly in our direction. She regarded Eve in silence. Just when I thought she would turn around and ignore us completely, she said, "She is not that much prettier than you, Eleanor. But her hands are much daintier and more feminine."

Eve looked at me with a raised eyebrow, but I shook my head slightly to let her know that she didn't need to play older sister and defend me. I was happy to have Helena score a point if it meant she was doing more than staring out a window or lying in bed.

Helena's bony fingers tapped against the arms of the chair. "But then again, how can one play the piano with such small hands?"

"I can't play at all," Eve confessed. "I always wanted to, but it was like I had two left hands."

I sat down on the ottoman and watched as Helena's lips curved. "Less competition that way."

I smiled to myself, surprised yet grateful to hear Helena defending me.

Eve laughed. "Oh, there were so many things she was good at, it wouldn't have mattered if there'd been one more."

Teri Weber stepped into the room, her face showing the tension we'd all been feeling since the accident. "Can I get some refreshments for anyone? Iced tea? And I made my chocolate chip cookies. They're Gigi's favorites."

I looked over at Helena, wondering if she'd heard Teri, and saw she was deep in thought.

"Yes, thank you, Teri," I said.

I watched as Helena's face became more animated than I'd seen for a while. "Eleanor told me that she was always getting you into trouble when you were girls and that all the worst ideas were hers."

Eve nodded. "Oh, definitely. It made life more exciting. I suppose we were both looking for something to change our lives, and I always depended on Eleanor to make that happen."

"Even if it meant falling from a tree and ending up in a wheelchair?"

Helena's voice lacked any malice, as if she really needed to know the answer.

Eve stilled. "Even then," she said. "Did she ever tell you that she almost died that day?"

"No. She has not." Helena sent an accusing glance toward me, while I just stared at Eve, wishing she'd stop.

Teri brought in the drinks and a plate of cookies, and I was hoping Eve had forgotten the question. She hadn't.

"When I fell," Eve said, "Eleanor let go of the branch she'd been clinging to, trying to get to me as quickly as possible. She hit the ground, and when the medics finally got there, her heart had stopped."

Eve looked at me over the glass of her iced tea, her violet eyes soft. "I never knew if she'd done it to try to save me or because she didn't want to live without me, so instead I simply blamed her for my own stupidity. In the end it was easier than trying to thank her for almost killing herself to try to save me."

"And you think it is possible to simply change your mind and pluck another chance at life right from the air?" Helena's hands were folded in her lap, like a psychologist listening to a patient.

Eve's delicate brow wrinkled. "We all make choices, Miss Szarka. And if it doesn't work out the way we wanted it to, we can spend a lifetime blaming ourselves or blaming others. Either way, we've spent a lifetime blaming instead of a lifetime doing other things." She rested her hand on her stomach. "This pregnancy has brought a whole new perspective to the way I look at the world. I think the possibilities for second chances are everywhere if we just look hard enough."

Eve focused on placing her glass on a coaster, avoiding our eyes as a confessor might.

I looked at my sister, wondering who this person was in the wheelchair next to me. Under my breath, I said, "Have you been watching *Dr. Phil*?"

Her violet eyes met mine as I smelled a hot summer afternoon and a dusty road. Very quietly, she said, "All good-bye ain't gone, right, Eleanor?"

I didn't say anything but remained transfixed.

"I heard her, too. I guess we were supposed to figure out what she meant on our own."

Helena was watching us closely, her eyes bright and clear, the shadows temporarily parted. She leaned forward, reminding me of the first time I'd met her, when she was trying to get me to leave and told me that I didn't look like a musician.

Using her most imperious tone, she turned to Eve and said, "I would like to know what it was like growing up with Eleanor. I would imagine it was very wearying."

I watched Eve and Helena as they talked, tossing in a word or two here and there, but enjoying listening to them taking turns being on the offensive and defensive in their discussion of me. I eventually gave up and simply leaned back and listened, my heart lighter than it had felt in a long, long time.

Later, after Helena had gone to her room to rest, Eve and I sat on the porch waiting for Glen to return and for news of Gigi. She put her arm around me, just as she had when we were small, and it was enough.

On the fourth day, Finn called, his words guarded, but I could still hear the hopefulness behind them. "The swelling has been steadily going down since last night, and her brain activity is normal. They're already talking about bringing her out of the coma."

"Oh, Finn," I said, my eyes squeezed tight, unable to think of any words that would say what I wanted to.

"It's still too early to say anything definitive, and the doctors are being very cautious in what they're telling us, but they're all very, very optimistic."

"When can I see her?" I said, no longer trying to keep the tears from my voice.

"As soon as she's out of the ICU. I'll come pick you up myself."

"I'm fine, Finn. I can drive Helena's Cadillac." I wasn't absolutely sure that I could drive without panicking at every horn or siren, but I'd figure that out later. I didn't want him to worry about one more thing.

"No. I'd rather know you're safe. And I need to be on the island. I need . . ." He paused. "I need to be there."

He didn't need to explain what he meant. I'd understood how salt water ran through some veins and not in others, like a blood type that identified those who belonged here.

"Call and I'll be ready," I said.

Neither one of us said anything for a long moment as we simply listened to each other breathe.

Finn broke the silence. "How is Helena?"

"The same." I had not told him Helena's story. It was not my story to tell. "She won't talk about Gigi and she's not eating or sleeping much, although none of us is doing much of either. But don't worry, the nurses are keeping a close eye on her. She did seem to perk up a little yesterday. Eve stopped by."

"Really?"

"Yeah. To see how I was doing. She brought a present for Gigi and me. I'll show you when you come home." *Come home.* The words hung in the space between us, undefined and undefinable. "We had iced tea and Nurse Weber's chocolate chip cookies. Tell Gigi that we've frozen some of the cookies for her when she's better." My throat seemed to thicken and I turned away from my phone so I could swallow without him hearing me.

"Helena called me," Finn said. "Late yesterday afternoon. She said she was supposed to be resting."

I almost laughed at the image of a ninety-year-old woman sneaking in a phone call to her nephew instead of napping. I sobered immediately when I began to think of *why*.

"She wanted to know where Magda's basket was."

"Magda's basket?"

A brief pause. "The basket under Bernadett's bed."

My hand froze on the phone as I remembered when he and I had gone through the contents of the basket in Bernadett's room and I'd thought that there had been something he wasn't telling me. My voice sounded thin to my ears. "You didn't tell me that's what it was."

"No. I didn't. I didn't think. . . ." He stopped. "I told her that you would get it for her."

"All right," I said slowly. "Why did she call it Magda's basket?"

"It had belonged to her, and she kept all of the old photographs in it, and other relics of the sisters' lives in Budapest. When she died, my father just stuffed it in the back of a closet, and when he died I found it and showed it to Helena, who told me to hang on to it for safekeeping. I think she may have added a few things before she gave it back to me, and I forgot about it."

Something seemed stuck in my throat. "How did Bernadett come to have it?"

He paused. "Last Christmas Bernadett mentioned that she was planning on putting a scrapbook together—for Gigi. And that she knew Magda had all the old photos. I didn't even look inside the basket when I brought it to the island when Gigi and I came for Christmas. I just . . . handed it to her."

Last Christmas. The last time Bernadett had played the piano and then closed the fall board and the piano top and silenced the music in the house. "And you didn't know what was inside?"

"Not all of it."

Like the businessman he was, he was not going to show his hand without me asking him to. I hoped his reasons were because he was trying to protect Helena and not because he knew more than he was saying.

"How did it get to be under Bernadett's bed?"

I felt him shake his head. "I think she put it there. She knew she was going to end her life and began to tidy up all the loose ends."

I thought of the planned meeting with Jacob Isaacson and the painting on the music room wall and wanted to ask him if he knew. Wondered if his silence meant that he did.

"Eleanor?"

"Yes?"

"This would be so much easier if you were with me."

I closed my eyes, allowing the warmth to spread through my body, pushing aside all other thoughts. For a moment. "I know," I whispered.

"I've got to go now," he said. "I'll call you later."

"Good-bye." I ended the call and found myself staring at the phone wallpaper for a long moment. It was a photo of Gigi in her life jacket, taken after our kayaking trip. She was smiling her trademark smile, her blue eyes hidden behind pink sunglasses. I could see her small fingers showing me how to take the picture with my phone, then move it to my wallpaper. I wanted to take that small hand and squeeze it and tell her what she meant to me. It was too late, of course. Like so many things. *I think the possibilities for second chances are everywhere if we just look hard enough.* Maybe Eve was right. And maybe an old woman with too many secrets to hold on to was a possibility I hadn't considered.

Tucking my phone into my pocket, I climbed the stairs to Bernadett's room to retrieve the secret keeper stored under a dead woman's bed.

CHAPTER 35

Helena

Nurse Kester had just finished tying my shoes when Eleanor entered the room carrying the basket. She looked different somehow. Not like one of those women in the before-and-after makeover photos in one of the women's magazines I used to hide from Bernadett. It was more like someone who'd learned to touch the sun and lived to tell the story.

"Finn called. He said that Gigi's getting better. That her brain function looks normal."

I pressed the heel of my hand against my heart to still the small fluttering there, as light as a butterfly, but enough of a sign to remind me that I was still alive. "Good," I said, as if that could encompass a journey to hell and back that I had embarked on when I had made Eleanor play the nocturne.

"Where are you going?" she asked, taking in my purse and shoes and the slash of lipstick I had asked Nurse Kester to apply to my thin lips. I knew it made me look clown-like, but old habits died hard.

"*We* are going to speak with Magda."

She frowned. "I'm not sure if I can drive. . . ."

"You will be fine. Or I could drive if you like."

"No," she said. "Never mind. I'm sure I can handle it. Will you want ice cream afterward?"

"Only if you are very good," I said. "And only if we can both find the appetite for it." It was the first time I had alluded to little Genevieve, and I saw her gaze sharpen. It was a small step, but it was a step nonetheless. Our visit from Eleanor's sister, Eve, had been an illuminating one. I had once thought that there could be no other relationship like the one I had shared with Bernadett and Magda, that there would be no one else who understood what it was to share the same soul.

But I had been wrong. Watching and listening to Eleanor and Eve had been like eavesdropping on a conversation between my sisters and me. It had been an unexpected gift, an opportunity to understand how two people could know the very worst about each other and love the other anyway. It had given me hope that if Bernadett had only given me enough time, she would have known this. If only the courage she had used to take a handful of sleeping pills had been spent in forgiveness instead.

After settling me into the Cadillac with the closed basket on my lap, Eleanor slid behind the steering wheel, studying it closely for a long moment before inserting the key and turning the ignition.

"You will be fine," I said. "The sun is shining and people will expect you to drive ten miles per hour because you are in a Cadillac."

She gave me a half smile as she put the car in gear, then drove slowly out of the drive with both hands clutched on the steering wheel like an old woman.

We parked at the church where we had the last time we had been there to visit Magda. It was not as hot, as it was still morning, and I seemed to have found a new energy, a new lightness of being. Still, it took most of Eleanor's strength and my own to hoist me out of the car.

"We forgot the red tulips," she said.

"Next time."

We made our way slowly through the graveyard as I silently castigated Magda for being buried so far away instead of insisting on something closer. I would never have been so inconsiderate. I suppose it was the prerogative of being the eldest.

I stopped near the grave site, at a small bench that was part of the memorial for a sixteen-year-old girl who had died more than a century before. Her monument was a tall fluted column, dressed in roses, that was missing its top half. I had seen such a thing before, this reminder of how life could be cut short without warning, and it brought me some comfort to know that there had been a reason for keeping me here for ninety years.

Or maybe I was not allowed to leave until I had finished what I had been sent here to do.

"Sit down," I said, indicating the bench. "This will take a while, and I think we are close enough to Magda that she can hear."

Eleanor did as I asked without complaint, and I hid my smile. I imagined her holding herself back, thinking me too fragile to argue with, too fragile to return a favor.

"I am too old for secrets, Eleanor. But not too old to believe that it is not too late to learn from our mistakes. I mourn Bernadett, but I pity her, too. Pity her because she ended her life before she had met her own Eleanor."

I put the basket on the bench between us but kept the lid on, amused at the confusion on her face. "I promised you my story, and so now you shall hear the rest of it."

In silence she took my hand and held it as I began to speak.

Eleanor

"I never saw Gunter again. I still tell myself that he could not remember where I was going in America and that he must still be looking for me. I wanted to believe that I would have felt something if he had been killed, like a tearing- or ripping-away feeling in my chest, and know that he was gone. But so much of my past was built on the foolish things only the young can sustain. Always believing that if we wish for something hard enough, it will come true. That we could plan to meet after the war and have that happen just because we made promises to the wind."

She sighed. "I think, deep down, I have always known that he was dead or he would have found me. In some ways, I suppose I am still waiting for him. He was the love of my life, as Benjamin was Bernadett's, and we were prepared to wait forever. There could never have been anyone else for us. So I continued to wait for Gunter as if he were alive and searching for me. To think otherwise would have taken away all of my hope. I saw that many times in Bernadett, her near hopelessness even though she tried to hide it from me. It was worse than death. Despite everything, I still believe that."

I squeezed her hand tighter, feeling the bones, as fragile as a bird's.

"Once in America, Bernadett got stronger, but her mind was tortured with thoughts of her Benjamin and Samuel. As always, she trusted me to take care of things, to find her Samuel. I wrote so many letters, to whomever I thought could help, and she would go with me to the post office each time I mailed one and would say a prayer before she put it in the box.

"But in those first years after the war, when there was no stable government in Hungary and the Communists were gaining power, it was impossible to get information. I lived in denial and would not look for Gunter, but I was desperate for information about Samuel and the children from the convent. We were in a state of uncertainty and waiting. I knew what had happened to Benjamin, but with Bernadett's fragile state of mind, I could not tell her. Even though for years every time she heard a car, she would rush outside to see if it might be Benjamin bringing her their son."

I studied her face closely, looking for signs of fatigue or distress, but I saw instead an odd calm, as if she had been waiting for this moment for a very long time.

Helena continued. "I could not rest, not knowing what had happened. Needing to know that Gunter's plan had worked and that all the children were safe. I had to believe it. Otherwise, I would lose all hope, and without hope I would have nothing. And then who would care for Bernadett?

"We had spent five years of waiting, and I saw my sister's health diminishing and I could not watch her suffer anymore. So I told another lie. I told her that I had finally heard from the Hungarian government in a phone call from the embassy in Washington. They had records that Samuel had been taken out of Hungary during the war, to a family in the Austrian Alps, a family with a mother and father and a brother and sister, and they lived on a farm and he was very happy.

"I made her believe that Samuel, who was then six years old, would not know her. Would only know his family, and that even if we could find him, to take him from the only family he had ever known would be cruel." She swallowed. "At least then I still believed Samuel to be alive. And that once everything was sorted out, I could go back to Budapest and bring him home to Bernadett. Then I could tell her the truth about Benjamin, when she could withstand the grief because she would have their son."

Tears tightened my throat. "You don't have to tell me any more if this is too hard for you."

She patted the top of my hand, as if she were comforting me. "It is all right, Eleanor. I need to do this. I just wish it had not taken me this long."

A dragonfly flittered from a small rosebush planted at the base of the monument, rising on unseen currents to land on Magda's grave marker. Helena and I watched as it sat on the marble, fanning its iridescent wings.

"Did it make her happy?" I asked, seeing the Bernadett in my mind dancing the Csárdás with flowing skirts and red shoes.

"Yes. If not happy, then content. That is when she began throwing herself into service to her church and community. She believed if she performed enough penance, they would come back to her."

"Atoning for her sins," I said quietly.

"Yes. It is not such a thing now, but she was always ashamed that she had a child without being married. Nobody would have married Benjamin and Bernadett then, as it was frowned upon by both faiths. But their love was strong. It created Samuel."

Helena's voice broke, and I moved to stand, to get her to stop. She shook her head. "Please. Let me finish. This is my penance. For perhaps not loving my sister enough to tell her the truth."

I shook my head. "No, Helena. You loved her enough to carry the burden of the truth all by yourself." I watched the dragonfly fan its wings, the sunlight filtering through, making them shimmer. "What changed?"

"It was the paintings that gave me away in the end. After all these years, it was the paintings." She shook her head. "I should have left them all with the Swiss farmer when I had the chance."

"But you didn't. Because you had promised Gunter that you would bring them with you."

"Yes," she said, her voice quiet. "Because I had promised him."

I frowned down at our hands, no longer able to hold back the question that had been burning in the back of my throat for so long. "You knew where the paintings came from, so why did you decide to sell some of them? Because you needed the money?"

She faced me, a hint of her old color coming back to her cheeks. "Is that what you think? That we sold paintings to live on all these years?" She shook her head. "No, it never came to that. And I have Magda to thank. She was the brains of the lot of us. When she came to the States, she brought all of our recording money with her and had her husband invest it, which he did. Finn continues to manage everything for me."

"But you did sell them."

"Yes. But not at first, and not for the reasons you are probably thinking. When we arrived here, I kept the paintings rolled up, just as Gunter had given them to me. But I was afraid they would get damaged after being rolled up for so long. So after a year, I decided to frame them and hang them, but I remembered Gunter warning me that I had to keep them hidden—from whom, I was no longer sure. So I framed them myself and hung them, then waited for him to come."

She sighed, and I allowed her to lean into me, trying to absorb some of the burden she'd been carrying on her narrow shoulders for so long. "For years I continued to write to the Hungarian government, and even to the Vatican, to find out what happened to the children and the sisters. I could not ask Magda's husband for help, as I did not want anyone to know all of the lies I had been living. I do not think he could have helped anyway. Everything was such a mess in Europe, so much destroyed, and then the Communists took over everything in Hungary. I kept writing, but I received no replies."

"And you still had all those paintings."

"I did. And for a long while I continued to believe that they had been rescued from St. Stephen's. It was easy to believe. The Holy Right Hand—the saint's relic that had been kept at the Basilica—had also been taken and hidden during the war, and I allowed myself to believe that I was doing a noble thing by keeping the paintings. I was glad the Communists did not have them and that I had played a part in saving them. Until one day." She paused. "One day when my sisters and I went to an art exhibit of the Dutch masters at the Gibbes Museum. There was a large section of van der Werff paintings, including three scenes of a pear tree in summer, spring, and fall. There was a little sign next to the group of paintings, explaining their origins and meanings. The sign read that the fourth painting, of the tree in winter, had belonged to the Reichmann family and was believed either lost during the bombings during the war or confiscated by the Nazis. But I knew that it could not have been lost. Because it was hanging on my dining room wall right then as I stood there."

"What did Bernadett say?"

"She didn't. She always took too much time in museums and was a room behind Magda and me. So I made up a story that I was feeling ill, and because she was always the good and dutiful sister, she agreed to leave. It helped that I did throw up on the way home, as the truth took hold of me."

A squirrel darted from an oak tree and ran across the sparse grass, pausing only to collect an acorn by the base of Magda's stone before scurrying away and disappearing up another tree. I noticed with some surprise that the dragonfly had not moved but almost seemed to be listening.

Helena cleared her throat. "I did not know what to do. So much time had gone by that it made me hesitate to admit that these paintings were in my possession. I was afraid I would be arrested. Mostly, I did not want Bernadett to know. It would have destroyed the small peace of mind that she had found serving the community. Yet at the same time I wanted to get rid of them, as if they themselves were tainted. I had to do something, to try to make it right. It was Magda's idea that I begin selling them—she always knew what to do. She at first tried to find the Reichmann family, to see if she could find a way to return the paintings without letting them know where they had come from." She was silent for a moment. "She told me what had happened to them, that the entire family had been killed. There were rumors that a child had survived, but she could not substantiate the claims or even find a name."

"Her name was Sarah," I said quietly. "And she did survive. She was Jacob Isaacson's grandmother."

"Ah," she said, looking at me with understanding. A small smile touched her lips. "I wish I had known. Then all that came afterward would never have happened."

"What do you mean?" I asked.

After a deep breath, she continued. "Magda made certain that I was careful to whom I sold the paintings, making sure the transactions were not publicized. Although, as you know, Mr. Isaacson apparently has sources that I was not aware of and found a way to track them.

"But every single penny that I have ever made from their sale has gone anonymously to children's and Jewish charities around the world. It is a very small thing, I know. But it was all I could do at the time. I was trying to honor the family and assuage my guilt at the same time, and for a long while it worked."

"Did you ever tell Magda the whole story? About Samuel and the children?"

Helena shook her head. "No. Only about the paintings, and Gunter. I could not burden her with the rest."

She lifted the lid from the basket between us, the gold letters of the Bible winking at us in the sun. *Rachel weeping for her children, and would not be comforted, because they are no more.* Our eyes met, and I said quietly, "It worked until Bernadett found out about what happened to Samuel."

Helena nodded. "In 1989, when the Iron Curtain fell, I wrote to the new Hungarian government, hoping to finally get an answer to what had happened to the children, hoping that finally I could reunite Bernadett and Samuel, even imagining he would have children himself and Bernadett and I could travel to meet them and they could meet their grandmother." She closed her eyes. "Sometimes lying to oneself is just as easy as lying to others." She shrugged. "The reply was quick. Within three months I had my answer."

I put my hand on her arm, letting her know that she did not need to say it out loud, the words I had already read. *They were deported to Auschwitz. All believed to have perished.*

"They never had a chance, you know." She paused and drew in a deep breath. "At the camps, they killed the children first. Because they were not useful. They took them off the trains, along with their mothers and the other women caring for them, and marched them straight to the gas chambers with promises of water." A shudder went through her. "I had killed my own nephew and other innocent children. I could not tell Bernadett. I could not. I should have destroyed the letter, but something held me back."

She turned the lid over, and with the nail of her left index finger, the one digit that had suffered less than her other fingers from arthritis, she plucked out a thick strand of woven grass and then another, revealing a hidden pouch inside the lid. I stared in surprise as a small brass key fell on the bench between us. "This was Bernadett's hiding place. It was Magda's basket; that is why Bernadett felt it safe to hide things here. Magda was always good at keeping secrets. Even after Magda died, Bernadett would find an excuse to see the basket. We all knew, of course, that she would put things in and take things out. Bernadett was always so easy to read. But I don't believe she ever thought we knew."

I remembered when I had been caught snooping in Bernadett's room. "The doors on Bernadett's armoire. Is that what the key is for?"

"Yes. It used to be in my room until I moved downstairs and there was not enough space. Bernadett had always admired it and asked to have it moved to her room. I did not think to remove the letter because she was never the kind of person who would attempt to see behind a locked door." The brass gleamed up at us in the sunlight. "Bernadett must have hidden the key here after . . ."

"After she discovered the letter," I finished for her. "But how did she find the key?"

"I attached it to the back of the van der Werff painting in the music room, where I knew Bernadett wouldn't find it—not that she would ever look for it. She had once asked me about the locked doors on her armoire, and I told her that the key was lost and she accepted that without question.

"But I wanted to be certain. I thought it was a good place to hide the key. Nobody paid any attention to the paintings except for me. Even the housekeeper knew not to touch them. At least until Bernadett decided she wanted to give a large sum of money to a charity that I did not approve of, and I told her no. I had known my sister for my entire life, yet I had forgotten how strongly she felt about saving the world. She would happily allow others to make her decisions for her, but if she saw an opportunity to help others, she would stop at nothing to make it happen. I think she learned that from Benjamin.

"She knew about Pieter van der Werff because of the exhibit and knew we had several hanging in the house and that they would be valuable. I had told her from the beginning that we were saving the paintings for the church from the Communists. After the Iron Curtain fell, I had to give her another reason why I had not returned them yet. I told her that I had been writing to the church in Rome for direction but that it might take years to determine where the paintings would go.

"I had already told so many lies that one more did not seem so bad. But it had been more than a decade, and she felt strongly about her cause and, I believe, most likely thought the church would approve of the donation on their behalf." She smiled softly, shaking her head. "I rarely came into the music room anymore, and I imagine she thought she could sell a painting behind my back without me noticing and then tell me afterward. She taught Sunday school to high school students at our church, and she asked one of her students to search online for the artist and his works."

"And that's how she found out about the portrait of the woman in the red velvet dress."

"Yes," she said wearily. "And that it was believed lost or stolen. That must have been how she found Mr. Isaacson, too—searching online for art dealers who were actively looking for art stolen by the Nazis during the war. She called him to meet with her and Finn without telling me. She thought I had done something terrible—as you had, and rightfully so.

"Bernadett gave me no hints about any of this. She was still teaching Sunday school and working in their music ministry. It was probably at this point that she went to the library in Mount Pleasant to find out more without telling me. She was always concerned about my feelings, and I imagine she thought this might have all been a mistake and she just needed more information. But then she removed the painting from the wall in preparation for Mr. Isaacson's visit."

"And discovered the key," I said. "And then the letter." I looked down at our entwined hands, imagining they belonged to the same person. "How did she confront you?"

She was silent for a long moment, and I sat still, holding her hand the only comfort I could give. "She brought me the Bible and made me mark that passage and read it out loud, and then she made me burn the letter, saying that I should have done so when I had received it. That she had been happy believing that her Samuel was out there somewhere, and that Benjamin might one day bring him back to her."

Helena was silent for a moment. "And then she simply prepared to die. I did not realize it at the time. All I could see was that she would not allow me to explain why I had done what I had done. I gave her time, thinking she would get to a point where she would listen. But she took the pills and there was nothing more I could say."

Her voice had lost its strength, and even though I had more questions to ask, I knew she needed to stop for now. "Are you ready to go home?"

She surprised me by not arguing. She simply nodded her head and allowed me to replace the key in the basket and put the lid on top before helping her stand.

We made our way to Magda's grave, the dragonfly suddenly bursting into life with a wild fluttering of its shimmery wings as it moved from one side of the stone to the other.

"I wish you could have met Magda," said Helena. "She was the smartest and most compassionate person I have ever known. Finn is very much like her."

She lifted her fingers to her lips, then pressed them down onto the headstone as she spoke quietly in Hungarian.

When she was finished, I asked, "Was that a prayer?"

"In a way," she said, turning to me with bright eyes. "It is what Magda said to me before she died, and it has taken me all this time to understand what she meant." She shut her eyes and was silent for a moment before she began to speak. " 'There is how we were before, and how we are now, and the time between is spent choosing which doors to open, and which to close.' "

The dragonfly hovered over us for a moment before taking off toward the old oaks with their shawls of Spanish moss. The old woman took my elbow as we began our slow progress to the car, allowing us both time to think about the doors in our lives, about the ones we had already closed behind us, and which ones still lay open.

CHAPTER 36

Eleanor

I lay in bed in my room at Luna Point, listening to the hum and whir of the air conditioner and hearing the words of an old woman in a quiet cemetery. The emptiness of Gigi's room beside me yawned its vacancy like a crouching presence, waiting to leap.

I had spoken with Finn several times throughout the day, and each time he reported an improvement in Gigi's progress. The swelling had gone down enough that they were going to bring her out of the coma. The next step beyond that was seeing if she could breathe on her own. We could not begin to contemplate any other outcomes.

Finally, I got out of bed and opened my window to the sticky night, hoping the music of the marsh would erase the fantasy noise of doors opening and closing in my mind. I paused, wondering if I was imagining the murmur of an approaching car, the airy light notes of a piano dancing in the night air through a car window.

The sound grew louder, and I leaned out as far as I could, listening closely until I could spot two headlights approaching beyond the pecan trees and moving toward the house. I stilled, recognizing the sounds of a Chopin mazurka and knowing who it was.

I ran down the stairs and through the foyer to the front door and threw it open just as the car pulled to a stop in front of the house, the piano music shutting off with the ignition, but the headlights casting two tunnels of white light across the drive, then fading into the place where the darkness and water met.

Finn opened the car door and stepped out, the ground crunching beneath his feet. I walked slowly across the porch, my steps tentative. The moon spun silvery shadows across the lawn, spilling into the creek as it slipped toward the river.

"Finn?" The word melted into the night, carrying with it all the hope and terror I had been holding on to.

"She's awake. Gigi's awake. And she's talking and asking questions. And her brain scan is normal."

His voice broke on the final word, but I saw the gleam of white as he smiled, trying to regain control.

I ran down the steps, feeling nothing under my bare feet, feeling nothing until I was in his arms and he was holding me, my face pressed into the warm space between his shoulder and his neck.

He lifted my face to the moonlight and kissed my wet cheeks, tasting tears I hadn't known I'd shed. He pressed his lips against mine, the stubble from his unshaven beard brushing my face, and I kissed him back, wordlessly telling him how glad I was that Gigi was going to be all right, and all the things I'd been holding back since he'd first told me about the night as a boy he had spent listening to me play the piano.

I pulled back, our breathing heavy between us, and felt the question in his eyes. I took his hand and led him up to the porch and through the door of the old house, closing it soundlessly behind us. We climbed the stairs and I paused only a moment before I pushed open the door to his bedroom.

We stood together in the darkened room, the glow of the moon from the windows filtering its light on his skin, across his gray eyes. His fingers touched my cheek and then my lips, and then I stepped back and slid my long T-shirt over my head, letting it pool at my feet.

I pulled back the sheets on the bed and lay down, watching in the half-light as he shed his own clothes, the moonlight moving against his skin. He slid under the covers next to me, his body warm against mine as he bent to kiss me.

We made love slowly, our touches knowing, as if we had both envisioned this moment for a long time, as if we knew the feel of each other's skin and the beating of our hearts. As if we knew we would have a lifetime of this, a lifetime of joining.

Afterward, as I lay in his arms, our legs entwined on the narrow twin bed, I stared up at the ceiling filled with the remnants of his childhood, the rockets flying through a space that never ended, remembering what he'd said to me the first time I saw this room. *I wanted to be an astronaut.*

"You should take flying lessons again," I whispered against his chest.

"Why?"

"Why not?"

His laugh rumbled beneath my ear.

I lifted up on my elbows to look in his face. "Because it's something you've always wanted to do. And if you can't remember why, you'll probably figure it out while you're up there."

"Okay," he said softly. "But only if you'll come, too."

"Why?" I asked, echoing his own question.

"Because it sounds like something you would have once wanted to do."

I smiled in the moonlight, feeling its cool touch on my face. "All right."

`He brought my lips down to his again, his kiss lingering, then held my head in his hands. "I love you, Eleanor Murray. I think I have loved you ever since my aunt Bernadett brought me to Russell Creek and I heard you play the piano. You bared your heart, and it was a beautiful thing to hear."

I rolled to my back, bringing him with me, his face hovering over mine. "And I think I have loved you since you first told me how you came back to listen."

He kissed me then, and we made love again beneath the planets and the rockets and the dreams of childhood that hung from the ceiling, and within the light of the silvery moon and the North Star that guided the lost toward home.

I awoke to full morning, with the sun shining brightly through the windows. Finn was gone but his scent lingered on the pillow, and as I pulled myself up to a sitting position my hand found a piece of wide-lined notebook paper with Finn's handwriting. He must have discovered the paper in the small desk drawer, and the image of him hunting for a pen and something to write on in his childhood desk while trying not to awaken me made me smile.

I'm going to the hospital to see Gigi. You looked so peaceful sleeping that I didn't want to wake you. I'll call you later and we can figure out a good time for me to come pick you up for a visit. I love you.

I closed my eyes, feeling the warmth of his words and the heat from the sun on my face. My eyes flew open as I realized that it was past early morning, and searched for a clock. An old electric clock radio sat on the nightstand, the orange digital numbers faded yet readable. Nine twenty-three.

I stumbled out of the bed, the sheets tangled around my legs. I hadn't slept that late in years, and since the accident I hadn't been sleeping at all. I imagined that the relief from the news about Gigi had given me enough peace of mind to sleep so soundly that Finn's leaving and even the bright sunshine had been unable to wake me.

After taking a quick shower and throwing on clean clothes, I raced downstairs to Helena's room, only to find Nurse Weber standing on a step stool with a measuring tape in hand in front of one of the windows.

She stepped down from the stool and quickly wrote a few numbers on a pad of paper. "Helena's out on the screened porch," she said, reading my mind. "She was up early this morning and has been waiting for you." She gave me a sympathetic glance as she moved the stool to the other side of the window.

I found Helena seated at the wrought-iron table, the sweetgrass basket opened in front of her, the photographs placed faceup in rows like a game of solitaire. She didn't look up as I walked in. "I did not think that Finn paid you to stay in bed all day."

It was almost a relief to have the old Helena back. Ignoring her comment, I pulled out a chair and sat down next to her, realizing why she was back to fighting form. "Finn must have told you the good news about Gigi."

She closed her eyes briefly and smiled. "Yes. I saw him this morning as he was leaving to go back to the hospital. It is very good news. For all of us." She looked at me with sharp blue eyes. "He seemed happier than I have seen him in years. And I do not think it was all because of Gigi."

I met her gaze without blinking, although I could feel the heat rising in my cheeks. I sat silently, waiting for what would come next and trying not to flinch.

Helena lowered her eyes to study the photographs on the table. "I can only hope that you were able to use some of the things we read about in those novels you insisted on checking out of the library for me."

My cheeks flamed even more. "I—" I stopped, knowing there was nothing I could say.

She glanced up at me. "I approve, by the way. Finn could make a much worse choice than you."

I rolled my eyes, but Helena had already turned her attention back to the basket. She reached inside and removed the silver rosary box and the Bible, then lifted out a few more photographs, flipping through them until she came to the one of the unnamed baby. She held it toward me. "This was Samuel."

I smiled at the picture of the cherubic boy with the toothless grin and dark hair, and my heart stretched and pulled as if I had known him, as if I had grieved for him for seventy years.

"And this is Gunter," she said, handing me the photograph of the soldier in the uniform.

"I know," I said. "Gigi and I found the basket, and I saw the name on the back."

She met my eyes without comment, then returned to sifting through the old photographs, letting them fall back onto the table like leaves. "All of these memories will be lost when I am gone. All of their stories. It will be as if they had never lived at all."

I held my breath for a moment, finding the courage to ask one more question. "So Finn knew nothing?"

Helena shook her head. "No. I was too ashamed to tell him. I knew he was troubled over Bernadett's suicide. He did what he could to honor her memory by keeping the suicide from public knowledge. But I could not tell him why. So many years had gone by that I had become comfortable with all of the lies. And Magda and Bernadett took my secrets to the grave."

I felt relief that Finn hadn't known, but I was sad in a way, too. I shook my head. "No, Helena. The memories won't be lost. Tell them to Finn." I closed my eyes, remembering Eve's words to me. "You are smart, and strong, and beautiful, and brave. That is your legacy, something Gigi will be proud of one day. It's where she gets her strength."

Her eyes met mine, and I saw new shadows in them, like clouds passing in front of the sun. "I would like you to tell Finn. I would tell him myself, but I am afraid I will not get the chance. I would not want to burden him now."

I looked at her with surprise. "I will tell him if you really want me to. But you'll have plenty of time to tell him yourself. Gigi is already planning your pink dress for her wedding, remember?"

She smiled weakly, her eyes moist. "I believe it would be easier for Finn to hear it from you. I am afraid that I will see the disappointment and grief in his eyes, and I do not have enough years left on this earth to be able to make me forget that." She patted my hand before I could protest. "Thank you, Eleanor. For everything you have done for me."

"For what?"

"For making me tell my story. Your sister said the most remarkable thing the other day. Something about the possibilities for second chances being everywhere if we just look hard enough. Everything that has happened will have meant nothing if nobody learns from it. And thank you for letting me bully you into playing the piano again. It hurt at first, to listen to you play. You reminded me so much of me and the way I felt about my music. But that was your story, and one you needed to tell so that you could heal, too."

"And what is my story?"

She looked through the screen, toward the river that had always flowed into the ocean, a constant as time moved inexorably forward. "That adversity in life does not rob your heart of beauty. It simply teaches it a new song to sing."

I took her hand and squeezed it, sharing grief over lives lost and choices made, of mistakes we had once believed to be permanent. My gaze fell on the photographs once more, and something Helena had said came back to me.

"Didn't you say that Bernadett had plans to make a scrapbook for Gigi?"

"Yes. But she died before she had the chance."

I smiled at her. "But you have time. And I do. And Gigi does. We can work on it together. You can tell the stories to Gigi, and I will write them down, and we will put the photographs and the stories in a scrapbook so that Samuel and Benjamin and Gunter and all the rest will never be forgotten. It is your legacy. It's Gigi's legacy. And there is much there to be proud of."

Helena's eyes misted and she blinked rapidly, and I watched as she struggled to control her emotions. "Would the scrapbook cover have to be pink if Gigi is involved?"

I pretended to consider it for a moment. "Probably. I hope that's not a problem."

We laughed together, and the sound carried out through the screen and up to the morning sky, where a great heron stretched its wings under the warmth of the sun.

Helena picked up the photograph of Gunter again and leaned back in her chair, studying it. "I would have liked to be a butcher's wife," she said with a sigh. "I would have liked to live within sight of Lake Constance and see the snow on the tops of the Alps in the middle of summer. I would have been happy."

"Are you happy now?" I asked, repeating the question Finn had once asked me and which I hadn't been able to answer.

"Yes. I think so. Or I will be when Gigi comes home. But all of my mistakes and all of my choices have brought me here to this place. To Edisto. And to Finn, and Gigi, and you, Eleanor. How could I not see my life as blessed?"

She gently placed the photos of Gunter and Samuel inside the basket, then began gathering the rest of the photographs, the Bible, the silver box, and the key, and stored them inside. Then I lifted the lid from the table and placed it snugly on top, a secret keeper with no more secrets.

CHAPTER 37

It was still dark when I awoke, Finn's steady breathing beside me. He had come back to Luna Point with me after we'd said good night to Gigi, and there'd been no discussion as we'd climbed the stairs together. He'd led me to my room, unwilling to sleep in a twin bed for another night. I watched him sleep for a long moment, breathing in his scent, then gently slid from the bed, unwilling to disturb him, imagining it had been days since he'd slept soundly.

I put my T-shirt back on, then padded through the dark room to the hallway, making my way to Bernadett's room. I had awoken with a single memory of a brass key falling onto the stone bench in the cemetery, the key to the locked armoire where Helena had hidden her letter.

But Bernadett had found the letter months before, and then while she was preparing to die, she had gathered her memories in the sweetgrass basket, along with the key in its secret compartment in the basket's lid, and hidden it under her bed. *So why were the mirrored doors in the armoire still locked?*

I opened the door and closed it quietly behind me, then flipped on the light switch. The small ceiling fixture cast a drowsy yellow glow across the room, not completely reaching the armoire on the far wall.

Helena had asked me to store the basket in Bernadett's room until Gigi was home and we were ready to start the scrapbook. It sat on the nightstand, next to the empty glass I'd seen the first time I'd been in the room, when I'd tried not to think of the woman who had died here and of the sister who had wished she could have gone with her.

I lifted the lid of the basket and spotted the key lying on top, nestled between the Bible and the silver rosary box. I took the key and moved across the room toward the armoire, feeling as if I wasn't alone or even directing my own actions.

The key slipped easily into the lock, and I pulled on the knobs of both doors, allowing them to swing open. I leaned back, allowing the light to reach its feeble fingers into the dark space, and saw an envelope. I reached in and pulled it out and stared at it for a long moment, as if this were all a dream, as if the envelope in my hand weren't real.

At first I thought it was Helena's letter, but she had told me that Bernadett had made her burn it. The envelope had crease marks across it, as if it had once been folded in quarters to fit inside a small space. A space the size of a hidden lining inside the lid of a sweetgrass basket. I looked closely and read the typewritten words:

Miss Bernadett Szarka
Edisto Island, South Carolina

I brought the envelope directly under the light, seeing now the yellowed condition of the paper and the three-cent postage stamp. The lack of a zip code or street address. With steady fingers I slipped the letter from the opened envelope, then unfolded the letter.

It was dated June sixteenth of 1951, and the return address was the German embassy in Washington, DC.

Dear Miss Szarka,

Thank you for your correspondence dated this last 4th of January, 1951, regarding information for a soldier in the Wehrmacht Heer 13th Panzer Unit stationed near Budapest in the summer of 1944.

I regret to inform you that Private Gunter Hans Richter, from the Bavarian town of Lindau, was killed in action on the 27th of August, 1944, during the second Jassy-Kishinev Offensive in Romania. We have no record of his burial.

Please do not hesitate to contact me if you should require further information.

My eyes only skimmed the name and signature of the official who'd sent the letter. I imagined him with wire-rimmed glasses and brutally short hair, a man who did not know that within his typewriter he held the power to change lives.

I wondered for a moment why Bernadett had waited so long to write and then recalled the Allied occupation of Germany following the war, and how the German embassy would not have reopened until at least 1950. I pictured her, waiting for news that diplomatic relations between the two countries had been reopened, and then sitting down to write her letter in secret.

Bernadett had known. She had known that Gunter had died, had known since 1951, yet never told Helena. I stared at the letter for a long time, seeing Bernadett writing her letter to the German embassy about Gunter, wanting to hear good news so she could share with Helena. Trusting that Helena was doing what she could to find Samuel and Benjamin. And, like Helena, when their respective letters arrived, she had recognized how despair can disguise itself as the truth.

I folded the letter and held it against my heart. I thought of the two sisters, at cross-purposes, each trying to hide a separate horrible truth from the other, each knowing that sometimes hope is all we have, and to lose that is to lose all.

I imagined Bernadett before her death taking the letter from its secret place in the basket lid and hiding it in the armoire before secreting the key just as Helena had done. It was as if she wanted it to be found eventually by someone besides Helena. It was part of their story. Their legacy of love and survival.

We would never know what happened after Gunter shut the door of the truck and watched Helena and Bernadett disappear into the darkness. Did he deliver the note? Did he warn the convent in time? Did they heed his warning? He had loved Helena and helped save Bernadett's life, and Helena believed that he would have done everything possible to save Samuel and the other children, unless extreme circumstances had prevented or circumvented his plans. There was so much we didn't know, so much we would never know. The secrets of the dead are always kept.

I turned at the sound of the door opening and saw Finn, his gray eyes full of questions. He came to me and I stepped into the shelter of his arms, still holding the letter against my heart. I laid my head against Finn's chest as he stroked my hair, and I began to tell him the story of a courageous woman with a fierce heart, and the story of the love between sisters that even death could not separate.

And somewhere in the dark night, redolent with the scents of the pluff mud and summer grass, amid the cries of a night heron and the chorus of thousands of insects, the sound of a door closing and another opening.

EPILOGUE

I smoothed down the burgundy wool of the skirt of my suit, glancing at the group of people assembling in the music room and in the foyer of the old house. The paintings had all been removed, the walls now wearing a pale cream that brightened the interior and welcomed in the light from outside.

Finn and Jacob Isaacson had been working on identifying and cataloging the paintings, researching their origins and returning them to the families they had once belonged to. It was a small thing, the return of property, considering all that had been lost. But it was one thing.

Teri Weber, brought in by the housekeeper, Mrs. Adler, to help with the refreshments, placed a large tray of her chocolate chip cookies on the dining room buffet next to the *mézeskalács* that Gigi and I had made.

I spotted Gigi in the music room darting across the foyer toward them, and I stopped her with a hand on her shoulder as she negotiated her way through the crowd in front of me. "Not yet. You don't want greasy crumbs on the keyboard or your fingers will slip all over the place. Believe me, I speak from experience." I smiled down at her. "I'll go put a stack in a napkin and hide them for you."

She beamed up at me. "Thanks, Ellie."

I hugged her to me, closing my eyes in silent gratitude. Our physical scars were healing, but I couldn't help a small part of me wishing that they wouldn't fade completely, like the scar on my finger from my fall from the tree, as if we both might need reminders of the battles we had fought and survived.

"Are you nervous for your first piano recital?" I asked.

"Just a little. I've done lots of ballet recitals but I'm never alone up on the stage, even though you're going to be with me turning the pages, but it's not really the same thing because you're not playing the piano, only I am, well, at least at first since I'm doing four songs and then you get to play a song all by yourself." She stopped to draw breath. "Are you nervous?"

I nodded. "Yep. I've never played in front of anybody besides your family and mine."

Her gray eyes widened with relief. "It's good to be a little nervous. God compensates those with a lack of talent with an overabundance of self-confidence."

I looked down at her as the large words slipped so effortlessly from her tongue, certain I'd heard those exact words before. "Did Madame LaFleur tell you that?" I glanced toward the dining room, where the woman herself, tall and dark haired and razor thin, stood by the table talking with Harper.

Gigi shook her head. "No, ma'am. Aunt Helena." She smiled again, then ran across to the front door, where her best friend, Teensy Olsen, was walking in accompanied by her mother.

Finn came up from behind and kissed me on the side of the neck just as I caught Lucy's gaze. She was sitting between Glen and Eve's wheelchair in the front row of chairs before the piano. She gave me the look that said, *That man is fine,* and I blushed. I turned to Finn, taking in the dark suit and gray tie. I supposed some things would never change.

"She's starting with the Csárdás," I said. "Are you sure I can't convince you to do an accompanying dance since you know all the steps?"

"Quite sure," he said, his voice soft as we both remembered the aunts who had taught him the steps to the Hungarian folk dance.

As a man I didn't recognize drew Finn's attention, Gigi approached with Teensy and her mother, Sharon. Sharon had bright red hair, with warm green eyes and a smile to match. "I have been looking for a piano teacher for Teensy forever. Gigi played one of her pieces for us when she was at our house last week, and I can only hope you will be taking on more students."

I smiled down at Teensy, who was at least three feet taller than Gigi and had bright red hair like her mother's. "I haven't really thought about it, but I'm sure we can work something out. I'm actually going back to school to get a teaching degree in music, but that won't be full-time."

"Oh, Gigi hadn't mentioned that. What are you wanting to do with your degree?"

"I'm hoping to work with an after-school music program in North Charleston for disadvantaged children. I've already started volunteering there."

Gigi jumped up and down, still clinging to Teensy's arm. "Just like my aunt Bernadett did in Hungary," she announced, repeating what her father must have told her.

"Yes," I said. "Something like that."

"Great." Sharon beamed. "I'll call you next week and try and set something up."

They retreated, and Finn and I began herding everyone into the music room, which now glimmered with light. The heavy drapes had been removed, and the walls repainted in the same hue as the foyer and dining room, forming a bright refuge for creating and enjoying music.

The love seat where Helena would sit to hear me play had been pushed back against the far wall and remained empty. I was glad, wanting to imagine her there now, listening.

Three months after Gigi came home from the hospital, Helena passed away peacefully in her sleep. We had completed the scrapbook a few days before she died, and I wondered if Helena had chosen to go then, her story told. Gigi had asked if she could continue placing photographs in the scrapbook, and I had agreed, knowing Helena would have, too. Gigi's life was a link between what had gone before and what was to come, the empty pages of the scrapbook like doors waiting to be opened.

In the end, Finn had not told her about Bernadett's letter, wanting to allow Helena to continue thinking of her Gunter out there somewhere, still searching for her. I pictured them together now, along with Bernadett and her Benjamin and Samuel, and Magda. I saw them dancing the Csárdás, the three beautiful Szarka sisters, together again.

The night before Helena died, I had played the nocturne for her again, and she had let me see her weep. It somehow made it easier for me to say good-bye to her, to this woman who had been through so much and taught me so much.

We had her cremated, as she had wished, and Finn and I would be bringing her ashes and Bernadett's to Hungary, where we would be going as part of our honeymoon trip. It would be the first time Finn had visited the place of his grandmother's birth, and I would get to see where the small house on Uri Utca had once stood, the house with the tiny room shared by two sisters and where the lives of so many had been permanently altered. We would stay in the hotel where the New York Palace Café still exists on the ground floor in all its splendor, just as it had in 1936, when their mother had taken Magda, Helena, and Bernadett there for Magda's sixteenth birthday.

We also planned to visit Poland, and Auschwitz, where we would lay a wreath of remembrance flowers on the train platform for Samuel, and another one to honor all the lost souls who stepped off the trains there and live now only in our hearts and our collective consciences.

We postponed the wedding until after Eve's baby was born so she would be more comfortable in her matron-of-honor dress. It would also give her more time to make my wedding gown. I showed her three of my favorites I'd seen in a bridal magazine and allowed her to surprise me. I knew it would be stunning. She actually had a waiting list of people needing custom gowns and costumes, assisted by our mother, who had learned how to use a specially designed computer keyboard so she could manage the accounts and client database. And give her opinions to Eve and me whether or not we needed them.

Eve was also making Gigi's maid-of-honor dress. It would have a wide skirt that twirled when Gigi turned, with lots of lace and tulle and sparkles, and it would be pink, of course. Gigi had at first suggested we wear our matching GEECHEE GIRL T-shirts as we marched down the aisle, but it had been Eve who dissuaded her with promises of a princess gown created just for her.

I escorted Gigi up to the piano and stood next to her, ready to turn the pages. I had told her this was the last time she would give a recital with sheet music, that real musicians played from memory. She had accepted this solemnly, although I felt that we were both relieved that she had sheet music this time so that we could do this together.

There was a rattling of paper as people referred to their programs, which Gigi and I had made. I stepped forward to announce the first piece, catching Finn's gaze, so full of love, and I nearly faltered. Then I moved back into my position and met Gigi's gray eyes—so much like her father's—and smiled as she began to play.

We live, we love. These are the choices we are given, to open doors or to close them. It is all we have, and it is enough.

Photo by Claudio Marinesco

Karen White is the award-winning author of sixteen previous books. She grew up in London but now lives near Atlanta, Georgia.

CONNECT ONLINE

karen-white.com
authorkarenwhite.wordpress.com
facebook.com/karenwhiteauthor

the time between

KAREN WHITE

A CONVERSATION WITH KAREN WHITE

Q. *One of the recurring topics in your books is the bond between sisters. What is it about sisterhood that provides so much inspiration?*

A. Because I grew up with three brothers, my lifelong wish was for a sister. I was horribly jealous of my friends who had sisters, knowing in my heart that my life would never be complete without one. My mother was the eldest of six children—five of them girls—and my fondest childhood memories are listening to my mother and aunts doing their "Southern sister girl talk." It is their voices and mannerisms that I hear and see in my head while I'm creating my fictional sisters.

Q. *Your books often play with real events or historical facts—did* The Time Between *have a real-life inspiration?*

A. For this particular book, I was inspired by a news story about two elderly twin sisters who'd once sung with Bing Crosby and were renowned beauties. And then, for some inexplicable reason, they stopped leaving their house, returning phone calls, and answering the door. This went on for years until they were found in their home, deceased from natural causes. They had died within days of each other. I wanted to know why they'd become recluses. What happened? This question kept on pecking at my brain, and I knew that I had the seeds for a book.

Q. *Why did you decide to make Helena and Bernadett Hungarian? Is Hungary a country you've ever visited?*

A. After deciding that the book would have World War II as a foundation of one of the plotlines, I knew I had to use Hungary. Hungary had a very unique and precarious position during the war. It was an Axis power, allied with the Third Reich as the lesser of two evils. The Hungarian government was more afraid of the Russian Communists than of Hitler, and so an uneasy alliance was formed. But it was because of this that the Jewish citizenry, although not immune, escaped much of the terror that Jews were facing in Nazi-occupied countries. At least until the very last year of the war, when Hungary tried to ally itself with the Allied powers and failed—leaving itself vulnerable to Nazi occupation, and the forced deportation of nearly 500,000 Jews in a three-month period in 1944. It is as unbelievable as it is heartbreaking, and I knew it would be a powerful backdrop for my story.

I did a lot for the research for this book, but I was lucky enough to schedule a trip to Budapest while writing it. I am so glad I did! I think the details and ambiance of the city really added to the "immersion" into the story that I like to provide for my readers.

Q. The story begins with a near-death experience—is this something that has ever happened to you or someone you know?

A. I have never had a near-death experience nor do I know anybody who has. However, when I was in middle school, I read my first account of a near-death experience and I've been fascinated by the concept ever since. There is so much documentation on the subject, from people from all over the world and throughout history, that it does give one pause. And for me, I knew it would be great fodder for a novel.

Q. There are no villains in this story, which is something the reader realizes once they "see" it from the other characters' points of view—is that why you decided on three different narrators?

A. Absolutely. When I first started the book, I thought I'd have only two narrators—Eleanor and Helena—since both plotlines revolve around them. But then I realized how important Eve's character was to both Eleanor's past and present. Seeing Eve through Eleanor's eyes made the reader very biased against her and I thought that made her very one-dimensional. The best way to flesh out Eve for the reader was to let the reader into her head.

Q. *Is it hard to write a story with no real villains, only protagonists?*

A. I write as true to real life as I can, and in real life—with notable exceptions—there are no completely good or bad people. Everybody makes mistakes, or bad choices. It's how we live with them that make us the people we are. Eleanor and Helena have made mistakes and bad choices—but they have learned from them and are more interesting characters because of it.

Q. *What was the hardest thing for you to write in* The Time Between*?*

A. Helena's story was the hardest part to write. It's truly heartbreaking. I had to put myself in her shoes, on a dark night with bombs falling from the sky, and figure out what she would have done with the information she had at the time—and there really was no other answer. The consequences were devastating, but not intentional. She's one of my favorite characters I've created because of how strong she is—how she was able to move forward despite the guilt she carried for so many years.

QUESTIONS FOR DISCUSSION

1. "The relationship between sisters is a little piece of heaven and hell. But we share the same soul." Do you agree with Helena's sentiment? How does this idea unfold over the course of the novel for each pair of sisters? Why is this relationship so complicated, so special? Are our siblings an extension of us?

2. From Eve's difficult pregnancy and Glen's and Ellie's affections, to Helena's and Bernadette's wartime tragedies, every character in the story seems to carry a burden of secrets. How do these secrets shape the story? Does airing them set the characters free?

3. Why does Eve wish for a child? Do you think it is wise or fair, knowing the risks? What trumps her own safety in her heart?

4. In the novel, we spend a lot of time moving in and out of Gigi's, Helena's, and Bernadette's bedrooms—what do these rooms say about the characters? Do you think this room defines or illustrates our lives?

5. What did you think was hidden in Bernadette's bedroom?

6. Why are the Gullah sweetgrass baskets, like the "secret keeper," so significant? What kind of magic do you think is woven into them at the time of their creation?

7. How do Helena and Ellie mirror each other in terms of the guilt they feel over the past? Is forgiveness possible for either one?

8. Why do you think the author chose the title *The Time Between*? What does it mean in the context of the story?

9. How does Ellie's caretaking of Helena transform them, even heal them, both? Why does Ellie stick with the job as Helena works to sabotage any relationship? When do things start to change?

10. Did you suspect any of the twists in the book? Which ones? From where did you think the paintings originated?

11. Were you shocked by the revelations about Ben's and Samuel's fates? Could you ever imagine having to make such a set of life-or-death choices—especially as a mother? Does knowing this background help you make sense of Helena's behavior? Do you think she did the "right" thing?

12. What does the Gullah woman mean by "All good-bye ain't gone"? What does it mean to Ellie? To Gigi?

13. What does it mean for Ellie to finally play the Chopin piece?

Vivien Walker Moise
Indian Mound, Mississippi
April 2013

I was born in the same bed that my mama was born in, and her mama before her, and even further back than anybody alive could still remember. It was as if the black wood of the bedposts was meant to root us Walker women to this place of flat fields and fertile soil carved from the great Mississippi. But like the levees built to control the mighty river, it never held us for long.

We were born screaming into this world, the beginning of a lifelong quest to find what would quiet us. Our legacy was our ability to coax living things from fallow ground, along with a desperate need to see what lay beyond the delta. A need to quell a hurt whose source was as unexplainable as its force.

Whatever it was that drove us away was never stronger than the pull of what brought us back. Maybe it was the feel of the dark Mississippi mud or the memory of the old house and the black bed into which we'd been born, but no matter how far we ran, we always came back.

I returned in the spring nearly nine years to the day after I'd left. I'd driven straight through from Los Angeles, twenty-seven hours of asphalt and fast food, my memories like a string guiding me home. The last leg from Little Rock to Indian Mound was punctuated by bright flashes of lightning and constant tornado watches on the radio. I kept my foot pressed to the accelerator as strong winds buffeted my car. It didn't occur to me to stop. I had a trunk's worth of hurts piled in the car with me that only my grandmother Bootsie could make go away. She would forgive those long years of silence because she understood doggedness. I'd inherited it from her side of the family, after all.

It was nearly dawn when the storm passed and I crossed the river into Mississippi and headed east on Highway 82 and into the heart of the delta. The hills and bluffs to the west disappeared as if a giant boot had flattened all the land between the Mississippi and Yazoo rivers, creating a landscape as rich and fertile as it was difficult to contain and control. This place of my ancestors was known to make or break a man, and I figured by now the scorecard was about even.

I've been a long time gone. Billboards and highway lights fell away, leaving behind empty fields and ramshackle structures swallowed by kudzu, turning them into hulking ghosts haunting the roadside. Sinewy cypress swamps randomly appeared as if to remind us of our tenuous hold on the land. The predawn flatscape flashed by me in shades of gray, as if the years had absorbed all the color, so that even my memories were seen only in black and white.

A therapist had once told me that my hindsight color-blindness was due to an unhappy childhood. I tried to tell him that I had never considered my motherless childhood to be *unhappy.* It was more of an accumulation of years filled with absence, that perhaps black and white were simply the colors of grief.

The rising sun had painted the sky pink by the time I passed the sign for Indian Mound, the first seeds of panic making my heart beat faster. I glanced over at my purse, where I kept my pills, wondering whether I could swallow them dry again as I'd been doing for most of the trip. My throat felt sore, and my hands shook. *I'm almost home.* I turned my gaze toward the dim light outside that seemed to swallow my car as I passed through it, and pressed my foot harder on the accelerator.

I slowed down, trying to avoid the increasing amount of debris tossed across the road, the tree limbs, leaves, and roof shingles that seemed to have been scattered by the hand of a careless child. I caught up to an old, faded red pickup truck as it slowed down at the bright flashing red and blue lights of a police car stopped in front of fallen electrical lines. A large, brindled dog, his lineage as indecipherable as the vintage of the pickup truck in which he sat, stared at me with a lost expression. A police officer guided our way around the danger zone, his other hand reminding us to slow down. As soon as he had disappeared from my rearview mirror, I sped up, passing the truck and maneuvering past a mailbox that stood upright in the middle of the highway as if it were meant to be there.

My tongue stuck to the roof of my mouth and I thought of the pills again, and how easily they could take away the pit of worry that had begun to gnaw at me. I went faster, clipping a tree limb with my left front tire and hearing a crack and a thump of the split wood hitting metal. I kept going, realizing that I was prepared to drive on the rim of a flat tire if I had to. *I've been a long time gone.*

I turned off the highway onto a dirt road studded with puddles and rocks. The road bisected a large cotton field, the furrows drowning in standing water. I remembered this road and had turned by instinct. It probably had a name, one we'd never used when giving directions to the odd visitor. We usually instructed visitors to turn right about one and a half miles past the old general store, which leaned to the left and still had a Royal Crown Cola sign plastered over the doorway even though it had been abandoned long before I was born.

The store was gone now, but I still knew where to turn in the same way my hair still knew where to part no matter how hard I tried to tell it different. But the road was the same, still narrow, with the tall white oaks—taller now, I supposed—creating a green archway above. Tommy and I used to race barefoot down this road, watching our feet churn up dust like conjured spirits.

My back tires spun out, bringing me back to the present and slipping my car off the side of the road. Panicking, I gunned the engine, succeeding only in digging the wheels further in muck. Although I knew it was useless, I gunned the engine two more times. I stared through the windshield down the tree-shaded road. It had taken me nine years to come back. I figured stretching it out for a few more minutes wouldn't matter.

I began to walk, my leather flats sticking to the Mississippi mud as if reluctant to let me go again. A murder of crows sprang up out of the trees, cawing loudly and making my heart hammer as I tried counting them, recalling the nursery rhyme Mathilda had sung to me as a child.

One for sorrow,
two for mirth,
three for a wedding,
four for a birth,
five for silver,
six for gold,
seven for a secret never to be told,
eight for heaven,
nine for hell,
And ten for the devil's own self.

I clenched my teeth, wishing I'd taken another pill. I glanced over my shoulder at the car, realizing too late that I'd left my purse. I'd almost decided to go back when a flurry of wings made me look up. Seven black crows, their inky black wings seeming wet in the light of the sun, swirled and dipped over me, cawing and cackling, then took off again across the field.

My throat stung as I walked faster, feeling light-headed as I tried to recall the last time I'd eaten. And then the trees by the side of the road fell away and I stopped in a large clearing with a wide, paved drive edged with centuries-old oak trees. The old yellow house of indeterminate architecture with columns and porches and an improbable turret and at least three different roof styles stood before me in all of its confused splendor. It was an anomaly among all the Greek Revival homes of the region, as peculiar and original as the women who'd lived there for two centuries. My heart slowed as if Bootsie were already with me, letting my head rest on her shoulder. I had come home.

Despite the storm, the house appeared almost untouched except for the litter of pink azalea petals that had been stripped from their stems and scattered around the drive and yard like fuchsia doubloons from a Mardi Gras float.

Grass blades stuck their tips out of standing water in the yard as if struggling for breath, the water reflecting the sky and odd yellow house. Its windows stared down on me with reproach, as if wondering at the audacity of the return of another Walker woman, my hubris in believing it wanted me back. But I'd lived my first eighteen years inside its walls and had run through the fields of cotton that surrounded it. This house was the only spot of color in my monochromatic memories.

I listened for the songbirds, as much a part of my memory as the landscape. Except for the crows, the only sound cutting the silence was that of dripping water as it fell to the ground from the eaves and chipped paint of the old house, and from the arthritic fingers of the oak trees. I slowly walked up the wooden steps to the wide porch, pausing to take off my mud-caked shoes and leave them by the side of the door, just as I had done as a child. I placed my hand on the large brass knob of the front door before deciding to knock instead.

I knocked twice, waiting for the tread of my grandmother Bootsie's footsteps, or the glide of my mother's bare feet. Or even the heavier treads of my older brother, Tommy. But all I heard was the sound of the water leaking from the house. *Drip. Drip.*

I hesitated for a moment, then reached for the knob. It didn't turn. In all of my years growing up, the front door had never been locked. I couldn't help but wonder if they'd known I was coming after all. I stood for a moment with my hands on my hips until I remembered it was a stance my mother had frequently used, and dropped them again. The air was heavy with the scent of rain and the boxwoods that had begun to creep over the porch railings unchecked.

I slid my shoes back on and crossed the drive to walk around the side toward the old carriage house that had been converted into a garage sometime in the twenties. I recognized Bootsie's 1977 white Cadillac convertible and my heart lurched with relief. A white pickup truck with an enormous toolbox in the bed that I assumed was Tommy's sat behind it, and next to it was a dark sedan that looked suspiciously like an unmarked police car. I didn't take the time to think about why it was there. I walked quickly now, no longer caring about avoiding puddles, needing to be embraced by my grandmother until I no longer craved my pills to soothe away the hurting.

I moved to the backyard, looking toward the rear of our property, toward the forest full of sweet gums and pines, the solid land giving way to the swamp and giant bald cypress trees that Tommy had once told me were over a thousand years old. A lone cypress tree had managed to take root on higher ground halfway between the house and the swamp, standing by itself among the sparse grass and haphazard pine trees whose scraggly branches always made them look bewildered next to the corded majesty of the giant cypress. I'd called it "my tree" as a child, and I longed to sit in the comforting shade of its branches again.

But the landscape had been altered. Limbs and leaves mixed blindly with papers and other indistinguishable man-made debris. A porch swing that I remembered had once hung on the front porch sat right-side up, its chains missing, in the middle of the yard. Close by, almost as if they'd been set there on purpose, were the two metal chairs that had always graced my grandmother's vegetable garden. They had once been a neon lime color, but sun and time had faded them into a disappointed green. With the swing, they formed a cohesive seating group, almost as if the wind had decided in the middle of its destruction to take a break.

I paused, feeling my equilibrium shift as if I'd just stepped off a moving sidewalk. I took in the three figures standing in the near distance, and then waited for my gaze to register what they were standing next to, blinking twice until I understood. My tree, the stalwart reminder of the best parts of my childhood, had toppled over, clipping the edge of the old cotton shed. The roots were singed black, with chunks of bark encircling the area. I imagined I could smell the burn ions in the air from the lightning strike, still feel the atmosphere pulsating with the power of it.

"Bootsie?" I called out, my walk becoming a run. Three heads turned in my direction just as another cluster of crows flew out from the dead tree, their shiny black bodies seeming to mock me.

I stopped in front of the small group, my breath coming in gasps, as we regarded one another, all of us looking as if we'd just seen a ghost. Nobody said anything as my gaze moved from one person to another, registering my brother's face, and then another man, and then my mother. Whereas Tommy wore jeans and an untucked shirt, like he'd just been roused from bed by the sound of a lightning strike, my mother wore a silk brocade cocktail dress taken directly from the Kennedy White House, complete with rhinestone earrings and matching bracelet and ring. I recalled seeing a photograph of her mother, Bootsie, wearing the same ensemble.

My mother turned to me with mild surprise. "Vivien, I know I've told you before that you should never leave the house without lipstick."

I stared at her for a long moment, wondering if there was more to this altered landscape than just a fallen tree.

My brother hesitated for a moment, then took a step forward to embrace me. He was ten years older than me, and almost a decade had passed since I'd last seen him, but now, at nearly thirty-seven, he still looked like the gangly and awkward boy I'd grown up with. Tommy's shirt was soft and worn under my fingers, and I clutched at the familiarity of it. "It's been a while." He didn't smile.

My lips trembled as I tried to smirk at his vast understatement, as if we both believed his words could erase nearly nine years of silence. "Hello, Tommy." I forced a deep breath into my lungs. "Where's Bootsie?"

His eyes softened, and I knew then that I'd lost more than just time in the last nine years. "You've been gone awhile." His gaze drifted to our mother in her cocktail dress and high heels and something icy cold gripped the area around my heart.

Before I could say anything, the other man stepped forward. Tripp Montgomery was as tall and slender as I remembered him, short brown hair and hazel eyes that always seemed to see more of the world than the rest of us. He wore khaki pants and a long-sleeved shirt and a tie, which only added to my confusion. I looked at him, wondering why he was there and hoping that somebody would tell me this was all a dream and that I'd soon awaken in my bed in the old house with Bootsie kissing my forehead.

"Hey," Tripp said, as if he'd just delivered me to my front steps after school. As if the earth had somehow stopped spinning in this corner of the world and everything was the same as when I'd left it. Except it wasn't.

"Why are you here?" I asked, plucking at one of the random questions I needed to ask to make the ground beneath my feet stand still.

His face remained impassive, but I thought I saw a flicker of what looked like sympathy pass through his eyes. "I'm the county coroner." He stepped back, allowing my gaze to register the gaping hole in the ground that the intricate root system of the giant cypress had once inhabited. The grass around the edges was blackened, wood and bark sprinkled like confetti around the wounded earth. And there, nestled inside the dark hole like a baby in its crib, were the stark white bones of a human skeleton.

My hands began to shake, my vision marred by mottled dots of light. I struggled to focus as I stared at the skull, unable to look away.

I forced myself to look at Tripp and saw that he was staring at my hands as if he knew why, like he'd always known everything about me without my ever having to open my mouth. I tried to clench my fingers into fists, but they were shaking too hard. The dots of light had now become streaks across my vision, and I tried to focus on Tommy again, but my mother's voice broke through the pounding in my head.

"Have you taken my car keys again, Vivien? I can't seem to find them."

I looked down at the dirty white of the forehead bone, now shimmering in the bright morning sun as if it were trying to speak to me. I started to say something, but the light suddenly dimmed and I closed my eyes as I felt myself falling, still seeing behind my eyelids the glow of white bone against dark, dark earth.